The Voynich Cypher

Russell Blake

First Edition

ISBN: 978-1480279452

Published by

Reprobatio Limited

Jesus said unto her, I am the resurrection, and the life:
he that believeth in me, though he were dead, yet shall he live:

John 11:25, 26 – King James Bible

PROLOGUE

2:38 a.m.. Two Weeks Ago – Dorset, England, The Abbey of St. Peter at Abbotsbury

Moonlight bathed the Abbey in an otherworldly glow as serpentine tendrils of foggy mist blanketed the countryside. The medieval buildings in the compound were blue-gray in the eerie lunar luminescence, and the encroaching vegetation appeared black instead of green. The Abbey was silent, with many hours remaining until activity on the grounds would begin, and only the dim illumination from a single incandescent bulb housed in an ancient rusted lamp above the massive stone entry hinted that the structures were occupied.

A dog barked in the distance, its throaty voice muffled by the thick haze.

The scarred brick well at the edge of the Abbey grounds, worn by the centuries and long since obsolete, blended with the landscape. But the guard who leaned against it, armed with a SIG Sauer 228 pistol, seemed out of place.

The crumbling aperture was surrounded by overgrown shrubs and weeds, rendering it virtually invisible. The sentry was dressed in dark army surplus camouflage pants and jacket, doing his lonesome duty on the latest of thousands of uneventful nights. He'd grown lax over the years, but in his defense, there was little to be actively vigilant against, save for an errant fox or badger that occasionally strayed into the vicinity. Even then the man didn't bother to shoo the furry intruders away.

Live and let live.

If a more boring or uneventful posting existed, he'd never heard of it. Still, a lifetime of indoctrination had molded him for guarding the Abbey's forbidden secrets, and that's what he would do, even if he privately thought it was pointless.

His instructions were simple: stand ready throughout the night at this hidden entrance to the Abbey's subterranean chambers. While part of him questioned why it needed to be guarded, and what, if anything, it required to be guarded against, he knew that if he was remiss in his simple function he would be punished in a brutal and medieval manner – some things hadn't changed over the eons. His first duty was to God, and after God, to the Order. And the Order had wisdom in its directives, even if he didn't fully apprehend them. His role was to do as he was told, which is why he was posted in the middle of nowhere, waiting for nothing to happen, just as it hadn't happened for centuries.

The edict to watch and wait came from the very top, so every night for almost a decade he'd maintained his vigil, performing his duty at the eleventh-century Benedictine monastery without question, just as his many predecessors had done before him.

❧

Wearing black cargo pants, rubber-soled paratrooper boots and a light black windbreaker, the intruder moved silently through the shrubbery – virtually invisible in the darkness. The perimeter motion detectors had been easily de-activated; the intruder had known where they were hidden, as well as their operating frequency.

The guard had finally settled into his usual sitting position on a weathered stone bench facing the brick opening and was surreptitiously listening to music on an iPod, tapping his fingers in time to the rhythm. He registered nothing as the intruder stealthily approached from the rear, a hypodermic syringe clenched in a gloved hand. At the final moment, sensing a presence, he attempted to spin around, but it was too late – the needle had penetrated his neck, its payload delivered with an abrupt depression of the plunger.

The man's pupils lost focus and took on a glassy stare as he slipped painlessly into unconsciousness, his head almost tenderly supported by the intruder as he slumped to the ground. After glancing around to ensure the scuffle hadn't alerted anyone from the Abbey, the intruder closed the guard's lids, ensuring his eyes wouldn't dry out during the hour he'd be in dreamland. Even after the surprise attack the man appeared at peace, other than having a faint expression of astonishment.

The intruder considered his inert form. *I don't envy you the headache you'll have when you wake up.*

Satisfied the guard was out cold, the intruder extracted a bundle from a form-fitted nylon backpack and clipped an anodized black rappelling wire to the well's sturdy iron cross-post, and after ducking into the brush to retrieve a rucksack with equipment in it, crawled over the crumbling lip and dropped sixty feet into the inky darkness below.

☙

The intruder dropped down the shaft and swung into a passageway that punctuated the end of the sheer descent, alighting soundlessly on the worn stone floor of the subterranean passageway before quickly scanning the area.

Hundreds of skeletons held silent vigil in cavities along the narrow crypt, all facing the spot where the new arrival stood; a phalanx of mute sentries to voicelessly witness the actions of anyone foolhardy enough to breach the stillness of the sacred burial space. The specters of the thousand-year-old remains generated no reaction in the masked figure, who was more than passingly familiar with the many faces of death. While the grim reaper wasn't exactly a friend, he certainly wasn't a stranger to the black-clad prowler, who'd ended the lives of enough miscreants to defy recollection.

The intruder stepped carefully past the groups of long-dead clergy, compelled forward by a more pressing mission than sightseeing in one of purgatory's antechambers.

Tracker 1x24 NV night-vision goggles rendered the darkness of the clammy chamber irrelevant; now the blackness was bathed in a greenish glow, with the level of detail similar to when having the lights on – had there been any lights – the only illumination would have come from the row of wall-mounted iron torch holders, with black smudges of gritty soot marring the stone ceiling above them. The departed had little use for modern conveniences such as electricity, and the old ways were still the best in the hall of the dead.

The only sounds other than the draft wafting through the corridors were the occasional rat scurrying about the bones and the trespasser's muffled footsteps moving stealthily towards the forbidden destination – the rumored 'Scroll Chamber'. Preparation for the early morning's adventure had included memorizing the layout of the surviving Abbey buildings and also the maze of catacombs beneath. The location of the Chamber was exactly one hundred twenty-two yards from where the abandoned water-shaft offered ventilation and egress – a fact that was pivotal now that the sanctity of the hidden recesses had been breached.

The most difficult part of the operation would take place at the Chamber – the advance intelligence had been clear. It would be guarded, both by a man outside its door and another within. A frontal assault was out of the question; the slightest slip and the interior sentry would sound the alarm, even if the exterior guard had been dispatched. No, a better approach would be required to achieve entry into the supposedly impenetrable room, although it too would require no small amount of luck to succeed.

Careful study of the almost impossible-to-locate ancient blueprints had provided the clue for an alternative means of accessing the Chamber – one that the guards and the friars were likely unaware of.

It would be obvious momentarily whether the strategy was a winner, or a dead-end.

ൟ

The Scroll Chamber was a small room, engineered to exacting measurements, and constructed entirely of stone blocks painstakingly hewn from a nearby quarry. Four meters by three, with not a centimeter of variation anywhere, its furnishings were modest, with only a dilapidated stool and a hand-carved stone table cleaved from the wall nearest the access door. Resting on this rustic ledge was a single cylindrical canister, twelve inches in height, resembling nothing so much as a coffee thermos – with the exception that common beverage containers were rarely constructed of medieval amalgams of oak and alabaster, embossed with crude Christian symbols and dire warnings in Latin.

The only occupant of the room was a tall man, also in the camouflage garb favored by the Abbey's protectors, whose immobile form was illuminated by a tiny battery-powered camping light he'd positioned on the table's edge. He was napping; his head drooped on his chest, and occasional rumbling snores disrupted the stillness. He was a young man, no more than twenty-five, heavily-bearded, with a scar on his forehead in the shape of a cross. This guard was also armed with a SIG Sauer automatic pistol – an incongruous anachronism given the nature of the room and the Abbey's monastic purpose.

A crudely rendered stone grid near the ceiling shifted upwards an inch at a time, six feet away from the slumbering man's head. It weighed over a hundred pounds, and yet it slid silently into the dark cavity behind it without so much as a scrape against the ancient stones of the Chamber. The slumbering guard hadn't stirred.

The intruder crawled out of the hand-carved tunnel and dropped lightly to the Chamber floor, pausing in a crouch, studying the *cruci fixus* on the guard's forehead before scrutinizing his eyelids, watchful for any sign of awareness.

Satisfied that the man wasn't an immediate threat, the silent trespasser's focus turned to the canister on the table, now only four feet away. The container was distinctly unimpressive considering what it purportedly held. It was almost a disappointment that the intelligence on its safeguarding was correct; no complex Indiana Jones-like counterweights to contend with, no medieval combination locks to breach. Nothing, except for the droning guard – the first priority if the mission was to be fruitful.

The intruder approached on catlike feet, another syringe at the ready.

A loose flagstone beneath a delicately-placed boot jarred the silence. The guard jolted awake with a start. The intruder lunged forward with the needle, but this guard was faster than the one by the well; he dodged the attempt at his neck and spun towards his assailant as he shook off the grogginess of sleep. He fumbled for his pistol, but the intruder snap-kicked his hand, audibly breaking the bones. The guard howled in pain and, not as adept in close-quarters combat as his attacker, he swung ineffectually with his good hand. The intruder dodged the awkward assault and delivered three successive blows to the tall man's solar-plexus, trachea and jaw. It was the throat-blow that stopped the guard mid-stride, and he staggered back against the door with a thud before crumpling to the floor.

The sound of his exclamation and body slamming against the heavy door alerted the other guard, and the rattle of keys scrabbling at the lock echoed in the now-still Chamber, followed by the guard's cries of alarm to the Abbey above.

So much for stealth. The intruder grabbed the canister and hastily shoved it into a streamlined backpack, then reentered the ventilation shaft and wedged the stone grid back into place.

The Chamber door heaved, but the weight of the unconscious guard held it closed. Within moments, more men were struggling with the door, and it grudgingly slid open. A shocked silence accompanied the discovery that the container was missing. The unthinkable had happened after centuries of vigilance – a locked room, a downed guard, and the cylinder gone, but nobody else in the Chamber. *How was it possible?*

One of the friars spotted a small lump of dust in a corner near the rock ledge that had been home to the Scroll. His trembling finger followed the path of gravity up the wall, ultimately pointing at the stone ventilation port. A cry went up, and half of the men ran out into the adjoining passageway, while the other half rushed to remove the heavy stone grid that barred the coal-black shaft behind it.

The intruder slipped along the crawlspace at high speed on a thin sheet of fiberglass with small rubber wheels mounted on the four corners – a modified low-profile skateboard, its ball-bearing axles rolling soundlessly. A second rappelling cord affixed at the starting point had proved a good idea for the return trip; the intruder traversed the entire length of the eighty-foot tunnel in seconds by pulling the makeshift trolley along the rope. The nylon line had also prevented confusion over which route led back to the catacombs – the shaft split in three directions at a central junction, but following the cord left only one choice.

The clamor of the guards exiting the Chamber reverberated down the passage where the prowler had dropped to the floor from the duct at the far end. Engaging the night-vision goggles again, the intruder easily found the harness dangling from the well's opening and, with a practiced motion, donned and secured it. The climb back to the top of the narrow shaft took several minutes of fiercely-determined exertion. At the end of the ascent the noise of pursuers fumbling through the hall below inspired a burst of stamina – the final twenty feet were conquered in a few seconds, just as the guards reached the bottom of the shaft, screaming in frustration. Shots echoed from the void, and bullets nicked the interior of the well's rim, but it was too late.

The nearly-invisible figure ran three hundred yards through the brush until arriving at a clearing – an ancient cemetery, possibly for the Abbey's service staff, or a long-departed farming family. The intruder glanced back at the Abbey, now glowing with illumination, every window streaming light into the gloom. The frantic roar of car engines starting shattered the still night over the foggy moor.

Perfect. The din would cover the sound of the getaway vehicle – a blacked-out obsidian Moto-Guzzi Stelvio NTX motorcycle hidden, for a fast escape, behind one of the battered headstones.

A gloved finger stabbed the starter button and the big motor cranked to rumbling life. The rider checked the backpack, ensuring it was tightly closed and safely strapped in place. It wouldn't do to have the canister lost on a trail somewhere in the English wilds.

No, the contents were far too precious to take foolish chances with. If the legends were true, the cylinder held the key to the most important secret ever known – a secret capable of changing the course of history.

Slamming the motorcycle into gear, the black-garbed rider sprayed gravel with the rear wheel and roared off into the night.

CHAPTER 1

Present Day, The Road to Lucca, Italy

Dr. Steven Archer Cross was having a very bad day.

His cell phone, wedged in its dashboard holder, signaled an incoming call just as he narrowly missed ramming his 2009 Porsche Cabriolet into a Renault sedan that had come to a skidding halt in front of him, blocked by a stalled VW Wesfalia covered with faded bumper stickers. The cars behind him slammed on their brakes and then stood on their horns in frustrated anger, as though somehow he'd conspired with the Renault and broken-down van immediately ahead. Steven had the Porsche's convertible top down, and he could feel angry eyes boring into the back of his head as he waited for an opportunity to pull around the immobile camper.

Eventually, one of the vehicles behind him took pity and waved him forward. He signaled and pulled past the log-jammed clump of vehicles to join the rubberneckers in witnessing another unlucky driver's misfortune. A tall man with curly brown hair and a faded Grateful Dead T-shirt stood by the side of the road, agitatedly talking on his cell phone. The look on his face telegraphed this wasn't the first time the Volkswagen had betrayed him.

Steven stepped on the gas as he drove away from the congestion, checking the digital dashboard clock as he accelerated through the gears. He caught a glimpse of himself in the rearview mirror, the wind buffeting his shaggy, light brown hair; the beginnings of hairline wrinkles on his tanned face framed his hazel eyes. Not so bad for forty-five, he reasoned, especially considering the mileage.

The road ahead of him opened up and soon he was tearing along at eighty, traffic having thinned to nothing. The vehicular crisis circumvented, he turned his attention to the phone and the missed call.

He reached for the keypad and hit the send button. His office manager Gwen answered.

"Hullo," she said in British-accented English, her Yorkshire heritage obvious even from the single word.

"Hey, sorry I couldn't pick up. I was a little busy."

"How busy can you be on a day like today?" Gwen asked.

"You'd be surprised at how much I have going on," Steven protested. "What's up?"

"A strange call came in a few minutes ago. The gentlemen said he needed to speak to you immediately," Gwen said.

"Okay…did you get a name?"

"Winston Twain. Mean anything?" Gwen asked.

Steven mentally file-referenced Twain. It was familiar, almost on the periphery of 'very important', but after racking his brain for a few moments the sensation of familiarity flitted away. Which didn't necessarily mean anything – he'd been scattered since…

No point dwelling on the unpleasant.

"Not really. What did he want?" Steven asked.

"Just said it was a matter of significant importance."

"Significant? Fine. What's his number?"

"He didn't leave one. Said he'd call back. He sounded like another Yank. I think the call might have been international," Gwen opined.

Steven considered Gwen's words – most calls of actual 'significant importance' tended to leave call-back numbers. Especially ones from the States, assuming her instinct was correct. Which it usually was. Gwen had been his office manager and handler since the inception of his software business three and a half years ago. She had an uncanny knack of being able to read people and was rarely wrong.

An uncomfortable silence hovered over the line.

"You're still going to jump today?" Gwen asked.

"Yes," Steven said.

"Jump out of a perfectly good plane, right?"

"Right."

"Dropping at thirty-six feet per second, at a speed of–"

"Stop it. I have to go," Steven protested.

"Cheers, then, and remember: what goes up…" Gwen disconnected.

As he fought the morning traffic towards Lucca, a city roughly half an hour north-west of Florence, Steven suddenly remembered what the name Winston Twain meant.

"I'll be damned," Steven muttered to himself.

Winston Twain.

Arguably the most respected cryptologist in the world.

CHAPTER 2

Thirty Months Ago, 20 Miles South of Florence, Italy

The rustic Tuscan country house seemed to glow in the bright noon sunshine; its mustard-tinged paint blended with the field of green and brown grass surrounding it, creating the illusion it was floating in a rusted verdant sea.

Two figures stood in a quiet embrace on the circular driveway's stones. A light breeze carried the scent of hay from a nearby barn, intermingled with the smell of garlic drifting from neighboring kitchens. Neither of the pair noticed. They kissed like newlyweds, which was hardly the case – it had been three years since they'd exchanged vows but to any onlooker it would appear that these were teenagers enraptured by the powerful glow of first love.

The woman's auburn hair stirred as she pulled away from the man and, rolling an elastic hair tie down her wrist, she drew her mane into a ponytail. He held her at arm's length, as though memorizing every detail of her face, and then hugged her close once more. They kissed again for a fleeting eternity.

The moment passed and the woman glanced at her watch. "Oh, Steven, I'm late as usual. Okay, this is goodbye for real this time. I have to go," Antonia exclaimed.

"Why are you abandoning me?" Steven asked in a theatrical fashion.

"*Caro*, it's only a weekend. And you could have come, but you changed your mind at the last minute. You and your hobby, too busy to keep a girl satisfied, so she has to find diversion elsewhere…" Antonia complained. Her English was fluent, yet the unmistakable Italian accent colored the cadence in a musical way.

"I wish I could go, but I made the arrangements for this meeting weeks ago, and I can't cancel. It's taken me a year to get the old bastard interested in selling, and he could change his mind at any time. You know I want to go with you," Steven declared.

"*Si, si,* I know. Oh well, then, it will be just me and my uncle…and perhaps the pool boy," Antonia said.

Steven knew better. Antonia's uncle, Dante, had a palatial home half an hour south of Venice, as well as ten-bedroom 'cottages' in Chianti, Naples, and on the shores of Lake Lugano. There would inevitably be dozens of relatives arriving for his seventy-fifth birthday celebration, and likely everything from visiting heads of state to a reunion of the surviving Beatles to commemorate another year on the planet for the patriarch. It wouldn't surprise Steven if, upon Antonia's return, she reported that the Pope had dropped by unexpectedly to wish Dante continued good health.

"Do try to have a good time, would you? I know how boring old Dante can be," Steven quipped, fully aware that the weekend would comprise non-stop revelry. "Maybe I'll take the train up and surprise you. I'm hopeful this meeting won't be a multi-day negotiation, but you know Italy…"

"Yeah, yeah. At least I have the internet. I'll tweet and let you know how the party is going," Antonia promised.

"I wouldn't mind giving you a good tweeting before you go," Steven fired back.

"There's nothing I'd like more, but I have to leave. Really, my little sparrow." She pulled him next to the car. "*Ciao, amor.* I'll see you in a few days."

Antonia kissed Steven's lips one final time, then opened the door of the silver Audi TT. He couldn't help but appreciate how magnificent her tanned, lithely-muscled legs looked as she climbed behind the wheel, her fashionably-cut skirt riding up to the top of her thigh. The engine burbled to life, and she shut the door and waved at him through the smoked window as she popped the transmission into gear.

Steven watched the little car pull down the drive and onto the small strip of pavement that passed for a road in their rural area. Antonia tore off as though the devil was on her heels – a sedate pace for her, he knew. He could hear the engine revving into the distance for a full minute before tranquility descended again.

You're a lucky man, Steven.

It was true. Three years ago he and Antonia had ducked out of the rat race and committed to prioritizing their time together over everything else. They'd roamed Italy for months before settling in Greve, where they could be in Florence within twenty minutes (if Antonia was driving) and yet were still well away from the hubbub of the city.

Not renowned for resting on his laurels, once they'd established their new home in the Tuscan countryside, Steven had become increasingly engaged in his burgeoning hobby of cryptography – pursuing it with single-minded focus until Antonia suggested channeling his energy differently. At her goading he'd started a boutique software company, which had quickly blossomed into a five person organization that managed the efforts of nine remote programmers in Russia, the Ukraine and India. Ironically, neither of them needed the income – Antonia's travel magazine sale had made her a small fortune, and Steven had accumulated enough in the market to never have to work again.

But that wasn't his nature. Steven had already retired once, after selling his original company while in his late thirties, only to discover that his personality required more stimulation than endless napping. After a brief but deadly dalliance with the U.S. stock market and a whirlwind education on the lethal factions that congregated wherever big money circulated, he'd switched his interest to the internet – at a time when social media was coming into its own.

That had ultimately resulted in his current venture, which was precariously close to a real job. The company was supposed to run itself, but he was still inexorably sucked into the day-to-day operations far more than he liked.

And he still had his hobby. The challenges involved in cryptography had grown from being light entertainment to borderline obsession. He'd spent countless hours working on medieval and Renaissance cyphers, and had gone so far as to write several programs for tracking character repetition and analyzing coded messages. Many of his weekends had involved trips to ferret-out original parchments, hundreds of years old, written in the cyphers that were fairly common from the twelfth through eighteenth century. Steven didn't get to spend as much time as he would have liked on it these days, what with the company seemingly going through one operational emergency or another, but he still took at least two days a week to work on his 'projects', as Antonia called them.

Which was why he was going to miss the party of the century, or at least, of this year, near Venice.

He'd been courting an octogenarian antique and rare parchment dealer from Bologna; his intention was to buy the man's private collection of parchments, some of which were the stuff of rumor – scrolls from

Morocco, thirteenth through fifteenth century England, Italy, France, and even some older works from Greece. These were museum pieces, rare and unseen, and would make perfect additions to Steven's growing collection. They'd been in the old man's possession for eons, many of them passed down from his father, who had also been in the business as well as being a counselor on rare documents to such entities as the Romanoffs at the turn of the 20th Century. This was a once-in-a-lifetime opportunity for Steven, although he knew that the truly valuable works would have long ago been committed to heavyweight private collectors from Russia and China. Still, this man's table scraps were probably as intriguing as the most highly-touted finds in the Italian trade, and Steven was anxious to seal a deal.

Steven checked his watch, a platinum Lange & Sohne perpetual calendar Antonia had gotten him as a forty-second birthday gift. He walked back into the house; his meeting wasn't until five o'clock that evening but he was impatient to view the old man's trove.

After a few minutes wandering aimlessly through the empty rooms, he resolved to go into Florence for a few hours to work out at his favorite Dojo. Steven's fascination with martial arts was still as strong as ever, and even though he was an adept in most of the disciplines, he loved the ritual of performing his workout. He patted his stomach – after eating Italian food for the last three years, he needed every opportunity for exercise he could get.

He packed a messenger bag with his Gi and a towel, then strode to the small stand-alone garage, which was crammed full of the junk he and Antonia had collected during their years together. After a few moments, Steven emerged pushing a battered Vespa motor-scooter – the ubiquitous transportation in the region – and struggled with the kick-start. On the fourth try it rattled to life and, after revving the motor a few times, Steven settled onto the cracked vinyl seat and made for Florence in a cloud of blue exhaust.

❧

Antonia loved the feel of the wind in her hair as she sped north on the highway that wound its way through the Italian countryside. She'd left the house just after 12:45 and, allowing for traffic and the odd unforeseen fuel and rest stop, she figured she could make it to Dante's house by 5 p.m..

The little Audi convertible's top was seldom up except when they went into Florence, and one of her guilty pleasures was to feel the sun warm on her face as she drove, admittedly far too fast, to one of her favorite places on the planet: Venice.

Even now, she felt the city possessed a majesty she'd never found anywhere else. True, it could get unpleasantly crowded with tourists in the spring and summer, but so could most of the larger cities in Italy. It was a necessary evil, and one she could deal with, especially if she was just visiting. She enjoyed the quiet of the country life she and Steven had together in Greve, but there was nothing like the magic of Venice to get the juices flowing.

Her mind wandered to the miracle that was their life together as she rolled through the hills – it really was a dream come true. She loved Steven deeply and completely, and she knew he would do anything for her – he'd more than proved that. And it was perfect that they'd turned the old farmhouse they'd bought into a rambling, Tuscan classic, lovingly renovating it while adding all the modern conveniences they both appreciated. It was large for the two of them – but they would soon need the space: only this morning she'd discovered, via the miracle of modern drugstore products, that she was pregnant.

Antonia had been so excited she'd repeated the test – both times had registered positive. There was no doubt. She'd wanted to tell Steven, but had composed herself and resolved to sit down with him once she returned – she knew enough about men that you didn't just announce you were going to have a family and then hit the road to a party. This was a serious step; one they'd discussed, but it had never seemed like exactly the right time…*eh, well, it's the right time now, no?*

After all they'd been through together, after she'd almost died in his arms, to create a life together – and see both of themselves in their baby's eyes – was almost too much to hope for. The circle of life was complete. They were safe, secure, healthy, prosperous, and Steven would be a perfect father…

Antonia was lost in her thoughts as she wound her way through the slopes north of Barberino de Mugello. As she twisted down the tortuous mountain highway her fuel light blinked and then illuminated. *Damn.* She'd forgotten to fill up. No matter, there was a station in a few miles, she was sure. Antonia passed a tanker truck making its way cautiously down the steep incline; as she swerved around it, she nearly collided with an old pickup that was barely crawling – in the fast lane, of course. She stomped on her brakes to avoid crashing into it, but the pedal went to the floor without any resistance. She slalomed around the pickup, nearly slamming through the guardrail, and checked her speedometer – 92 MPH. Her mind racing, Antonia downshifted, and the car gradually slowed. At least she could use the transmission to brake – it was just her luck that something would go wrong on a Saturday, when most mechanics were closed for the weekend.

Antonia pushed the thought aside. She could make arrangements once she'd found a gas station. At worst, she could have Dante send a car for her. It would be annoying and inconvenient, but sometimes that was how life was.

She downshifted again, slowing the little car to 60 MPH, then 50, and pulled off at the exit she thought led to a fuel station. She coasted along and glanced to her right – she could make out a service station sign through the olive trees. At least that's what it looked like – she couldn't be sure, but she thought it must be. She studied the map on her in-console GPS, looking for the icon that signified a fuel stop. *Aha! She was right. There was one an eighth of a mile away.*

Temporarily engrossed with the GPS, by the time Antonia registered the overloaded semi-rig hurtling down the frontage road at her, it was too late to do anything but scream. She instinctively pumped her non-functional brakes, and then, instantly realizing her mistake, tried to accelerate.

She almost made it.

Antonia only had a split second before the massive truck rammed sideways into her little roadster, crushing it like a soda can. Her final thoughts were that it was too soon, that it wasn't fair, and that the precious life inside her would never see the light of day.

Then everything went black.

&

Steven pulled back into the driveway of his home, his impatience and anxiety at the upcoming meeting with the rare parchment dealer blunted by the physical exertion from his martial arts workout. He checked his watch and realized he only had twenty minutes to prepare for his guest.

He threw open the front door, tossed his bag onto the entryway hall table and hurried to the bedroom, stripping off his damp top as he went. He grabbed a button-up shirt and a pair of khaki pants from the closet, and cranked the handles on the shower, knowing it would take a couple of minutes for the water to reach a comfortable temperature. The plumbing of the old house had been a continual source of annoyance and was next on their list of items to be redone – they'd been holding off on it because they wanted to be gone when the floors and walls were gutted to replace the ancient pipes. As with most projects in Italy, what should take two weeks would inevitably take two months, so one had to get used to it and become resigned to the reality of the pace of the country.

Steven stepped under the stream of tepid water and quickly and efficiently rinsed himself clean. He heard the sound of a car moving up the drive as he exited and hurriedly dried off, ran a comb through his hair, and pulled on the shirt and slacks. He was still tucking in his shirt when the front knocker sounded the early arrival of his guest.

Steven opened the door and greeted the old man, who stood outside the entryway clutching a battered metal toolbox to his chest. Behind him was a new Peugeot sedan with a lanky driver leaning against the front fender, a cigarette dangling from his lips as he scanned a newspaper he'd brought for diversion.

Steven welcomed the dealer into his study and moved the accumulated books from his large rectangular table, making space to examine the ancient man's trove. The old man carefully placed the box on one edge of the workspace and opened the top before removing five parchments, each lovingly ensconced in a clear plastic sheath for protection. Steven studied each hand-crafted treasure in turn. All were obviously genuine and very old. The first was a Greek document from approximately 800 A.D., and the following four were from the twelfth and fifteenth centuries. All the documents were written in cyphers, which was why Steven was interested – his collection was exclusively encrypted parchments from the seventeenth century and earlier, with a preponderance of work originating from Italy and England.

Steven spent a half hour discussing the various parchments with the dealer, all of which had been in his family's custody for several centuries. The initial asking price was multiples higher than what Steven had calculated the true value to be, which was not unexpected. He invited the wizened dealer into the dining room to partake of some vintage port, and they sipped the seventy-year-old wine with approval as they negotiated back and forth. Eventually, they arrived at a price both could live with – considerably more than Steven had hoped, but still within reason. Delighted that he'd struck a bargain so quickly, he ducked back into his study and wrote a check for the dealer, who exchanged the toolbox of parchments for the payment.

Their business concluded, Steven bade the old gentleman farewell and walked him to his car, where the driver was still standing in the same position as when they entered the house – the only giveaway of the passage of time, the seven cigarette stubs collected around his feet. Steven and the dealer said their goodbyes by the side of the vehicle, which were cut short by the jangling of the phone in the kitchen. Steven waved at them and sprinted back to the house, but the phone had gone silent by the time he reached it.

That was sort of how his whole day had gone – he felt like he'd been running a few minutes late since he'd woken with Antonia an hour past their usual time. He returned to his study and surveyed the parchments, ruminating over which one he would begin to decrypt first. The phone started ringing again. This time he made it into the kitchen by the fourth ring and snatched the handset from the cradle of the heavy mid-Seventies base station.

Outside, the olive trees stirred in the careless breeze as the day's warm light faded. The flocculent clouds drifted lazily across the mackerel sky as the sun made way for the encroaching night. It was an idyllic dusk in the valley, a thing of tour book photos, travel brochures and chocolate boxes.

Inside the house, the telephone handset clattered to the floor, and an otherworldly moan echoed around the rustic stone walls; an animal sound of raw, tortured pain.

CHAPTER 3

Present Day, Palm Desert, California

Winston Twain glumly regarded the phone on his desk, which was nearly completely blanketed with papers, reference books, and two laptops. He groaned out loud and then noisily slurped at a cup of Earl Grey tea before he resumed studying a letter addressed to him by Dr. Steven Cross. He appraised the concise script with approval and nodded to himself. He'd just gotten around to studying a note Cross had sent him about a working theory on the Voynich Manuscript: an obscure document from the Middle Ages written entirely in an indecipherable code – a code that Twain had dedicated himself to trying to decrypt for the past thirty years.

The study's screen door moved slightly as a light wind hummed through the room. Twain wheeled around and looked out at the desert night as the door once again settled into place. Twain had lived all over the world, but swore by the Coachella Valley and the surrounding desert, only a two hour drive from Los Angeles. The sun had long since set over the mountains that jutted eleven thousand feet into the sky, and Twain was burning the midnight oil, as was his custom. It was the perfect time of year in Palm Springs – late May – when the temperature rarely deviated from ninety-three degrees at the height of day, dropping into the sixties at night. He preferred the tranquility of night for contemplation and rarely slept more than five hours now that he was of a certain age, which afforded him ample time for his projects as the rest of California slept.

Twain wheeled his chair around and, again, considered his desk and the materials of a lifetime scattered across the top of it. Most of the area was occupied by a high-resolution copy of his fascination – the Voynich Manuscript – which, in loosely strewn unbound form, covered every inch of a work surface in desperate need of reorganization.

Lost and re-discovered through the centuries, the Voynich was a seemingly innocuous hand-printed and illustrated series of chapters – quires – written in a cypher that had rebuffed the efforts of the best minds in the cryptology field. While it was, at a cursory glance, apparently devoted to equal parts herbalism and astronomy, the actual text remained a mystery. The odd-looking volume was entirely written in an unknown language using unfamiliar symbols. Page after page, quire after quire.

Early 20th century theories had speculated that it was gibberish, an elaborate hoax, but later analysis confirmed that the character repetition and sequencing was too symmetrical to be a hoax language. The oddly-formed calligraphy and seemingly fantastical illustrations had confounded the best efforts of the best in the field, maddeningly keeping its secrets through the ages.

The original of the Voynich had long been on display at the Beinecke Rare Book and Manuscript Library of Yale University and was, in fact, the most popular document in the collection. It continued to be a subject of rabid fascination for many cryptologists, as it had been ever since it had been made public by Polish-born antique book dealer, Wilfred Voynich, in 1912. As with several of his colleagues, deciphering the Voynich had become a lifelong obsession for Twain; its pull was just as strong as when he was a young officer returning from the Korean War. His specialty had been code-breaking for the military, so it was almost inevitable that he would be drawn to the most notorious riddle in cryptography. But what had begun as a conviction that he'd be able to crack it in a matter of months gradually became a multi-decade odyssey of twists and false starts. He'd grown sadly accustomed to illusive progress transforming into dead-ends, with any forward movement ultimately resulting in him being slammed into a brick wall, no closer to a solution than at first.

Cross had formulated an interesting theory – one that Twain himself had considered before discarding as non-disprovable, and therefore useless as the basis of a scientific hypothesis, but he wanted to understand how an amateur like Cross had arrived at such a complicated and innovative conclusion. The level of reasoning required to reach it was significantly more advanced than anything he'd come across in recent memory. It had impressed him by virtue of its brash brilliance.

Ah, well, Twain thought. This Dr. Steven Cross was not even part of the formal cryptology community – he wasn't a member of any of the professional organizations, and he'd never published; the call had been made primarily as a courtesy on Twain's part – because he was in a good mood. A good mood indeed because today, after what he'd just acquired, the world would soon be turned on its head.

The Voynich Manuscript had never been closer to being deciphered – by him, Winston Twain – since its creation.

A noise made Twain turn – the back door to his garden study had swung open.

"Hello, who's there?" Twain called out. "Natalie, is that you?"

Silence.

"Hello?"

He peered down the dark hall to the back porch and was about to dismiss his premonition when he detected motion at the edge of his awareness. Twain's eyes widened in horror as a hulking figure stepped from behind an antique armoire.

"Good morning, Professor Twain," the huge, hirsute man named Sia Amieri said, in a hoarse, heavily-accented whisper that was almost inaudible. "We need to talk."

Twain's pupils dilated to the size of pinheads.

He swallowed with difficulty – he knew what a visit from the menacing giant meant, and he understood instantly that this was going to be the last day of his life.

CHAPTER 4

Present Day, Lucca, Italy

Steven's mind raced over the implications of a call from Professor Winston Twain. He'd forgotten about the letter he'd sent about his tentative theories on the possible origin of the Voynich Manuscript – a document that was a legend wrapped in an enigma. Steven had spent the better part of a year studying it, but had made no more progress than anyone else, which was to say, none at all. Over time, his interests had shifted elsewhere, and that period of mourning for his wife, interspersed with feverish efforts to untangle the manuscript's puzzling code, had receded into a hazy memory.

Steven pulled down the road leading to the main terminal of the Scuola Paracadutismo Lucca, the parachuting academy that was his ultimate destination this morning. For its elaborate name, there wasn't much to it. The total campus consisted of a very small hangar with a tiny office attached on the periphery of the airport. Several Pilatus PC6 single engine airplanes were taxiing toward the runway, while one plane – the plane he would be jumping out of – prepped for take-off. Steven killed the momentary twinge of fatalism in his mind that intruded when he saw it and resumed his former ruminations.

Winston Twain and the Voynich Manuscript.

Twain and the Voynich were practically synonymous in the cryptology community. The man was near-legendary in certain circles, considered equal parts savant and dreamer, due to his near-compulsive fixation on decrypting that which had stumped his peers for decades.

A bouncing young brunette in a short denim skirt and a pink tank top approached him as he wheeled to a stop in front of building. She brandished a clipboard and seemed to float with each step.

"Are you *Dottore* Cross?" the girl asked cheerfully in Italian, beaming a smile.

"Yes," Steven replied in near-fluent Italian.

"We were waiting for you!"

"I got held up on the road."

"Okay, no problem. But we have to hurry. We're on a tight schedule."

She led Steven directly to the airplane and introduced him to the pilot, Tomaso Caldieri, and his 'jump-buddy', Paolo. A third man, Giorgio, nodded silently from the rear of the plane.

"Sorry I'm late," Steven said.

"No problem," Tomaso assured him. He finished his pre-flight checklist and turned to regard Steven, who had climbed into the back of the plane and was hurriedly donning an orange jumpsuit Paolo had handed him. "Let's do some flying, shall we?"

"And jumping," Paolo chimed in.

They closed the transom door, and within a few seconds the engine sputtered to a start before leveling to a roaring hum. After a brief taxi, the little plane sped down the runway and was airborne.

"We'll be at twelve thousand feet in about fifteen minutes," Paolo said to Steven as they soared into the sky. He was already putting on his parachute and preparing Steven for his first tandem jump. Paolo briefly took him through the drill. He would harness himself to Steven and they'd skydive together, with Paolo manning the chute and Steven, presumably, enjoying the ride.

Steven was doing this for one reason: a desire to push the envelope and experience things he'd shied away from. Antonia had been a big believer in trying new things, and since her death, Steven had made it a point to schedule something that took him out of his comfort zone at least once every ninety days, as a tribute to her memory as well as a mechanism to force him out of the doldrums that had become his customary state since the accident. So far, he'd conquered scuba diving, had learned to rappel, had run a marathon, and acted as a mentor to several underprivileged kids in Florence. Today was skydiving.

"Don't worry," Paolo said, smiling. "Very rarely does anything go wrong." Paolo had mistaken Steven's silence as fear.

"That's very comforting," Steven said, as he snapped back to the present and fiddled with the harness around his chest and waist.

"Accidents are almost unheard of. The odds are very much in our favor," Paolo said. It sounded almost like he was trying to convince himself as much as he was trying to reassure Steven. "So here's how this is going to work, Dr. Cross."

"Call me Steven."

"What's going to happen, Steven, is in about two minutes, Giorgio here will slide the door open, and then Tomaso will give us a Go-Green on that light." Paolo pointed to the small bulb above the door. "We'll take a moment, and then it's boom, out of the plane!"

"How long until we get to the ground?" Steven asked.

"Terminal velocity is around a hundred and twenty miles per hour, give or take wind, drag and a few other things, but I'd say it will be about eight minutes. It also depends how long you want to freefall – how long we drop before I pull the chute."

"I'll leave that up to you."

Paolo grinned, then turned Steven towards the door and harnessed himself to Steven's back. Giorgio gave a thumbs up.

"One last question," Steven said over his shoulder.

"Fire away."

"What if something does go wrong? Like the chutes fail to open?" Steven asked.

Paolo contemplated the question. "If that happens, you'll never have to worry about anything ever again."

Sensing that Steven was less than amused, Paolo cleared his throat and unfastened the harness. Free of Steven once again, he turned and patted two handles on his parachute.

"This is the ripcord. It deploys the main chute." Paolo gestured to the white handle.

Steven nodded.

"And this, what they call the lolly-pop, is the secondary emergency ripcord." Paolo tapped it for emphasis. "Now you know where both ripcords are. Ready to jump?" Paolo asked, moving to reconnect himself to Steven.

"Might as well get it over with."

The plane reached its cruising altitude and the green light illuminated. Giorgio gave an okay sign and then pulled open the plane's sliding panel.

Wind pummeled Steven's face, and in spite of the goggles he winced involuntarily.

Paolo negotiated both of them toward the opening. Steven looked down and saw miles of nothingness.

Then he felt a push in the small of his back, and he was falling, face first into the void. His stomach churned, and for a moment he couldn't breathe.

"Relax!" Paolo screamed at him over the roar of wind.

They dropped for seemingly ever towards the ground below. Paolo hadn't pulled the chute yet, determined to give Steven his money's worth. Steven forced himself to calmly look down at the approaching earth, and for a moment it felt like he was floating, though his intellect told him that they'd already achieved terminal velocity, as did the way the wind tore at his jumpsuit.

He almost began to enjoy the odd sensation when a massive jolt slammed into him, and he felt pain lash his face as something tore across it. They abruptly spun into a spiral, and Steven spat something out of his mouth.

A feather.

He craned his neck and saw a ragged flock of geese, stunned and panicked, hundreds of feet above him as Steven and Paolo continued their fall. Then the birds were out of sight, continuing their journey.

Steven's focus became a dizzy whirl of confusion. He was no longer floating in a quasi-dream state. They were tumbling out of control. The spinning was disorienting, and he battled to stay calm even as the shriek of the wind deafened him.

"Paolo!" Steven screamed.

Paolo didn't answer.

Steven yelled again, but still got no response. He elbowed his expert savior several times, to no avail. Paolo was either unconscious or dead.

The ground was approaching faster. Steven drew a deep series of breaths and forced himself to concentrate on reaching the rip cords he knew were on either side of Paolo's harness.

He groped behind his back with his right hand, trying to get to the main handle, but his arm couldn't quite make it no matter how he strained, and the ripcord remained out of reach by a scant few inches. It wasn't working. He shifted to his left arm and stretched for the lolly-pop handle of the emergency chute.

No go.

He looked down at his harness and calculated that one of the connecting straps would have to be detached so his arms had more flexibility. Steven intuitively understood the risks involved, but didn't see an alternative.

He reached to the harness clip on his left side and pulled the safety belt release.

With a lurch, half of his body now dangled from the one remaining strap securing him to Paolo. He supposed it was too late to wonder about how many foot pounds of resistance a single belt could take before snapping – hopefully at least several more than he was about to subject it to.

Steven turned on himself, still tumbling head over heels in tandem with Paolo without any perspective or line of sight, and concentrated on the emergency handle.

His left arm now free, his fingers felt for the grip. They felt the distinctive form and wrapped around it, and he yanked the cord as hard as he could.

For a moment, nothing happened.

Then his whole body jerked abruptly upwards, and something in the small of his neck tweaked painfully. He looked up to see the chute opening above and grabbed at Paolo's harness just in case the sole strap was preparing to give way. Fortunately they were still connected.

Reassured he was secure, he returned his gaze to the ground, now only six hundred feet below. He fought to adjust himself so that when he landed it would be on his feet. That turned out to be easier than he'd anticipated; with the braking effect of the chute he had more control. Now the trick would be to avoid snapping his spine when he slammed into the ground with Paolo unconscious.

The earth drew closer, and he made out three people below, hands outstretched, waiting to assist him.

He hit the ground upright, and while there was a jolt, there was no anticipated pain of a twisted ankle or sprain. But almost instantly his legs collapsed under him and he rolled on the ground atop Paolo's body before coming to a stop, spitting out dust.

"*Mierda*!" someone yelled, and suddenly three pairs of hands were pulling at him, unsnapping harness straps and the cords linking Paolo's pack to the parachute.

"Never seen anything like that!" another man said.

Steven tried to stand up, but couldn't. Visions of himself paralyzed in a hospital bed flashed across his mind, and then he realized it was because he still had two hundred plus pounds of Paolo strapped to him.

"Unbelievable. I've heard of bird-strike on small planes, but nothing like this," yet another man exclaimed in Italian.

"One for the record books," the first declared as he fumbled with Steven's harness.

The men heaved Steven, struggling for breath, free from Paolo, then he abruptly found himself standing on very shaky legs.

"Are you all right?" a burly man asked as he put both hands on Steven's shoulders and looked him straight in the eyes.

Steven nodded, then collapsed onto both knees and vomited.

"Your equilibrium's shot. It will take a while to get adjusted. The nausea's normal," the man explained.

Steven managed a nod as spasms racked his body, and it was with relief that he finally heard the approaching ambulance arriving from the nearby hospital.

* * *

After an hour of observation and an X-ray of his neck, Steven was released with instructions to take aspirin for any pain and to come back if the discomfort lasted more than a couple of days. He'd declined the offer of a whiplash collar – the attending physician had said it was optional in his case. No permanent damage had resulted from the strike or the hard landing, and the doctor had put a Dramamine patch below his ear to control the dizziness before signing him out. Paolo wasn't so lucky – his spine had been badly twisted after hitting a goose, and one of his legs was fractured in three places following the landing.

The front desk nurse in the emergency room called him a taxi, and Steven sat on the bench by the sliding glass doors, an ice bag held to his still-aching neck. Minutes dragged by. He extracted his cell from his windbreaker and dialed his office number.

Gwen answered. "I'm guessing from the caller ID that you made it in one piece?"

"You're a funny lady."

"I'm told that all of the time. I'm thinking of buying a tent and taking it on the road." Gwen paused. "How was it?"

"It was close."

Gwen's tone changed to one of genuine concern. "You're kidding…"

"No, I'm not. I wish I was. I'll tell you all about it later," Steven said. "Listen, did Professor Twain ever call back?"

"No. Where are you? Are you all right? Do you need anything?" Gwen sounded disturbed.

"I'm fine. Mostly. Listen, do me a favor. Look the Professor up and see if you can locate his number. His full name is Winston G. Twain. If my memory serves, he's in the Palm Springs area of California. I wrote him a letter a year ago, but that's all I can remember. Palm Springs, or Palm Desert. If you can't find him, I can root around for the address in my desk. I probably still have it," Steven said.

"Okay. You don't sound so hot. You're not coming into the office today, are you?"

"I'll play that by ear," Steven replied. A siren drowned out the call for a few moments.

"Good Lord, Steven. Are you at a hospital?"

As the taxi pulled up to the glass doors, the driver looked around, irritated, as though he'd been waiting for his fare for half an hour. He spied Steven and gestured impatiently.

"I have to go now. Call me as soon as you get a hit," Steven said, and then hung up.

He wasn't in much of a mood to chat.

CHAPTER 5

Present Day, Tel Aviv, Israel

Two days after Steven nearly plummeted to his death in a field near Lucca, Colonel Gabriel Synthe glanced casually at the date on his watch as he passed through a suburb ten miles from the airport. He frowned. It was exactly six years ago that he'd resigned his position with the Mossad. He'd committed the date to memory, filed away – along with countless other unmentionable data points accumulated over a long career of savagery in the name of God and country.

He'd made a decision to never forget the circumstances surrounding his resignation, so he figured he might as well memorialize the date as well.

It was the day of his last assassination.

The Palestinian, Nassar, had been stretched out on the bed in his hotel room, near the Place de l'Opéra in Paris. He was suspected by the Mossad hierarchy of planning a car bombing that had killed four people two years earlier outside a synagogue in Jerusalem, and later, the strangling of the Prime Minister's cousin while she was enjoying her vacation near the Black Sea. The Mossad had gotten a tip that he was meeting with a terrorist cell in Paris, and Synthe had been selected for the operation, which would require planning and delicacy, in addition to ruthless efficiency.

He had contemplated using poison, but after getting the lowdown on the hotel had instead opted for the simple and effective. When Synthe's contact at the front desk received an order for room service from the terrorist, Synthe intercepted the errand and showed up at Nassar's hotel door in person, dressed as service staff, carrying a tray with a platter cover and a towel on it. When Nassar opened the door, he'd curtly gestured for him to bring the food in, and Synthe had obligingly moved into the room behind him with the tray. As Nassar turned his back to close the door, Synthe drove the razor-sharp carbon fiber blade of his custom-made stiletto into the base of his neck. Nassar crumpled to the carpet, his spinal cord severed at the junction of the spine and skull. Synthe then calmly withdrew the knife and drove it through Nassar's left eye, into his brain.

Nassar's head had convulsed twice, then lay still, blood pooling on the carpet beneath his twisted frame.

The entire episode had taken eight seconds.

Synthe then carefully moved to the bathroom and washed his weapon in the small sink, taking care to also rinse the blood from his hands and right sleeve. He pulled off the pair of translucent latex gloves he'd donned in preparation for the messy errand and methodically removed his bellman's jacket, folding it carefully before slipping it and the gloves into a plastic laundry bag the hotel provided for guests.

Synthe studied himself in the mirror. He winced as he tore off the mustache and sideburns that he'd affixed with theatrical adhesive and then dropped those into the bag as well. Now he looked like any one of millions of non-descript forty-something year old men wandering the busy French metropolis, wearing a Versace knock-off dress shirt and fashionable black slacks.

He had returned to the room and poked the corpse with his foot, more out of habit than anything. Satisfied that Nassar wasn't going to spontaneously come back to life, he walked to the door and listened carefully for any movement.

Nothing.

Synthe spied the terrorist's wallet on the dresser and quickly moved to pocket it. Brutal robberies were not unknown in large cities – a sad but unavoidable fact of life. Nassar would be just another in a long string of quickly-forgotten burglaries that had taken a turn toward the violent and, after a few days of no progress, would be largely abandoned by the police. He had no fear of getting caught – the security cameras had conveniently stopped working several days before and the maintenance company couldn't make it for a week. Yet another unfortunate coincidence for the police in an entropic universe.

Senses tuned to detect any threat, he cautiously opened the door and scanned the hall in both directions. Nothing. The area was empty.

Within two minutes, he was on the sidewalk with his bag of goodies, making for the Metro at a leisurely pace.

That same afternoon at the embassy, he submitted his report on the operation and then tendered his resignation. His superiors had been surprised, but ultimately, accepting. Everyone burned out eventually. It was impossible to predict what would trigger it, but it happened, and when it did, all they could do was let the operative try to make it in private life; and if he failed, have a position available for him behind a desk running his own gambits in the field with younger, more resilient agents doing the dirty work.

Synthe had taken the train to the South of France to spend a week amongst the rich and beautiful before flying to Tel Aviv, where he'd been met by his new employer and briefed on his odd new assignment.

Six years was a long time, and yet it seemed like yesterday.

It wasn't so much that killing Nassar had been memorable in any distinct way. Rather, it had been so mundane, so routine, it barely stood out from a host of other sanctions he'd carried out during his career.

That's why he'd had to commit the date to memory.

Lest he completely forget, and Nassar became just one in a long blurred lineup of hateful faces whose last living impression had been Synthe's icy stare.

Synthe looked out of the window of the black Lincoln Town Car at the throngs of carefree pedestrians enjoying an early summer day in Tel Aviv. It had to be nice, living in the innocent world of the civilian. He sometimes wished he could rejoin it and then banished his daydreaming – what was the point? His life was what he'd made it, and there was no turning back, which was why he was now sitting in an armor-plated sedan taking him to a meeting with one of his current employer's other operatives.

Something serious had happened in the past week, and his superior was not happy.

Synthe thought back to the meeting that had preceded his resignation from the Mossad, and his first encounter with the man known to him only as 'The Sentinel'. Two weeks before he'd assassinated Nassar, Synthe had attended a meeting with this shadowy figure, who had approached him through a contact with another intelligence service. Synthe had been curious, based on the veiled suggestion that a highly-paid position was available to an operative with his experience, and had allowed the courtship to proceed from the seemingly chance discussion with his counterpart at an embassy cocktail party to a lunchtime meeting at a deserted coffee bar several miles from the city center.

Synthe had arrived at the rendezvous at the small outdoor café at the agreed-upon time and had been greeted by a dignified older man in a perfectly-pressed Italian suit of expensive tailoring. They were the only ones in the small, walled courtyard of the establishment, and the disinterested waiter disappeared after bringing them their order of espresso.

"I presume we can have this discussion in French, Colonel Synthe? I believe you're fluent in the language?" the man asked in the Gallic tongue, obviously aware of Synthe's linguistic capabilities.

"That's fine." Synthe had always been a man of few words.

"Or we can speak English, or Italian, or Russian. I understand you're equally comfortable in these as well," the man said, not so much a question as a statement.

"Whatever. It is of no consequence. But I see you've done your homework," Synthe acknowledged, willing to accede professional courtesy at what was obviously a thorough background check into a high-ranking Mossad asset – an organization that was notoriously tight-lipped about all aspects of its personnel.

The older man smiled, a sort of dry grimace, his message of being able to access the most sacrosanct data in the Mossad efficiently delivered. He carefully lifted his little espresso cup to his lips and sipped before speaking.

"We can dispense with social niceties. You're a busy man, and so am I. I'm called the Sentinel – perhaps a bit melodramatic, however, it's a formality which has been observed for a long time, and I'm not going to end the tradition now."

"The Sentinel. Okay, fair enough. What can I do for you, Mr. Sentinel?" Synthe asked, just a hint of humor in his voice.

"The organization I represent has a position of considerable importance which has become vacant, and you were identified as being a potential candidate for filling it. The job is heading my group's security force and overseeing all aspects of its operations. The irony is that even though it is a tremendously important position, your duties would be virtually non-existent. Your predecessors have literally never had to do anything but be prepared," the Sentinel explained.

"Interesting. A position with almost no work involved. Sounds intriguing," Synthe said noncommittally.

The Sentinel reached over the table, picked up Synthe's untouched espresso and set the cup on the ledge next to them, along with his own. He leaned to one side, then placed a dark brown ostrich-skin briefcase on the table, turning it so the latches were facing Synthe.

He nodded, indicating that Synthe should open it.

Synthe did and studied the contents without reaction.

"Two hundred fifty thousand dollars – six month's pay. The position draws a five hundred thousand dollar a year salary," the Sentinel stated flatly.

The Mossad didn't pay a fraction of that sort of money, even at its upper tier. This 'Sentinel' now had Synthe's complete and total attention.

"And what would I be expected to do for this generous stipend?" Synthe asked.

"Wait," the Sentinel responded.

"*Wait*? That's it? Wait for what?" Synthe's usually unreadable composure slipped, just for an instant.

The Sentinel knew Synthe was hooked. He slowly closed the valise and turned it back towards him. After methodically securing the latches, he placed it carefully by Synthe's left leg before returning their coffee cups to their table. He studied Synthe's face for several moments, and then nodded.

"Wait for a moment I pray will never come. And participate in security planning for a holy object that is of considerable importance to my organization – an ancient group that is entrusted with the safekeeping of this relic," the Sentinel explained.

"I presume I'll have to leave the Mossad if I choose to accept your offer," Synthe observed.

"That is correct. Your allegiance would need to be to our organization and no one else. You would have a month to decide how best to resign without revealing to anyone why you did. In return, you will have your position for life."

"I'll need to understand who I'm working for. If I'm going to make a lifetime commitment, I want to understand the game and the players," Synthe said.

The Sentinel had agreed and proceeded to explain the details. Established in the sixteenth century, the Order of the Holy Relic was a clandestine offshoot of the Roman Catholic Church. Its mission was to ensure the protection of the Church's most valuable secret, which was housed in an obscure location in southern England. The Order recruited its security force from outside of the Church, as it required skills that weren't part of an ecclesiastic curriculum.

"You don't need to know more than this right now. If you accept my proposal, once you are no longer with the Mossad I will provide further information you'll require to carry out your duties. Again, most of which will consist of waiting."

Synthe had already made up his mind. It was a no-brainer. *Do nothing for a half mil a year?*

"I accept."

The Sentinel nodded again and finished his espresso. He pushed back his chair and rose, preparing to depart.

"We will call upon you occasionally. Security matters that will demand your presence. This will consist of what will seem to be dreary meetings. Perhaps at another point down the line, you will be asked to perform somewhat more dramatically. I trust you'll be up to the task."

"I shall *wait* for your call."

The Sentinel smiled tightly again, turned, and exited the courtyard, moving deliberately through the café before disappearing into the pedestrian traffic on the street outside.

In the intervening six years, Gabriel Synthe had been called upon exactly three times – and these were for secret Order meetings in Paris, where one topic was always the focus of attention. The small, obsolete abbey in southern England. Though Synthe had been present at the meetings, he had never been required for anything more than to comment on the various security measures employed to secure the location.

Following his resignation from the Mossad, Synthe's existence had settled into a comfortable retirement as he collected his half million dollars a year and waited for something to happen. He busied himself in the outside world by devoting himself to a small school he'd opened as an instructional facility for self-defense training, specifically: Krav Maga – the special brand of martial arts developed for the Israeli military.

It had been a peaceful, if extraordinarily boring, six years. Synthe lived modestly, had saved most of his salary, and so was now relatively well-to-do, with his accumulated savings totaling well over two million dollars.

But he'd gotten a panicked call a few days earlier from the Sentinel, who gave him the barest details and advised him to be ready for an in-person meeting. He was to rendezvous with Diego Luca in the parking lot of the

Tel Aviv airport, on the north end of the terminal, near a sewage swamp which was notoriously odiferous, guaranteeing they would be the only ones in the area.

As the car wove through traffic, a twinge of anxiety told him that this meeting with Luca would need to be handled very carefully.

The unthinkable had happened. The Order's precious sacred relic was gone, and Synthe was going to be required to lead the charge to recover it. He had never really believed that anyone could penetrate the security measures in place at the Abbey and make a grab for the Scroll. Given the agitation, and Diego Luca himself coming to Tel Aviv for a rendezvous, apparently Synthe had called that one wrong. That rarely happened.

But he wasn't sure exactly what the Order expected him to do about it now.

Synthe glanced at his watch once again.

He was early for the meet.

CHAPTER 6

As Deputy Grand Commander to the *Pauperes Commilitones Christi Templique Solomonici* – the Knights Templar – Diego Luca was the last in a long line of men who bore their hidden duty throughout their life, serving silently and with unquestioning loyalty. As the second most powerful officer in that shadow organization, he was responsible for the administration of a group which, supposedly, had expired centuries before; he was a ghost, a rumor in the hushed halls of the Church, a murmur at the highest levels of the Masonic order. It was common knowledge that the Knights Templar had met with extinction in the Middle Ages, and Luca was chartered with ensuring that history was never disturbed with even a hint of their continued operation.

The Templars had existed in secret after their public dismantling and persecution in 1312, when the few surviving members loyal to Pope Clement V agreed to become the clandestine arm of the Church. The order had aroused considerable resentment because of its power and financial success, so this newly created group would remain hidden, carrying out its duties in obscurity rather than in the public's eye. Rumors would occasionally circulate of Templars in action, but they were always quickly hushed-up by the Church – which got to write the history books. Within a hundred years the Templars became nothing more than a legend, and from that point to the present, they would remain a shadow group that answered only to the Pope.

Beyond coordinating their affairs, Luca's duties also included working in tandem with the Order of the Holy Relic, which, as tradition demanded, had to be afforded the greatest respect and reverence. Why, Luca could not really say – but that had been the multi-century edict handed down to those who had risen to the ultimate levels of authority. It had been that way forever, and there were some tenets one never questioned.

But centuries of calm had been overturned during the last few days. The Chamber Room at the Abbey had been breached and the Scroll had been stolen. The perpetrators remained unknown, although just today, the name of Professor Winston Twain had surfaced through the repentant, albeit forced, confession of a wayward member of the Order. That would have ordinarily been sufficient for Luca to mobilize resources; however, almost as soon as they'd discovered the professor's identity, they'd been alerted that he was dead.

That brought them to a standstill – impotent – during the greatest crisis the Order had ever encountered. Which was why Luca was now in a car on his way to a meeting with Colonel Gabriel Synthe, a man who he disliked on principle. Synthe was an atheist and believed in nothing, as far as Luca could tell. That absence of faith made him a loose cannon. If you believed in nothing, then you were the center of the universe in your own mind – a state of affairs that was anathema to the beliefs Luca had devoted his life to protecting and nurturing.

A man without belief in God, or conviction in a supernatural realm outside of his own scope of understanding, was a danger. A man who operated on rogue solipsism, who negotiated through life as a virtual narcissist, could therefore only be motivated by the coarsest of principles.

Diego Luca sighed as he sat in the back of his limousine. His driver, Brother Misto, navigated silently to the meeting destination. The phone in the center console of the back seat warbled.

Luca picked it up. "Yes, sir," he said in a voice barely above a whisper.

The voice that responded was deep; soothing, but forceful. Luca recognized it as the Religious Protector, His Beatitude Metropolitan Justinian – the head of the Knights Templar worldwide.

"I assume we have little progress," the Religious Protector stated without rancor.

"That is correct, sir. The traitor wasn't in good health, and he didn't provide any real information before he slipped into a coma, beyond his interaction with Professor Twain."

"I understand from the transcript that he did have some things to say – they just didn't make any sense," His Beatitude observed.

"Yes. If you've read it, you know all about the gibberish. 'Eyes are upon you' and 'beware Rosenkreuz and Loyola'. I think the poor man was trying to throw out anything he could think of to shield himself from blame. I can't see how the Rosicrucians have any hand in this, nor the Jesuits."

There was a beat as the voice on the other end of the line made a humming sound.

"Perhaps. I'm calling to underscore that it's critical that you and Colonel Synthe cooperate completely with each other, my son. You are aware of the importance of the Scroll, but you do not know its full significance."

"Your eminence has never seen fit to include me in this confidentiality," Luca said.

"Not you, nor others of your rank and stature before you – you shouldn't take it personally," the voice said consolingly. "But the Scroll *must* be recovered, and obstacles to that recovery must be surmounted at all costs."

"Understood. I'll work with Colonel Synthe closely until the matter is resolved," Luca said – perhaps too forcefully, he thought.

"Keep me advised."

That was the second telephone conversation that the Religious Protector and Luca had conducted in the past few days. It was unprecedented.

Luca knew precious little about the Holy Scroll, even after the briefing that followed his promotion to his rank in the Templars. The sum of his knowledge could fit in a thimble – that it was sacred, that the Order was to protect it at all costs, and that it was part and parcel to the Voynich Manuscript. He was also aware that the language of the Voynich was regarded as an important and yet unsolved puzzle at the highest level of the Church, but he didn't know why.

Regardless, he had his marching orders, and he would do what needed to be done. Luca was sixty years old, possessed of piercing blue eyes and a powerful build running to fat. He considered himself a principled individual, erring towards pragmatism.

As they approached their venue, Luca stared ahead at the car Synthe had arrived in and prepared himself for the dialogue to come.

"This is fine, Brother," Luca said to his driver.

The limousine came to a halt. Luca got out. Synthe was smoking a cigarette and lounging against his own vehicle, his expression wary as he watched Luca approach him. *Perhaps he, too, is leery of this meeting*, Luca thought.

The Grand Commander stopped a few feet in front of Synthe, and both men sized each other up.

"Good to see you again, Colonel," Luca said.

"Yes, you too," Synthe said.

A moment of silence hung in the air before Luca spoke again.

"Have you been apprised of the nature of this meeting, Colonel?" Luca asked.

"Other than the loss of the relic, not a thing," Synthe said, tossing his cigarette away and standing to his full height of over six feet, no longer lounging. "I assume I'm here to kill someone."

Israeli humor, Luca surmised.

"Not exactly," Luca said. "I'll bring you up to date on what's transpired so far."

Luca relayed briefly what they'd gleaned about the theft of the Scroll and the ongoing investigation of possible perpetrators, including the recently deceased professor.

"Then it's worse than expected. We don't have much to go on," Synthe said. "Was Twain murdered, or was his death coincidental to these events?"

"Unknown at this time," Luca admitted. "We do know that he has a daughter, but where she might be…" Luca shrugged. "We're trying to find her."

Synthe considered this. "And the purpose for my presence here is?"

"To alert you that, as of now, every waking moment needs to be directed to recovering the Scroll. This unfortunate event took place on your watch. It's time to earn the substantial pay you've been collecting. You have a suitable background for this sort of investigation – I don't. But hopefully, together we can figure out who has the Scroll and recover it before any damage can be done," Luca concluded.

Synthe stood in silence, wondering what had been set in motion.

"I'll be available twenty-four-seven to assist in whatever way you need."

"Perfect. I'll brief you on the steps we're taking now that we know Twain is dead. Time is of the essence on this," Luca advised and motioned for Synthe to join him in the limousine.

The unlikely pair entered the car and shut the door, their conversation shielded from interruption. A jet roared overhead, its cargo of passengers blissfully unaware of the chaos that had been unleashed by a seemingly inconsequential theft of an obscure ancient parchment.

CHAPTER 7

Steven Cross secured the door to his flat and set out on his daily walk to his company's offices. It was a gorgeous early summer morning in Florence; the streets were abuzz with pedestrians hurrying to work. Motor scooters roared down the narrow streets, their angry whining combining with the shouts of laborers unloading delivery vans double-parked with cheerful illegality along the sidewalks.

Steven had sold the converted farmhouse in Greve after Antonia's accident – every moment there was too painful a reminder of a life cut disastrously short by an ugly trick of fate. After three months sitting virtually immobile in the living room, staring at his books and the stack of ancient parchments that were the only reason he hadn't been in the car with Antonia, he'd decided to move somewhere new, where her ghost didn't come to visit every morning and stay till he dozed off late at night. So he packed up his valuables and located a flat in downtown Florence that was sufficient to his needs, and listed the country home with a realtor. An American couple had jumped at the asking price, and soon the house was just a memory. Like so much of his life.

He stopped at his favorite bakery and bought two baguettes of rustic peasant bread, then moved down the block to the café that was his regular morning haunt while he scanned the paper. His Italian was excellent after five years in Italy, and he diligently practiced speaking and reading it at every opportunity. Languages had always come easily to him, although as he'd got older everything became a little harder.

Steven paid his bill and grabbed a second cup of coffee to go, then stepped out onto the sidewalk to continue his trek towards the office.

Only something wasn't right. He wasn't sure what it was, but he was getting the tingle at the back of his neck that was a sixth sense he'd developed while in the military – and it was rarely wrong. Impulsively, he turned a corner on a street that led away from his office and circled the block, adding five minutes to his journey. Well worth the extra time because his vague uneasiness had become a certainty.

Steven's survival instincts were sounding an unmistakable alarm. He'd picked up a tail, a gray sedan shadowing him. He'd confirmed his suspicions through rudimentary tradecraft he'd picked up from films and books – he stopped at a shop window, ostensibly to study the merchandise on display, and watched in the reflection as the vehicle came to a stop fifty yards down the street. Why he was under surveillance by parties unknown was a mystery, but from past experience he knew this sort of thing was never good. Steven resumed his walk and the sedan followed at a discreet distance.

Whatever this was, Steven was now in full alert mode. In his past life he'd made powerful enemies, on Wall Street as well as with organized criminal elements, and while it was unlikely that after this many years he would have resumed being an active target, the possibility never entirely disappeared. He'd resigned himself long ago to the idea that there was always that chance.

This morning, as he walked from his apartment to his office, the notion that a vindictive foe from a past life was stalking him seemed remote, yet the vision of the stealthy vehicle told him he wasn't being paranoid. Still, any kind of attack on him seemed unlikely. Not in the open like this, in a district filled with witnesses, and with too many variables that could compromise the success of a hit. The bad guys generally came after you when there was nobody around. He didn't think things had changed much since his last adventure – his bullet scar was painful evidence that he had some small familiarity with how these things played out.

The street traffic thinned as he entered the less commercial section of Florence his offices occupied, and he abruptly turned into an alley on his right – a shortcut – glancing behind to see if the car was still dogging him. It wasn't until he'd already committed to that course that he saw the far end of the alley was blocked by a low-slung delivery truck with its emergency blinkers on.

The mouth of the thoroughfare was suddenly filled by the sedan, which came to a halt after it turned the corner when the driver realized there was insufficient space to continue, owing to the way the street narrowed. Steven stopped and turned towards the darkened windshield – he couldn't make anything out but the pale oval of the driver's head. The car and Steven faced each other in a silent standoff.

Another moment passed. A kit of pigeons flapped up from behind four recycling crates and soared past the hood and then above it, disappearing into the sky. Feathers and dander created motes of dust in the morning sunlight that flooded into the mouth of the alley, casting a surreal, hazy effect around the stationary car. Trapped and unable to move forward any further, but lacking sufficient width for anyone to get out, the vehicle reversed until it reached a point where the doors had reasonable clearance. After a few moments, the front passenger door of the car swung open.

Here it comes, Steven thought.

To his surprise, the figure that exited the car was a woman. She didn't bother closing the door – Steven could hear the dim beeping emanating from the vehicle. The sunbeams slanting down momentarily blurred most detail except her silhouette, but as she moved into the alley, he registered that she was young, with jet-black hair spiked in a euro-punk style. As she approached him, with a steady, measured gait reminiscent of a gymnast or a dancer, Steven could make out her face in more detail. She was strikingly beautiful. The glinting of her nose-piercing and the small tattoo of a broken heart below her left ear lent an air of the exotic – the pseudo-goth look definitely gave her an aura of freaky danger, which he supposed was the intent. She looked Slavic, with high, pronounced cheekbones. But perhaps her most striking feature was her eyes, which were a stunning violet. He'd never seen anyone with eyes that color, and he vaguely wondered if she was wearing contact lenses.

Steven automatically completed his threat assessment and didn't register anything overt. Her hands were empty, and her outfit didn't have a lot of hiding places for weapons – she wore a skin-tight black jumpsuit crafted from suede that left little to the imagination and calf-height black leather boots boasting four-inch heels. He calculated she was all of five foot three including the boots, and although the ensemble was stunning, it was hardly what he would have imagined as first choice for a morning assault using hand-to-hand combat.

Though there was an initial hardness to her gaze and demeanor, Steven realized it wasn't an air of antagonism; rather, it was one of self-confidence. She stopped in front of him and appraised him with open curiosity before finally speaking.

"Steven Cross? Dr. Steven Cross?" she said in a voice that was soft as velvet, and discordant with the steel-girder edginess of her cyber-punk look.

"Yes," Steven said carefully. "But I have the feeling you know that already."

The corners of her mouth twitched, and then she smiled…though it was a troubled smile that didn't convey friendliness as much as something else Steven could not immediately identify. *Sadness? Yes…sadness…*

"Very astute, Dr. Cross," the woman said. She extended her hand. "My name is Natalie Twain."

Steven stuffed the baguettes under his left arm and extended his right hand. She grasped it with a strong yet feminine grip, Steven noted; again, incongruous to the rest of her demeanor. And then her name made him do a double-take.

"Natalie Twain? Any relation to Professor Winston Twain?" he said, still shaking her hand.

She nodded her head.

"Professor Twain was my father."

"He called me a few days back, and my office team tried to track him down, but without success – he must have an unlisted number," Steven said and then stopped. "Did you say Professor Twain *was* your father?"

"Yes, Dr. Cross. Was."

Steven continued to stare.

Natalie nodded, reading his unspoken query. "My father is dead," she said quietly.

Steven continued to take her in, and he could see her eyes, originally so piercing and uncompromising, were now softer in appearance…more vulnerable, somehow less impervious to scrutiny.

"I'm sorry," Steven said.

"So am I," Natalie said. "But not as sorry as I plan to make the people responsible."

"I don't understand."

"Dr. Cross," Natalie said softly. "My father's death wasn't an accident."

Steven was taken aback, but held Natalie's stare.

"Ms. Twain…I'm sorry to hear that, but I have to ask – why are we talking?"

"Because, Dr. Cross," Natalie said, "I believe you – and I – are both in very real danger. I need twenty minutes of your time. Please don't say no. Your life may depend on it."

CHAPTER 8

Sia Amieri sat behind the wheel of a silver Lexus that had been provided to him by his mentor and employer, Dr. Morbius Frank. He gazed out at downtown Tehran, Iran, after a grueling travel session that had spanned from New York, to Los Angeles, to Palm Springs, then back to L.A., and a rather circuitous voyage home by way of Singapore, to Mehrabad International Airport.

The car had been waiting for him in the lot where Frank had indicated, the keys handed to him by an eager attendant who treated Amieri as if he were a visiting dignitary. Amieri knew that his benefactor was greatly respected in Tehran, although Frank was a British citizen. His dealings with the regime included petroleum, international banking and arms, and Frank had access to the most rarified corridors of power. Frank had homes and offices in Tehran, England and Canada, and his influence seemed to be boundless.

Amieri drove on Meraj Boulevard, heading for the Azadi Tower, where they were to meet. He took in the impressive piece of architecture, still half a mile away; the Tower, built entirely of white marble, thrust fourteen stories into the sky. Amieri was no stranger to the region, having been born and raised in Iraq, and having crossed into Iran many times on clandestine missions in his past – a brutal one spent as an interrogator and assassin under Saddam Hussein's iron rule in Iraq, and then later as a freelance killer for anyone willing to meet his price. His benefactor had rescued him from certain execution at the hands of the new regime and offered him an alternative future to one that would be measured in hours before ending at the barrel of a pistol.

Amieri had known since he was a teenager that there was something different about him, something wrong. He gravitated to the notorious Iraqi secret police because he enjoyed hurting others; a large young man who would carry out the most offensive tasks without question was valuable – something his early mentor, a captain in the Mukhabarat, had recognized immediately. Soon, word of his ruthlessness spread beyond the agency, and he became the most notorious killer it had ever spawned. But all the while, Amieri was plagued with guilt. Not for what he'd done, but for his enjoyment of it, which his childhood upbringing condemned. He'd been secretly relieved when he'd been arrested and sentenced to die – at least there would be an end to the madness. Then Dr. Frank had appeared; the only person who'd ever truly understood.

Over the years, since what Amieri thought of as his salvation by the father he'd never had, he'd grown increasingly slavish to Frank and would have taken a bullet in the face for him. Frank's appearance in his hour of need had been like that of an angel for Amieri, who was offered both a better life and a path to atonement.

There is always punishment, Dr. Frank would tell him on occasion. *If not corporal, then that of the soul.*

Amieri only hoped he would not cause his benefactor anger after what had happened with Professor Twain. Frank hadn't negated the possibility of torturing Twain to extract information as to where the Scroll was – but neither had he tacitly endorsed the old man's murder.

The professor's demise had taken him by surprise. Amieri was unaware of Twain's health problems and had been shocked and alarmed when the old man had gone under. Amieri had barely gotten started interrogating Twain before he'd died, so Amieri could legitimately take the position that his death had been an accident. Frank had not been interested in discussing the details on the telephone – his instructions were simply to meet with Amieri under the Freedom Tower, and all would be discussed in short order.

Amieri was not fearful of the slings and arrows of Frank's anger.

His greatest fear was that his surrogate father would be disappointed in how he had handled things.

That would be the worst punishment Amieri could imagine.

❧

Four thousand feet above the Caspian Sea, a Hawker executive jet was on final approach to Mehrabad International Airport. There was slight turbulence, but this was to be expected in this flight vector; the updraft from the Caspian was notoriously churlish when it came to airplanes descending over its capricious waters. Dr. Morbius Frank, however, was accustomed to the bounce. His gaunt countenance didn't look up from his *Financial Times* even as the plane lurched several times – his pilots were the best, and he had more pressing problems than nervousness over a spot of rough air.

He was initially furious with Amieri about the old man's death, but the big assassin was really just a child and had to be handled delicately. And perhaps it was his fault, at the end of the day, for not approaching Twain in person about the abrogation of their mutual agreement on Scroll ownership. Amieri had simply done what he did best – extracting the required information from those who were reluctant to be forthcoming.

"I'm not angry with you, my son," Frank had reassured Amieri from his home in London when Amieri had called from the hotel in Palm Springs where he had taken a room before meeting Twain.

"He was sick, Doctor," Amieri continued to insist. "I was not that harsh in my approach. There was no way of knowing he had an aneurism–"

"I'm confident you were not overzealous. You always apply judicious pressure. I appreciate that. This was simply an unfortunate and unforeseeable complication."

"The Scroll was not there. I searched the place, top to bottom, without being too obvious. I know you didn't want to leave any trace," Amieri said. "It wasn't in the house."

"We'll find it," Frank cajoled. "My suspicion is that the daughter has it. There's no other explanation that makes sense. Twain was a virtual shut-in, and the only one he trusted was the girl. My investigators confirmed that he didn't have any safety deposit boxes, but the daughter does, so it's not difficult to see where she fits in this. I'm sure that when we find the girl, we find the Scroll."

"Do we know where she is yet?" Amieri asked fervently. "Because once I get my hands on her–"

"We're working on it. My network is handling this even as we speak," Frank said. "I will share more once we meet in Tehran."

That had been three days ago. He wished he could turn back the clock and confront Twain himself about the change in plans on the Scroll, but nobody got to do things over. Frank had been occupied by other matters – critical matters that demanded his attention and which would come to the fore once the Scroll was located and the translations from it were obtained. It was a shame things had rapidly gone from controllable to chaotic, but in the end he'd prevail. He always did.

Frank felt a renewed sense of confidence as the buildings of Tehran loomed below. His team was pulling out all the stops in their search. Twain's daughter would be located. Of this, Frank was sure.

He just hoped that they would find her before the Order of the Holy Relic got to her first.

CHAPTER 9

Steven opened the door to his offices for Natalie, fumbling with the baguettes and coffee while Natalie walked into the building, clutching a leather bag.

Gwen Peabody rose from her desk and briskly approached Steven, taking the bread from him and glancing at the new female arrival.

"Hullo," Gwen chirped at her.

Natalie only offered a nod. Steven glanced around the red brick interior of the old building, which had been gutted and converted into a single large workspace. The section nearest the entrance housed a reception area and a group of computer stations, arranged in a semi-circle on the polished concrete floor and occupied by the other residents of the office. All three now turned to regard Steven.

"Hello, gang," Steven said. He turned to Natalie. "Ms. Twain, I'd like you to meet Gwen Peabody; she's my office manager and is responsible for anything that goes right in my life on a day-to-day basis."

"Nice to meet you, Gwen," Natalie said. "Natalie Twain."

Gwen made the connection instantly. "Ah, immediate relative, I would guess, of Professor Winston Twain. His…daughter?" She appraised Natalie more closely. "Or granddaughter?"

"The very same. His daughter," Natalie answered.

"He called our office the other day. How is your father?"

"At peace," Natalie said cryptically.

"Professor Twain passed away a few days ago, Gwen," Steven said softly, and then looked to his three other employees.

"Oh," Gwen said, deflated, and at a momentary loss of words. "I'm…so sorry."

"Thank you," Natalie replied.

Steven turned to his team, who were watching him expectantly.

"Ben Walker, Will Donahue and Sophie Lipton," he introduced.

Sophie, a stout black woman of twenty-six, whose fondness for Italian pastry was clearly evident, smiled and raised an eyebrow. "Pleased to meet you, Natalie."

"Likewise," Natalie replied good-naturedly.

Ben smiled and said, "We're the tragically underpaid and perennially overworked elves who make the software work. I'm Ben, and that's Will." He nodded his head in the direction of Will, who was busily typing on his keypad even as he glanced at Natalie in acknowledgement. Ben was tall and lanky, even seated, and had a scar running from his forehead down to his lower lip. Will was thin and pale, with a three day growth of sparse beard, and iPod headphones blaring metal music in his ears.

"Nice to meet everyone," Natalie said.

"Natalie, let's step into my office; this way, please…" Steven moved ahead of her to a room at the far end of the cavernous work area.

Natalie strode behind him, still holding her soft leather satchel.

Gwen looked to Natalie. "May I take that for you?"

"Thank you, I'm fine," Natalie said and then followed Steven into this office, closing the door behind them.

Natalie took a seat in front of Steven's desk. For a moment there was only silence, as he reclined in his chair and sipped his coffee. Steven and Natalie regarded each other. Natalie's gaze was impassive, inscrutable.

Steven put the cup to the side and folded his arms while leaning forward in his seat. "All right, Ms. Twain. You have my attention. Why is my life in danger, and how can I help you?"

Natalie lifted her satchel and placed it on Steven's desk.

"Call me Natalie. Please." She paused, appraising him, and then continued. "I – I'm not sure where to start, so I'll just begin with my father's death. I believe that he was murdered by a man named Morbius Frank. Dr. Morbius Frank. Does the name mean anything to you?" Natalie said.

Steven searched his mental rolodex, but nothing flipped in terms of recognition. "No. Should it?"

"He is, aside from being behind my father's murder, a businessman. A businessman, adventurer, self-described archeologist and philanthropist, and a billionaire. A trust fund baby to an oil magnate dynasty – one of the largest in the United Kingdom."

Steven nodded. "I don't recognize the name, but I get the point. He's rich and powerful…and you think he killed–"

"Two weeks ago, Frank funded an operation for my father to obtain a religious artifact which Frank had learned was intrinsic to the Voynich Manuscript. I *know* you recognize that."

Steven leaned back and his demeanor changed. "Of course. It's only the holy grail of cryptology. But the Voynich's been at Yale for decades. What relic could possibly be connected with it? I know everything about it, and there's nothing but the manuscript and mountains of speculation as to how to crack the code – something nobody has ever done."

"It's something that my father said could help decipher the Voynich. He believed it was the key, in fact, to a mystery that dates back six hundred years."

Steven studied Natalie quietly, but inside, his heart had just shifted gears into overdrive; his normal sinus rhythm shot from sixty to a hundred in just a few brief moments. "Go on, Natalie."

"The artifact is known as the Holy Scroll of the Abbey of St. Peter at Abbotsbury in Dorset, England. Have you heard of the place?"

Steven nodded. "Heard of it? I visited the Abbey on a tour ten years ago. But there was no sacred relic there that I can remember. Are you saying this artifact is in the Abbey? I'm still not following the logic."

"It was there, deep in the hidden catacombs beneath the grounds. But no more," Natalie said. "The Holy Scroll was liberated two weeks ago."

Steven shook his head. "Ah. So it was stolen. And your father had something to do with this?"

"Liberated," Natalie corrected.

"Liberated. Sure, okay. And this 'Holy Scroll' was 'liberated'…by your father? I would have imagined that he wasn't a particularly, er, nimble man, given his years…"

"He didn't do it himself, but I know that he and Dr. Frank arranged it. But what's important is that my father retained possession of the Scroll on the understanding that Frank would be able to share the information it contained once it was decrypted."

"And you believe your father was murdered because Frank wanted the Scroll for himself. Did Frank steal it after killing your dad?"

"No, he didn't."

Steven considered this, the hair on the nape of his neck prickling. "Then where is this holy artifact, and how do you know so much about all this?"

"I have it," Natalie said, answering part of the question. She glanced at her bag.

Steven studied Natalie, and then his eyes slowly moved to the satchel. Natalie had his full and complete attention.

"Did Professor Twain…your father…have time to analyze this Holy Scroll?" Steven asked quietly.

"No, but…" Natalie hesitated for a moment.

"No, but what?" Steven persisted.

Natalie opened the satchel, removed a piece of paper and handed it to Steven. Steven took it and opened it.

The paper was the letter that Steven had sent to Winston Twain a year before, articulating his theory on the origin of the Voynich Manuscript.

Steven perused the document and a chill ran down his spine.

The letter was partially smeared with blood.

The blood of the late Professor Winston Twain.

❧

Steven studied the letter in silence, and then squinted as he tried to make out a handwritten note that the Professor had scribbled on the left hand side of the letter. He read it aloud: "Theory wrong, but close. Call Cross, have a chat."

Steven looked up at Natalie. "Then he hadn't ignored my letter after all."

"No," Natalie said. "He didn't. I found the letter under his head. When he died…" Natalie paused, and swallowed hard. "When he died, his head collapsed on the desk, and your letter was under it. The coroner said he died of a massive aortic aneurism, and that he probably broke his nose when it hit the desk. That's why–"

"Yes, I understand," Steven said and looked at the bloodstained letter again. "But now I'm really puzzled. You keep saying your father was murdered by Frank, and yet you just described a congenital defect as the cause of death. Those don't add up. Either he was killed, or he died of natural causes. Which is it?"

"I believe that he was being tortured when the aneurism ruptured. The coroner also found some unexplained abrasions on his hands, but ultimately said they were inconclusive. I don't think they were. I believe Frank lost patience and came for the Scroll," Natalie insisted.

Steven sighed. "You realize that's completely impossible to prove, right? I mean, you could also theorize that the devil was having a drink with him when his aorta burst. It doesn't make it so. I'm not trying to be difficult…"

"I can appreciate your skepticism. But it doesn't change my opinion." She gestured to the letter in Steven's hands. "I wanted you to see this first because you need to know that my father respected your skills," she said.

"I'll take that as a high compliment. But none of this really sheds any light on whether your father was able to study the Scroll and make heads or tails of it," Steven said matter-of-factly.

"I'm sure he didn't. My father and I were close, and he hadn't called to tell me of any significant discovery. If he found something new about any of his projects, he would call me immediately. He was like a child. Always excited, always wanting to share with me first."

Steven offered a sympathetic smile. "I can understand that."

She gave an almost imperceptible nod of thanks.

"How did you come by the Scroll?" Steven asked.

"He gave it to me before he died," Natalie said. "He insisted that I safeguard it as soon as he had it in his possession." She stared at the Picasso lithograph on the wall behind Steven's head. "It's almost as if he knew someone would be coming after him sooner or later."

Steven frowned.

"What?" Natalie asked, noticing the change in his expression.

"If your father and Frank had an agreement to share the Scroll, why would he kill him? Assuming your torture theory is right."

"Because my father, for all of his failings, was in the end a religious man. He was torn – his academic side wanted to decrypt it, but he didn't want to do anything overtly sacrilegious or damaging to those who shared his faith. I know it caused him a great deal of anxiety. Once he'd seen the Scroll I think his conscience got the better of him, and he told Frank that the information contained in the Scroll was best left undiscovered," Natalie said. "My father told me that he was going to sell his entire retirement portfolio of stocks and bonds, as well as his summer home in Aspen, and give Frank back his money so there could never be contentions that Frank had any claim on the Scroll."

Steven let out an exasperated sigh. "Let's say I completely buy all this and agree that this Frank is a monster. The obvious question is, how can I help you? What do I have to do with any of this, other than having written a letter even I forgot about? And how do I even know that the Scroll, which I've never heard of until you mentioned it, has anything to do with the Voynich?"

Natalie silently extracted a battered container from her bag, easing off the lid as she regarded Cross from across the desk.

"My father did describe how the Scroll was connected to the Voynich," Natalie said at last.

Steven nodded indulgently. "Okay, I'll bite. We've come this far. What did he say was the link?"

Natalie carefully took out a sheaf of parchments from the canister that were clearly hundreds of years old. He'd seen enough medieval documents in his time to recognize the signs of antiquity, as well as the distinctive scent of centuries past.

"My father told me that the Holy Scroll was one of the missing chapters of the Voynich Manuscript, Dr. Cross," Natalie said slowly. "Quire 18, to be precise."

The room seemed to spin for a few moments as Steven took in the details of the dog-eared parchments in Natalie's hands. His eyes roamed over the ancient canister, then returned to the quire. This was impossible. It was akin to someone walking in off the street and unfurling a lost Rembrandt. The missing section of the Voynich had disappeared early in its life, along with another chapter, quire 16, and even though there were vague rumors of forbidden knowledge that periodically surfaced when one studied the history of the document, nobody had ever seen the lost pages. Through the ages, speculation as to their contents was sparse and often contradictory. They were phantoms, nothing more.

"Quire 18…are you…are you sure this is what your father told you?"

"Yes," Natalie said. "He put its date at around 1450."

Steven couldn't believe his ears.

In front of him was the lynchpin – the key – to solving one of the greatest mysteries the world had ever known.

CHAPTER 10

"May I see it, Natalie?" Steven asked, his voice catching on her name.

Natalie handed him the pages across the desk. His hands were steady, thankfully not betraying the surge of adrenaline, as he took them from her.

Steven carefully unfurled the document and spread the sheets on his desktop, which was empty except for a telephone, his computer and a coffee cup full of pencils and pens.

The vellum was in remarkable condition, showing inevitable minor degradation after weathering the ages, but beyond that, in extraordinary shape. He glanced again at the canister. It had done its job admirably, protecting the treasured Scroll from the elements so that, even now, the document was pristine.

The distinctive pseudo-alphabet used in the Voynich was unmistakable – the glyphs were unique. The first pages were filled with the unusual, and yet to Steven, familiar, illustrations that were in keeping with the medicinal character of quire 19. Steven knew most of the quires from memory, having devoted hundreds of hours to study them. The Scroll was definitely consistent with what he would have expected quire 18 to look like, although there was something odd about the drawings; something niggling, but off. He studied them closely, but couldn't put his finger on what he was sensing. The harder he scrutinized them, the further away the elusive sensation got.

"What do you think?" Natalie walked around the desk and stood by Steven's side as he pored over each page. He was jarred back into the present by her proximity, and he could detect a subtle aroma of cinnamon emanating from her skin, along with a hint of fragrance, a light floral perfume. Steven realized his focus had slipped even as he simultaneously had a burst of insight: Natalie smelled extremely good.

He shook off the thought. "Based on a cursory look, I'd agree it's the Voynich. I don't think there's any doubt about that, based on the drawings and the calligraphy, not to mention the age. Your father would have recognized it as such instantly. But I'm not seeing anything that's jumping out at me as earth-shattering, beyond the fact that these pages exist at all," Steven explained.

"Take your time. There has to be something here," Natalie pressed.

Steven shook his head. "Why? Why are you so convinced these pages hold some sort of solution to the Voynich, when they appear to be almost exactly like the other two hundred forty pages on display at Yale?" Steven reached over and moved his computer mouse. The large flat screen monitor blinked to life. He typed in a password and selected a folder labeled: 'Crypto' and then drilled down until he got to one marked: 'VMan'. He opened a web browser, and within a few moments the screen was filled with high-resolution images of the pages of the Voynich Manuscript. He quickly went to quire 17 and scrolled through the photos, which looked similar to the pages on his table.

Ignoring Steven's question, Natalie said, "Quire 17 doesn't have any nudes in it, and neither does 19. Maybe there's some significance to the two nude women in 18?"

"Then perhaps there's some significance wherever they appear in the manuscript. If there is, it's defied researchers, including me, since the Voynich surfaced. I think that's a dead-end in terms of something unique to this quire." Steven stopped and turned to Natalie, their faces only inches apart as they both hunched over the desk. "Why don't you answer my original question, Natalie? Why are you convinced there's something special in these pages?"

She held his gaze, then moved a few feet from him – the proximity was too intimate for her to dodge Steven's reasonable query.

"My father was killed for them, and Frank considered the Scroll to be priceless," she stated flatly.

He shook his head. "You *think*. You're of the *opinion* he was killed for them. But you don't *know*."

"I know," Natalie insisted.

Steven decided to let that go. There was nothing to be gained by pointing out the difference between a strongly-held conviction and a provable fact. He knew the tone she had adopted, and logic was the wrong approach if he wanted answers.

"Okay. I believe you're convinced your father was killed for these pages."

"Don't patronize me, Dr. Cross," Natalie admonished him, pain and anger now evident in her eyes.

"I…look, I'm sorry. We're getting off on the wrong foot here. What I meant was I believe you. But you came to me because you obviously want my help in figuring out what the significance of these pages is – I didn't come to you. But if you trust me enough to show me this stolen quire," he held up a hand to silence her protest at the word 'stolen', "you're going to have to trust me enough to tell me everything you know. Otherwise, I'm fumbling in the dark, and that won't do either of us any good." Steven stopped, waiting to see what effect an appeal to reason would have on Natalie.

She hesitated, then looked away. "This was important enough to have armed guards protecting it for hundreds of years in a secret section of the Abbey," she revealed.

"How do you know that?" Steven demanded.

"I'm not inventing it. My father and Frank discovered a lot about these pages. Enough to pay millions of dollars to get their hands on them," Natalie concluded.

"Millions? Are you kidding me? They couldn't give the Voynich away forty years ago. That's why it was donated to Yale. It had no value, other than as an historical curiosity…"

"That may be, but I can assure you that my father was not a foolish or impulsive man, and his partner in this, Morbius Frank, is as ruthless and cunning as they come. They both believed that they were getting the bargain of a lifetime by paying seven figures for information that enabled them to get their hands on the Scroll. Whatever the Voynich may or may not be worth, it's clear that there's something in these pages that's far bigger than you can imagine."

"It sounds like you know a lot more about this than what you are letting on, Ms. Tw…Natalie."

"Here's what I know. This canister contains a secret so important that even more than five centuries after the Scroll was written it was still being guarded twenty-four hours a day by an elite order of the Catholic Church. Year after year, through wars, famines, plagues, changes in governments and ideologies, the secret was kept, and generations of protectors lived and died," Natalie explained.

"That sounds far-fetched–"

She held up a hand. "You've listened to me so far; hear me out. It's also pretty far-fetched that an American woman would show up on your Italian doorstep with missing pages of one of your fascinations, isn't it? I know how unbelievable this must sound, but everything I'm telling you is the truth."

"Who were these 'protectors', Natalie? And how do you know what you claim you know?" Steven asked.

"Just let me finish. They call themselves the Order of the Holy Relic, and they don't exist in any church records. My father learned of them from Frank, who'd spent decades cultivating contacts and following up on threads and rumors. Eventually, he found a chink in their armor and was able to confirm that the Order was still active. From what my father explained, it had to do with money. Frank met with my father multiple times and revealed to him that, whatever the Scroll was, it was connected to the Voynich, which is where his knowledge came into play. That's how the uneasy partnership began, with my father vetting all the information Frank had unearthed."

"You're serious about all this? A secret society protecting a relic so powerful the world would end if it ever got out, and it winds up in your dad's lap?" Steven wasn't trying to be rude, but to say it danced on the edge of credibility was tame.

"Dr. Cross, I've never been more serious about anything in my life. My father was the smartest man I've ever met, and he was every bit as skeptical as you, but by the end of this, he understood every word I just told you to be completely true." Natalie reached for the Scroll. "Maybe coming here was a bad idea. I don't know what I was expecting, but you're not it. This was a mistake. I'm sorry to have wasted your valuable time," she said, gathering up the pages.

"Whoa. Wait a second. I'm expressing justifiable skepticism at some unbelievable claims. I don't think that's unreasonable. So before you run off the rails here, just give me some time to absorb all this. The parchment appears to be genuine, so that's a huge plus in favor of your story," Steven offered.

"It's all true, and I can tell you that I'm in danger now because of what I know. And yes, I need your help, but I'm also trying to warn you that you're also at risk because of the letter you wrote to my father. Frank, or whoever he had murder my father, had to have seen it, and my father's interest in the letter couldn't have escaped them, given that he was reading it when he was killed."

"*If* he was killed," Steven corrected.

"*When* he was killed. And that means that you'll be on a shortlist, because they don't know where the Scroll is, or what it really contains, or who my father was having help him. So this isn't just about me or some crazy conspiracy. This is about the same people who killed my father showing up on your doorstep to find out what you do and don't know. I'm betting Frank's henchmen don't ask polite questions and then apologize for disturbing you. These pages were worth millions to them. You really think they won't torture and kill to get them?" Natalie asked.

"I'm not say–"

"What you should be asking yourself are two questions: how lucky do I feel, and how much do I enjoy breathing? Because, as of now, I'm here to tell you that right or wrong, you're going to get that visit from Frank's goons, and it's not going to be pleasant. You won't be walking away from it, Dr. Cross. I'm sorry to be the bearer of bad news, but it's true. It didn't take me long to find you, and it won't take them long either. You're wasting time right now that neither of us has," Natalie stated.

He had watched her as she argued her position, and his gut said she believed what she was saying. Steven was a good judge of character, and she was obviously agitated, and afraid, and needed his help. Or believed she did. Which, in the end, was the same thing – at least for now.

Steven wondered how likely he would be to entertain this sort of outlandish story if the person telling it didn't also happen to be beautiful, in addition to having presented him with the cryptology equivalent of the Holy Grail. He had to admit that she made a persuasive and passionate case. And she did smell awfully good.

Not to mention that if she was even partially correct, he had just landed in the middle of a shit-storm of epic proportions. If Frank had actually paid millions for the Scroll, it didn't matter how much of the rest of the story was accurate. People would kill for that kind of money. And Steven didn't want to test his luck until he knew more.

"Let's say I believe you, or at least that I buy some crazy bastard might believe the Scroll is worth killing over, if he was nuts enough to pay through the nose to get it. What can I do about any of this? I run a boutique software company, not some sort of professional code-cracking outfit working for the NSA," he protested.

"I'd like you to do an in-depth study of the pages, and if you spot anything that makes you uneasy or seems like it could contain a clue, tell me. I see you still think this is hysteria, and I agree it sounds crazy, but please, please believe me that the truth is much worse than whatever you're thinking is plausible. Can you please take some time and really examine the Scroll? Or is there somewhere we can go that nobody knows about, where we'll be safe while you look it over? I have a villa I'm renting outside of town we can use…" Natalie offered.

Steven mulled over the invitation. There were worse things he could imagine besides spending the day at Natalie's villa. It wasn't like he had a ton of work piling up – things had been quiet for the last month, and the team was running on automatic pilot.

Natalie's cell phone rang. She glanced at the screen and answered it.

"Yes?"

"A car with two ugly-looking goons just parked thirty yards from the front entrance of the office you're in. They look professional. See if there's another way out of the building. I'll meet you after you're clear." It was Frederick, her driver.

Natalie hung up and looked around urgently. "Is there a back way out of the building?" she asked Steven. She scrambled to gather up the Scroll and return it to the canister.

"What? Why?" Steven demanded.

"That was my driver. We have about sixty seconds before you learn the hard way that this danger is very real. There are two thugs approaching the front entrance, and they're not here for computer training."

Shit. He regarded her eyes. They were steely, with no trace of panic, but also completely earnest.

"There's a back emergency exit by the storeroom next to this office."

"Let's go. Unless you want to stay and discover I wasn't exaggerating," Natalie said.

Steven made an instant decision. "Follow me." He moved to the office door and called out to Gwen, "If anyone comes looking for me, you haven't seen me for a few days – I'm on vacation until next week in Switzerland, with no way of contacting me until Monday, all right?"

Gwen didn't miss a beat. "Have a lovely holiday."

They pushed their way out through the rear exit. Steven called Gwen's cell as they sprinted through the alley behind the building and out onto the larger street a hundred yards away.

"Gwen. If two men come in looking for me, please be very careful, and very convincing," he started.

"Yes, sweetheart, of course I can make lunch today. Say at two o'clock?" Gwen replied, sounding breezy, like she had not a care in the world.

"Did they show up?" he asked.

"Yes, of course I can," she replied.

"Do you need me to call the police?" Steven responded.

"No, can't chat right now. I have some visitors I need to speak with," she said.

"So no police?"

"That won't be necessary. See you at lunch. *Ciao*!" Gwen said and hung up.

Steven glanced at Natalie.

"You were right. Are my people in any danger?" he demanded.

"I don't think so. It's you they're after. They'll want to keep low key until they find us, and not arouse any suspicion. It's just their bad luck they came to kill you when you were on holiday," Natalie said.

Two minutes later the gray sedan pulled up next to them. Steven and Natalie climbed into the back.

"We're clean," she said to the Frederick, and Steven noticed that, even so, the man spent a lot of time studying the rearview mirror as they lost themselves in Florence's perennial snarl of traffic. "Dr. Cross, this is Frederick. He's been with the family since I was a child."

Frederick nodded at him, eyes still darting from the rearview mirror to the side mirrors between glancing at the road in front of them.

Steven didn't get the feeling he was talkative, so he opted for silence.

Ten minutes later, Steven's cell phone rang as they rode through Florence's outskirts on the way to the villa. It was Gwen.

"So, luv, did you rob a bank or chop up some supermodel?" she asked by way of greeting.

"What are you talking about? Are you okay? Who were those guys and what did they want?" Steven pressed.

"They were detectives with the Florence police. They were very interested in your whereabouts, but wouldn't say anything besides that they needed to speak with you as soon as possible, as they put it, to 'assist them with their inquiries'. I asked them what inquiries and they gave me some line about not being free to discuss it," Gwen explained.

"That's bullshit. I haven't done anything. Did they show you any ID or leave any contact information?" Steven's mind was racing over possibilities.

"One of them flashed a shield, but I didn't have a lot of time to study it. Could have been a traffic warden's badge for all I know. The one odd thing was that they had to write down a phone number for me to contact them if I spoke with you. If they were police, you'd think they'd have had printed cards…"

"I agree. They're probably private investigators or something like that," Steven confirmed. He didn't feel like speculating with Gwen about what he meant by 'something like that'.

"Well, they weren't happy that you're on holiday for a week, but what can I do about it? I'm just a lowly receptionist. I merely answer phones and clean out rubbish bins, and occasionally bring the high-and-mighty coffee." Gwen had a typical British dry sense of humor.

"Do me a favor and e-mail me the number and have the lads run it through the crisscross directory to trace it. Get me any info they come up with," Steven requested.

"What's this all about, Steven? Seriously." Gwen's tone had changed.

"I don't have any idea, Gwen. That's what I'm going to try to find out. This morning I was minding my own business, buying bread and coffee, and now I'm darting through back doors…"

"With girls wearing outfits straight out of The Matrix. I know it has to be tough on you, luv. Do try to keep your spirits up through all this," Gwen observed sweetly.

"It's not what you're thinking," Steven protested.

"It never is," Gwen responded. "Call me if you need anything, and enjoy your holiday. Do be careful, and try not to overexert yourself or pull anything. You're not a young man anymore."

"Don't I know it. Thanks for the well wishes. I'll talk to you later. Let me know what the crew finds out about the number," Steven fired back.

Natalie regarded him with one eyebrow cocked.

Steven summarized the discussion. She shook her head.

"They got to you awfully fast. I'm not surprised. Everyone's playing for high stakes here. Now do you believe me?"

"Let's just say I'm still gathering data, but the scales are tipping in your favor," Steven acknowledged.

"Hallelujah…" Natalie sighed, rolling her eyes.

Steven sank into the ample seat and fiddled with the center armrest. Natalie didn't seem to scare easily, he reasoned, and was obviously extremely smart, judging from her oration in his office. He wondered how familiar she was with the Voynich.

"Since your father was one of the leading experts on the Voynich, I'm presuming you know quite a bit about it?" Steven floated as a trial balloon.

"*One of? One of* the leading experts? He was *the* expert. Nobody else could hold a candle to him on the topic," she corrected.

"Sorry. You're right, of course. But my question is, how up to speed are *you*?" he persisted.

"What do you want to know?" she asked innocently.

He waited without speaking.

She gave him a neutral look and cleared her throat. "The Voynich Manuscript was discovered, or rather re-discovered, by rare book dealer, Wilfred Voynich, in 1912, here in Italy. He got it from among the possessions of a top Jesuit general who'd recently died. It's two hundred forty pages written entirely in an unknown language, which most cryptographers agree is some sort of a cypher, although what kind remains unknown. The author remains a mystery, as do the illustrations, which depict unknown species of plants, prescriptions or recipes, nude women and astronomical data. The parchment was carbon-dated to roughly 1430, although it's possible that the vellum was created then, and it was written at some later point. There are many theories as to who wrote it, and why, most of which have fallen apart over the years. And it's no closer to being decrypted now than it was a century ago, when it first resurfaced." She stopped. "Did I leave anything out?"

"Wow. That's the most succinct description I've ever heard. I usually take a lot longer to describe it," Steven said.

"That's probably because you get caught up in the minutiae, like 'word entropy', which isn't relevant to a general overview," Natalie countered.

"*Touché*. Did you happen to pick up any of your father's thinking as to who the author was, or what language was used as its basis?" Steven asked, genuinely curious.

Natalie's demeanor became guarded. "He didn't like to speculate. Over the years, he considered and then rejected several possibilities, but in the end I'm not sure he really had a favorite. I do know that he believed it wasn't a fraud, as some earlier 'scholars' of it posited," she concluded.

Steven was impressed with her grasp of the document's intricacies. There were few people in the world he could discuss the Voynich with who had any idea what he was talking about ten seconds into the conversation.

"What about speculation that the whole thing was concocted by Edward Kelley?" Steven countered.

"To fool John Dee, or Emperor Rudolf? Not a chance. The text doesn't in any way resemble a random character set or an invented language. The likelihood is close to zero. No, it may be a mystery, but it isn't a hoax," Natalie pronounced with certainty.

Steven considered her comment.

"I happen to agree, by the way. As do the majority of the cryptology community," Steven said.

They sat in silence for a few minutes, watching Florence's outskirts glide by and the countryside south of it appear outside their darkened windows.

"Aren't you concerned that whoever is tracking you might have discovered the villa you're staying at?" Steven asked, changing the subject.

"Not a chance. I got it from a last minute rental pool on the internet and paid for it with a wire from an untraceable bank account in Austria. It's as clean as anything in the world gets," Natalie assured him.

"What about your flight from the States? That has to show up somewhere."

He knew a few things about the precautions one had to take in order to stay below the radar, and they were not only difficult to master, but most amateurs blew it by hoping that the data was so massive it could never be sifted to reveal their moves. Hope was a lousy strategy, he'd learned.

"Not if you have several passports and identities," she explained, as if addressing a schoolboy.

Steven had no pithy rejoinder. She was right. He just never imagined she might have multiple IDs. He made a mental note not to underestimate her – between her grasp of the Voynich, and her obvious fluency with the nuances of anonymous international travel and payment methods, she'd just demonstrated she knew more about those arcane topics than all but a tiny fraction of the population.

He stole a glance at her, sitting next to him, absently looking through the car window as they got onto the highway leading south. All that, and wrapped in an edgy, knockout, suede-clad package.

Steven had the sensation that he was already in whatever this was to a point way over his head. But the contents of Natalie's satchel, as well as the woman herself, ensured he'd have to keep pushing forward to see where the road led. At least for a while longer.

CHAPTER 11

The villa was a typical higher-end rental owned by a British couple who used it July and August and leased it out during the ten months they weren't there. Four bedrooms in two stories, it came fully stocked and with maid service every three days. Located near San Casciano, it was ten miles from Florence, but could have been on a different planet, with none of the bustle or crowds of the larger city. As they pulled down the long, manicured drive, Steven was reminded of his and Antonia's place in Greve, a scant few miles southwest of them. He forced the tide of memories back into the mental cell he'd built for them – it would do no good to go down a road of wistful regret when there were more pressing matters to attend to.

Studying the house and seeing no other vehicles, Natalie spoke to Frederick, after placing her hand on Steven's to stop him from getting out of the car. Steven noted that her skin was warm, and that her nails were short, with black nail polish.

"Frederick, would you please take a look inside and ensure we haven't been disturbed? I'd hate to think we could have been tracked, but…"

"Give me a second. I'll call you if it's all clear. If I don't call within two minutes, get out of here," Frederick said, leaving the car's engine running.

Natalie exited the back seat and assumed the vacant position behind the steering wheel. Steven realized she was taking the situation much more seriously than he would have. Then again, his father hadn't just been murdered, and a large part of him didn't know what to make of Natalie's story. Much of it sounded like a paranoid adventure cooked up by a bored rich girl; an invention to make the everyday seem more vital and dangerous. Seeing how careful both she and Frederick were being, he decided to reserve judgment before dismissing their concerns as frivolous.

"You never mentioned why your father involved you in all this. Did you work with him?" Steven asked, filling up the uncomfortable silence with chatter, the warmth of her hand still tingling on his.

"I was the only one he trusted. He led a solitary life, and other than a few close friends, I'm the only one he had. My mom passed away eleven years ago. I was a large part of his support system."

"Did you live with him?" Steven inquired.

"No."

There was no further explanation. Steven figured she was drawing a line beyond which she didn't want to go. He made a mental note not to delve into her personal life.

Her cell warbled. She listened for a moment, then hung up.

"All's well. Let's go inside. Are you hungry? The place is loaded with every kind of delicacy you can imagine," Natalie offered.

"No, I'm good. Maybe in a few hours." He hesitated. "Why don't you tell me a little more about this threat while I look over the Scroll? I'm still fuzzy on parts of it…"

"Come on in and I'll break it down for you," she responded over her shoulder as she made her way to the front door.

Steven followed dutifully after her, admiring the view.

The interior of the villa was the usual rustic Tuscan finish so popular in the area, all terracotta flooring and exposed wooden beams on the ceiling. Natalie moved into the dining area and opened the satchel, extracting the cylinder and carefully removing the Scroll before spreading the pages on the dining table.

"Do you have a magnifying glass?" he asked. "And can we get some more light in here? Maybe a desktop lamp, or worst case, a flashlight?" He looked around the room. "Oh, and do you have a computer with internet access? I'll need it for research."

Natalie nodded and pointed at a laptop that was on the kitchen bar counter. Steven walked over and was soon online, typing rapidly. He pulled up a site and was reading intently when Natalie returned after a few minutes with a hinged desk lamp and a rectangular magnifying glass. She plugged in the lamp, watched it flicker to life, and turned on the overhead lights for good measure. Steven noticed she didn't open the curtains on the dining room window. She apparently valued her privacy, especially while sorting through stolen parchments. Which reminded him.

"So, who exactly stole these for your father? Maybe that's a good place to pick up the story…" he started, as he closed the web browser and moved to the dining table and the quire.

"*Liberate.* My father had someone *liberate* the Scroll from where it was being kept by those to which it no more belonged than to me. Let me just start at the beginning and you'll realize why I'm so cautious about everything," Natalie protested.

"Why don't you? I hope you don't mind if I interrupt you occasionally with a question or three," Steven countered.

"No problem. All right. First, you have to understand that my father would have never, ever engaged in the theft of anything. Liberating an article of historical significance from a group which had itself liberated the item in order to come into possession of it is a different matter. The lost quire was removed from the Voynich centuries ago, only a few years after the document was created. It was stolen and locked away from prying eyes by a faction of the Catholic Church," Natalie explained.

"Ah, yes, the mystery sect. You know, it's strange, because I've never heard of this 'Order of the Holy Relic' even though I'm more than passingly familiar with every medieval secret society that ever existed," Steven protested.

"Nobody has heard of it. That's its whole objective. It's a top secret splinter faction with tremendous resources, supported at the highest level of the Church – the first director of the group, who is always known as the 'Sentinel', was handpicked by Pope Nicholas V after he'd crushed a plot to displace him from the Papacy. After Constantinople fell to the Turks, he created the Order and dedicated a stipend to its ongoing operations," Natalie continued.

"That would be around 1453 or 54. Fair enough. Although how do you know this?" Steven probed.

She looked at him with thinly-veiled annoyance. "As I already explained, Morbius Frank co-opted a member of the Order and put him in touch with my father. He filled in the group's history, or as much as he knew of it. Almost everything about the Order is shrouded in mystery, even to members. Besides its origins, my father discovered that its charter was to keep the Scroll in its possession, hidden forever."

"Now out of its possession, technically speaking," Steven observed. Natalie glared at him. He ignored it and continued. "You're telling me that this parchment will not only drive Morbius Frank's minions to hunt us down, but will also bring the full weight of the wealthiest organization in the world to bear in order to recover it?"

"Exactly."

"If you're right about even half of this, you'll never be safe as long as you have the Scroll. Am I missing anything?" Steven asked.

Natalie walked around the table and stood next to Steven, studying the pages intently.

"Where are you going to start?" she asked.

He considered the question.

"I think the first thing we need to do after I have a chance to examine it thoroughly is to make copies and store the original someplace safe. It's not a good idea to be handling vellum that's almost six hundred years old. It will degrade in no time – the chemicals from our skin and the atmosphere will start eating away at it. We shouldn't really be handling it at all, and ideally it should be stored in a humidity and temperature-controlled unit," Steven explained.

"I know all that. I already made copies of the Scroll – super high-resolution color copies, which I printed out and also have on disk. But I wanted you to see the actual pages, in case there's something the copies didn't pick up, or there's some tell-tale only the originals show."

Natalie's father had probably given her all the same admonishments about handling the originals, so he let that one lie.

"Good. Then I'll just need some time to look these over. There's something about the grouping and illustrations that I find strange, but I can't put my finger on it. Give me some time and maybe it'll come to me," he said.

"You're here for the duration, so take as long as you like, Dr. Cross."

"Steven. Please, Natalie, call me Steven. But I'm not sure what you mean by the duration…"

She stared at him like he was an idiot. "Steven, I thought this was clear. You're not safe. Frank's people, the Order, and anyone helping them will be looking not only for me, but also for you. The visit to your office was just the start. Whether it's fair or not, or even makes sense or not, you're in danger because your name was on that letter, and there's nothing you can say or do that will change that. I'm sorry, but the way I see it is we're going to be spending a lot of time with each other, *for the duration*, until we either solve the puzzle and can figure a way out of this mess, or they find us and put an end to it all." Natalie didn't need to expound on what she meant by putting an end to it all. Her implication was clear.

Steven hadn't fully considered the ramifications of their predicament, but he did so now. If, and that was a big if, she was correct about a shadowy sect hunting for them both, not to mention a billionaire's murderous henchmen, they were in an impossible situation.

He rubbed his chin. "Don't take this the wrong way, but aside from your say-so, do you have any proof that what you've said is true? I'm not questioning your veracity, so don't take it the wrong way, but is there anything else you haven't told me that might be more solid than rumors of a secret group and speculation about your father's death?"

Natalie sighed, clearly exasperated. "You're looking at a section of the Voynich that's been hidden for hundreds of years. My father was dead seventy-two hours after taking possession of it, and his partner's enforcement thugs have been overturning every rock they can find to locate me – I've gotten multiple warnings on that front from my contact network. You've just been visited by two gentlemen who were extremely interested in your whereabouts. Precisely what more do you need to know?" she asked.

"We don't know for sure what that was about…" Steven protested, but she grabbed his arm to quiet him.

"There are two possible explanations. First is that I'm crazy, and this is all an elaborate hallucination of mine, and we're in no danger of anything worse than dying of boredom while you study the rarest document in the world. The alternative is that I'm telling the truth, and it's as bad as or worse than I'm saying, in which case it's going to require every bit of luck and skill we can muster to be alive tomorrow. I think you need to decide which it is, because right now you're wasting time on an issue I thought was decided," Natalie fumed.

She was right. It was A or B. Either way, it would do no harm to examine the Scroll thoroughly – at worst, he was trapped in a Tuscan villa with a stunning *femme fatale* who favored Catwoman suits and had the most amazing eyes he'd ever seen…who might also be kind of crazy. Actually, that wasn't the worst case scenario, but he didn't want to think about the second possibility just yet.

"I'll admit you're persuasive, Natalie. Let me get to work on these and see if I can spot anything that would be a giveaway or a clue. But as you know, the Voynich's kept its secrets for a long time. I'm not sure how much I can do in a day," Steven parried.

"Better get busy, then. This is our only shot, on the off-chance that I'm not as nutty as a Christmas fruitcake," she said, and then beamed a thousand kilowatt smile at him before turning and leaving him to his work.

ঌ

As the day wore on, Steven took Natalie up on her offer of lunch and was pleasantly surprised at the spread she set out. Organic green salad, gnocchi pesto, dry salami, rigatoni in a four cheese sauce, all accompanied by a passable bottle of chianti.

They ate on the small, brick-built outdoor breakfast patio off of the kitchen, which had a sturdy rustic pine picnic table and two benches. Natalie and Frederick sat across from him, making strained small talk about where they could go from Italy to ensure her continued survival. Steven had probed for some more information on her background, but the attempt had been met with a polite but firm rebuff.

Steven wondered what the exact nature of Natalie and Frederick's relationship was – she seemed far more relaxed with him than Steven would have expected her to be with a driver, and he seemed to know everything she did about their current adventure, even though he limited his commentary to a few terse words. As with much that had occurred over the last half a day, Steven figured he'd discover more in time and contented himself with savoring the gourmet meal while thinking through his examination of the Scroll.

"Are you making any progress?" Natalie asked after he thanked her for lunch, clearly having resisted the urge to raise the subject throughout the meal.

"Perhaps. The glyphs look the same as the rest of the Voynich, but they're arranged in a different format, almost like short descriptive paragraphs. That would be consistent with several other quires, but there's just something that strikes me as unusual about this set. I haven't yet been able to put my finger on it, but I'm working on it," Steven summarized.

"If you have a breakthrough, I'm all ears, Steven. I'm thinking I'll take a nap while you're working – Frederick can get you anything you need," she said, yawning ever so slightly into her cupped hand.

"I'll try to have the whole thing wrapped up by the time you wake up," Steven said easily as he re-entered the dining room.

After spending several hours poring over every nuance of the parchment pages, the truth was that Steven was no closer to deciphering the Scroll than when he'd first laid eyes on it. That wasn't unexpected, although a part of him felt disappointed. It would have been wonderful if it had inspired a Eureka moment. But in his experience, that wasn't how things worked. He was very good and had honed his skills over the years, but there were no secrets to decryption only he knew – much of the time it was simple trial and error. One painstakingly looked for patterns and tried known examples of encryption techniques that dated from the same period, hoping that it would yield a solution, or at least a direction to follow. But the Voynich had always been inscrutable, impervious to all efforts to decode it. Even after the best in the field had done their best, there had been no breakthrough. Plenty of theories, but no solutions.

He wearily rubbed his hands over his face and stood back from the dining room table as he stared at the collected pages. There was so much data to incorporate, and no obvious place to start. This was an almost impossible task, and he wondered absently why the Order had spent so much energy guarding what on the surface appeared to be just more Voynich cypher. It made no sense. He began pacing in frustration, his gaze wandering absently over the Scroll as his mind raced. There was something there, but so elusive…

Wait a second. The crest on the final page of the Scroll, under the elaborately drawn roots of a mythical plant. That looked vaguely familiar.

Steven racked his brain to recall why he'd felt a stirring, or where he'd seen the crest before. It was a tiny depiction of a labyrinth, which seemed out of place in this seemingly medicinal chapter. He concentrated on it, searching his memory banks for the recollection, but couldn't place it. He continued pacing. *That crest. What was the significance?* For that matter, what was the significance of any of the illustrations, depicting everything from elaborate, nonsensical plumbing diagrams replete with bathing nude women, to cosmological diagrams of unfamiliar or fantastical galaxies or constellations, to plants that appeared to be hybrids of the real and the invented?

Whenever he spent long hours studying the Voynich, he always felt like he was being sucked down a dark rabbit hole into an upside-down world where nothing made sense. Today's efforts were no different.

And yet that symbol. He'd seen it before.

Steven moved to the computer and, from online scans of the complete document, spent an hour looking at every illustration in the Voynich. The labyrinth didn't appear anywhere, so he hadn't seen it before in the Voynich. Frustrated, he switched strategies and loaded a search engine, then proceeded to pore through countless results for medieval astrological and astronomical symbols. There were tens of thousands, and he quickly acknowledged the futility of trying to find the needle in the haystack. But he knew he'd seen it elsewhere during his travels. Could those have been coded clues that would decode the Voynich? Anything was possible, and Steven realized he wouldn't have thought twice about the symbol if he hadn't seen it in quire 18.

Think, dammit. It's an emblem – almost like a coat of arms with the circular labyrinth depicted as the central element.

It was right on the periphery of Steven's awareness. But the harder he focused, the more fleeting it became.

This isn't working.

Steven knew he'd need to stop trying to force it and wait until the gears meshed and the answer came to him. But knowing and doing were two distinctly different things. Increasingly frustrated, he decided to go for a short walk to clear his head. After alerting Frederick, he made his way down the long drive, taking in the vineyards and olive trees surrounding the property.

The summer sun felt good on his face; by its angle, he realized that it was going to be evening in just a few hours. That raised the question of what he was going to do. If Natalie was right, his best option was to stay at the villa until further notice, but there was a part of Steven that wasn't comfortable allowing an ephemeral threat drive him underground. His life for years had been spent in a sort of hiding, always looking over his shoulder, and he'd only recently become comfortable that he had nothing more to worry about. Then this slammed into him. It wasn't fair.

Steven was jolted out of his daydream by the deep boom of a nearby gunshot. He swung around and found himself facing an old man, seventy yards off, holding a turn-of-the-century shotgun. He was shooting at the crows, trying to drive them off his property. Steven waved at him. He waved back. There were few things like the Italian countryside, where just a few minutes outside of a major town you could find farmers discharging guns with nobody batting an eyelid.

What a weird country. He continued strolling, amid a reverie of his old place in Greve, haunted by Antonia's restive ghost and his own disturbed dreams, and realized there was a part of him that still missed living in rural tranquility. Just as quickly as that image flitted through his consciousness, the familiar sequence of recollections began their bittersweet parade – those last moments, kissing and holding Antonia, watching her race off in the Audi, thinking it was just another routine day when, in reality, the final minutes of her life were ticking away. If it hadn't been for the ancient book peddler, he would have also been crushed by the huge–

The book collector. His box.

Steven stumbled, then turned and ran like a madman back to the villa. He burst through the front door to find Natalie standing in the kitchen, her nap over, making herself a cup of tea.

"I know where I've seen the Voynich crest before," he announced, only mildly winded from the sprint back.

"That's amazing!" She peered at him. "What Voynich crest?"

Steven realized that he hadn't shared with her any of his postprandial speculations. He beckoned to her, and she joined him at the table where the Scroll was laid out.

"You see this small drawing on the last page? The one that looks like a highly-stylized circular labyrinth in a shield-shaped exterior?" he asked excitedly, tapping the parchment delicately with his index finger.

"Yes. I see it, although to me it looks a lot like the rest of the drawings. What's the big deal about it?" Natalie asked.

"I've seen it before."

"You already said that. But why is that such exciting news?"

"Because of where I've seen it," he responded.

"Where have you seen it?"

"On another parchment, also written in a cypher, but one that's been decrypted," he announced.

"And…" Natalie gestured with her hand: like, whenever you're ready to tell me the meat of it, proceed.

"Decrypted by me." Steven could see she still didn't get it. "I have the parchment."

CHAPTER 12

"You're saying that this little emblem, or whatever it is, is similar to some parchment you worked on?" Natalie summarized, surprised at the direction events had suddenly moved in.

"No, I'm saying that it is the exact same crest as on a medieval parchment that I own – I bought it along with four others from an antique book dealer several years ago. One of the oldest families in the business in Italy, and perhaps all of Europe. They've been at it for hundreds of years, and many of the older pieces in circulation have moved through their hands at one time or another if a sale was involved. This parchment was part of the family's private collection, which comprised mainly obscure and historically insignificant documents. The only reason it's now noteworthy is because of the drawing. Otherwise it would just be a run-of-the-mill fifteenth century coded letter that was drafted using a fairly complex substitution cypher. The pisser is that I actually consigned it to a rare book company six months ago, with some of my others," Steven explained, then shifted his attention to the Scroll. "If you look at the crest, you'll see that it's an eleven-circuit labyrinth. Not sure if that has any significance…"

"What does that mean?"

"See the path? If you count the rings, you'll see that there are eleven levels. Older labyrinths tend to be simpler. This is similar to the one in Chartres Cathedral in France," Steven explained.

"So it's a maze…some sort of a puzzle?"

"No. Labyrinths have well defined paths. Mazes don't – they're intended to challenge the intellect with numerous dead-ends. With labyrinths, the symbolism is deeper. The only decision with a labyrinth is whether or not to enter it. Everything else is about the trip through. In a way, this could be a veiled reference to beginning a tortuous journey…"

"Do you remember what the parchment said?" Natalie asked.

"Not really. It…it simply wasn't anything particularly noteworthy. At least not then. I just put it onto the curiosities pile and went about my business. At the time, I had a lot going on…I'd just lost my wife in a car crash, so I wasn't really that involved in much of anything for a while…"

"I'm sorry, Steven." Natalie said quietly.

"It was two and a half years ago… Anyway, the point is, I've seen the parchment and I'll need to get hold of it as soon as possible, because it may hold the key to deciphering the Scroll, or at least could put us on the right path." Steven looked at his watch. "Shit. I'll need to make a call. If he's in town, I should be able to get the dealer to scan the document and send it to my e-mail. Let me give it a try."

Steven consulted his phone's address book, and after a few moments, conducted a hurried call in Italian. When he hung up, he was smiling.

"Mission accomplished. Framboso, the dealer, hasn't sold it yet. He promised to get a high resolution scan to me by the end of the day," Steven said.

"You're sure it's the same crest?" Natalie asked.

"Positive. But I have another problem, and I think we need to deal with it sooner than later. My passport and cash are in one of several large safety deposit boxes at a bank in downtown Florence, where I keep my parchment collection. It's completely secure and climate-controlled." He stared at the crest closely, nodded, then turned to Natalie. "The bank's open until five o'clock. I'll need it anywhere I go in Italy, or if I have to cross a border. Come to think of it, it might not be a terrible idea to put the Scroll in one of the boxes at the same time. If you've got scans, there doesn't seem to be anything on the originals that wouldn't be on an image. Your call, but you're welcome to use one of my boxes to store it," Steven offered.

Natalie hesitated. Steven could tell she was torn. His invitation made sense, but she wasn't completely willing to give up possession of the Scroll. Too high a price had already been paid for it.

Steven let the moment pass. When push came to shove, it wasn't his problem – the Scroll wasn't his property. Then again, it wasn't really hers, either. She hadn't paid millions for it.

"I'll bring it with me and make a decision once I see the security. Not all banks are created equal," she observed, dodging the moment of truth.

"If we're going to make it with any time to spare, we better hit the road. Oh, and I think it would be a good idea to stop by my flat so I can get a shaving kit and clothes. Especially if I'm going to be on vacation for a while," Steven said.

"That's a terrible idea, Steven. They might be watching your place."

"Natalie. You said they'd be following up on me as a routine lead, which would be one of many, I'd think. So the likelihood of someone being there, watching the flat with twenty-four hour surveillance, is slim. In fact, the longer I wait, the higher the probability they'll get interested in it," he insisted.

"If you're hell bent on it I can't stop you, but remember I told you I don't like it. From my perspective it's an unnecessary risk. Can't you have someone else go over and pack a bag for you, and then they meet Frederick someplace crowded? They won't be looking for an older man. That's just one of many ways to solve the problem," Natalie proposed.

"I'll make the decision later," Steven said, echoing her earlier comment on the Scroll.

Natalie decided not to press the point. She carefully gathered up the pages and returned them to the canister. Glancing around the table to ensure she wasn't overlooking anything, she nodded to Steven.

"All right. We're ready. Tell Frederick where the bank is, and with any luck, we should make it before five," she said.

Traffic was the usual late-afternoon snarl, with the angry insect-like buzzing of motor-scooter engines flooding the streets. Honking on some of the larger roads was a near constant as two-wheeled scooter-nauts with a death wish darted from alleys and wove their way through the procession of cars. Sirens screamed in the distance, announcing that one of the daredevils had mistimed a move and would be heading to the hospital or the morgue.

They arrived at the bank with fifteen minutes to spare. Steven escorted Natalie into the modern lobby of the restored building and through the computerized security system for the safety deposit boxes. Once they were in the vault, he fished around in his pants for a set of keys and methodically opened one of the larger compartments, taking care as he extracted a three-foot long, foot high metal box and set it on the table in one of the adjoining private rooms.

After they were both seated, Steven opened the lid. Natalie gave an involuntary shiver from the air-conditioning; the breeze outside was fresh, as early summer in Italy could be, but the room was borderline cold. He removed a plastic document container and retrieved his passport and a wad of euros – fifty thousand of which he kept in cash out of force of habit. There had been a time in his life when he carried that much around with him on a routine basis, but that had been over half a decade before, and the two bundles of bills felt strangely heavy to him now. He weighed them both in his hands, then replaced one bundle, putting the other into the zip-up pocket of his lightweight windbreaker along with the passport. Natalie watched him silently.

"The vault is temperature controlled at sixty-seven degrees year round, and the air-conditioning keeps most of the humidity out of the air, so for storing parchments it's a good situation. Ideally, I would build a storage unit of my own and have more precise control, with a backup generator in case of loss of power, but for as small a collection as I have, that would be silly," he said.

"How many parchments do you keep here?" Natalie asked.

"Forty-five, at last count. I have four of these drawers," Steven explained.

They exchanged glances. Steven looked at her quizzically – it was time to make the decision about leaving the Scroll in the bank. A quiet struggle went on behind her eyes as she weighed the risks of allowing the two million dollar document out of her sight, in the safety deposit box of a man she'd just met. Eventually, she nodded at Steven.

"I suppose it would be best if we left it here. But I think it would be appropriate to put me on the security list so I can access the box if something, well, goes wrong or happens to you…" Natalie reasoned.

"Fair enough. We can sit down with the manager on the way out. We should get going." Steven smiled. "Looks like we're going to have to trust each other a little."

"That's not so easy for me to do."

Steven decided not to go there. Whatever was playing behind those violet eyes, it could do so without his intrusion. He reached across and placed the Scroll container delicately in the drawer before closing and locking the top, then carried it over to the bank of compartments and replaced it with a slam of the door.

They stopped at the manager's desk, but he'd gone home early, so they were faced with another hurdle. Natalie sighed and, shaking her head, strolled to the front entrance. What was done was done.

"We can come back tomorrow and put you on the list, Natalie," Steven offered, following her to the exit.

"Sure. I'm not going to worry about it now. Let's get going,"

They walked down the block to where Frederick had the car waiting. Natalie turned to him.

"I want to try to talk you out of going to your apartment, Steven. It's a really bad idea. We can get you whatever you need at any of a hundred stores in town. There's just no reason to take the risk I can see," Natalie said.

"Well, I can think of a big one, besides liking my own stuff. The software program for decrypting parchments I came up with is on my PC at home, and if we want to get to the bottom of all this, it will be an essential."

"Shit. Okay, now I get it. Do you have it anywhere else? At your office?" Natalie asked.

"No, because when I'm at work I'm generally working. Not trying to decrypt medieval manuscripts," Steven explained.

"Then I see why it's worth the risk. Guess we don't have much choice," Natalie admitted.

"Not really. Trust me when I say I don't want to take a bullet in the back to get a software program. I'm sure it'll be fine."

They drove the seven minutes from the bank to his flat, which was one of five in the old three story building. On Natalie's instruction, Frederick parked a block away. Steven got out of the car, stopping Natalie as she opened her door.

"It's probably a bad idea for us to be seen together, Natalie. If anyone is watching my place, your presence there would make my involvement in whatever this is undeniable. Let me go in, grab some stuff, and I'll be back in a few minutes, okay?"

Natalie sank back into the seat. "Fine. I'll stay here."

Steven began the walk to his flat, which was around the corner and a hundred yards up the block. He ambled along unhurriedly, watchful of any surveillance, but didn't spot anything. Maybe Natalie was being sensationalistic. Then again, there was the matter of the two men who'd been at his office just a few short hours before.

He approached his building's entry and didn't note anything amiss. Steven slid his key into the creaky old lock, which fought his right to enter with customary Italian ennui. Once inside, he moved to the stairs that led to the second floor.

His cell phone jangled, startling him. He peered at the screen as he climbed the stairs. It was Gwen.

"Hello," Steven said.

"We got a fix on the phone number those two men left for you, mighty bwana," Gwen chirped glibly. "It's to the southern precinct of the police. Looks like they were telling the truth."

He digested the information. "They were cops after all? What did they say they wanted?"

"Just that they needed to speak with you as soon as possible," Gwen reminded him.

"E-mail me the number and I'll give them a buzz. And thanks, Gwen," Steven said.

"Are you still going to be 'on holiday' for a week?" she asked cheerfully.

Steven considered the question. The men were real detectives, so Natalie's entire story was beginning to look pretty shaky.

"That remains to be seen. For now, consider me gone, and I'll call you if anything changes," he offered.

"Okay. Be careful," Gwen said.

"Will do. I remember your advice – don't strain anything," Steven said.

He arrived at his second floor landing and made his way down the old, poorly lit hall. The first door on his right opened, and the nosy old superintendent, Mrs. Salarno, fixed him with a disapproving gaze.

"I heard your voice on the stairs. I hope everything's all right, *si*? Nothing too valuable is missing?" she said, hands on her hips.

"Mrs. Salarno. How lovely to see you. I'm afraid you have me at a disadvantage. What are you talking about?" Steven asked politely, puzzled by her statement.

"I called the police when I heard the commotion in your flat. This morning, right after you left. I thought maybe you were having problems, so I knocked on the door, but then the noise stopped and nobody came to the door, and I thought, 'that's not right'. I called the cops right away. They were here for a few hours. I told them where your office was. Didn't the lazy jerks come by?"

Steven tried to absorb her rapid-fire account. "Police? Here? And what noise?" Steven looked down the hall towards his front door.

"I let them into your flat. I hope you don't mind. And I stayed with them to make sure they didn't make off with anything," Mrs. Salarno assured him.

Steven gently pushed past the woman and made his way to his door, which had a notice affixed to it from the local police along with a business card inserted into the door jamb. He withdrew the card and pocketed it, glanced at the notification, and then unlocked the handle. Nothing could have prepared him for the vision that greeted him.

The flat looked like it had been torn apart by vandals. Papers were strewn everywhere, drawers hung half opened with a few upended on the floor, and a flower vase was broken on the coffee table. Steven sensed a presence behind him and turned to face Mrs. Salarno.

"I stood here and made sure they didn't touch anything. I figured you'd rather clean up yourself than have the police rummaging through all your things," she said.

"This was the way they found it?"

"Exactly the way it was. Like I said, I heard a commotion, and I suspected the worst because you're always so quiet. There are some broken items in the kitchen, too, which is probably what made the noise. Either that or the drawers." She paused, taking in the shambles. "It's a shame that even in this area we're having robberies. When I was a girl, it was safe enough to leave your front door open. Not now."

Steven ignored her, eyes roaming over the shambles of his living room while madly processing the implications. Maybe Natalie wasn't so crazy after all?

Or maybe Natalie's associates had done this?

What did he know about her, anyway? She'd appeared as if out of a dream, with a wild story and outlandish claims, and convinced him in no time to literally run away with her. She'd mischaracterized the two cops as goons intent on doing him harm, perhaps innocently, or possibly as part of some scheme he wasn't aware of.

He didn't get the sense that she was deliberately trying to mislead him, but that was hardly dispositive. The bottom line was that Natalie was a question mark, and he'd have to keep his guard up until he understood more – sparkling violet eyes or no.

Steven skirted the worst of the debris and moved to his computer station. The laptop was gone. That was a big problem. Not only because all of his personal files were on it, but also because it housed the decryption software.

Steven surveyed the clutter, shaking his head. What a mess. He supposed he'd best call the cops and file a report listing the stolen items, which would mean doing a full inventory. Maybe later. For now, he needed to grab some clothes and go to his storage locker downstairs.

He threw together a duffle bag with a week's worth of clothes and a shaving kit and then moved to the front door, where Mrs. Salarno was in residence.

"Mrs. Salarno, thank you so much for sounding the alarm on this. Who knows how much worse it would have been if it wasn't for you." Steven complimented, hoping to be rid of her. She seemed unwilling to leave, so he gently guided her by the arm into the hall.

"If you need anything, you knock, *eh*? It's a disgrace this can happen in this neighborhood," she complained.

Steven nodded in agreement and thanked her again, and then, when he heard her door squeak shut, closed his flat and descended the stairs to the ground floor, where he walked to the back of the long vestibule and unlocked a scratched wooden door. Dank, musty air hit him in the face as he swung it open, and he brushed a cobweb out of the way to turn on the light switch. Two low voltage fluorescent bulbs dimly lit the area, which held five locked storage stalls.

He approached the nearest and unlocked the padlock, swinging the hinged piece of dusty plywood and propping it open with a garbage bag of indeterminate junk he'd been storing for years. He rummaged around among the boxes until his hand felt the distinctive edge of a desktop computer, which he grabbed and lifted free of the cartons. When he'd stored it he'd had the presence of mind to tape the keyboard and mouse to it, along with the power cord, so he was good to go. Steven could use the monitor still sitting on his computer station; all that remained was to hope the old CPU would fire up.

He closed the storage stall and returned to his flat, where he dusted off and then set up the PC. While he waited for it to boot, he went to the bedroom and got a blank CD-ROM from a box in the closet. Upon his return, the screen was proudly displaying a set of icons he'd last seen when he'd moved into the flat. He quickly searched through them until he located the file he was looking for and then began downloading the contents. He hadn't bothered to save the decryption results for the parchment with the crest and silently kicked himself for his sloppiness. Now he'd need to perform the whole analysis over again, which would be a chore, given that it was processing-intensive. The last time, he remembered, it had taken days.

That gave him an idea. Maybe he could use the company computers to run the program overnight. He invested in the very latest technology for the programmers, changing out the systems every year for cutting-edge advents. One of the office computers could crunch the data in a third of the time Natalie's little laptop could. He picked up the phone on his computer desk and pressed a speed dial number. Gwen's voice answered.

"Hey. Is Sophie still there?" Steven asked.

"She sure is."

"Perfect. I need her to clear the decks on one of the new systems and run a decryption table for me. I can e-mail you the program in a compressed folder and send a separate file with a scan of the document. Can you get Sophie to do that for me?"

"I'll let her know. You ever find out what the coppers wanted to talk to you about?" Gwen asked.

"There's been a break-in at my place. I imagine they wanted me to identify what was stolen."

"Break-in? Did they get anything?"

"Far as I can tell, just my laptop. Not much else worth stealing, unless you want to try to stuff a big screen TV or monitor under your arm. But they messed up the flat pretty badly. Looks like a couple of mountain lions were mating in here," Steven shared.

"Was there anything critical on your system?"

"Not really. It's all password protected, but anyone with some time and knowledge could get through that. Mostly just BS. Still, it's annoying," Steven groused.

"I'll bet."

"I'm going to send the program over and the document a little later. I don't have internet access at my house. The bastards tore the jack out of the wall and stole the modem. God knows why. Anyway, call me when it's done. Thanks, Gwen."

The CD door popped open, signaling that it was finished. Steven logged off the computer and, surveying the damage to the flat once more, he decided there wasn't a lot more he could do other than clean up. He powered down, pocketed the CD, and lifted the duffel over his shoulder. Glancing around a final time, he shook his head in disapproval at the mess.

He would need at least a full day to get everything sorted and put back in place. *What a pain in the ass.*

He tromped down the stairs and out onto the sidewalk, preoccupied with new doubts about Natalie. Steven thought he was a good judge of character, but you never knew. He'd have to be on guard in case she had mischaracterized her involvement and had simply engineered circumstances to get him to decrypt the Scroll. It had been sheer luck he'd remembered a parchment with the labyrinth symbol on it, although there was no telling how many documents like it were in circulation. Could be only that one, or could be dozens.

He rounded the corner and approached the car, still parked in the same place. Steven was startled when the trunk popped open. Soundlessly interpreting the unspoken instruction, he tossed the duffel into the boot and closed it before moving to the rear door, which Natalie had swung ajar for him.

"Took you long enough," she complained.

"Yeah, well, I had some odds and ends that needed tidying up," he responded, watching her face closely for any sign of reaction. She looked at him blankly, obviously annoyed by his glib rejoinder. If she knew anything about the break-in, she was an Academy Award-level actress. He detected nothing but impatience to get going.

Steven regarded her exotic face, noting again in the close proximity that she smelled like a small slice of heaven. Whatever that was, it was a winner, he mused. Or maybe it had just been an awfully long time since…

Best not to go down that road.

"We need to get to a computer so I can check my e-mail and send the program to my office so they can hammer on it. Any ideas?" he asked.

"There's an internet café up two blocks," Frederick said. "We passed it earlier."

Natalie gave Frederick a thumbs up. He pulled into traffic, which was now heavy from the evening rush hour.

Across the street, a whippet-thin man with heavy acne scars marring his hard-chiseled face murmured into a cell phone as he lit a cigarette and pretended to consider a pair of chocolate leather women's riding boots in a shop window. He took in the car and the license plate, as well as the heavily-tinted windows and the way it rode low, and passed the information to his associate.

"I think it's him. I trailed him from the flat. I wish we had some photos so we could be sure," the man muttered into the mouthpiece between puffs.

"We're trying to get access to the motor vehicle database for a license photo, but there's nothing else I've been able to find. The man obviously isn't much for social media. Pity. Facebook's made everything easier…"

The man glanced around and then moved to the street as a motorcycle pulled to the curb. He tossed his smoke into the gutter and climbed on, and the driver gunned the engine before slamming it into gear and pulling into the clogged traffic a dozen car lengths from their quarry.

CHAPTER 13

Steven and Natalie entered the internet café, which was filled with students and tourists, and approached the bored, heavily tattooed and pierced girl behind the shabby counter. Steven wondered what circus she was planning to join – with fluorescent blue hair, four nose-piercings, a chain of skulls inked around her neck, a perpetual sneer and an attitude that rivaled the most arrogant baristas in town, there was little chance of her winning the title of Miss Florence Congeniality. Italy invented dismissive annoyance, and it was practically a rite of passage to be shown just how little you mattered by a whole phalanx of shop workers and restaurant staff eager to make the point. Their hostess had taken the leitmotif to heart. In spades.

Steven negotiated for the use of a computer, and soon he'd verified that the dealer had sent him a scan of the ancient document. He opened the large file and studied it – there in the lower right-hand corner was the identical crest to the Scroll's. There could be no mistake. He typed a rapid series of keystrokes, and in an instant the bits and bytes were winging their way to the office, along with the program to decrypt it. Once they had paid for their internet time, Steven held the door open for Natalie. Frederick had pulled the car around the block because there were no spaces. Natalie fiddled with her phone while clutching the satchel as they made their way back to the car. Steven leaned over to her and whispered in her ear.

"Don't look back, but I think we've picked up a tail."

Natalie's expression didn't change. She edged closer to him as she walked easily by his side.

"Should we duck into this café? It'll buy us time and we can confirm it. I'll call Frederick and ask him to go round the block and eyeball the exterior," Natalie suggested, and then without waiting for an answer, dialed Frederick's number. She murmured a few words of explanation into her phone and then palmed it.

They swung into the busy café and moved to the back of the long room, which featured faux bohemian décor, replete with black and white photos of beat poets adorning the walls. Jack Kerouac glared from one; Allen Ginsberg scowled from another. Steven felt as though he'd been transported to the late 50s-era Greenwich Village, which was oddly incongruent with modern Florence, yet the place was packed, and the din of animated conversation filled the air along with the rich aroma of coffee. Natalie's phone chirped while Steven scanned the room as though looking for a table, his eyes darting to the front door and picture window seemingly as an afterthought.

Natalie hastily fielded the call and hung up.

"Looks like two men. Professional. Staked out on either side of the front entrance, roughly twenty yards apart. Frederick doesn't think we'll be able to shake them. Any ideas before I have him start shooting?"

Steven studied Natalie and realized she wasn't joking.

He glanced around the back bar to the kitchen area and then grabbed her hand.

"Come on."

They pushed through the stainless steel double doors, past several puzzled servers, and found themselves in a frenzied dishwashing area next to a bank of ovens. The supervisor approached them and fired off a burst of staccato Italian, demanding to know what they were doing. Steven, pretending to be a tourist, merely shrugged apologetically as his eyes scanned the back of the kitchen and landed on a corridor leading into the depths of the building. He peered down the hall and saw an exit door, no doubt the delivery entrance, and elbowed Natalie gently. He hoped those following him didn't have a larger team than the two out front.

Steven glanced back over his shoulder in the direction of the dining room and saw a man struggling past the wait staff, the doors momentarily swung open by a woman carrying a tray filled with dirty cups. The irate kitchen manager made as if to physically remove them from his little kingdom, and Steven had to make a split decision.

"The back. Now. They're coming," he whispered, and Natalie ran towards the rear exit, Steven in tow. The dishwashing staff stopped what they were doing and stared as the odd couple raced for the garbage area.

Steven hit the door with his shoulder, wrenching the lever handle as he did so, and they spilled into a small alley. They heard a commotion from the kitchen behind them. Steven didn't wait to confirm that it was their pursuer. He darted down the street and spied a large, centuries-old building under refurbishment, the rear entrance barred by a slab of flimsy particle board held in place with a chain. It looked like there was just enough room for them to get in. Steven gestured to Natalie, who hurriedly slipped through the opening. Steven quickly followed, and they found themselves in a dimly lit, gutted area undergoing renovation. The construction crew had long since gone home, and the only sounds were the rumble of traffic from the far end of the building where it faced onto a major boulevard. They hastily pushed past the hanging construction tarps and ladders towards the street noise, probing their way through a maze of half-finished rooms and halls cluttered with bags of plaster and wood planks.

A rattle echoed through the area as their pursuer struggled with the rear entrance. If they couldn't find a way out they were trapped, and Steven resolved himself to a possible fight with adversaries of unknown competence, who could very well be armed.

"Be as quiet as possible. We need to find a way out the front," Steven whispered.

They crept past a tall ladder and a rotary table-saw on a makeshift stand. Footsteps pounded from a distance. Natalie glanced at Steven's profile – jaw set, eyes narrowed to slits as he focused on finding an exit.

An explosion of feathers startled them both as a sparrow sought escape, hurling itself against the tarps before disappearing into the cavernous darkened space above. Dim light from the waning dusk filtered through the broken windows, providing scant visibility. The footsteps slowed to a more cautious cadence, drawing closer.

Steven gestured to a spot ahead that was brighter, and the sound of cars grew louder as they made their approach. The footsteps behind them ceased. Steven cautiously picked up a three foot section of wood beam and motioned for Natalie to continue towards the opening. He remained behind, sliding his body into a recess in the wall, waiting for his stalkers to show themselves, his improvised club at the ready. After what seemed like an eternity, the crunching of plaster underfoot sounded from a few yards down the hall, and then a silhouette materialized in front of him.

The pursuer didn't register the movement in time, and by the point he did, it was too late. The wood beam landed squarely on his head, dropping him instantly. Steven listened for evidence of another assailant but heard nothing. The other man must have stayed in place outside the café or had gone into another building.

Steven crouched and felt the man's pulse, barely making out his shape in the darkness. The beat was weak and fluttering, but there. He'd live, although he'd feel like a piano had landed on him when he regained consciousness – Steven could just make out blood streaming down the side of the man's head. He surveyed the surrounding floor and spotted two weapons his assailant had dropped – a square box and a pistol. He scooped them both up and soundlessly eased himself to where Natalie would be waiting.

When he arrived at the front entrance, also secured haphazardly with some wood and a cursory length of chain, she was nowhere to be found. Natalie had disappeared. He glanced down at the white plaster dust that coated everything and saw the distinctive outline of her boots leading out onto the street, beyond the barrier. He wondered whether he'd be able to make it through the space and then heard noise from somewhere in the building's depths and resolved to try. It didn't sound like he had a lot of time.

Steven barely squeezed through, emerging onto a busy sidewalk with pedestrians hurrying along, anxious to get home. He scanned the sidewalk but didn't see Natalie.

Great.

A horn honked, and Frederick slid to the curb next to him, the rear door swinging open before the car had completely stopped. Natalie's distinctive aroma floated into his awareness even before he'd made it to the car, drawing him like a bear to honey.

He climbed in, pulling the pistol from where he'd concealed it under his shirt, and examined it.

"An air gun." He cracked the breach and extracted a small, blue-feathered dart filled with a dark amber fluid. "Want to bet that's knockout juice?"

She hefted the box he'd set on the seat. "This is a stun gun. Which makes sense – they want you alive so they can interrogate you. They'll only kill you once they understand what you know," Natalie reassured him.

Steven absorbed that. "What do we do now?"

"I think it's safe to say that they're on to you. Your home and office are off-limits. They must have made the car, so we'll need to ditch it and get another one. Frederick can handle that. My vote is we go back to the villa, make dinner, and rinse the construction dust off while he deals with it.

How long will it take for your office to run the decryption analysis?" Natalie asked.

"Should be done by morning, with any luck. But are you sure that these people can't find you tonight?"

"You're the one who picked up the tail, not me. The trip to the flat was a bad idea. I understand you needed to get the software, but everything in life has a risk, and the risk there was of you being followed. We knew that. And now we dealt with it, so other than the problem of us being confirmed together on a visual by our pursuers, we're clean. But you can't go anywhere near your usual haunts. Hopefully this was a wake-up call for you, and you realize I haven't been overstating the danger."

Steven listened to her calm, measured cadence, absent any trace of emotion, and nodded.

"I believe you."

In the tranquility of the now deserted office, Sophie's fingers flew over the keyboard as she set up the encryption software to perform the analysis on the file Dr. Cross had sent. She'd been a programmer for close to a decade, having been somewhat of a child prodigy, which had earned her a full scholarship to Stanford. Those had been heady times and had validated the many hours of sacrifice her mother had invested so she could pursue her interest in technology. A scholarship had been the crowning achievement of her life, and she'd graduated with a 4.0 average before going to work for Microsoft.

When she'd been recruited to work for Cross's group it had been a no-brainer. Live in Florence, a location redolent of the exotic in a country she'd always dreamed of visiting, for the same salary as being another faceless cog in a corporate machine in Washington, where it rained constantly and costs were through the roof? No contest. Of course, there had been logistical issues to deal with, not the least of which was her mother, who had been fighting cancer for the last two years. She'd gone into remission after an aggressive course of chemotherapy, but her health had been precarious ever since, and Sophie was her sole means of support other than disability income and a meager Social Security allotment. They'd quickly burned through her mom's savings over the course of the health battle, and Sophie had stepped in and bridged the shortfalls. But that had cost her dearly, and the expenses were still piling up, even with the health insurance. Her mother was now living with her in a two bedroom apartment, and Sophie's life revolved around work and attending to her needs.

The screen indicated that the software had begun the comparisons as it studied for pattern recognition and tried countless possible substitution cyphers in myriad languages. It was a processing-intensive program that Steven had written in his clumsy, amateurish manner, which could only be sped up by distributing the various computing tasks across the three most powerful systems they had. Steven might have been a visionary in some respects, but a coder he wasn't, and the program was one that would take a week of full time operation for a single CPU.

Sophie gazed at the screen in dismay and made a silent resolution to herself. She would approach him whenever he got back, casually, and see if he was interested in having her optimize the program at an equitable hourly rate. It might take up all her nights for the next few weeks, but she was willing to make the sacrifice. She had to generate money somehow. It had affected her sleep for the past month, as she plotted the course of her savings versus her expenses – it was grim picture that would see her underwater within a few more weeks.

She tore open a bag of barbecue-flavored potato chips and popped a fistful into her mouth, washing them down with a swig of cola. Sophie knew she was a little heavy. Okay, more than a little heavy. She was easily eighty pounds overweight, which was getting dangerous for her. Her doctor had cautioned her to cut back on calories and start exercising, the only real fix for her pre-diabetic condition, which was teetering on the brink of going full-blown. But food was her comfort and solace, and it was her constant companion now, just as it was her father, lover and confidante. She didn't need a pet. She had chocolate.

The primitive little icons Steven had filched from some off-the-shelf shareware annoyed her, just as everything seemed to lately. She knew it was nerves, coupled with a creeping awareness that ignoring the reality of her financial situation wasn't going anywhere good. It was getting to the point where she'd have to start maxing out all her credit cards – that was a downward spiral that always ended badly. She understood the effect of compounding and recognized it worked against her.

Sophie had considered asking for a big raise, but in the current financial climate, that wouldn't fly. Steven was already paying her at the top of her pay scale and had been overly generous in subsidizing her health insurance to include her mom. That amounted to thousands of dollars per year he was shelling out due to sympathy over her situation, which she appreciated. But in the end, if her problem wasn't solved, it would ruin her. It was an unfortunate situation all around. She had to do something, and do it quick, or she'd wind up drowning in a financial ocean that had the capacity to devastate both Sophie and her ailing mother.

She hated the choices she was going to have to make, but in the end it was family first. When all was said and done, it was about survival. And Sophie had someone depending upon her.

Stabbing at the monitor button, she shut down the screen in preparation to leave for the night. Glancing at the chips, she shrugged to herself and poured the remainder into her mouth before balling up the bag and tossing it into the trash. *Waste not, want not.* Sophie grabbed her small purse and moved to the front entrance, fishing her keys out so she could lock up. It was going to be another lonely night on the couch with Mom, watching pirated movies. Not quite the life she'd aspired to, but it was out of her hands.

CHAPTER 14

Colonel Gabriel Synthe lit his twenty-fourth cigarette of the day from the glowing ember of his twenty-third and blew a cloud of rancid smoke at the ceiling of his home office. He coughed a rasping exclamation, but didn't hesitate from drawing another deep puff into his lungs to quell the spasm. He figured that he was probably on borrowed time, so what was the point of quitting now?

He contemplated the phone conversation he'd had a few minutes earlier and considered not making the call he knew by rights he really should. He just didn't see much point, and naturally was resistant to reporting to the insufferable fool he'd been saddled with. Still, it would probably wind up harming more than helping if he sidestepped it, so he reluctantly dialed the number and listened as it rang.

"Any progress?" Diego Luca asked, by way of opening.

"Of a kind, I suppose. I just got word that Twain's daughter has been located."

"That's wonderful news!"

"Maybe not. She's hooked up with a third party, who we're trying to get more information about. And there's a further complication. Someone tried to follow them, and it didn't go well," Synthe rasped, noisily exhaling another cloud of smoke.

"Start at the beginning. Where is she?"

"Florence. Italy."

"What the hell is she doing there?" Luca demanded.

"That's a great question. For now, it's an unknown. But we're working on it."

"*Working on it.* I see. And who is the mystery third party?" Luca asked.

"He's a local entrepreneur, a Dr. Steven Cross. But the first checks into his identity are odd."

"In what way?"

"He didn't exist until five years ago. Before that, there's no data on him. It's like he came out of nowhere," Synthe reported, stubbing out the cigarette in an old terracotta flowerpot he used as an ashtray.

"Italian records are notoriously unreliable. Probably a quarter of all the people in Italy don't have history. It's not like the U.S. or the rest of the European Union. Things in Italy are more, you know, old-fashioned."

"Great. Well, here's what we know. He owns a small software company. He's got money. Lots of it. His wife, Antonia, died in a car accident a few years ago, and he inherited a bundle. He's forty-five, healthy – there are no medical records to speak of – and he has no debt. Leases a flat, and that's it. Nothing else," Synthe said disgustedly. He felt the cigarette pack on his desk and shook his head – he was down to the last cigarette.

"Hmm. A question mark," Luca said. "All right. What's this about someone following her? And what did you mean by it not going well?"

"Someone, presumably after the same thing we are, entered a construction site after they did, but didn't get a chance to leave. When we picked up the girl's trail yesterday, I dispatched a small team to see what they could find. We were able to trace her from a bank account she must think is anonymous, which it would be, under ordinary circumstances but we have reach in a lot of unusual areas. Suffice to say, money always leaves a trail. Always."

"Why not just scoop her up?" Luca asked.

"Because we don't know whether she's got the item. Nor do we know what her game is. All we know is she's vacationing in Italy and has a friend. That's not a lot to go on. If we move on her at the wrong time, we're done. We lose the chance she could lead us to the…to our objective."

"I understand. But what happened to the follower?"

"Either she, or her friend, knocked the man unconscious. We don't think he, or any of his associates, know where she is." Synthe chose his next words very carefully. "This morning, there was a police report that someone had broken into Steven Cross's home. A burglary, they say."

"What?"

"It wasn't us. But that tells me that whoever is doing the surveillance might have known about her friend earlier than yesterday. It's troubling – we seem to be playing catch-up to a group that's one step ahead of us. We need to change that," Synthe concluded, his information exhausted.

Luca could hear Synthe lighting a cigarette. Filthy habit for a degenerate atheist. It figured.

"Is there anything else?" Luca asked.

"We're doing research on Cross, and we'll be following the followers now that we know they're on the board. But at present there are many unknowns. That's not good. As you know."

Synthe spent another few minutes discussing logistics before terminating the call. Luca was a conniver, he decided, and the man was growing emboldened by his mandate to work with him – the tone of their interactions was increasingly becoming one of Synthe playing the role of subordinate to Luca's insufferable position as his superior.

The only really interesting news was that Cross and the girl appeared to be on the run, and Synthe knew where they were using as their home base. That single bit of information could well wind up being a critical piece – and at present it was the only real break they'd gotten.

He leaned back in his executive chair and stared at the paint flaking off his ceiling from the constant stream of toxins being blown there, day after day. It, like his soul, was rotting away, largely due to his own actions. He smirked humorlessly to himself as he considered the metaphor.

Nothing, he knew, lasted forever.

❧

Natalie had been unfazed by Steven's account of how he'd knocked the man who'd been following them unconscious. She had studied the air pistol and stun gun with only mild curiosity. As someone who had been on the receiving end of attempted assaults before, Steven found the response unusual. She should have been shaken by such a close brush with violence, and yet she'd continued to exude that unabashed tranquility – a quiet confidence that betrayed no anxiety. She was either extremely tough, or a sociopath, he reasoned. Even he, who had been in the military for several years and had been in numerous deadly situations, was shaken by the implications of surveillance and a near miss on a kidnapping attempt.

Natalie looked like she'd just woken up from a night's restful sleep, refreshed and ready to go to the gym. He'd never seen anything like it.

Frederick kept scanning the mirrors, and several times made abrupt turns into small streets then doubled-back, checking for any followers. He was clearly very good at what he did, causing Steven to wonder again exactly what his full job description was.

"We'll get out a few miles from the villa and get a taxi. We don't want the car anywhere near the villa anymore. Frederick will get new wheels for us by tomorrow morning. Won't you, Frederick?" Natalie smiled at the driver, and their eyes locked in the rearview mirror. He nodded.

"So, you think those were Morbius Frank's men?" Steven pressed.

"Yes, or the Order. In the end it's probably the same. Whoever it was, we have to expect the worst. If you don't have any pressing reason to stick around Florence, we should make tracks out of the area tomorrow. I'd say tonight, but that isn't practical until we have a different a car. Now that they know I'm here, with you, it isn't safe in Florence for either of us." She paused.

Steven didn't say anything. Natalie took a closer look at the stun gun.

"This is Iranian. Not one you usually see. First one I've ever come across up close," Natalie observed.

"You know the different types of stun guns that well?"

"Let's just say that at one point in my life it was of interest to me." If Natalie was trying to create additional mystery surrounding her, it was working. "It's different than civilian models. These are for the military and secret police."

"Forgive my ignorance, but what's the difference?"

"Civilian devices are designed to incapacitate. They give a zap and then stop unless the button's pressed again. These are built to not only incapacitate, but to continue delivering a series of charges to keep the target down for a long time." She waved it around casually. "Or to torture."

"Torture."

"In some countries, the police torture in order to get suspected perpetrators to cooperate – they find it far more useful than civilized techniques. Devices like these are built for that application."

"Seems like you know an awful lot about them. What did you say you did for a living, Natalie?" Steven asked, only half joking.

"I didn't." She leaned forward to Frederick. "Drop us at that little restaurant we passed yesterday that I said looked cute, okay? We'll cab to the house from there."

Frederick nodded, never stopping his perusal of the mirrors on an automatic circuit – rear, right, left; rear, right, left. Steven was getting dizzy following it. Then again, if he'd been treating this more seriously he would have spotted the surveillance at his apartment. He was usually good that way, and it annoyed him that he'd dropped his guard and gotten lackadaisical. There had been a time not so long ago when he was so finely-tuned he would have had internal alarms going off the second someone had scrutinized him; just as when Natalie had begun her shadowing.

He resolved to get back into the old habits.

Being rusty could cost him his life, if Natalie was right.

And it looked at this point like she was.

❧

At four-forty a.m., the computers stopped processing and went silent, their decryption job finally completed. Sophie's whirred for a few additional minutes as it committed the results to a new folder, then closed down the program, automatically putting itself into sleep mode.

The parchment was decrypted, awaiting human eyes to interpret the data.

CHAPTER 15

Steven woke to the sound of a rooster crowing nearby and for a few seconds was disoriented. Then the whole adventure came rushing back to him. He was in a rented villa, being hunted by shady miscreants intent on torturing him, while in the company of a modern Mata Hari with a mysterious past and beautiful eyes.

His phone indicated it was seven in the morning. He sighed, and then focused on meditating: a practice that was second nature to him. Steven felt the immediacy of his surroundings fade away, and soon he was in a void, absent any thought or mental images. After twenty minutes he felt a stirring and returned to conscious awareness, slowly coming back into the world, his nerves alive and again processing sensation.

Swinging his legs off the bed, he debated going for a morning run, but decided that it probably wasn't the day for it. They had a lot to do, not the least of which was getting away from Florence as soon as possible. Steven peered through a gap in the curtains at the driveway and saw a silver Audi sedan parked in front of the house. Frederick had been busy last night.

Steven shuffled to the bathroom and showered, reflecting on the prior evening as the hot needles of water invigorated his skin. Natalie had proposed having dinner at the restaurant, and they'd lingered over an excellent bottle of Cabernet once their pasta entrées were through. She'd opened up a little, offering glimpses of her past, tantalizing slivers of an at-times rebellious and unconventional adulthood. Natalie had hinted at a background in law enforcement, although she was reluctant to go into detail. But that explained her comfort with weapons and her lack of agitation over their brush with violence.

He fingered the bullet scar on his leg, recalling how long it had been since he'd had to contend with being hunted. Antonia and he had nearly been killed when they'd first landed in Italy, in the small hill town of Todi. That seemed a lifetime ago, but it had only been six years.

Steven snapped back to the present and shut off the water. There was no point in throwing himself a pity party. Antonia was gone, and with her his interest in women. Until now. He had to admit that there was something about Natalie that had gotten to him. Not just the obvious visceral appeal, although that was potent. No, it was more the combination of her looks and her personality. Some elusive quality that was difficult to pinpoint, yet powerful.

She was as unlike Antonia as she could be. American, tattoos, goth look, accustomed to rough situations. And wildly smart, he remembered from their discussion of the Voynich. It was quite a cocktail, and Steven would need to keep on his toes to prevent being lulled into comfortable relaxation. He still wasn't sure whose side she was on, although he was leaning more towards betting she was on his since the attack. But the truth was that she was on her own, and part of his job over the next few days would be to figure out where he fit in that scheme.

He toweled off and donned some fresh clothes, inspecting himself in the mirror. Not too bad – looked at least five years younger than he was, on a good day. Things could have been worse, he supposed. Steven repacked his shaving kit into the duffel and zipped it closed.

His phone rang. He glanced at the screen to discover it was from the office. Gwen's voice chirped at him when he answered.

"Your results are in on that task you had Sophie run. You want me to e-mail it to your account?" Gwen asked.

"Yes, please. How long did it take to finish?"

"Let me ask. I got in a bit late today, and everyone was here before I made it."

Steven heard her move the phone away from her mouth and call out. She was back on in a few seconds.

"Just before five this morning."

"Wow. That was quicker than I expected," Steven said.

"Sophie co-opted everyone's computers, so it was a distributed effort," Gwen explained.

"Ahh. Thanks, Gwen. And listen. If anyone else stops in looking for me, I've decided to extend my holiday indefinitely."

Gwen paused. "Well now. You must be having a ball," she remarked dryly, stressing the final syllable.

"It's not like that. I can't really explain because I don't know much more, but it isn't what you think," Steven finished lamely.

"No. Well, I'm sorry to hear that. She looked like such a sweet young innocent thing. Really about the age of a daughter, if you'd gotten started young."

Gwen was obviously not happy with the new arrival. She'd always been protective of Steven, but this was the first time he'd detected jealousy.

"I'll continue to think of her as a daughter, Gwen. Thanks for that reminder," Steven assured her.

"You can always have her call you 'Daddy' or 'Papa' to keep you centered," Gwen offered. "Well, then, I'll be e-mailing your findings to you now. Was there anything else you needed…Papa?" Gwen finished sweetly.

"That should do it. I'll check in later."

What the hell was that all about? Just when he thought he had enough trouble, something new surfaced. Now Gwen was getting territorial about Natalie? There was nothing going on there. And nothing between Gwen and Steven, either. It was all a big zero.

Could Gwen have somehow detected that Steven's interest in Natalie wasn't purely altruistic? It seemed like she knew things before Steven did. It would have been more efficient if Gwen had just sent him a list of what he was going to do every day. That would have been more useful than veiled innuendo.

Steven put his duffel onto the bed and moved to the bedroom door. He smelled the distinctive odor of strong coffee and…eggs. His mouth started watering on the way down the stairs, and he realized he was no better than a dog this morning. He was starving. Gwen's mocking voice echoed in his head. *Yes, old boy, you're a dog, all right – 'Papa'.*

He smiled at his internal dialogue as he swung into the dining area. Natalie looked up from her position at the table, her hands cradling a cup of steaming brew.

"You're certainly in a bright mood this morning. Nice to see – you had a good night, I take it," she commented, noticing Steven's grin. He stifled it and grabbed a cup of coffee.

"A little rest can do wonders." He took a cautious sip. "The results are done. The office is sending them to me," he informed her, suddenly all business.

"That's awesome. Let's get you online and cranking. You in the mood for some eggs? OJ?" Natalie offered.

"That would be great. I'm famished for some reason. Scrambled is good." He moved to where the laptop was sitting and quickly logged into his account. "I've got the code. This will take a while to download. It's a big file," he explained. Natalie shifted to behind the breakfast bar and began preparing eggs. Steven looked up at her. As if reading his mind, Natalie paused.

"Don't get used to his. I usually don't do breakfast. And windows are definitely out of the picture."

"What? I didn't say anything. I was just admiring your…multi-faceted talents," Steven teased.

Natalie ignored him. "Three eggs do the trick?"

Without waiting for an answer, she cracked three and whipped them into a froth before pouring them into the hot skillet. Steven chose to remain silent, tapping his fingers impatiently while the file downloaded over the slow wireless connection.

"So what's your deal, Steven? Are you single? Seeing someone?" Natalie asked.

What was that all about? Had he been that obvious? It seemed that every woman he was in contact with could read his innermost thoughts. So much for his inscrutable poker face.

"I'm widowed. Two and a half years ago…"

"I know that. If I could find you on the street, I did that much background-checking. No, my question was, are you seeing anyone now?" Natalie pressed.

"Why? What's it to you?" Steven volleyed.

"We may be gone for a while. A long while. I have no idea how anything is going to turn out, but I do know that Morbius Frank won't stop until he has the Scroll and its secret. The Order is going to be the same way. So if you have someone you're seeing and you try to stay in touch, sneaking in a call here and there, it will endanger us both, as long as we're together," Natalie explained matter-of-factly.

Steven digested this. His imagination had been running away with him. The idea that Natalie was interested in him was ludicrous, he supposed. She was at least fifteen years younger, maybe more, and doubtlessly had men fighting to get her clothes off every time she went out. The notion that she'd be drawn to him was some delusional male-menopausal fantasy. She was just trying to assess his liabilities.

"Nobody special," he admitted.

Her eyebrow cocked again.

"And your receptionist? Gwen? Nothing going on there?" she asked disbelievingly.

"My office manager?" Steven corrected. "Don't be ridiculous."

"Why not? She clearly likes you, and she reacted to me like a cat dropped in boiling water. You could see her back arch from across the room," Natalie observed.

"I think you got the wrong impression of Gwen. She's a professional, and we're not…we're not an item. So don't worry."

"Seems like there's some unfinished business there, whenever this is all over, Dr. Cross," Natalie said.

"Thanks for the dating tip, but that's not an option. It's not something I'm interested in."

"Women, or Gwen?" Natalie asked simply.

Steven was momentarily flummoxed. This wasn't at all the discussion he was expecting first thing in the morning, with teams of assassins hiding behind every bush.

"You missed your calling as a high-pressure interrogator," Steven advised.

The computer pinged, and he returned his attention to the screen.

"Ah. The file's finished," Steven announced, saved by the bell. He turned his attention back to the little laptop screen, and Natalie let the touchy subject drop.

Ben skulked to the bathroom, casting a furtive glance at Gwen and Sophie. He was having a rough day again, and the paranoia was setting in even after he'd done his maintenance dose of heroin that morning before making it to the office. He despised himself for his weakness and the constant dull ache of pain that was his legacy from the horrible accident that had left him scarred. If he'd been paying more attention that night he would have seen the car swinging out of the driveway, and instead of striking it with his motor scooter and flying thirty feet through the air to bounce against the cold cobblestones like a broken ragdoll, he would have braked in time, or swerved and dodged it.

He'd played the scene over in his head many times, nearly every night for the seven years since that fateful evening. As he was recovering in the hospital, his bones broken and his skin shredded, after three operations to repair the internal injuries, he replayed the incident, and each time he made a minor adjustment, or had been going slower, or had been paying more care to the road – and less to his fiancée, Sabrina, whose arms had been locked around his waist, distracting him with their warm embrace.

They'd met at university, where he'd been finishing up his doctoral thesis for a Ph.D. in computer science and she'd been majoring in political science. At first there had been little in common – she a native of Sienna, only in the big city of Florence for her studies, and he, an American expat who'd decided to live abroad and who shied away from social situations. They'd met at a mutual friend's party and, other than an immediate and powerful physical attraction that had resulted in her joining him in his dingy little apartment that first night, they hadn't really found much to talk about. And yet one night turned into a week, and then into six months, and ultimately a discussion of marriage.

It was an odd pairing. Sabrina was stunning in a no-makeup, naturally-beautiful way that could stop traffic even in a city filled with gorgeous women, whereas Ben, while decent-looking – his nose a little too big, his eyes a hair too close together – was naturally withdrawn and introspective. She was the life of most parties, whereas he was a loner, but somehow circumstances conspired to bring them together, and their passion could have powered a small city. By the time their first month together had passed she was living with him, and both were convinced this was it.

When his scooter had crashed into the VW, he'd flown over the front fender and hood. Sabrina hadn't been so lucky, and her trajectory had carried her headfirst into the car's roof. The emergency medical technicians who'd appeared on the scene within ten minutes said she'd died instantly from the broken neck and had probably felt no pain. That was slim consolation to Ben, whose waking hell on earth was only relieved by the ever-present morphine they'd given him for the pain. Once he'd been discharged, he'd been weaned off the meds and given less powerful painkillers, but they had virtually no effect, and his suffering had been ongoing.

The counselor at the hospital had been of the opinion that much of his discomfort was mental, but Ben didn't see how that theory helped or changed anything. He was miserable, physically and spiritually, and even after the plastic surgeons had repaired him to the point where he didn't frighten small children, he'd felt like his life was over and he was running out the clock on a tortuous existence.

The first time he'd smoked heroin it had numbed the pain, and by the time he'd moved to skin-plinking, his chemical romance was firmly established. It was only a matter of time before he'd moved to shooting up, the progression inevitable. Ben wasn't stupid, and he understood that he was dancing with the devil each time he injected himself, but a part of him was dead, and the drug helped him get through the day. Heroin was plentiful in Italy, a function of the trafficking from North Africa and Afghanistan, so he never had any problems copping. But the cost was a killer – it took ever larger doses to achieve the same effect, and he'd watched his meager savings leak into his arm. He'd tried reducing the amount gradually, but in the end it was no good, and he now found himself in a different kind of hell.

He was still one of the fastest and best coders around, making a more than livable wage, but when the hunger was riding you like a pony it was never enough. And his weekly sexual holidays with the working girls cost him dearly as well. Since the accident, he hadn't sought out any company other than that of professionals. He knew that there was no way a broken, addled and addicted wreck would be able to attract any kind of a mate, so he didn't waste his time in a depressing, doomed-to-failure pursuit, preferring to stay with the prostitutes who would pretend he was normal as long as he could afford their charms.

He splashed some water on his face and studied the scars in the mirror, wondering how long he could continue like this. He needed to figure out how to get his hands on more money, or every day would be this kind of purgatory, where the dose was never sufficient to make him feel good and barely kept the howling void at bay.

Ben was loyal and thought of himself as a basically good man, but the monkey on his back had its own agenda. And the monkey needed its medicine. No medicine, and the withdrawals would come, and perhaps worse, the dreams – the recollection of Sabrina, fun and filled with life, and then the crumpled heap of lifeless flesh next to a car door, the victim of half a second's carelessness in a lifetime of perfectly-timed events.

Whatever it took, he wanted to avoid the dreams.

Dreams of Sabrina, glaring accusingly at him with only half a face.

CHAPTER 16

Sia Amieri's oversized frame filled the doorway of the private detective's offices in Florence. Seated in front of the mouse-like investigator, Dr. Morbius Frank was all polished relaxation in his hand-tailored lightweight navy blue suit, worn, as was his custom, with no tie, the shirt opened one button, with a red cravat hugging his neck. The investigator, Paolo, was explaining the steps he'd taken, while Frank nodded periodically in approval.

"Besides that, I also have two of my staff making inquiries with Cross's employees, as instructed, to see what sort of accommodation can be reached for helping us with anything of potential interest," Paolo explained.

"I'm not price sensitive…within reason," Frank underscored.

"Yes, and I've shared that. Perhaps it would help if we knew precisely what we were looking for?" Paolo suggested, for the second time during the meeting.

"That's the problem, isn't it? I'm not completely sure. Anything related to cryptography, or ancient parchments. Failing that, information on where Cross can be found."

"I think you'll agree that I've been quite thorough. I'll pass everything along to your associate, just as you wish." He shot a nervous glance past Frank to where Amieri stood impassively by the far wall, in tan slacks and a dark brown leather jacket. "I would hope we have something within a day or two, at most. We're doing everything we can. Now we just need to wait for the fly to come to the spider," Paolo assured him.

"Time is, alas, our most precious commodity at the moment. Please stay in touch, and get me whatever you find, no matter how seemingly inconsequential," Frank ordered, then pushed himself to his feet, ignoring Paolo's outstretched hand. The tense moment passed, and Paolo exhaled a sigh of relief when the pair had vacated his office. The money was stupendous, but both men exuded pure menace. He'd bent the law before, which is why Frank had contacted him, but even so, these two were in a completely different league than his customary jilted wives or corporate espionage clients. They stank of death, which Paolo recognized as clearly as he understood the value of their cash. In troubled times like the present, he couldn't be as selective about his customers as in times of prosperity – and Frank was paying top dollar.

Which in the end, was what mattered.

Paolo lifted the telephone handset from its cradle and dialed a familiar number.

Natalie peered over Steven's shoulder at the screen.

"What does it mean?" she asked.

"It's the first step. The program established a character substitution pattern, so now we have a cypher. The problem is that we need to organize the letters into something coherent. That will take a little while, but I seem to remember that this was written in Latin, so that will shorten the time required for me to figure it out. It was a long time ago, but I still remember the basics of this document. Give me some space and some quiet and I can nail it," Steven advised.

"You have the floor. I'll go pack. We need to make tracks sooner than later."

Natalie left him to his devices. He entered the string into the program that would perform the painstaking process of trial and error to structure the seemingly gibberish letters into a lucid order. Soon, he had the Latin organized coherently, and it was just a matter of translating it so it made sense.

He studied the familiar words. "*Occultumest…*"

When Natalie returned from her bedroom with her bags in hand, Steven was finished with the translation and was surfing the web to make sense out of the cryptic message. He looked up and was momentarily taken aback by a Natalie with long brown hair. She looked like a different person, which he supposed was the whole point of the wig. He quickly regained his composure and fixed a look of concentration on his face.

"Well? How's it going?" the new, improved Natalie asked.

"I translated it. But it's not like a street address. Remember, this was written almost six hundred years ago."

"What does it say?"

Natalie approached him, and he held up the sheet of notepaper where he'd scribbled his findings.

"Translated, it reads: 'Six paces from Alexis in the middle basilica stands a crucifix. Illumination into the sacred text is near the savior's head on the cross'." Steven scratched his ear. "I think that's pretty clear, no?"

"That's it? It might as well say: 'Follow the doves to the wall of silence'. How do we figure out what it means?" Natalie asked.

"This is the second hard part. Just decrypting it would have been a multi-week or month process if I hadn't written this software program, and organizing the random letters into coherent script is no small feat. It helps that I remembered this was in Latin, otherwise we would have needed to increase the complexity for the program, to make it compare the letter series to all the idioms being used at the time the parchment was written; that would have taken some serious time. We're actually well ahead of where we could reasonably expect to be," Steven explained. He could see she was disappointed, but he'd just accomplished the near-impossible, so he felt a little defensive.

Natalie seemed to sense he was on edge and said nothing. She went to the coffee pot and prepared more while he stared at the seemingly meaningless clue. He entered some of the key words, hoping for a hit, but didn't get anything. He didn't even know where to begin.

"This part is going to take a while. I need to run different word combinations into the search engines in the hopes something comes up. It's trial and error, with no guarantees. And Natalie? This was written in the mid to late 1400s. It's quite possible that whatever it's referring to was destroyed over the years, or forgotten. I wouldn't get my hopes up. That, and we don't even know what country it's referring to, much less city. Latin was used everywhere by the Church. Whatever the message is directing us to could be anywhere in the known world of the time," Steven warned. "Be that as it may, I have a program that will do these comparisons at high speed. It's on the disk I loaded onto this computer. I'll have it churn through the data over the next hour. Maybe we'll get a hit."

"It seems like a long shot," Natalie said dejectedly.

"Everything in cryptography is a long shot. There's no such thing as instant results, at least not that I've found. Sorry. It is what it is."

Steven tapped in a few commands, and a crude screen popped up. Peering at his notes, he entered all of the words from the message into the fields, and then hit 'Enter'. The computer began working, and he returned his attention to Natalie.

"We need to stick around the villa until this is done; it's going to access online search engines and record the results. Want to get some air?" Steven invited.

"Sure. It's not like I have anything else to do."

They walked slowly along the driveway, enjoying the sun's warmth on their skin. Natalie broached the obvious subject.

"What's your preference for new places to hide?" she asked, only half serious.

"Let's see if we can get a fix on where the parchment is directing us," Steven answered humorlessly.

They meandered across the road and turned towards town, the gravel on the shoulder crunching beneath their feet.

"I'm sorry you're involved in this, Steven. I know how odd it has to feel being pursued when you haven't done anything wrong," Natalie said – the closest that she'd come to apologizing.

Steven hesitated, glancing at her profile.

"The wig isn't bad, but I like your real hair better."

The corners of her mouth twitched, and her nose crinkled.

"Why, thank you. Are you always such a smooth talker with the ladies?"

"It's been a while…and believe it or not, I know exactly what it's like to be on the run from powerful enemies," Steven offered.

"I don't think you do. Not like this. These people will torture and kill you. That's their mission – to find the Scroll, get everything you know, and then terminate you."

He paused, considered his response, and then forged on with it.

"In another life, I had everyone from organized crime syndicates to intelligence services trying to kill me. I've taken bullets. Trust me. I know what it's like," Steven stressed.

She stopped. Steven turned to face her. A moment seemed to pass between them.

"I couldn't find out much about you when I was checking. I suspected there might be a reason for that when you took down our tail without breaking a sweat. Care to share?"

He chose his words carefully. "A while ago, I pissed off the wrong groups, trying to fight odds I should have walked away from. I disrupted a very lucrative scheme, and it wound up collapsing at considerable cost to these groups, so they tried to take me out. These were very dangerous adversaries. Not some jealous husband or impatient loan shark. I'm talking world-class bad guys. And I'm still here. They aren't. Or at least, most of them aren't."

She appraised him as he spoke.

"Perhaps I misjudged your temperament. Sounds like it isn't a good idea to underestimate you, Dr. Cross."

Steven didn't have any glib responses. They resumed their stroll.

"I'm thinking we need to stay in Italy. We don't want to trigger any alarms with your passport. Agreed?" Natalie asked, returning to her original topic.

"That's fine. Maybe a bigger city where we'll blend in easily. Bologna, or Milan, or even Rome…"

"I've heard good things about Bologna. If you're okay with that, barring something materializing with your software program, I'm for going there. We can drive," Natalie said.

He rolled his head, relaxing the taut muscles in his neck, then looked over at her. "Beyond running, do you have a plan?"

"Sure. You figure everything out, we learn the secret of the Scroll, and then…"

"…and then?" Steven asked.

Natalie stopped walking.

Steven softened his voice. "Natalie, there's a big hole in all this, even if I'm successful in decrypting the Scroll. That hole is that you don't have a plan, beyond reacting. Let's assume we figure this out. Then what? Or being more realistic, let's assume we don't. That we never learn what the Scroll says. What do we do? When will you, or I, ever be safe?" Steven stressed.

Natalie didn't speak. Her eyes glistened momentarily.

Steven pressed on. "I've been through this kind of thing before." He kicked a piece of gravel into the adjacent field. "This is a massive dislocation that will change everything. There's no scenario I can see where we return to the way things were. Our lives are permanently altered, as of now, with no going back to normal, whatever that was. Just accept that, and we'll both be better off."

"I hadn't thought about it like that…"

"Look. If you're correct, and the Order is real and coming for both of us, they won't stop. If it's a group that's been protecting the Scroll for over five hundred years, can you imagine any circumstance where they give up? And how about Frank? Regardless of whether you give him his two million back, you told me yourself the man's filthy rich and obsessed. In what scenario does he just walk away?"

Steven turned and began moving back to the house. Natalie increased her pace, quickly catching up to him.

"I…I'm sorry, Steven. I didn't involve you on purpose. It's the letter to my father that got you sucked in…"

"Natalie. I'm a big boy. I understand that. I'm not looking for who to blame. I'm worried about how to survive, not just today, but ten years from now. Assuming you're right, it's going to take every bit of luck and skill we have to make it through this. Fortunately, I've got enough money to last a lifetime, but I need to move it around so it stays off the radar. But I realize I'm going to have to walk away and never look back." Steven rubbed his face and sighed. "I've done this before. It's tough. The sooner you realize what you have to do, the better. One mistake and you're screwed. You can never slip up. Ever."

Natalie digested his words as she trudged along beside him. Her tough exterior had cracked, just a little, and Steven saw a hint of vulnerability where before there had only been strength. He knew what she was going through. She'd been so busy pursuing the secret of the Scroll, hell bent on somehow avenging her father, that she hadn't considered the larger picture. Either that, or she had, and decided to push off acknowledging reality until she was more prepared to deal with it. But Steven had once before been forced to throw everything in his life into a bag and run, and once you'd been through it, you never slept the same, and a part of you was always mentally prepared to do it again. In some ways he was the worst possible target to pursue because he'd been there and remembered all the lessons.

"This sucks," Natalie muttered.

"You can say that again."

Overhead, a few birds hung languorously in the air, wheeling around the field before the farmer came on duty with his ancient shotgun. The sun kissed the vines of the neighboring parcel: a picture of rustic serenity. Other than the fact Natalie and he were being hunted like rats, it was a beautiful day.

Steven checked his watch. The program might have finished. Time to get back to work.

Frederick was carrying Natalie's two bags out to the car when they approached the house; he nodded at them in greeting. Steven again wondered what the man's story was.

"What's with Frederick? What's his deal?" he asked Natalie as they entered the house.

"Frederick was with my father for almost twenty-five years. I sort of inherited him when my father died. He was at the house when I arrived to claim the remains and said he wanted to help me."

"Not very chatty, is he?"

"Not really."

"But I'll bet he's a hoot on karaoke night…"

Natalie laughed. "Frederick just isn't loquacious. He never has been. But he's fiercely loyal and would do anything for me. He's completely fearless. Ex-Green Beret. Went to work for my father in the mid-Eighties straight out of the service and never had another job. He'd follow me anywhere," Natalie said.

"That's good, because he's going to need to be with you for a long time. His life is also over as he knew it. You get that now, right?"

"I'm there, Steven. I just need a little time to absorb the concept. I've had a few other things on my plate…"

Steven moved to the computer and began staring intently at the screen. "Bingo."

"What?"

"Change of plans. We're not going to Bologna," Steven declared.

"We aren't? Where are we going?"

"Rome."

CHAPTER 17

"Why Rome?" Natalie asked.

"That's what pops up with ninety-six percent certainty as the likely location described in the parchment. Specifically, the Basilica of San Clemente. One of the most ornate churches in Rome. Among its most noteworthy features is that it's built on top of a fourth-century basilica that acts as a pseudo-basement, which is itself built over a first-century Roman home, complete with pagan worship room. And it has several noteworthy examples of art, one of which is of St. Alexis. I've heard of it, but I need to do some more research. Does your phone get internet access? Can we access the web while we're on the road – plug the computer through the cell phone?" Steven asked.

Natalie nodded. "That will work. Although you can surf using just the phone."

"Screen's too small or I'd take you up on it." He closed the laptop and quickly readied it for departure. "This way, I can read up on San Clemente while we're en route. I don't see any more reason to stick around here."

He carried his bag out to the car, where Frederick stood, expressionless, near the sedan. The trunk popped open, Frederick having pushed a button on the key fob. Steven carefully placed his duffle beside Natalie's bags. Another smaller suitcase sat to the side, presumably containing Frederick's gear.

In a now familiar ritual, Natalie slid into the back seat, and Steven followed. The trip to Rome would take three to four hours, depending on traffic.

Once they were underway, Steven connected the laptop to the web and began searching for everything he could find on the old church. There was precious little to go on. The site was only a few blocks from the Roman Coliseum and appeared to be impenetrable, with bars on every window and security lighting and razor wire running across all roof areas. Steven shared this with her. Natalie retrieved her phone from the laptop and made a hushed call. She murmured for a few minutes and then terminated the discussion and plugged Steven back in.

"Who was that?" Steven asked.

"You'll see. I have some contacts in Rome. They'll work on finding someone who can help us with the basilica."

Steven assessed her blank face, which betrayed nothing.

"You seem to have an extraordinarily developed network, Natalie. I'm surprised."

"I've traveled in some interesting circles. You aren't wanted by Interpol for any reason, are you?" she replied.

"No. Why?"

"The man I called is very innovative and can arrange for virtually anything, but he's naturally suspicious, so you can expect that you'll have a background check run that's far more thorough than what I did. If you're an international criminal, that wouldn't be so good," Natalie explained.

"What does he do, this innovative friend of yours?"

"This and that. Doesn't like to broadcast exactly who he works for, but I think it's safe to say he's no stranger to alphabet agencies."

Steven processed that. "And he can help us? Do you trust him?"

"Absolutely. We have history," she declared, and left it at that.

Natalie was proving to be increasingly surprising: she didn't flinch at violence and had contacts with the CIA or someone similar. He wanted to probe more, but sensed this wasn't the time, so returned to his research while the car sped down the freeway.

The church's lower levels were only discovered in 1857, but that didn't necessarily mean anything. Whether the author of the parchment had known about it in the mid-1400s had little to do with whether that knowledge had died with him. History was filled with gaps, and Rome's was no different. Once the middle-level basilica had been rediscovered, the order of Irish Dominicans, who were the facility's caretakers since 1667, had excavated it, along with the first-century building beneath it.

At the time of the parchment's authorship, the basilica had been under the stewardship of monks from Milan, who were of a newly created order – the Augustinian Congregation of St. Ambrose. If the author had been a monk in that order, it would explain why the mystery was hidden in the middle level. That a secret passage had been crafted to access the hidden church-beneath-a-church didn't particularly surprise Steven. That period of history was filled with intrigue and persecutions, so prudent clergy trusted no one and kept their own counsel. And that the knowledge had somehow been forgotten over the centuries was consistent with the original monks being displaced by the Dominican monks from Ireland – who would have been regarded by the Italians as not-to-be-trusted, unwelcome interlopers.

Steven couldn't imagine what might be hidden in the basilica, or whether whatever it was had withstood the elements and ravages of time for over five centuries. He didn't want to discourage Natalie, but he knew the chances were far from good. Still, they'd do whatever was necessary to eliminate any doubts. He could tell Natalie would never quit – she reminded Steven of himself in that regard. She was determined.

Most of the websites were regurgitations of the same information, drawn from a few books as well as from the site's official web page. Steven quickly exhausted the online resources and was soon back to square one. He'd need to make sense out of the cryptic message, but couldn't see any way to do so until he was inside. Hopefully he'd see something that made it relevant, because as of now, he was at a dead-end.

Halfway to Rome, Natalie's cell chirped an incoming call. Steven had downloaded all the websites that were of interest, so didn't need the web any longer. Natalie unplugged the laptop cable and answered. After a brief discussion, she gave Steven an okay sign and disconnected.

"We'll be doing a tour of the facility today and then meeting with my friend's contact. He says we can trust the man with anything. We should be in Rome within two more hours, tops, so we can do the tour this afternoon, then meet with him after, at five. And he set up an apartment for us near the church," Natalie reported.

"Wow. You don't waste time."

"I don't think we have any time to waste. We have no idea what our opposition is up to, so we have to assume the worst. Don't you agree?"

"I think we're probably safe, for now. Nobody has the parchment but me. So we should be fine from here, as long as we don't telegraph our moves or do something stupid," Steven reasoned.

"I agree. But I want to move fast. A high-velocity target's harder to hit," Natalie said dryly.

Steven couldn't disagree. The lady had a point.

When they arrived in Rome, Frederick drove them directly to the Basilica of San Clemente and dropped them off at the end of the block. After an hour wait in line, their tour began, and the group was herded through the present-day basilica. Natalie and Steven listened as the bored guide recited the details of the building in a tone that indicated he'd rather be anywhere on earth besides leading the tour. After a perfunctory period in the upper church, they descended to the middle level – the fourth century structure that had been excavated to the point where the original layout was evident. They moved along with the rest of the group, and Natalie quietly tugged on Steven's sleeve when they passed into the main hall and were greeted by frescoes and mosaics, one of which was: 'The Legend of St. Alexis'.

"That has to be the Alexis the parchment refers to," Steven said.

They inspected the surrounding area but saw nothing promising – no crosses, and a large area of the floor was cordoned off where it had collapsed into the lower level.

"Maybe there's another Alexis in here?" Natalie whispered.

"Possibly. We'll know in a few minutes when the tour ends. Or maybe the cross is long gone. That was one of my fears," Steven murmured back to her.

Natalie swung slowly around, estimating mentally where six paces would be in all directions, and saw nothing. Not on the ceiling or floor, or on the walls. There was no crucifix.

"What do we do?" she asked.

"Keep your eyes open. Let's look on the other side of the wall, in the left gallery. Maybe there's a cross in there."

They obediently followed the throng into the farthest gallery, where there was a hole in the floor with a barricade around it. The gallery contained more art, but again, no crosses. The tour meandered in the middle for a few more minutes and then made its way to the lower level of the site, with its first-century Mithraic worshipping chamber and a host of small apartment-like cubicles. Natalie was fidgety and anxious to leave – the tour couldn't end soon enough for her once they'd finished with the middle level.

As they returned to the main floor the crowd quickly dispersed, and Natalie and Steven found themselves on the sidewalk, debating their options.

"We need to get inside when nobody's around and do a real search," Natalie immediately advanced.

"That would be great, but how? And not to be a pessimist, but there's the very real chance that whatever used to be there, assuming this is the right place and I didn't miss something with my software, hasn't been there for eons. In which case the Scroll might as well be on broadcast TV because there's no hope of decoding it."

"I understand, but we have to try. I'm going to see what our contact can do for us. It shouldn't be that hard to get in. Money buys a lot of cooperation," Natalie observed.

They walked two blocks to a small café. Natalie had made a call en route. Ten minutes after sitting down and ordering, a balding, stylishly dressed olive-complexioned man in his fifties approached them, smoothing his moustache and straightening his collar as he did so. His blue blazer and gray slacks lent him an air of aristocracy, as did his aloof bearing.

He caught their eye and moved to them.

"Ah, you must be my meeting! Welcome, welcome. Is this your first visit to Rome?" he greeted in good English. "My name is Daniel Franchesso. Danny to my friends."

Natalie shook his hand and gestured to a seat.

Steven shook hands perfunctorily. "A pleasure. It's our first time."

Danny ordered a double espresso and prattled about the glories of Rome until the waitress brought his coffee and departed. He fished out a package of cigarettes and offered them to Steven and Natalie, who declined. He shrugged and returned them to his pocket.

"Filthy habit, and it will kill me, but I can't help myself. Now, how may I be of assistance? Our mutual friend indicated I was to do whatever I could," Danny told them.

"We need to get into the Basilica of San Clemente, after hours. We'd like some time in the middle level without being disturbed," Natalie explained.

Danny's eyebrows arched, but that was his only reaction. He didn't ask why. "Oh. I thought you were going to ask for something easy, like an audience with the Pope." He smiled, revealing yellowed teeth. "A joke, of course." Danny gave them a look that was anything but funny.

"Can you do this?" Natalie asked.

"I don't see why not. I'll need to spread around a little money, and there will probably be conditions, but in Rome, anything can be done if one is flexible…and generous," Danny assured them. "I have your phone number. Let me do some exploration and see what I can come up with. In the meantime, here's the key to the apartment. Your friend, David, said you can use the safe house for as long as you need it."

Danny slid a key wrapped in a piece of paper with an address scrawled across it to Natalie. She nodded and took it, tucking it into her purse.

"Whatever cash you need to get us into the church, consider it approved." Natalie eyed him. "Our presence here is not to be discussed, with anyone. Is that clear?"

"Absolutely. I don't even know who you are. But whoever, I never saw you. Si?" Danny quipped.

"I'm glad we can rely on your discretion. Please call when you have something for us. We're available twenty-four hours a day," Natalie finished.

Danny swallowed the last of his coffee before pushing back from the little table and rising. "I'll be in touch. Enjoy your stay," he said and then turned, walking away as if without a care in the world.

Steven and Natalie exchanged glances.

"What do you think?" Natalie asked.

"Who's David?" Steven countered.

"The friend I told you about. His real name is Moody, but he uses different field names. In Italy, he's David." She paused. "What do you make of Danny?"

"Seems on the level, but smarmy. Maybe that's good. I don't trust him, but then again, I don't trust anyone right now. As long as he doesn't know anything more than we're a mystery couple looking for a midnight rendezvous in the church, we should be fine." Steven stopped. "Although I think it's a rotten idea to stay at the apartment he's lined up. That's one of the weak links in this."

"I trust Moody implicitly, Steven. We've been through a lot together."

"Maybe, but we don't know Danny from a taxi driver. Even if your Moody is pure as driven snow, if Danny isn't, for any reason, we lose. I think I'd rather make my own arrangements. Call it an insurance policy," Steven advised.

Natalie mulled over his point.

"Maybe you're right. Let's find someplace else."

CHAPTER 18

Natalie and Steven settled in at the hotel they'd selected by the Spanish Steps plaza, a large, multi-storied affair in a renovated older building. Steven was in Natalie's room, using the laptop, when her phone rang.

Danny explained to them that he'd found a contact at the church's security company and had made an arrangement for three thousand dollars to get them half an hour alone in the middle level, on the understanding that they couldn't take anything out and didn't harm any of the art, subject to prosecution. A meeting was set for one a.m.. Danny offered to supply a ride if they wished, but Natalie declined. She told him they'd be at the side entrance of the church at one. Danny would meet them to ensure there were no last-minute problems at the basilica.

They ate at a little restaurant a block from the hotel that the manager had recommended and were pleasantly surprised to find it a world-class eatery. Both avoided any wine and instead had mineral water with dinner, prompting a sneer from the surly waiter.

Steven had studied the online blueprint of the site and plotted a rough circle that equated to a radius of six paces from the fresco. He hoped they would find something they'd missed in the crush of tourists on the tour, but the way things had been going, he wasn't hopeful. A part of him believed this was all for naught, but he wouldn't tell Natalie that. She'd had enough body blows in the last week, between her father dying and being hunted all over the planet.

When they returned to the hotel, they agreed to meet at twelve forty-five in the lobby. They silently rode up the elevator to their floors, lost in their separate thoughts. Back in his room, Steven brushed his teeth and took a fast shower, hoping to get some rest before their basilica adventure started. But once on his bed he found himself tossing and turning on the unyielding mattress, unable to sleep for the few hours before their rendezvous.

The prior time his life had been uprooted, he'd had Antonia to keep him company and partner with him on the journey, which made things easier. Now he was alone and in the same situation. There was no alternative he could see to abandoning everything.

Steven shifted uncomfortably on the bed, willing the unbidden thoughts away, but to no avail. His mind was racing on its own course, fueled by adrenaline in anticipation of the night's forthcoming events. In spite of his best intentions, it wouldn't be denied.

He could tell that Natalie hadn't digested all the ramifications of their predicament until their discussion that afternoon. If Frank was as murderous as she'd said, and the Order was as persistent as could be expected, given their history, they'd never stop hunting them. No matter where he went or what he did, he would never be safe, nor would Natalie. She wasn't his problem, but still, she had forced her way into his consciousness. Unfortunately, their discussion hadn't yielded any insights into what she intended to do, other than reinforcing that she was playing it all by ear.

Much as he'd tried, Steven couldn't figure Natalie out. She seemed tough as titanium, but with a vulnerable streak that flashed to the surface occasionally. That was a powerfully attractive combination to him, which was obvious, given how hard a time he had concentrating whenever she was near. It was probably for the best that there was no chance for them. The last thing Steven was looking for was any kind of a relationship – it was too soon after Antonia – but even so, he was intrigued by Natalie's violet eyes and overall aesthetic.

But was it really too soon? An internal voice whispered the nagging question. It was approaching three years since the accident. Was it really too soon to be interested in another woman, or was that just an excuse for remaining disengaged, a spectator in life rather than a participant?

He rolled over, trying to banish the pointless speculations. She was too young for him, and he knew it. His mind was just punishing him with empty possibilities based on delusions of vitality.

At half past midnight, he pulled himself off the bed and changed into black slacks and a dark blue shirt, pulling on his lightweight black windbreaker as an afterthought. He automatically checked to ensure the room safe was secure as he pocketed his valuables, then closed the door behind him and descended to the lobby. Natalie was already waiting for him, now back to wearing her black suede jumpsuit. He tried not to notice how well she filled it out, but lost the battle when she walked ahead of him to the entry doors.

Frederick pulled up at the curb right on time. As they sped away, he wordlessly handed Natalie a small bundle of tools – a flathead screwdriver, a putty knife and a cordless battery-powered jeweler's drill. She inserted the various items into her knee-high boots, which, while awkward, effectively concealed them. Steven watched her preparations with interest. They'd been told they couldn't remove anything from the church, but nobody had said anything about what they could bring in. He hoped whoever they were paying off wasn't too much of a stickler for formality.

They pulled to a stop around the corner from the side entrance of the basilica, the only vehicle on the deserted street. Steven and Natalie cautiously got out and proceeded up the block. When they turned the corner, they saw a single car parked at the far end of the building. Danny's distinctive frame approached them from beneath one of the dim streetlights.

"Good evening. I trust this will work for you?" he asked.

"Perfect, Danny. I appreciate it," Natalie said.

"I just handled the payment to security – we can settle up later. Now, remember the rules. No removing anything, no defacing the art. Beyond that, you have thirty minutes to explore or do whatever you like in the middle level. The guards will stay in the upper level, so you'll have privacy, although they'll do a quick tour with you once your time is up to confirm everything's still there and that you didn't damage anything. Is that all clear?" Danny warned.

"Don't mess with the art. Don't steal anything. I got it," Natalie confirmed.

"That's about it. I'll introduce you to the guard and then I'm going home. We can meet tomorrow to handle the money. Good luck."

They followed Danny to the side entrance, where a few minutes later a pale face peered at them through the bars. Danny fired off a soft burst of Italian, and the guard's face relaxed. Seconds later, the lock turned and the old iron door creaked open. Danny nodded to them and left them to their devices, strolling casually back to his vehicle while lighting a cigarette.

The guard motioned for them to enter as he scanned the street to ensure they were alone. The bars slammed shut behind them with an ominous finality, echoing in the empty church. Gesturing with an outstretched hand to signal silence, he guided them to the stairway that led to the lower levels, then did a pat-down of Steven, pausing when he found his phone and keys. Next, he performed a cursory inspection of Natalie's small black clutch purse before handing it back to her. One look at Natalie's outfit had convinced him that if she was hiding anything on her person he'd need an X-ray system to find it. Satisfied, he pointed to his watch.

"Thirty minutes," he said in Italian. "You know the rules, *eh*?"

Natalie looked at Steven uncomprehendingly; he tersely summarized the man's message for her. They nodded, and he opened the two wooden doors that shuttered the foyer for the stairs to the lower level. Once they were through, he closed them again. They heard a chain wrap around the handles. Steven experienced a moment of foreboding but it quickly passed. It was only a half hour, and they'd soon find out whether their mission was a dud or a winner.

They stepped down the stairs into the dank middle basilica, the walls of which were mostly worn stones and crudely-made brick held together with mortar, with odd patches of plaster covering stretches where it hadn't yet crumbled away. They made their way quickly through the first gallery, which ran perpendicular to the main chamber. The middle level, much like the upper modern church, was composed of a large central room punctuated by a series of supporting columns and arches, with a long, narrow gallery on either side.

From their position across the main room, Natalie pointed at the fresco of Saint Alexis on the far wall, near the entry to the left gallery. They moved soundlessly across the floor. Once at the fresco, Steven paced off six long strides – five feet each – and after fishing a small stub of chalk out of his pocket, made a light mark on the floor. He walked twelve paces in the opposite direction and repeated the process. They both moved away from the fresco and inspected the ceiling, floor and the two walls on either side, by the chalk marks. There was no cross anywhere. Steven strode into the left gallery, the wall of which was the back side of the fresco, and after counting the paces to the entryway, repeated the calculation process. Natalie watched him, and they peered at the two points. Nothing. Just ancient stone walls dotted haphazardly with art.

Frustrated, they moved back into the main chamber and stared at the Alexis fresco.

"Like we saw today," Steven whispered, "there's no cross. Now, either that means that this is the wrong place, and I somehow garbled the parchment data, or in the last five hundred years a cross in this room was removed."

"What if it was painted on the wall and over time the plaster came off? Most of the walls are just bare stone, but you can see some of the original plaster in places, like the frescoes," Natalie said, kneeling as she extracted the tools from her boots.

"Anything's possible, but we could just as easily speculate that it was somewhere on the floor in a six pace radius. Point is, that's a lot of space to cover. If the cross was a statue on some sort of a base, it's long gone. I'm afraid the short answer is, looks like we're screwed."

"Maybe a pace is more like a yard?" she mused.

"No. It's five feet. Even in 1450 the yard was well understood as a unit of measurement. If the parchment had meant yards, it would have said yards."

Natalie walked to the wall near the first chalk mark and lightly tapped on the stones with the handle of the screwdriver, starting from the bottom and moving as high as she could reach. Steven watched her stretching on her toes. He absently wondered what her workout regimen consisted of. He felt a stirring and quickly shifted mental gears.

She shook her head and made a noise, then moved to the far chalk mark and repeated the process. Steven decided to occupy his wandering eye in some other fashion than ogling his partner in crime and walked to another fresco at the far end of the chamber – this one of Saint Clemente celebrating mass. According to his watch, they'd burned seven minutes. This wasn't going anywhere.

"Steven. Come here," Natalie called.

He spun around and moved to where she was crouched by his second chalk mark. "Look up at the ceiling. Is that what I think it is?" she asked.

He squinted in the meager light, then rooted around in his pocket for his phone. He selected the flashlight function and a bright beam of light stabbed into the darkness above them. There, faintly embossed in the plaster remnants, was the unmistakable labyrinth crest from the Scroll. Natalie and he exchanged a look, and she redoubled her tapping on the wall below it. The wall was solid stone and mortar.

"Kneel down," Natalie urged. "I need to climb onto your shoulders and try higher up the wall. That's the crest. There has to be something here."

"What if it was a stand-alone cross on the floor below it…which is now gone? Or what if it's up in the ceiling?" Steven asked, crouching down as he did so.

"Then we'll borrow some scaffolding and get up there somehow." She threw her legs around his head and, once in place, tapped the top of his skull. "Giddy up, big boy."

Steven ignored the erotic implications of having Natalie straddling his shoulders and obligingly stood. She couldn't have weighed a hundred pounds, so it wasn't much of a burden. He noted that even her suede jumpsuit legs smelled good, while she busily tapped against the wall with the screwdriver. After a few seconds, the tone of the tapping changed.

"I think I found something. Hold still," she instructed and began chipping at the mortar. Dust and chips landed on Steven's face. He closed his eyes and spat out the small bits that had found their way into his mouth. After several minutes of this, she nudged his shoulder with the screwdriver blade, which he grabbed as she retrieved the battery-powered drill from her boot. The little motor whined alarmingly, but the grinding bit ate through the old mortar like it was butter. Eventually the din stopped, and Natalie slid the drill back into her boot. He blew mortar dust from his lips and shook some fragments off his head.

He heard something above slide grudgingly out of the wall, then Natalie handed the object to him. It wasn't a rock, but rather a ceramic block crudely molded to look like one.

Natalie squinted at the cavity. "There's something in here, in a cubbyhole. I…Steven, I don't want to ruin it…"

"Take my camera and get some photos. Then we can figure out how to extract whatever it is without damaging it."

Steven fished his phone out of his pocket and handed it to her. A few seconds later the blinding flash went off, once, then again.

"Okay. You can see it clearly. Let me down for a second."

Steven obliged, kneeling on the floor so she could get off his shoulders. They both looked at the image on the tiny screen.

"It looks like a parchment," Steven said. "The bad news is that it's going to be in terrible shape after five centuries in these damp walls. It's a kind of miracle that it's even intact," he warned. "It looks like it's folded in half. See if you can gently lift it out, and we'll place it here on the floor and have a look at it. I'd use the screwdriver."

Natalie nodded and, screwdriver in hand, hopped back up onto Steven's shoulders, wedging her feet under his armpits as he gripped her legs. Within a minute, she'd painstakingly slipped the metal blade under the document and extracted it from its hiding place.

"I'm clear," she said, then as Steven kneeled, both watched in horror as the ancient parchment tumbled from its precarious position and fell to the floor, where it shattered into six fragments. The ancient vellum had indeed degraded to the point where it was as brittle as an eggshell.

Natalie gasped as Steven gently set her down, then held her back from the small pile of rubble.

"Don't breathe. Give me the putty knife," he instructed.

Natalie did as asked, and he cautiously flipped over the shards of the old document, piecing them roughly together. He unfolded the area that was doubled across the broken lower sheet, and it split at the fold. Steven gently eased that piece against the rest, creating a badly broken single page with faint coded writing on it. To Steven's eye, it was the same code as the one that had led them there. With a trembling hand, he took several more photos, checking to ensure they were of adequate resolution to be analyzed later.

The clattering of the chain on the doors in the stairwell foyer above them jarred their moment of triumph.

Steven dropped the phone back into his pocket and whispered to Natalie, "Grab the stone and set it back in place. Hurry."

He handed the coarsely crafted rectangle to her and knelt down again, swinging her up onto his shoulders and moving back towards the wall. He heard the scraping of the block as Natalie re-wedged it into place. More debris hit him in the face. Finished, she patted his head and he crouched so she could jump down. Just as her feet hit the floor, they heard the door swing open upstairs and a soft voice call out. Steven peered at his watch – their thirty minutes was up. He looked down at the parchment and saw with horror that his boot had crushed it into an unrecognizable pile of dust, intermingled with the tiny mortar specks from above. Moving quickly, he brushed the debris away from the wall, off into a dark corner at the far end of the chamber. Natalie quickly followed suit as they heard the heavy footsteps moving down the stairs and into the far gallery.

She looked up at Steven's face and began lightly patting it in an effort to remove most of the telltale powdery residue. The footsteps neared the opening to the chamber, and she hastily moved a few paces away from the area, pulling Steven along by the hand. As the steps neared the main room, she pulled the zipper of her jumpsuit to her navel, threw her arms around Steven and kissed him full on the lips, her tongue finding his with a small moan.

The guard shuffled into the hall and cleared his throat. Steven and Natalie looked up at him, visibly startled. Steven wasn't faking the surprise, and his tousled hair and expression clearly radiated shocked guilt. Natalie pulled away and hastily pulled up her zipper, allowing the man to catch a good glimpse of one perfectly-molded breast in the process. She cleared her throat and flashed a beaming smile at the entranced guard, then also smiled at Steven, who was struggling to regain his composure.

"*Eh*, so your half hour is over. Let's have a look at the paintings to make sure you didn't damage anything." The guard leered at them both. "I hope it was worth it for you, *si*?"

Steven smirked in what he hoped was a lascivious manner. "Oh, it was, my friend. It was. *Si*."

The guard performed a cursory inspection of the frescoes; satisfied that nothing had been touched, he motioned to them to accompany him up the stairs, muttering to himself and shaking his head along the way. Americans were an odd bunch. Who else would pay several thousand dollars to screw in a church basement? Then again, whatever floated your boat, he reasoned. If he had the money and a willing partner like this minx of a woman, he'd pretty much do it wherever she wanted, as well. When love was in the air, you didn't question it…

Natalie took Steven's hand as they mounted the stairs to the upper level. After thanking the guard and slipping him an extra hundred dollar bill for his discretion, they stepped out onto the empty street. Steven listened as the heavy iron security door closed behind them, sheltering the church's treasures from blasphemers once again. Natalie was suddenly all business and detached her hand from Steven's before moving down the block.

When they reached the corner of the building, they peeked around and confirmed that Frederick and the car were still there, waiting patiently for their return. The street was empty, with only a few streetlights glowing in the darkness. Steven followed Natalie to within a few yards of the passenger door, when he abruptly stopped and grabbed her arm. A man's leg protruded from the bushes to their right, part of the church's hedges.

What the hell was going on? Steven spun Natalie towards him and held his fingers to his lips before moving to the vegetation. A quick inspection revealed Frederick's body lying twisted in the dirt, the telltale marks of stab wounds on his torso, his white shirt and black jacket gleaming with blood.

Steven reached into the bushes to confirm there was no pulse, then jerked Frederick's weapon free of the shoulder holster – a Ruger SR9 semi-automatic pistol. Steven guessed by the still-wet blood he'd been killed no more than ten minutes earlier. Beyond him, in the space near the rear of the building, another man lay in a pool of his own fluids, also clearly dead.

Natalie was reaching for the car door when Steven hissed at her, "No. We've been blown. Leave the car. We've got to get out of here; it could be rigged."

He grabbed her hand and they set off at a run, away from the church and the death that had suddenly surrounded them. The empty street gave no hint of pursuit, but still they ran like the devil himself was behind them.

CHAPTER 19

Diego Luca answered the strident ring of the cell phone without needing to ask who was calling. Only one person had the number of this new telephone, and that person was Colonel Gabriel Synthe. He stabbed the phone into active mode, rubbing the sleep out of his eyes as he noted the time displayed on his bedside clock. One forty-five in the morning.

"Yes?"

"There's been a development. I thought you'd want to know," Synthe reported.

"A development?"

"We installed a tracking device last night on the target's car once we pinpointed them from the girl's wire records – at a villa near Florence – and went on full alert when she left and drove to Rome today. We don't know why she did, but we were following the car, which was our only lead. It arrived at the Basilica of Saint Clemente a little less than an hour ago. That seemed irregular, so I had two of my contractors dispatched to establish in-person surveillance."

Luca took this in. "Yes, yes. And…?"

"The woman and her new companion entered the basilica at one, and the driver remained outside."

"They went into the basilica? That's impossible. It's closed at night."

Luca knew this particular church well. It was only a few miles from Vatican City, where he had resided much of his life and where he even now had been roused from his sleep.

"Closed or not, they disappeared into the church. Fifteen minutes later, all hell broke loose."

"Damn it, man. Spit it out. What happened?" Luca demanded.

"Two men approached the target's vehicle and killed the driver. When they saw the murder, my men took action," Synthe finished.

"Took action?"

"They shot one of the assailants dead, and they believe they wounded a second, but he got away on a motorcycle. They pursued him for several kilometers, but he managed to give them the slip in the smaller streets."

"Are you telling me that the Basilica of Saint Clemente has become a bloodbath?"

"The street outside certainly is," Synthe confirmed.

Luca absorbed this. "What was the girl doing in the church?"

"That's something I could use your assistance with. I assume you have considerable sway in Rome. It would help a great deal if you could see whether there was security footage from inside. Right now, we're dead in the water. We've lost track of the girl, and we don't yet know who else is involved, but whoever it is has no compunction about killing."

"I'll deal with the security cameras. I'll call you back as soon as I know something. Are you still in Israel?"

"No. I'm en route to Rome now. I should be in town within two hours," Synthe replied.

"Do you have any leads for re-establishing surveillance on the girl?" Luca demanded.

"I have men watching the spots the car visited several times before they hit the church. Two different hotels. Those are our best hope. But I don't have to tell you that a hit team showing up at a Roman church in the dead of night moves this situation into a new and critical phase. And obviously, they'll now be on full alert, as will the girl. This is quickly spinning out of control."

"Let me remind you, Colonel, that the overwhelming priority is to recover the Scroll. There is no higher calling. Having said that, I cannot condone killing for any reason," Luca stressed.

"Even if the men involved are butchering those who can lead us to the Scroll?" Synthe fired back.

Luca exhaled a long, pained sigh. "It would seem that providence is testing us. I'm not saying that your contractors acted inappropriately under the circumstances. But I want to stress that I do not want any more killing. There is always another way."

"Perhaps. But if an armed assassin points a gun at our only lead, there may be more bloodshed. I respect your moral stance, but in field work, sometimes ethics aren't consistent with reality."

Synthe couldn't believe this idiot was taking some religious-based turn-the-other-cheek stance in light of the stakes, with very real killers using lethal force within spitting distance of a sacred place. What was he expecting Synthe to do, shame the killers into behaving? Embarrass them into stopping the slaughter? Synthe barely controlled his anger at the arrogantly superior tone Luca was using. He didn't have time for this shit.

Synthe decided to enlighten him. "Look. I'm running this operation because I have decades of experience. Sometimes field work calls for difficult decisions to be made in short time periods. To find the Scroll, we need the girl alive. If someone appears ready to kill her, it's either stop the killers with whatever force is necessary, or watch our only chance of recovering it vaporize. At which point we have no idea whose hands it falls into, or for what purposes it will be used."

"I…I understand. I just don't like it."

"It would really help if I understood what the Scroll contained," Synthe said.

"That isn't mine to impart. Even I don't know. But it is the most important secret the church has," Luca assured him.

"Fine. Then you can expect it to get messier. Because I can guarantee you that the men who killed the driver aren't playing by any morally-constrained rules." Synthe exhaled in frustration. "I'm wasting time. If we run into another situation where deadly force is necessary, should I use it, or shall I instruct my men to watch helplessly as the killers butcher the girl?" Synthe demanded.

Luca paused for a long time. "In the end, if you must use force to defend yourself or the girl from armed assailants who have demonstrated that they intend to kill, then you must do what you must. However, I'd prefer to avoid it if at all possible," Luca said.

Synthe smiled. They were all the same. The politicians and the desk jockeys always wanted to avoid blood on their hands, but couldn't achieve their ends without it. This pious ass was no different. He could hide behind the cross and his cassock, but in the end he would do what he had to in order to get his way. It was the history of the world. The pacifists always needed someone like Synthe around when it got ugly and would quickly distance themselves when the emergency was over.

"I understand. Now, if you don't mind, I need to get back to work. We're knee deep in this, and it's not going to fix itself," Synthe snapped.

"Call me as soon as you have information on any surveillance footage from the church. It might help if we knew what they did inside."

Luca hung up and rubbed the sleep out of his eyes as he considered this latest development. The game had obviously changed to one of overt violence, and he was torn. Colonel Synthe was the ideal man for the job if bloodshed was involved, he had no doubt, but how far could Luca allow things to progress before he called off Synthe's dogs? They were now in water far deeper than ever before, and his heart knew that they had crossed an important line, even if the killing had been in defense. There had to be another way.

The biggest problem they faced was that they couldn't be sure that the girl even had the Scroll or knew anything about it. Her movements had been suspicious, but for every possibly nefarious explanation there was also an innocent one – although he couldn't think of a lot of reasons for her to be in the basilica at night – but still, the reasons were speculation at this point. As it was, they had lots of guesswork but precious little solid fact. The only thing Luca could be certain of was that someone was trying to kill her, and that he was now in the thick of it. A place he didn't want to be.

Luca began making the calls that would result in his getting the security footage, assuming there was any, by morning. Any chance of sleeping had gone since the ringing of the phone.

Sia Amieri sat on one of the two chairs in his hotel room, a small plastic case on the bed in front of him. He held the towel against the crease where the bullet had torn through his side, goring through the fatty flesh of his waist and taking some of the muscle beneath with it. The wound was painful, but hardly life-threatening. He'd been through far worse.

Amieri unscrewed a tiny, single serving bottle of Finlandia vodka he'd found in the mini bar and poured it on the wound, wincing as the alcohol burned the bacteria away. He'd threaded the needle of the hotel sewing kit with dental floss, an old trick from his operational days. It was far stronger than thread and wouldn't bio-degrade, making for perfect stitching material. Fishing line would have been better, but he didn't have any, so he'd make do with floss.

The bleeding had slowed to an ooze. Steeling himself for the ordeal to come, he put a washrag in his mouth to bite on and started sewing the wound shut. It had been a while since he'd had to do so, but it all came back to him as the needle punctured the ragged edge of the tear. Like riding a bicycle. His eyes streamed from the pain as he pulled the floss through and began closing the wound, but he continued on, machine-like. There was no point in delaying the inevitable, and the sooner he was done, the sooner he could get back out and deal with the girl.

Five minutes later he spat the rag onto the floor and moved to the bathroom to rinse the blood from his hands. He'd need to change his shirt and pants and get some water and fruit juice to replenish his fluids. He'd lost a fair amount of blood, but was no worse for wear. Which was lucky. Two inches to the left and it would have been a different story.

The attack on Amieri had come as a shock. He'd lost his local contact in the shooting, all of which had been with silenced weapons, telling him he was dealing with professional adversaries. Which could only mean one of two things – either the girl had pulled in some sort of pro help via unknown channels, or the Order was on the ground and willing to engage in a lethal manner. In the end, it wouldn't make any difference – Sia Amieri was an unstoppable force of nature. And he wouldn't be surprised again.

He powered up his cell phone and called Dr. Frank.

"Speak," Frank's distinctive voice answered.

"I lost my associate here to gunfire, but eliminated the driver," Amieri said dispassionately.

"And the girl?"

"I was ambushed by unknown assailants. I took a bullet and had to take evasive action," Amieri explained.

"I see. And I repeat my question. What about the girl?"

"I lost her. For now."

Silence on the line radiated disapproval more than any scolding could have. He'd failed his master yet again.

"What will you do to find her?" Frank demanded.

"It's a given that as soon as Cross contacts his office, we'll hear about it. That's just a matter of time. He had to run without any time to take precautions, so he'll need to stay in touch with them. I'll await the inevitable," Amieri said.

"I'm not so sure." Frank shifted gears. "Do we know if they found anything in the church?" he asked.

"We have to presume it's the clue that Cross's decrypted document pointed to."

"That's what I'm afraid of. We don't know if he's seen the Scroll, but if he has, and this parchment is related, which we have to assume it is, then we now have no idea if he's cracked the code or not. We need to do better than we've been doing."

Frank had his own cryptologist on call in Russia who had made short work of the data the office had sent to Cross, which Frank had gotten shortly after Cross had received it. The Russian had tried Latin as one of the possible languages right off the bat because of the age of the document, and from there he'd come to the same conclusions Cross had – although in addition to immediately putting the Basilica of Saint Clemente under twenty-four hour surveillance, Frank had also dispatched a team to a second possible location in France, just in case.

But now they knew Rome was the right call, and they'd have to stay on top of Cross to keep track of Twain's daughter's whereabouts. If Frank had ever had any doubt about Cross's involvement with the girl, this ended it; he had to assume that there was only one reason she'd sought him out – to decrypt the Scroll. Frank silently cursed his luck so far. If he'd been just an hour or two earlier, he could have been ahead of this instead of reacting to events.

Amieri winced as he splashed more alcohol on the sutured gunshot wound. "I won't disappoint you again. Just tell me where to go, and I'll get them."

"I know you will, my son, I know you will. Leave your phone on. I'll be in touch as soon as we have more information," Frank said soothingly before disconnecting.

Frank reclined in his leather executive chair and glared through the window of his home-based office at the London night skyline. Thank God he'd had the presence of mind to get some assets moving in Florence when he'd figured out that Twain's daughter had flown the coop in the States. It had been a reasonable assumption that she might seek Cross out, given the obvious respect her father had for his progress on the Voynich – the letter and a few notes Amieri had photographed made clear that the Professor believed he was a significant new talent. Cross had been a question mark until Frank's men in Florence had placed him with the girl in the internet café. It could only mean one thing.

Frank had been late to that party, but because of the steps he'd taken, he would know whenever Cross contacted his staff back in Florence, which he'd have to do sooner or later, following his abrupt departure. There had been no signs of anything at his apartment, leading Frank to conclude that the contact with the girl was recently established.

Frank had the sensation of events accelerating. Perhaps it wasn't terrible that Cross was in the picture. His parchment had likely provided a missing puzzle piece they'd never suspected, and it would hopefully save them time once Frank got his hands on the Scroll. He suspected that, even without it, he could eventually decode the Scroll if he put a team on just that and spent whatever it cost to have them do nothing else, but if he could save the expense and effort…

So much the better.

He glanced around his richly appointed suite and spotted the bottle of eighteen-year-old scotch on the marble bar. Why not? He'd never been closer to solving the ultimate ecclesiastic mystery. It was now almost a foregone conclusion, as the noose tightened on Cross and the girl. They were now running, alone, their driver dead, with Amieri and presumably the Order in hot pursuit. Besides which, it would help him sleep. Maybe a double just to be safe.

Frank poured three fingers into a crystal tumbler and sipped the amber spirit, savoring the rich smoky taste as it burned its way down his throat. He felt a quickening and smiled to himself. Years of research were about to pay huge dividends.

It was just a matter of time until the trap was sprung and he had the Scroll's secret in his possession. Which would make him the most powerful man in the world if the whispered rumors were even close to being true.

CHAPTER 20

Steven slowed the pace once he and Natalie were two blocks away from the church. Other than a few random drunken pedestrians they were the only ones on the long streets, lined with four and five story centuries-old residential buildings. They hadn't spoken a word since they'd bolted. After walking one more block, they hailed a taxi and told him to take them to the Roma Termini – the main train station. Even at two in the morning it was sure to have plenty of traffic, and Steven hoped it would be easy to find someplace to sit and collect themselves and digest what had just happened.

He'd expected Natalie to be in shock, but she remained calm and was barely winded from the sprint. Once in the back of the taxi, she adjusted her wig and, in a hushed whisper, asked Steven what had happened. Steven told her that Frederick had been murdered – stabbed to death, with his presumed assailant dead only feet from where he'd fallen. She nodded, no change in her expression.

"What do you think happened?" she asked in a monotone.

He regarded her cautiously. "Obviously, somehow, we were tracked. But I have no idea how. Regardless, you have me officially convinced that we're in deep shit."

"Glad it finally dawned on you."

"After this, I'm a believer," Steven observed.

Natalie stared without focus through the taxi window as they rolled along the late-night downtown streets. She frowned. "I'd say we have a real problem now. Rome's a big place, but not big enough."

"I know."

Natalie went silent, obviously upset over Frederick, and Steven let her be. She needed to deal with it in her own way, and his mind was racing over the ramifications of the attack, as well as on the ancient message they'd found. They sat quietly, lost in their respective thoughts for the duration of the trip. Even at the late hour, traffic was stop and go, thanks to the late night party crowd, exacerbated by an accident that brought their thoroughfare to a standstill.

The driver finally pulled up to the station; they paid him, tipped him and climbed out. A bank of lights bathed the entrance in a blinding glare at the front of the massive contemporary steel and glass terminal.

Inside, they headed for a fast food restaurant whose familiar golden arches twinkled in welcome. Once seated, two sodas before them, Steven breached the topic that was nagging at him.

"We need to get back to the hotel. Now."

"That's the worst idea I've ever heard. We don't know how much whoever killed Frederick knows, but we have to assume it's a lot," Natalie warned.

"True. But I need my passport and money, which is in the safe. And if we want to have any shot at decrypting our find, we'll need the program I loaded on the laptop. We're pretty much boned without those. We have no chance of traveling without my papers, or of figuring out what the basilica's parchment says without the computer."

"Steven…that's a real problem. We can't just traipse in there without attracting attention."

"True. But I have a plan. Sort of." Steven proceeded to fill her in on his thinking. She sat quietly, and then nodded.

"It could work. But a lot of things need to go right."

"I know. But I don't think we have any other options. And the longer we linger here, the more time our attackers have to regroup and stake out the hotel. I say we go in now and take our chances," Steven pressed.

"Okay. I go in first, take the elevator to the third floor and wait for you by the fire exit at the end of the hall…"

"Right. We can check the street for any surveillance on our approach. If there isn't any, we're still ahead of them, and we grab our stuff and get out. If there is, we'll need a plan B. Which I haven't thought of yet. But having Frederick's gun is a decent equalizer."

"I don't like it, but I guess there aren't any other options. Why don't I go in and clean out both our rooms, and you keep watch on the street?" Natalie asked.

"And what if someone's waiting in one of the rooms?" Steven countered.

"I'll take the gun," Natalie offered.

Steven considered it. "Have you ever used one?" he asked.

Natalie shot him a scornful look. "Steven, there are a lot of things you don't know about me. Maybe if you're good I'll tell you a few. One you might find interesting is that I graduated top of my class at Quantico," Natalie said.

"Quantico? You were FBI?" Steven asked incredulously. Natalie looked like a lot of things, but a Fed wasn't one of them.

"It was a while ago, but yes, I spent six years with the Bureau as a Special Agent. I know how to use a gun…and I've used one more times than I care to remember. Probably a lot more than you ever have."

He looked at her with new appreciation. "You may well have. I suppose it sounds like I'm being a complete chauvinist if I insist we do this together…"

"Correct. Now that's settled, let's stop the back and forth and get to the hotel before they have a chance to stake it out. I just wish I knew how they tracked us to the church," Natalie groused.

"There are only a few possibilities, and none of them are good. Either they followed the car somehow, or Danny tipped them off."

"What about your office?" Natalie asked.

"Impossible. All they sent me was the decrypted parchment. But it hadn't been translated from Latin or assembled into anything intelligible. That's the weakest possibility. I'd put my money on either the car, or your friend's Italian contact has a big mouth. Those are far more likely."

"No point in speculating. We can worry about Danny later. Let's go do what we have to do," Natalie said, sliding out of the hard plastic booth. "I'll be right back. I'm going to hit the ladies room. I don't think I'll need a toolkit in my boots, and I can move a lot faster without the drill cutting into my ankle…"

Upon her return, they exited the restaurant and approached the cab line. A sleepy man with an elaborate turban grunted a welcome as they slid into the back seat. Steven gave the driver instructions to drop them by the

Spanish Steps, a block and a half from their hotel, and once they were underway, he surreptitiously handed Natalie the gun. She expertly flipped the safety off and then slipped it into her clutch purse, with a wary glance at the driver, who was engrossed with setting a new land speed record in the noisy little Fiat and had no interest in his passengers. They lurched around several corners and were at the large plaza within a few frantic minutes. Even at the late hour, pedestrians lingered in the area – drunks, lovers, vagrants, petty thieves and several police officers.

Natalie and Steven moved in the direction of the hotel, eyeing their surroundings for any hint of danger, but saw nothing suspicious. Fifty yards from the hotel, Steven murmured his safe combination in her ear and slipped her his room key. Natalie broke away, as agreed, and sauntered unhurriedly to the front lobby while Steven leaned into a recessed doorway and kept watch. He scanned the neighboring buildings, but didn't detect any surveillance. The only good in any of the night's surprises so far was that at almost three in the morning it was hard to loiter and keep an eye on the hotel without being noticed – a fact he was keenly aware of as he stood sentry, too exposed for his liking.

Five minutes of waiting turned into ten. Steven began to get worried. His room was on the third floor facing the street, and he didn't see any lights on. After another few minutes, he decided it was taking too long. He made his way to the lobby entrance, where he nodded to the night man before taking the stairs up to his room. On the third floor, he eased cautiously down the carpeted hall, his footsteps mercifully hushed. When he reached his door, he tried the handle, but it was locked. He strained to hear anything, but it was silent inside. Torn, he decided to chance a soft knock. He whispered into the door jamb.

"If you're still in there, open up. It's me."

A few moments later the door opened. He pushed past Natalie into the dark room, where her bags lay on his bed, with his partially packed.

"What's taking so long?" he complained.

"I had to get my stuff and make sure nobody was waiting to kill me. Then do the same in here. It took a while. Besides which, your junk is all over the room – laptop over on the desk, shaving kit strewn everywhere in the bathroom, clothes in the closet, papers in the safe…" She eyed him. "Who hangs their shirts and pants when they're only going to be in a hotel for one night?"

Steven ignored her and hurriedly threw his belongings into his duffle. He was finished in sixty seconds. He did a quick scan of the safe to ensure she'd removed everything, then moved to the window to peer out. Natalie was making for the door with her bag when he turned to her.

"Slow down. There's a problem. Looks like we've got company."

"Shit. How many?" she asked, setting her bag down and extracting the pistol from her purse.

"Three. But hold off. It'll take them at least a minute to get up here, assuming the desk doesn't stop them. Follow me," he whispered as he pushed past her, shouldering his bag.

He cracked the door, peeked out and verified the long hall was empty. Alert for sounds of pursuit, he motioned to Natalie. The elevator motor sounded noisily. They jogged past it towards the fire stairs at the rear of the hotel as the old lift creaked to their floor. Steven pushed the heavy steel fire door open and they stepped onto the concrete landing. Natalie looked warily down the dimly-lit stairwell to the ground floor two stories below and then shrugged at Steven. They descended the stairs without hesitation, taking them two at a time. In a few moments they were at the street level. Steven eyed the door to the lobby, then moved away from it to the metal emergency exit door.

Which was chained shut, with a padlock securing it in place.

Perfect. Far be it for an emergency exit to be usable in the event of an emergency. Better to keep intruders out by rendering it impassable to those fleeing from an inferno.

Natalie pulled on his sleeve and gestured at the fire axe hanging on the wall.

The pounding of the heavy steel edge against the lock sounded like an amplified battering ram. Fortunately, it was a relatively flimsy clasp, and after three blows the shattered padlock hit the concrete floor with a clatter. Steven quickly tore the chain from the handle and shouldered the door open.

The klaxon shriek of the hotel's alarm wailed into the night as they ran down the alley towards another small street, away from the plaza. After turning the corner, Steven stopped and moved cautiously back to watch the rear exit. Three men emerged from the hotel and scanned the street before hurriedly splitting up – two sprinting to the plaza and a lone man moving in their direction. Steven estimated he was two hundred yards away.

Doing a quick calculation, Steven motioned to Natalie to get moving. She silently took her bag, and with a glance, nodded and jogged away, the sound of her boots on the cobblestones echoing from the dark buildings' façades.

Steven pressed himself into a doorway and waited. After what seemed like forever, his patience was rewarded by heavy footsteps scraping along the street.

One man, as expected.

Steven heard him pause at the intersection, and then after a few moments of hesitation, the footsteps continued down the larger thoroughfare – he hadn't made the turn. Steven listened as the clumping sound of pursuit receded into the distance, then detached himself from the building and ran down the dark sidewalk in Natalie's direction.

She was waiting for him at the next corner. They put another block between them and any danger before hailing a slow-moving taxi and piling in, their bags hastily crammed into the back seat next to them. Steven told the driver to take them to the train station; within a few moments they were pulling away to the relative safety of the terminal.

Natalie kept her eye on the side mirror for any signs of a tail. She relaxed after a few minutes, but still looked worried.

"That was too close," she said.

"I know. But the important thing is we're safe. For now."

"True, but that can change pretty quickly. Once we're at the terminal, let's switch cabs and find a hotel somewhere on the outskirts of town. I have three passports with me. We can book under a different name than I used at this hotel. That should be good for at least one day, while we figure out what we're going to do next," Natalie suggested.

"I think we're better off at the train station. I'll need a few hours to decrypt the basilica clue, but it should be a lot easier than the parchment because I already know the substitution letters. It's just a matter of entering them into the program and running the software to see what comes up in Latin, and then translating it. Let's hope this one's a little more specific."

"Can you do that at the station?" Natalie asked.

"I'll have to. I don't like the idea of checking into a hotel at three in the morning. We don't know what kind of resources we're up against, and if these clowns have clout with the police, it's conceivable they could call the area hotels, scouting for late bookings. I don't like the odds that there will be more than one couple checking in without a reservation in the wee hours of the morning." Steven paused. "The terminal will have crowds and, within a little while, the early morning rush should start. I think it's a safer bet. When we get there I'll change my shirt and put on a baseball cap, and you can do something with your wig." Steven glanced at her. "And maybe slip out of the Catwoman suit into something less…formal."

Natalie smiled. "I have some jeans, so no problem. And you're probably right about the hotel. I'm tired, but not so much I want to take any more stupid chances. I think we've had enough brushes with danger for one night," Natalie said. "But what's wrong with the Catwoman suit? You don't like it?" Her violet eyes bored through him.

"I didn't say I don't like it. I said that it may be too, uh, distinctive. My thoughts on your getup have nothing to do with it," Steven said, flustered.

"Worked pretty well with the church guard," Natalie observed, and then let it drop.

They both obviously still remembered the basilica kiss, even if it was part of their cover. But now wasn't the time or place to explore that.

Still, Steven could taste her in his mind's eye and vividly recall the way her skin and breath smelled, as her tongue darted…

No point in dwelling on it.

❧

"They escaped?" Synthe seethed into the phone.

"Yes, sir. They cleared out of their rooms and slipped out the back. We searched for them, but it was no good. Way too large an area for three men, once they were out of the hotel," the voice reported. "I'm sorry, sir. It was only a matter of seconds. We almost had them."

"That's like being almost pregnant. It's a meaningless statement." Synthe calmed himself. "Where does this leave us?"

"We're expanding to our contacts in the police, and by morning we'll have several assets working the day shift at Interpol. Hopefully we can get something on one of their cell phones, or be alerted when Cross contacts his office."

"Keep me informed. So far we've been outflanked by these two, and now we have an additional player who's proved they'll kill. We need to get the girl and her new friend and take them off the field. If we don't, I have a feeling the other guys will, and then we're out of luck," Synthe underscored.

"I understand. We're actively working it. I'll check in when I know more," the voice said, and then the line went dead.

Synthe lit a cigarette and noisily blew a plume of smoke at the desk lamp in his hotel room. The situation was rapidly deteriorating. He paced for a few minutes, considering the ramifications of the new wrinkle, muttering to himself as he cursed their luck.

He stubbed out the cigarette and moved to the bed, where he programmed his phone to wake him in two hours. He'd pulled many all-nighters when he'd been in the field, but he'd been younger then. The years had taught him the value of being rested.

Synthe leaned back against the headboard and closed his eyes, trying to shut off the barrage of thoughts. He'd grown accustomed to sleeping sitting up, and now couldn't do so any other way.

Yet another example of how his decades of service in the Mossad had affected him.

He switched off the bedside lamp and looked at his watch. Three forty-five.

It was going to be a long day.

CHAPTER 21

Steven sat slumped over his laptop in the arrival area as though waiting for an early morning train. The terminal had a fair number of people in it: mostly shifty-looking loiterers and the late night fringes of society that frequented train and bus stations. The few police patrolling seemed to be oblivious of him. That made sense – it was too soon, and they hadn't actually broken any laws. Although there was always the chance that someone would pull some strings and get an All Points Bulletin issued, it seemed highly unlikely if their intentions were to remain a secret. Besides which, Steven was barely recognizable now that he was wearing a hooded sweatshirt pulled over his NY Yankees baseball cap. The ensemble was completed with nondescript black cargo pants, and he could have passed for early thirties, or even younger, at a glance. The attire was miles from what a cryptologist or a technology CEO would reasonably wear.

Steven glanced up as he sensed Natalie's return and ventured a fatigued grin. She looked like she'd just awoken from eight solid hours of rest, dazzling in a multicolored lightweight sweater and jeans. The wig was now pulled into a pony tail, and the change in her appearance from the goth-princess he'd met two mornings ago was striking. It was hard to believe this was the same woman, but the intense violet eyes were unmistakable.

She appraised him as he tapped at the computer's keypad.

"Any progress?"

"I entered the photos from the basilica and did a glyph-by-glyph comparison, then recreated the text and fed it into the software." He touched the screen. "It's processing, after which I'll need to translate it from whatever it spits out in Latin."

"How long do you think it will take?" Natalie asked.

"Maybe an hour – it will check for all permutations, which could turn out to be a lot. No way of knowing until it tells me it's done. If I didn't have the program, it would be weeks."

"Is there anything I can do to help?"

"Could you get me a cup of very strong coffee? I'm not used to staying up all night, and I'm starting to drift…"

Natalie nodded. "Relegated to the coffee girl. Fine," she teased.

"You can sit here for a while and stare at the blank screen telling you the task is only fifteen percent complete while I go get some," he offered.

"Know what? I'll take you up on that. It will probably do you good to stretch your legs. Do you mind?" she asked.

"Not at all. Nothing will happen with the software until it's done, and that will be a while. You want anything? Java? Muffin?"

"Please, no pet names." She studied Steven's blank expression. "Sorry. I'm a little punchy too. I was just playing. Sure, I'd love some coffee. Lots of cream, three sugars, please."

Steven wordlessly handed her the PC, careful not to kick the power cord from the outlet.

He adjusted his hat. "Hot, white and sweet. Got it." His eyes twinkled. "See? I can play too."

Without waiting for a response, he departed in search of liquid sustenance. Nothing was illuminated but the fast food restaurant they'd stopped at earlier. Steven bought two coffees and two croissants, which had just come out of the oven. He looked at the wall clock as he waited for his order. Four-eighteen. Either very late, or very early. It would start getting light around six-thirty, so they had a ways to go until dawn.

How had circumstances gotten so crazy in under forty-eight hours? Two days ago, he'd woken up like he did every day, shaved and showered, and had given no further thought to his upcoming day than to hope he wasn't bored to death. Since then he'd been chased twice, had bludgeoned a man senseless, been forced to run for his life, had set hands on the rarest parchment on the planet, taken a gun from a dead man, slept in a strange villa, fled a hotel in the dead of night, and kissed an incredible woman he barely knew.

Her tongue probing into his mouth had awakened a side of Steven that had been dead for over two years. He wasn't sure he was ready for it to be roused in such an abrupt manner, but now that it was, he couldn't stop thinking about it – when he wasn't consumed with the puzzle of a lifetime and calculating how to escape execution by centuries-old secret societies or murderous billionaires.

The soft feel of her full, lush lips and urgent tongue, the scent of her dewy immediacy, the hard curves of her supple, pert, inviting–

Steven mentally shook himself. *That's enough of that.* Mooning around like a high school boy with his first crush wouldn't do either of them any good, and occupying his limited mental resources with fantasies of Natalie seductively peeling off her skin-tight jumpsuit to reveal her perfectly-sculpted nudity, tattoos heralding her passionate, wanton shamelessness…

Stop it. Now. Enough.

The girl behind the counter, who was all of seventeen, regarded him oddly. Steven supposed she saw plenty of old perverts on the graveyard shift, but still, it made him feel grungy and lecherous. She slid the cardboard tray with two coffees and a bag of croissants across the counter to him with a look that clearly said she was afraid he'd pounce on her if she didn't snatch her arm away.

Yes, he'd come a long way in the last forty-odd hours. Now he was scaring random females with his newfound Uncle Touchy leer. *Great.* Hard to add that to the resume.

He realized that his internal dialogue was veering into unexpected areas and attributed it to the fatigue and post-chase adrenaline crash. It had been a long time since he'd had to run from pursuers, and he'd almost forgotten how many inner resources it consumed.

Natalie had seemed almost unaffected by the day's events, except for Frederick's death, which Steven had watched her quickly digest and compartmentalize. He understood because he also dealt with grief and pain like that, especially during times of crisis. Getting bogged down in emotion was a luxury those on the run couldn't afford and came at a cost that could be lethal if you hesitated at the wrong moment or missed a vital danger signal. He'd seen the pain in her eyes when she'd taken the gun from him in the taxi, but she'd quickly bucked up and done what was necessary. A rare trait in most people, much less a gorgeous young ingénue with sex appeal that wouldn't quit.

Steven forced himself to swallow some of that compartmentalization medicine and stuffed his daydreams about Natalie's charms behind a mental door, which he shut with commitment, if not enthusiasm.

He returned with his bounty and sat across from Natalie, who was staring at the silent computer screen as if to command it to complete its task through sheer force of will.

"Did it flash the decrypted message alert?" Steven asked, handing her the coffee.

"Will it do that?" she asked, eyeing him skeptically.

"Absolutely. Oh, wait. I never downloaded that update. Sorry."

She fixed him with a quizzical stare. "Did you just make a funny?"

He couldn't keep his composure, and just a hint of a smile flashed across his face.

"I've been told my sense of humor is one of my most endearing traits," Steven tried.

"Don't quit your day job." Natalie shifted her gaze back to the screen. "When will you know that it's finished?" she asked.

"Seriously? It will default to a screen that says processing complete. Very low-tech. Once that's done, I'll have a file with the contents organized into the three likeliest combinations of words, which I'll need to translate. Although in my experience the top choice is usually the right one."

Natalie emitted an impatient sigh and set the computer to one side. She tasted her coffee with a slurp.

"So what drives a young woman to become an FBI agent?" Steven asked, sipping his own coffee gratefully.

"Honestly? I got fascinated with the idea after seeing Silence of the Lambs, and one thing led to another," she said.

He studied her serene expression. "Are you F-ing with me?"

A trace of amusement crossed her face at his choice of terms.

"Steven, trust me when I tell you that you'll know when I'm 'F-ing' with you. And this ain't it."

He decided to let that ball go by without swinging at it.

"You joined the FBI because of a movie?"

"It's more complicated than that, but that's basically my story. I graduated from Duke University with honors in three years and decided on getting my JD in half the usual time. At some point during that whirlwind I saw the movie, and I thought, 'That's what I'd like to do.' After I passed the bar, I applied to the Bureau, and they accepted me. The rest is history."

"You're an attorney, too?"

"Don't hold that against me."

"And you said you were with the FBI for five years?" Steven asked.

"Technically, six. But half the first year was training."

"I hope you don't mind my asking, but how old are you, Natalie?"

She hesitated. "Just turned thirty-one. I focused on financial crimes to start with, but quickly moved into specialized field work. The financial stuff was too boring. So I weaseled my way into becoming a mob specialist. Tracking hit men."

"Why did you leave?" Steven asked.

"I'm not a good team player, and the FBI is all about teamwork and politics. That, and it's still somewhat of a boy's club, which makes it tough for a girl to get ahead – even though half their ads feature politically-correct, racially-and-gender-mixed models, the truth is it's still mostly white men who run things. I loved the field work, but hated the political jockeying. So I quit after sewing up a huge case. They were sad to see me go – when I graduated from Quantico I was chosen to receive the Director's Leadership award. I was one of their model success stories." She took another taste of coffee. "I quit being a Special Agent two years ago and almost entered a convent to better serve the church. And in case you're wondering, I'm still a virgin," she confessed.

Steven's mouth actually fell open at her nonchalant recitation. She smiled at him.

"*Now* I'm F-ing with you," she said. She leaned over and picked up the sack and rooted around in the paper bag for a croissant.

The laptop beeped.

"I think that's for you," Natalie said.

Steven moved to her side and put the computer in his lap. He quickly pulled up a screen and opened a file.

"Let's use your phone again. I need to translate these from Latin," Steven said.

Natalie plugged it in the laptop and within a few seconds they were online. He fed in the data to a translation engine and saved the results.

They both peered at it on the screen.

"Huh?" Natalie exclaimed.

"I told you not to expect too much on this first go around."

"What does it mean?"

"My job, such as it is, would be to find out."

CHAPTER 22

Steven scratched his head. The message didn't make a lot of sense.

"From holy Januarius' crypt, three paces from the olive harvester points the traveler to the path, five hands above the trinacrium." Steven groaned. "I'm tired. Is it just me, or is this gibberish?"

"Remember the last one. On first blush it wasn't obvious. Aren't you going to run it through the computer and see what hits for likely locations? It worked with the basilica."

"You're right. Sorry. I'm just running low on steam," Steven apologized. Suddenly he felt beat.

"Too bad we can't use Moody's apartment. But given the circumstances, seems like a poor idea," Natalie observed.

"That's an understatement."

"Maybe we can get a room once it's light out. It doesn't have to be in Rome. Or we can take a train somewhere for a few hours and sleep onboard."

"You know what? That's not a bad idea. We can get first class seats to somewhere in Italy and catch up on our rest. And they have internet on board." Steven brightened. "I'm sorry. It's just that this requires a lot of mental focus, and when I'm exhausted…"

"No need to apologize. You're not a young man. I completely understand," she said in a neutral tone. Steven cocked an eyebrow. "I'm F-ing with you again," Natalie deadpanned.

"I got that. Let's go over and see what time the next train to anywhere leaves," Steven said, closing the laptop. "We can run the search while we sleep."

They proceeded to the ticket windows, where they were greeted by a surly man with a low patience threshold. After a few curt sentences back and forth, Steven was able to glean that the next train for Milan left in under two hours. He asked about other destinations, but the ticket vendor seemed annoyed at having to answer questions, and brusquely slid a laminated paper timetable under the window to them before resuming reading his magazine. Natalie gave the man a black look, which he cheerfully ignored.

"We might as well run the search while we wait," Natalie said and held out her hand for the laptop. Steven handed it over and she plugged it into her phone again. They moved away from the ticket area, and Steven sat, typing in a series of commands – then the little computer began searching online for relevance.

"Train for Milan doesn't leave till 6:15 a.m.. You mind if I get a little shut-eye while we wait?" Steven asked, more a statement than a question.

"Help yourself. If you can sleep on those plastic seats, you're entitled to. There's no way I can," she complained.

"Right now I could sleep through a Metallica concert."

They moved to a waiting area near the ticket window, and within a few moments, Steven's head moved down toward his chest, and he was out.

❧

Steven ran down a long hall roughly hewn from polished black stone. Obsidian, he realized, even as he registered the scrape of claws behind him. Something was gaining on him, and it had murder on its mind – he could smell an odor of death, of carnage, wafting over his shoulder, driving him on as he blindly raced down the dark passageway. Ahead in the distance a torch flickered smoky illumination, revealing an ancient wooden door; heavy, held together with rusting iron studs and brackets, its surface scarred by long vertical grooves. As he neared it, a part of his brain noted that the scores were symmetrical and could only have been left by razor-sharp talons.

His body slammed against the door, but it wouldn't give. He grabbed the torch and spun around, waving it in front of him, the better to make out his stalker. The gleam of giant, wickedly serrated mandibles thrashing the air, drooling a thick, stinking mucous appeared out of the murky depths of the passage; a long spiked claw shot at him with lightning speed, as his eyes went wide with horror–

He was shaking.

Being shaken.

"Steven. Wake up. The computer's done with its search."

He groggily cracked one eye open, and then forced both wide, blinking from the glare of the overhead lights in the increasingly bustling terminal. He tried to focus on his watch. After a few seconds, he saw that he'd been asleep for just over an hour. His neck was stiff. He rolled his head cautiously, reaching up to rub the muscles at the top of his shoulders. Natalie ignored his plight and thrust the laptop at him.

"It's finished," she repeated.

"All right. Let's see what we've got," Steven said, taking it from her. "Huh. Not a whole hell of a lot. Although we do have a bit of luck. It's obscure, but it's really the only hit that makes sense. 'Holy Januarius'. There is a Saint Januarius…"

"I've never heard of him. Then again, I'm not big on saints," Natalie admitted.

"No reason you should have. I've never heard of him, either. Our biggest problem is that his remains are in Naples. On first take, we'd have to go there to find what amounts to his crypt. But that's deceptive because a lot of these saints and popes were entombed elsewhere originally, and then later had their remains moved to their current resting places." He performed a series of rapid keystrokes. "Ah. See? We search further, and while his remains aren't in Rome, sure enough, there's a reference to an obscure crypt that housed his corpse for a time in one of the Roman catacombs."

"I hate catacombs."

"Not many people get warm and fuzzy when it comes to underground burial chambers. But Rome has miles and miles of them. Most are located along the Appian Way – the original road that led into Rome and connected the Roman Empire. It was forbidden to bury anyone within the city walls, so the locals came up with a way around that by excavating massive tunnel complexes to house the dead just outside the gates. When the Christians were persecuted by the Romans, before Christianity became the state religion, they used the catacombs to hold secret worship ceremonies." Steven paused, staring at the screen. "The only problem is that this one is closed to the public, and the location of the entrance is a secret. That, and I have no idea what the message means. But it's the only hit on the terms that has any relevance."

"Then we need to go there. Wherever it is, we need to find it and get in," Natalie said excitedly.

"That didn't go so well the last time, as I recall. And we can't afford to use Danny to grease the wheels anymore, so we're on our own."

"I'm not so sure about that. I've been waiting to call Moody and tell him what happened. He might have some ideas. And he'll be able to give us a read on exactly how trustworthy Danny really is. If Moody thinks it wasn't him that rolled, I'd believe him – he's a very careful man, and he wouldn't send us into harm's way. I say we wait until I talk to Moody and see what he proposes. It can't hurt."

"No, it probably can't. Although I'm reluctant to trust anyone right now. There are probably hotels around the Appian Way that we could check into without sounding any alarms. Fortunately, it's not far from this terminal," Steven reasoned.

"Really?"

"Maybe two and a half miles. Assuming that this catacomb is anywhere near the others. Most of them are in the same general area."

"Just a few miles? That's nothing. Let's go," Natalie said.

"I think we're better off waiting until it's light out. It'll still look suspicious if we show up at a hotel without a reservation before dawn."

"Wow. If only you had a computer and could go online and make a reservation for early check-in, say around eight this morning…then it wouldn't look at all weird. Just a couple getting in early after an all-night flight," Natalie suggested sarcastically.

Steven didn't say anything for a few seconds.

"Did I mention I don't process well when I'm exhausted?"

"I got that. Let me know what you find…" Natalie stood. "I'm going to the little girls' room. Oh, and just get one hotel room – use the name Linda Jenkins. That will take care of any problems we could run into getting two rooms. They'd want your passport for the second room."

"Linda Jenkins. Got it."

Steven rubbed his eyes, then did a quick search for hotels near the Appian Way. There were a few within a mile, and he found one that was modern, large and had plenty of vacancies. He was just finishing up as Natalie got back.

"I've been thinking. I want to call Moody right now and get it over with. It's after midnight in Virginia, but I think this rates a call. I don't want to have to wait seven more hours. We're in a footrace, and the sooner we make it to wherever we're going, the better." Natalie shrugged. "I'm sorry you're tired – I'm tired, too – but I really feel strongly about this. If Danny's bad we need to know it, and if he isn't, we need to get him working for us as soon as possible."

He looked at her, standing with her hands on her hips, her jaw set with determination. Steven was too tired to fight about it. He unplugged the phone from the computer and handed it to her.

"Knock yourself out. I'm going to get some more coffee. You'll probably want the same order, right?"

Natalie nodded, already pressing the phone to her ear.

Some of the cafés in the terminal were putting out small tables, gearing up for the morning crush of commuters making their way into the bustling capital. Steven stood outside one as the tired-looking man who was probably the owner of the nearest one set out a few chairs and then motioned to Steven to approach the counter. He ordered two lattes and waited as the man steamed the concoctions. Fumbling with some change, he paid the proprietor and made his way back to Natalie, who was finishing up the call.

"Would you? That would be awesome…but you really don't have to. No, it's not that. I just don't want to drag you into anything that's not your problem. All right. It's your funeral. I appreciate it. Let me know when you arrive. And, Moody? Thanks again." Natalie glanced at Steven and hung up.

He silently handed her a cup.

"Moody says there's no way Danny tipped anyone off. He's been a trusted asset for fifteen years, and there's never been any question of his loyalty. Moody swears by him. I think we can rest easy on that. I told him what happened with Frederick and gave him a brief outline of what's going on, and he volunteered to fly over to help out." Natalie hesitated. "That would be invaluable, Steven."

He sipped the rich brew and then asked the question that had been burning since she'd originally referred to him. "This Moody is going to fly across the Atlantic on a moment's notice to get involved in a dangerous situation in a foreign country that involves the most powerful organization in the world? That's some friend. Mind if I ask what exactly the relationship is?"

"I do mind. It's none of your business," she snapped and then seemed to reconsider. "Moody and I met when I was in Quantico. We dated for a while, but it never went anywhere – I wasn't interested in him that way, I guess you could say. He was, but it didn't pan out. But we've remained close ever since, and he's a good man. It doesn't hurt us that he's pretty high up in the CIA."

Steven didn't betray any emotion.

"He's twenty-five years older than me, Steven. It wasn't meant to be. I think we can leave it at that." Natalie suddenly sounded defensive, more like a teen having to answer to a parent than the confident woman he'd spent the last two days with.

"Natalie. The guy's a spook. I don't know much about them, but are you sure he's completely disinterested and just pursuing this as a favor to a 'friend'? It may sound overly paranoid, but you've got me convinced now that your story's true, which means the manuscript could in fact hide a secret that some would do anything to get their hands on. What makes you think that a government wouldn't take a side in this to curry favor with the Church?"

"Steven, you're not paranoid. If it was anyone else but Moody, I'd say you have a point. But you don't know him. I do. For almost a decade. I trust him like I'd trust my father," she replied evenly.

"If you're wrong, it could be our lives."

She gave him a look he'd come to know well even within the scant time they'd spent together – the old Natalie was back with a vengeance.

"I'm not wrong."

CHAPTER 23

Blue flashing lights flickered along the basilica's side street, where three police cars, a detective's sedan, and the coroner's wagon blocked the broad drive. A handful of officers stood at the edge of the yellow police tape that sealed off the crime scene. Bright spotlights were mounted on stands along the perimeter, bathing the bodies in a cold, white glow. The forensics team was processing the area, and as the dawn's uneasy light pervaded the Roman sky, the cleanup crew was anxious to get the corpses moved – before the city came to life and they had a crowd-control situation on their hands.

Rome was as dangerous as most large cities, but even so, it was unusual to have a stabbing victim as well as a gunshot fatality on church property. The two detectives chartered with investigating the mess were not optimistic about their chances. A late-night passer-by had phoned in the report, but nobody had called about any gunfire, which was strange, following a densely-populated area shooting. Either everyone in the nearby apartments was deaf, or a silenced weapon had been involved.

The two homicide detectives watched impassively as the crime scene personnel methodically pored over the vicinity of the assault. Both detectives had been working the Rome beat for decades and so had seen everything. The older, taller of the two, Emilio Carruzo, leaned in to his partner. Neither man had shaved for three days.

"What do you think? This wasn't a robber – both victims were packing guns. Maybe a Mafia hit?" he asked his companion.

The smaller, olive-skinned man, Detective Guillermo Farrallio, spat into the gutter then fished a packet of cigarettes from his jacket, pausing to light one with a stainless steel zippo before responding.

"Could be, but there's too much that doesn't make sense. Where did the stabbing victim's gun go? He's got a shoulder holster; he was armed. But the other stiff got close enough to stab him, what, four times?" Guillermo gestured with his head. "And the stabber also had a gun he didn't use, preferring a knife. The way I see it, the stabbing victim gets out of the car, is waiting for something, and the stabber sneaks up on him and gets him with the knife. But why wouldn't the victim have heard him?"

"Lots of possible explanations. There's no point in speculating. At least we have a few good footprints – looks like a size forty-four man's boot."

"What about the blood further down the street?"

"I bet we'll find it's not from either of these guys," Emilio said. "That means a third assailant, and also at least one more shooter. My hunch is the stabber somehow got the jump on the driver, maybe while he was distracted by a second or third guy, stabbed him to death, possibly after a struggle, and then a shooter took out the stabber. Maybe the shooter was in the car, maybe not. There's no cordite smell, but the shooter could have exited the vehicle when the scuffle started and opened up."

"The driver still had his wallet on him. It's not a robbery. And there's the question of what happened to his gun…"

"Again, numerous possibilities. Someone came along after the fact and stole it. Or he didn't have it with him, although that's not likely, given the holster. Or maybe the shooter took it, or the second assailant. There had to be two," Emilio mused, running the physics of the altercation through his head.

"I agree. No other explanation for the blood over there. But it could have been the stabbing victim who shot the man down the street as he ran away or approached the car, or was stabbed while preoccupied with his quarry and, as his dying act, shot his killer, too. Then someone came along and took the gun, or maybe the quarry returned for it once the driver was down?"

"Forensics will be able to figure that out by the blood. But my gut says two hitters, the driver, and a fourth mystery shooter, who may have taken the gun with him. Could be it was used in some other killings…"

Guillermo looked glum. "We pretty much have nothing right now." He threw a poison look at the forensics team before taking a last drag of his smoke. Glancing absently at the smoldering butt, he spat again, and then threw it into the street.

"We know from his driver's license and passport that the stabbing victim was American," Emilio said. "Frederick Marshall. We'll run the ID and see what we come up with. And we'll dust the car for prints and run those through Interpol. But right now, the best lead we have is the boot prints, which will only matter if we get a suspect…"

"We're not even close unless someone shows up to confess. But maybe the prints will tell us something. Maybe whoever has been in the car knows something. Could be this is drug related – most of these kinds of killings are. But with no witnesses, it's not looking like a fast-solve case. Another problem to deal with." Guillermo sighed, the weight of the world on his shoulders as usual.

His taller partner eyed him with restrained amusement and then returned to studying the scene. It was definitely a curious one.

❧

Danny's phone rang at seven-thirty a.m., just as he was stepping out of the shower. He quickly wrapped a towel around his waist and trundled into the bedroom to answer it.

"Danny, it's Natalie. Sorry to call so early."

"Ah, yes, Natalie. How are you? I trust your adventure last night went well?"

"Not really, Danny. We have a situation."

Natalie explained what she knew about Frederick's death and the unknown assailant. Danny listened without comment until she finished.

"Any idea who it was, or how they found you?" he asked.

Natalie decided not to share too much. The less he knew the better. "As David told you, I have some ugly characters looking for me. It was probably them. As to how they found us, that's a mystery…"

"Where are you?" Danny asked.

"Someplace safe. But I need your help with one more item," Natalie said and then told him what she wanted.

Danny didn't seem surprised by the request. "Praetextatus, *eh*? I've heard of the catacombs. Not an easy one," he said. "It's not open to the public."

"So you can't do it?" she asked.

"I didn't say that, did I? No, anything can be done, but it will take some digging and a decent amount of money. How much I won't know until I start checking with people. Do you have a budget for this?" Danny asked.

"Whatever's reasonable. Can you call me whenever you have something?"

"Of course. I understand the urgency. You want access as soon as possible, preferably today. Is that correct?"

"Absolutely. Thank you, Danny."

❧

Steven and Natalie walked into the hotel at eight, looking as though they'd been on flights all night. The desk clerk regarded them with little interest as he processed Natalie's reservation and took her cash. The hotel was modern, all stainless steel and angles, with a decidedly business orientation. It was large, with a hundred rooms distributed over five stories, and another tired couple arriving wouldn't raise any eyebrows.

The bellboy escorted them to their room, and after a few minutes of perfunctory orientation, they were alone. Steven flipped the 'do not disturb' sign onto the doorknob, then locked and bolted it so a maid couldn't intrude on their rest. He turned and faced Natalie, who was sitting on the king-size bed.

"We can do a Clark Gable deal and hang a blanket between us," he suggested.

"Are you afraid you'll be attacked? I can stay up with the gun if it's a problem. Keep the boogeymen away…" She threw him an obviously fake smile.

"I'm going to take a quick shower," he said, ignoring the sarcasm.

He peeled off his clothes and hosed down, mildly distracted by Natalie's proximity, but exhausted. Steven didn't think he'd have too much problem falling asleep, even with her next to him. It was a big bed, and they were adults. She'd correctly pointed out that it would look odd if they asked for separate beds, and he'd conceded the point. Unless she climbed on top of him, he'd be out within a few minutes, and he was willing to take the risk that his raw animal magnetism wouldn't overpower her good sense. And if it did, he knew martial arts and could defend himself…

Steven toweled off and pulled his clothes back on, trying to remember whether he'd put a T-shirt into his duffel when he'd packed it. That seemed like a month ago.

When he emerged from the bathroom, Natalie had removed the wig and was rummaging in her bag. He noted that, even after the long night she looked great, especially without the wig. She'd pulled her shirt off and was wearing only a tank top and jeans. His impression of her physique being a toned one was validated – she looked like a gymnast, but with important curves in the right places. Steven quickly shook off that line of thinking.

"My turn," she said, then slipped past him and shut the door.

Steven retrieved his T-shirt and hastily changed his underwear, then closed the heavy curtains and climbed into bed. The last thing he registered as he drifted off to sleep was the sound of the shower turning on. He was dead to the world almost before his head hit the pillow.

CHAPTER 24

A trilling jolted Steven awake. Natalie's cell phone was clamoring. As she stirred beside him and reached for it in the dark, he tried to make out the face of the bedside clock. Four-fifteen p.m.. A little under six hours of sleep, which he supposed was better than nothing. He listened as she had a brief conversation, then he felt the bed shift as she got up and moved to the table. The blackout curtains ensured the room was as dark as midnight.

"Shut your eyes," she called to him before flicking on the light. He groaned and rolled over, away from the table, but not before catching a glimpse of Natalie in her tank top and a pair of bright green boy shorts.

It was a good look.

She took a few notes, repeated: 'six o'clock' several times and then hung up. The light stayed on, much to his dismay, and she returned to the bed, this time sitting on it and facing him.

"All right, big boy, wakey wakeys. We've got a date with destiny to get into the catacombs at six. That means if we hurry, we have enough time to get something to eat and make it to our rendezvous," she said.

He peered at her, sitting cross-legged, reading her notes on the slip of paper.

"That was quick. Where are we supposed to meet him?" Steven asked.

"Another catacomb, somewhere near here. San Calisto. Apparently, it's a popular destination. Big tourist stop."

He nodded. "It's the largest catacomb in Rome. Famous, partially because of the Crypt of the Popes, where quite a few of the early popes were buried."

Natalie studied his face. "How do you know so much about it?"

"I did a three-day tour of Rome's sights and sounds five years ago, and that was one of the stops. On the Appian Way, not far from this hotel. I remember it because of the gift shop. At the time, I remembered thinking that it was hokey. For some reason that stuck with me."

"We have to get going. Don't want to miss our meet," Natalie said.

He closed his eyes. "You do this one without me. I'm going to sleep some more."

She swatted him with her pillow. "Come on. We're leaving in five minutes. I'll buy the late lunch. You're welcome."

Steven opened his eyes to the vision of Natalie walking over to where her jeans lay. An elaborate tattoo of a highly-stylized parrot adorned her right shoulder, which Steven found made her even more alluring as she paraded around wearing little more than a smile.

"You use the bathroom first. I'll only take a second," he said, not wanting to get out of bed with evidence of his interest prominent. She glanced at him, her eyes seeming to flit across the blanket, then wordlessly collected her jeans and wig and moved to the bathroom.

They had their late lunch in the hotel restaurant, which did nothing to improve the reputation of hotel food, and then waited patiently for a cab. When it screeched to the curb in front of the hotel, Steven shook his head. Even after over half a decade in Italy, he still hadn't gotten used to the driving ethos, which treated every moment behind the wheel as a competitive race.

The trip to the San Calisto catacombs took ten minutes, and soon they were standing near the dreaded gift shop, among swarms of tourists from all over the world. The crowds were thinning as the day drew to a close, but it was still unpleasant to be in the milling concentration. After a few minutes of anxious waiting, Danny materialized from the road and honked, waving from his window. They opened the rear door and climbed in.

There was no preamble. Danny eased the car onto the Appian Way and spoke to them over his shoulder.

"I got a telephone call from the police today. Someone at the church talked and, without admitting anything, pointed the finger at me. Your prints were on the car at the murder scene, and they now record them in immigration whenever you enter the country, so they have your names. They naturally were wondering what I knew about you. I told them you contacted me on a routine surveillance job and requested help with after-hour access to the basilica. Beyond that, I knew nothing about you, or why you wanted to get in. Maybe it was a kinky fetish thing. They seemed satisfied for now, but I think it would be wise if you left Rome as soon as possible."

"I'm sorry, Danny. I didn't mean to cause you any problems. We had no way of knowing that we were tailed or that murder was a possibility," Natalie soothed.

"Be that as it may, I'd make myself scarce. They asked for a description and I gave them as generic a rendition as possible. The truth is, I don't know anything about you. When they asked how you found me, I said through the phone book. I have an ad."

"But why are they spending so much time on us? Surely they don't think we killed Frederick?" Natalie asked.

"They said you were 'persons of interest'. My guess is that they've got nothing else, so they're focusing on the details they do have. If you'd taken the car instead of leaving it there, they'd have had zero. It's the prints that connected you. Otherwise you'd have just been a mystery couple I helped with a problem, who I know nothing about."

"All right. How much scrutiny can we expect?"

"I talked to a contact in the department and, right now, they've only circulated your names to the force, which will trigger a cursory hotel check for your names. If you don't turn up in a day or so, you can expect things to escalate, especially if they don't find any leads on the killer. They may be slow, but they aren't completely inept."

"Then for now, we're okay. But your advice to get out of Rome isn't bad," Natalie acknowledged.

They passed through fields surrounding small residential developments until they arrived at the gates of a vineyard surrounded by a seven-foot high brick wall, with an ancient, crumbling building at the far end of the property. A man in overalls waited for them at the gate and, seeing Danny, opened it a few feet. Danny parked in the driveway and turned to face Natalie and Steven.

"That's Umberto. He'll take you to the catacomb entrance. You'll have an hour to view it. Here's a flashlight…" He opened the glove compartment and checked it before handing it to Natalie. "He told me there are a few lights strung down there, but they haven't been used in nobody knows how long. They were installed as a temporary measure decades ago. Remember, it's a historical site, so no vandalism, right?"

"Fine. But how will we know the crypt we're looking for?" Steven asked.

Danny shrugged. "Beats me. Ask Umberto. He knows the layout as well as anyone. They're on his family's property. If he doesn't, you may find that this was all for nothing. There are a lot of passageways down there, from what I hear. Some of the catacombs go for many miles. Hopefully, you'll find your way in and out with no problem. It would be a shame to lose you…" Danny smiled. "Don't worry. Umberto says he hasn't locked anyone down there yet."

They got out of the car and shook hands with Umberto, a wiry man in his sixties with deeply tanned skin and dirty, graying hair. Steven and he exchanged greetings as they walked down the drive. Fortunately, Umberto knew the crypt they were interested in. He described the rough location and told them to look for the elaborate frescoes of birds and grapevines.

They approached the old building, in modest disrepair as so much of Rome was, and he led them through a brick corridor to an old iron door. He flourished a key ring and made a big display of unlocking the rusty deadbolt. The lights were already illuminated. He gestured to them to descend the rough stone stairs into the murky chambers below. Umberto reminded Steven that they had one hour, holding up a single finger for emphasis. Steven nodded, then led the way, Natalie following close behind.

The air had a leaden feel to it, smelled of dank earth. The corpses had long since been removed to cemeteries, and yet there was a lingering taint of death. Centuries of housing the bodies of the dead had left their indelible mark on the catacombs, and this one was no different.

They made their way carefully down the passageway that Umberto had directed them to, which was hewn from limestone and fortified in sections with ancient brickwork. Natalie edged closer to Steven as they moved past chamber after chamber, through a never-ending hall punctuated by tomb cavities with long forgotten inscriptions. Eventually, the art on the walls changed, as Umberto had told them it would. At the junction of the main passage, they came to a large crypt – if Umberto was right, that of Januarius. Most areas were elaborately painted with third-century scenes of vineyards and birds. Steven and Natalie had the same impression as they studied the art: where did they even start?

"I think it's safe to say this is it," Natalie whispered, taking in the marble and frescoes.

"Yes. But there's a lot of detail here, a lot of images. Let's work this in sections. You take the left side, I'll take the right, and we can double our progress. Use the flashlight – I've got the light in my phone. We're looking for something to do with olive pickers; maybe a carving or a picture," Steven reminded her.

Natalie took the light and began her investigation. They pored over the walls, searching for anything that might be consistent with the cryptic message from the Basilica of San Clemente. It was slow going, and some of the paintings had degraded to the point that they were unrecognizable. Steven was getting that sinking feeling in the pit of his stomach again – it seemed pointless to be playing detective six centuries after the clues had been created. He was amazed that they'd gotten this far, and to expect to progress any further was a kind of madness. Too much time had passed – there were too many variables; too much entropy at play.

After twenty minutes, Natalie called out, "I've found something."

"What is it?"

Steven was reluctant to leave his position, fearing that he'd lose track of what he'd already inspected, requiring him to start all over again.

"It's a painting of men picking something. Could be grapes, or…olives."

"Okay, I'll be there in a sec. Let me just mark where I am." Steven fished out his trusty piece of chalk and made a line on the floor before joining Natalie, who was shining the flashlight on several images. Birds perched upon ornately drawn vines, replete with authentic-looking flowers. At the bottom, several men were going about their business, which involved harvesting of some sort.

Steven peered at one in particular. "That's an olive picker, all right."

"How do you know?"

"The central figure? He's on a ladder. And you can just make out a tree – it's faded, but it's there. You wouldn't need a ladder for grapes – only for olives, which grow on–"

"Trees." Natalie finished the thought and smiled. "We found it! What was the rest of the message?"

"…three paces from the olive pickers points the traveler to the path, five hands above the trinacrium," Steven intoned.

"Three paces. That's fifteen feet, right?"

"Yes. Let me walk it off," Steven said, a hint of excitement in his voice. Maybe there was a chance, after all…

He took three long steps along the wall in one direction; he marked the floor, then reversed and took six, marking that spot as well.

"Five hands above the trinacrium," he murmured, studying the drawings.

He went over the first area carefully, but there was nothing of note. No labyrinth crest. Nothing. Moving to the far side, he stopped at the base of the wall. There was a new, more modern painting amongst the vines: a small depiction of an island, crudely painted, in the rough shape of a triangle. Sicily, the island where Saint Januarius had died. Steven examined the image more carefully.

He knew the Romans had associated Sicily with the classic symbol of Medusa's snake-topped head, three running men's legs sprouting equidistant from the rough circle of the mythical woman's face. That odd image was referred to by the Romans as the trinacrium. Even to this day, the symbol was part of the flag of Sicily, although absent Medusa's countenance.

The crude painting's presence on the wall would have had no meaning to anyone looking at it, or perhaps it would have seemed to be some untalented artist's homage to Januarius's place of death – had it not been for the basilica message. Certainly, had Steven been studying the crypt absent that information, it wouldn't have meant anything special. But now, armed with the cryptic clue, the island took on a new significance.

Five hands above the trinacrium.

Each hand was roughly four inches. Five hands, twenty inches. Steven slid his fingers along the ancient wall, and sure enough, there was a subtle change in the texture of the surface, where the plaster had worn off and been repaired. Steven suspected that there was considerably more to it than that. He knocked on it with his knuckles and confirmed it was hollow. Natalie moved to where he was studying the spot and extracted her screwdriver and Dremel.

"Are you thinking what I'm thinking?" she asked.

"Seems like they enjoyed hiding things in walls back in the fifteenth century," Steven observed.

Natalie rapped on the area in question with the screwdriver blade. A few chunks of plaster flew off. Five hundred years of dampness had rendered it crumbly. She hacked at the spot with the screwdriver and then fired up the little battery-powered jeweler's drill, grinding through the plaster and mortar behind it with relative ease.

After ten minutes, she'd excavated a spot eighteen inches wide by six high. Dust caked her arms and top. As she stepped back and brushed herself off, Steven wiped away the worst of the debris in the hole and peered into the opening.

"There's something in there, but it's not a parchment. Do me a favor and hold the flashlight for me, and I'll see if I can get it out," Steven said.

"What is it?" Natalie asked.

"I don't know. Hard to tell with all the dust. Give me a second," he said, handing her the light. She shone it into the aperture, and Steven tentatively reached inside.

He jerked his arm back with a shudder as a large black spider scuttled up his bare arm. Natalie swatted it away and stepped on it while Steven worked to bring his racing pulse back to something approaching normal. They exchanged a look.

"Do *you* want to get it out?" Steven asked, only half joking.

"You're the expert. Besides, I'm not a big spider fan," she said.

"Thanks for knocking that one off me. I think it was some kind of tarantula. That could have ruined my day," Steven observed.

"I was just trying to save myself from having to carry you out of here. You looked about ready to faint."

Steven steadied himself. The adrenaline response from the arachnid racing up his arm had his hands shaking a little. He took several deep breaths. "Mind handing me the screwdriver?"

Natalie complied, and he carefully slid it along the edge of whatever was lying in the hidden recess. It shifted a little, and he wedged the entire blade under it and pried it up. The distinctive sound of metal-on-metal grated. After reassuring himself that there were no more spiders – deadly or otherwise – he reached in and grabbed the hidden item. It was heavier than he was expecting. He slid it out and found himself holding a burnished metal plaque covered with dust. Steven noisily blew it off, creating a small cloud and causing both of them to cough.

"What is it? What does it say?" she asked.

He studied it. "If I'm reading this right, it's the key to deciphering the Scroll. Look – see the symbols? It's a substitution cypher, but it looks like it takes two glyphs to compose one traditional letter – and even then, the glyphs before and after change the letter." He wiped at it with his hand. It was a deep brown color, with the letters and glyphs etched into the metal by hand. “It’s a brass alloy. That’s why it didn’t degrade other than the surface patina, and why it’s so heavy. Someone went to a lot of trouble to create a record that wouldn’t be lost to time,” he said, hefting the plate.

Natalie shifted closer to look at it. “It’s got etching on both sides,” she noted.

Steven turned it over and examined the lettering with interest. Here, finally, was the solution to the code that had stumped cryptologists for centuries. And now he would get the honor of being the first man in history to decrypt not only the Voynich, but also the Holy Scroll.

Then the lights went off.

CHAPTER 25

Steven froze, ears straining for any hint of threat. The catacomb was impenetrably dark. Even after thirty seconds of standing motionless his eyes didn't adjust. He could hear his heart beating in his ears like kettle drums, and when Natalie shifted her feet the sound seemed to be amplified fifty-fold. Steven slowly slipped the brass tablet into the back of his pants so his hands would be free for whatever was happening. He felt Natalie edge closer and do something, and then heard the distinctive snick of the pistol as she chambered a round. Then a pale wash of illumination lit their area with the flick of the flashlight switch. Steven gestured for her to turn it back off – if there was a threat, there was no point in hanging a neon light out for an assailant to find.

A sound echoed in the far distance; a muffled thud that barely reached them. Then, just as suddenly as the lights had gone off, they flickered back on. Steven held a finger to his lips so that Natalie wouldn't speak, and then, quietly as he could, moved to the entrance of Januarius's crypt. She followed, gun at the ready. Once they were free of the tomb, they stopped again, listening for any evidence of company. Silence was their sole companion in the halls of the dead.

Natalie slid past Steven to take the lead, weapon clasped in one hand before her, the flashlight in the other at its side, ready to flick on should the lights fail again. She moved gracefully, sure of her steps and yet soundless. They were still several hundred yards from where Umberto had opened the door for them.

Natalie held up a hand and signaled for Steven to stop. A scrape sounded from far down the passageway. Another noise echoed, this time closer.

Someone was approaching. Natalie motioned to Steven to move into one of the cavities along the way and slid herself into a depression across the passage from him. They both held their breath as footsteps moved along the stone floor, approaching their hiding place.

When Umberto shuffled into view, Steven nodded his head in warning, and Natalie quickly slid the pistol back into her purse. Steven cleared his throat, and Umberto almost fainted.

"What the hell are you trying to do? Scare me to death?" he demanded, hand clenched to his chest.

"I'm sorry. No, we were spooked by the lights going off. My young companion got frightened. What happened?" Steven countered. Natalie shot him an annoyed look at his using her youth as the reason for their fright.

"I was fiddling with the wiring, where it's coming apart from age, and I guess I tripped something. But I got it sorted out in a few minutes. I apologize for that. Anyhow, your time's up, so we need to get going, *eh*?" Umberto tapped on his watch crystal with a dirty nail.

Steven nodded.

"The tombs are fascinating, Umberto," Natalie said. "Really. They seem to go on forever. Have you ever cataloged everything in here?" she asked, turning a beaming charm on as she pressed close to the man.

"Yes, well, they are interesting, *no*? I haven't spent much time down here in forever. As a younger man, yes, and there are still more tunnels below us, but now I have things up in the real world to attend to. These are just a curiosity for me at this point in my life. I keep watch over the entrance to make sure no vandals get in and collect a meager salary from the state for doing so, but other than that and the occasional exploration by a few interested academics, nobody has been down here for years."

"We can't thank you enough. It's always been my fiancé's dream to visit, and now you've helped make that a reality," she said.

Umberto grinned. "You're a lucky man, *eh*, my friend?" he said to Steven.

"So I've been told." Steven smiled back in as neutral a manner as he could muster.

When they reached the top of the stairs it was dusk, getting darker by the second. Steven gave Umberto two hundred dollars as a symbol of his additional gratitude, which made the old man happy. Whatever Danny had paid, and he was sure they'd be getting the bill soon enough, it was worth it. The cool metal of the tablet rubbed against his back, covered by his shirt, as they ambled unhurriedly down the path, Umberto's eyes boring holes in Natalie's jeans.

"You think he heard anything, with the drilling?" she murmured to Steven as they approached the gate.

"Nah. He was more interested in you than in anything we were doing in the crypt," Steven said.

"Old pervert," she said, her tone good-natured.

"You seem to be surrounded by them," Steven said, regretting the joke even as he uttered the final words.

"Occupational hazard for a woman in Italy, it seems," she fired back.

Steven cast a glance over his shoulder, noting that Umberto had disappeared back into the building's gloom. They moved up the long drive, and Steven slowed his pace as they neared the road, then gripped Natalie's arm to stop her. He didn't know what it was, but he had a bad feeling. It could have been nerves from the scare in the catacombs, but he didn't want to take any chances. And his senses were telling him that something was wrong.

"Let's circle to the edge of the property and check out the road from there," he whispered.

Natalie's eyes flashed understanding, and she extracted the pistol from her purse as they moved down one of the long rows of vines. Several hundred yards further they came to a side wall delineating the periphery of the property, and Steven motioned for Natalie to approach. She did, and he boosted her foot so she could climb over to the neighboring property. Steven jumped and scrambled over the wall, to find himself in another massive field of vines and olive trees. The frontage was another brick wall running parallel to the road, the same as the catacomb. They moved to a gap in the wall and peered out.

It was already so dark that it was hard to make anything out. Steven pointed a hundred yards away, to where they'd entered the catacomb vineyard. Instead of Danny's car, a van was parked twenty feet from the gate with two men standing beside it. Both had the distinctive shapes of pistols in their hands.

"Let's keep moving," Natalie advised. "This field's huge. If we go to the far edge and climb over the wall there, they won't see us. The bend in the road should provide cover. We'll be out of their field of vision."

Steven nodded agreement.

They walked for five minutes before reaching another, smaller service gate. Natalie looked through the bars and confirmed that they were clear, so

Steven repeated the process of boosting her over the wall before following her. They found themselves on a road darkened to the point where it was barely recognizable, the tall trees that lined it further blocking the dim light from the low crescent moon. Natalie took her cell phone from her purse and called Danny's number, but it went straight to voice mail.

"He's not answering," Natalie complained.

"I think it's safe to say that he either turned us in or they got him. Either way, we have to assume he's a hostile now." Steven checked the time. "It's seven-twenty. We're maybe a mile from the hotel. I suggest we hoof it, given the welcome committee at the other gate."

"It's a nice evening for a walk," Natalie observed as she set off across the road to one of two intersecting streets.

A car sped by them after they'd crossed. A police cruiser, which slowed down as it passed and then stopped. The brake lights flashed, and then it reversed to where they were walking. Natalie reached into her purse, but Steven stopped her.

Two officers were in the car, and one rolled his window down and addressed Steven.

"Pretty dark out for a walk, *no*?" he said.

Steven nodded. "We're just out exploring, and the night rushed in on us."

"Where are you headed?"

"To our hotel. It's a nice evening for it," Steven explained.

The cop looked Natalie over, then grunted. "Have a good one," he said, and then they pulled off down the road.

Steven and Natalie let out audible exhalations and exchanged worried glances. They needed to make tracks and get out of the area.

After walking several hundred yards up a smaller street, they set off in the direction of the hotel. It took twenty-five minutes to make it, and the first thing Steven did once they were in their room was to carefully clean off the brass tablet. While Natalie watched him, he painstakingly photographed both sides so they'd have a record if they had to ditch it somewhere.

Natalie's phone rang, startling them both. She checked the number and answered.

"Moody. Am I glad to hear from you," she said.

"You sound odd, Natalie. What's going on?" Moody asked.

Natalie explained about their missed rendezvous with Danny, the two mystery men, and the situation with the Roman police.

"Sounds like it's time to leave Rome. Let me see what we have in the way of safe houses elsewhere in Italy and figure out how to get you some transportation. I'm staying at the St. Regis downtown. I'll get on the horn and call you ba– wait a second. Natalie. Did Danny have your cell number?" Moody asked.

"Yes. We needed a way to stay in touch. I called him a little while ago but he didn't answer."

"Listen to me carefully. Get the numbers you need off your phone and dump it. Immediately. Call my hotel in four hours from a pay phone. I'm checked in under the name Stan Gardener. I'll get you a new, clean cell. The Italian equivalent of the NSA has the ability to track cells to within a few feet, and we don't know what kind of strings the group that's after you can pull. Let's assume they've got Danny and will have your number shortly, if they don't already. That's a very real danger. What about this guy you're with? Does he have one?" Moody asked.

"Yes, but he hasn't called anyone."

"Same drill. Pull the contacts and lose it in a river. But treat this as a serious threat. Do it now. I'll talk to you in four hours."

Natalie explained about the phones after she'd finished the call.

"Shit. I know this stuff, Natalie. I'm just rusty. He's right; we have to get rid of them immediately. I'll send the photos to my PC, and then we'll ditch the phones. We should probably check out of this hotel, too, just in case they start looking for places that are proximate to the catacombs."

Natalie nodded and immediately set about packing her bag. She was done in two minutes. It took Steven a little longer while he sent the image files from his phone. Finished, he placed the plate into his duffel.

"Let's get a cab. Any ideas?" Steven asked.

"I think we should grab dinner while we wait for Moody. I've heard dinner in Rome can take three hours, so let's get near the St. Regis and find a place where we can blend in."

"You're on."

They made their way down the stairs to the rear section of the hotel near the pool, where, after dunking them in the water, they disassembled the phones and jettisoned them in a dumpster by the hotel restaurant.

It took them thirty minutes to make it the few miles in the evening traffic, and when they got near the St. Regis, it turned out to be three blocks from their favorite train station. The driver pulled to the curb in front of a building with an elaborate façade. They paid him and exited, waiting until he'd pulled back into traffic before walking down the block to find a restaurant.

ঌ∽ও

Danny's head hung against his chest as blood drooled from his badly mangled face onto his shirt front. He struggled for breath, his lungs laboring to get air, each inhalation causing a white-hot lance of pain due to broken ribs. His hands were bound behind his back; he'd long since given up trying to free them.

He was going to die. That much he already knew. Everyone did eventually, but Danny never imagined it would be in this manner, over something he had no real part in. A small piece of his brain told him this wasn't possible; it had to be some kind of horrible mistake – but the intensity of pain reminded him it was real. The big man had subjected him to far worse than he'd ever dreamed he could live through, and he had no hope left that he'd walk away.

Sia Amieri stepped towards him and slapped his face several times, bringing him back to full consciousness. Danny looked up, his eyes swollen nearly shut from the beating.

Amieri sneered. "I can make this last all night if you want. Again. The girl. Where is she staying? The phone number doesn't answer. No more lies. How do you get in touch with her?" he demanded.

Danny didn't know what he needed to say to make the agony end. He shook his head weakly.

Amieri slapped him. "I'm tiring of this. You gave me a number that's no good. You told me stories. I sent two men to the place you said they would be and nobody showed. That, and there's no catacomb anywhere – there's no building or entrance where you said you dropped them off, just a private vineyard. My patience for your lies is at an end. Tell me where you are supposed to meet them, or so help me God you'll wish you'd never been born." Amieri watched the bloody froth bubble from Danny's nose, noting the light pink color. A rib must have punctured a lung. The man wasn't going to take much more. "Tell me what I want to know, and I'll get you to a hospital. I'll drop you at the emergency room, and you'll live. You'll see another birthday, or maybe another anniversary with your wife?" Amieri glanced at the wedding band. "Or your mistress?"

Danny wanted to tell him. He wanted to tell him more than anything. But there was nothing to tell, beyond what he'd already said. Danny had admitted that he'd been given the girl's contact information by his CIA handler, whom he knew only as David, and had run the errands for her as instructed. He'd even given up the location of the safe house, but nothing seemed to satisfy his torturer.

Amieri slammed him in the head again with a bear-like hand, rupturing his eardrum and causing blinding pain, then he moved away from Danny with a look of disgust. He fished a cell phone out of his pants pocket and made a call.

Morbius Frank answered with a barrage of questions. Amieri struggled to answer them.

"No, there's nothing new on the girl. The investigator insists he's told us everything. I passed her phone number on to the contact you gave me, and he should have a fix on the location any minute. But beyond that, I dispatched two men to the supposed rendezvous spot and there's nothing there but dark vines and an old gate. No girl." Amieri hesitated before telling Dr. Frank the worst news. "He says he got the girl's contact information from a CIA operative. Known only as David."

Frank digested the revelation. CIA changed everything, increasing the danger level as well as the possible resources the professor's daughter had at her disposal.

"CIA? Hmm. Not completely surprising, given what we now know about her background. We must proceed carefully. Finish this and dispose of the body so it won't be found for a few days. And call me as soon as you have news. This isn't going well, my son. You must be faster, yet more cautious. New players on the board are not a good thing for us. We cannot afford to lose this game. Am I completely clear?"

"Yes, sir. I will do as instructed. Hopefully the contact with the police will get a location on the phone, or Cross will contact his office. I won't fail you."

"Carry on, then."

Amieri stabbed the phone off and walked over to a makeshift table in the corner, where he reached for a five-foot length of braided yellow nylon rope. He looped a knot in it and then wrapped it several times around each hand. Amieri pulled it taut as he stepped back to the investigator, who was fading in and out of reality.

"You've been granted an end to your ordeal, my friend," he said from behind Danny and then quickly flipped the rope over his head and wrenched the knot into his esophagus, crushing it instantly. Danny's body stiffened and convulsed for thirty seconds before it slumped inert, life having given up its futile battle for a few more seconds' reprieve.

Amieri walked around the chair and regarded the dead man's face with marginal interest. Satisfied by the beginning of cyanosis tingeing the corpse's lips, he flipped the rope into a corner. He exhaled loudly, having held his breath while close to the dead man, who'd lost control of his bodily functions over the course of their discussion. With any luck it would be a week before anyone came across the investigator's remains.

In the end, the man hadn't known much. A pity.

His phone rang. It was Frank's contact with the Roman police, who was running a trace on the girl's phone. He jotted down the name and address and grunted before hanging up. It was amazing what they could do with technology.

Time to pay a visit to their hotel.

CHAPTER 26

"Moody. Give me some good news." Natalie cut to the chase in typical fashion, the pay phone held against her ear.

"We need to meet, but not at the hotel. I haven't been able to get hold of Danny, so I'm assuming the worst. Are you nearby?" Moody asked.

"Yes. Pick a spot and tell me when. We'll be there," Natalie said.

"The Arch of Constantine, by the Coliseum. Twenty minutes?"

"See you then."

It was just after midnight when they arrived, but there were still groups of tourists taking photos in front of the famous illuminated marble arch, memorializing for posterity that they had been there, in the shadow of greatness. Steven shifted his bag from his left shoulder to his right and tried not to check his watch every two minutes. After what seemed like an eternity, Natalie nudged him with her elbow. A tall, ruggedly handsome man with closely-cropped silver hair moved cautiously towards them, his shoulders squared with a military bearing. Natalie gave him a big hug, which he accepted with a slightly embarrassed look, and then turned his attention to Steven. Steven extended his hand.

"You must be Moody. I'm Steven."

"A pleasure. Mind if we walk while we chat?" Moody said, clearly not asking.

"Love to," Steven responded.

Natalie hefted her bag, and Moody took it from her, lifting it with ease. They strolled unhurriedly away from the Coliseum, its ancient presence hulking in the background. Moody reached into his jacket pocket and handed Natalie two phones.

"Merry Christmas. Those are clean," Moody assured them. "I did some checking. The police interest in you is increasing, and I don't think I'd wait for it to escalate. We have a safe house in Mestre, just across the lagoon from Venice, I can make available until things cool down. There's no countrywide alert, and nothing's gone to Interpol yet, but there's no telling how this plays over the next few days. Now, would you mind telling me exactly what you're into here, so I can get a better handle on it?"

Natalie glanced at Steven and then gave Moody a summary, omitting only that they were close to solving the puzzle of the Voynich. Steven and Natalie had discussed how much disclosure to make, and they'd agreed that if Steven had a positive reaction to him, they'd give Moody all the data. The jury was still out, so Natalie kept to their agreement.

"Hmm. A centuries old secret sect of the Catholic Church is after you because of a document your father came into possession of, through questionable means, the 'liberation' of which was financed by a billionaire who will stop at nothing to beat them to the punch. Is that about right?" Moody asked dryly.

Natalie frowned. "Put that way, it sounds crazy, but let's not forget someone killed Frederick, and Danny's gone missing – and there were a couple of goons waiting for us this evening. Plus, we were followed in Florence and only got away because Steven took one of the pursuers out," Natalie reminded him.

Moody studied Steven's profile as they continued their walk.

"You're quite resourceful. What's your background?" Moody asked Steven.

"I'm an entrepreneur and amateur cryptologist. But I've been doing martial arts for years, so I'm pretty handy when it comes to close quarter self-defense."

"I'll say. Any military service?"

"A few years. Wasn't for me," Steven said, wanting to end the inquiry there.

"What do you make of this situation?" Moody pressed.

Steven stopped and turned to him. "I thought Natalie was nuts when she first came to me. Then I had a chance to look over the parchment, and it was as she described. Before long, we were being chased. That's more data in her favor. But seeing Frederick stabbed to death outside of the church was the clincher. We've stumbled onto something very important to the groups Natalie is convinced are involved, and they'll do anything to recover their treasure and protect their secret. Whether or not it's worth killing for doesn't matter if they believe it is," Steven said.

Moody nodded slowly. "I've known her for a while, and I trust Natalie's instinct on this." Moody turned to her. "Get out of Rome now. You'll be safe in Mestre, and if you need to travel, you've got plenty of choices. Between Venice and Milan, there are flights anywhere in the world. I'd say, drive to Mestre before the cops start paying real attention, and we'll figure it out from there. Make sense?"

"Perfect sense, as always," Natalie said deferentially. "Might be easier if we had a car, though."

Moody handed her an envelope. "Inside are directions and an address for the house, a key, and the valet stub for a black Alfa Romeo at my hotel. Wait half an hour before picking it up. It's got a full tank of gas, and all the paperwork's in the glove compartment. Registered to a corporation in Genoa." He cleared his throat. "I'm going to stick around Rome for a day or two and see if I can figure out what happened to Danny. Then I'll meet up with you in Venice. I'll call before I show up on the doorstep. If you drive fairly fast, you should be able to make it in seven hours."

"Thank you so much, Moody. You're a lifesaver," Natalie said.

"You'd do the same for me, so no sweat." He looked morose. "I hope you're wrong about what you're up against. Last time I checked, the Church swings a lot of weight, especially in Italy. Although I find it hard to believe they'd resort to murder..."

"That was probably Frank's people. I have no doubt he killed my father. He's got a reputation as a ruthless and mercurial businessman. Towards the end, my father wanted less and less to do with him," Natalie explained.

"No point in belaboring it. I'll see what I can find out. You two drive safely, and we can touch base once you're at the safe house," Moody said, glancing around casually to ensure they weren't under surveillance. He handed her back her bag.

"Nice meeting you," Steven said, trying for enthusiasm.

"Likewise. Hang out here for a few minutes, playing tourist. I'm headed to the hotel."

With that, Moody forked off onto a path leading back to the Coliseum and blended quickly with the foot traffic. Natalie slid the envelope into her purse.

"What's your problem with Moody? Or do you just ordinarily suck at meeting new people?" Natalie asked.

Steven was taken aback. Was it that obvious? He framed two or three defenses in his mind.

"Sometimes it takes me a while to warm up to people," he said simply.

"You better accelerate the process. If you didn't notice, he just saved both our asses."

"Without putting too fine a point on it, mine wouldn't need saving if you hadn't gotten me involved," Steven fired back.

Natalie stopped walking. "I suppose you think Frank would have just invited you for tea when he found you? Do you still not get this? It's nobody's fault. Sometimes things happen. This just happened to you. You can either mope about it and alienate my closest allies, or get your shit together, knock off the dick thing, and play nice," Natalie warned.

"The dick thing?" Steven repeated.

"Two males in the same sandbox, threatened and unsure of each other. We don't have time for this. If you don't mind, lose it."

Steven had no snappy rejoinder to that. Natalie was right. Worse, his dislike for Moody stemmed from the idea that maybe in the past he'd been intimate with Natalie. Which was juvenile bullshit. It wasn't as if Steven was dating her. True, he thought she was hot, and smart, and very, very sexy. But lust wasn't the same as having a claim. Her point was completely valid – it was time to knock off the attitude.

"You're right. I'm sorry."

Natalie resumed walking. "Wow. He admits when he's made a mistake. There may be hope for you yet," she said and picked up the pace, leaving Steven to play catch up.

They killed time ambling around the arch and down several of the boulevards, and after the agreed-upon half hour Steven dutifully presented the valet stub to the attendant at the St. Regis. They'd agreed he would collect the car and then pick her up a block away, on the off-chance anything unexpected occurred during the process. Thankfully, there was no drama, and after paying the equivalent of thirty dollars in parking fees and tip, he was ensconced behind the wheel of the small sedan, wheeling his way to Natalie. He pulled to the curb to a symphony of horns behind him, and she quickly slung her bag into the rear and climbed into the passenger seat. Moody had been thoughtful enough to include a road map of Italy in the glove compartment, and after a few minutes of battling their way out of downtown Rome, they were on the freeway to Mestre, the lights of the capital receding in the rearview mirror as they sped to their next hiding place.

Steven was anxious to decrypt the Scroll, but knew that it was more important to get them out of harm's way. Besides, it wasn't the kind of project he could do in a moving car with dim lighting. He needed a controlled environment to first absorb all the glyph combinations and decode the Scroll, and then make sense out of whatever it said. He was under no illusions that it would be a finger snap, but a part of him had the familiar buzz of excitement he felt when he was getting close to solving a puzzle. Whatever the Scroll was hiding, soon he would be one of the few people in the world to have ever known it.

He wondered silently what terrible secret could have been worth spending centuries to protect. In the end, it was useless to speculate.

Glancing at the dashboard clock, he calculated that if they were lucky they'd make Mestre by nine a.m..

CHAPTER 27

The teenage couple swigged the last of the bottle of Lambrusco, the boy anxious to get to the night's main event, the girl also excited, but more interested for the moment in having a cigarette. The boy had a better idea. He'd gotten his hands on a small wedge of greenish-black opiated hashish from Afghanistan, reputed to be an incredible high by the dealer he'd bought it from.

The two sat on the stairs of the dark building while he carefully broke off a chunk the size of a pencil eraser. The girl watched with interest as he pulled out a pouch of tobacco and some papers, and then made a hand-rolled cigarette with the sticky resin liberally crumbled into the tobacco. He closed up the tin foil packet, sealing the remaining drug, and slid it into his sweatshirt pocket, pausing before lighting it to sniff the creation.

He held it out to Theresa, tonight's hoped-for conquest, who had just turned fifteen and was bursting with youthful experimentation.

"This is great shit. You can smell it. See?" the boy, Luciano, said.

Theresa sniffed it with approval. "Wow. You're right. It smells awesome," she said, not quite sure what it was she was supposed to be appreciating, but game for anything after the better part of a bottle of cheap sparkling wine. Luciano was really cute, with a devil-may-care attitude that had half the girls in school pining for him. At this point, he could have held out a piece of rat poop and she would have expressed enthusiasm. She giggled inwardly at the thought and gave him a beaming smile.

They lit the joint and took deep hits, holding in the smoke for as long as they could before noisily exhaling. At first they didn't feel anything other than the rush from the nicotine as their blood vessels constricted, but after a few minutes, a euphoric tingle of relaxation flooded their senses. By the time they'd finished their smoke, both felt wonderful.

Luciano leaned into Theresa and kissed her, eyes closed as he savored her taste. She responded with ardor, and before long he had his hand up her shirt as she moaned encouragement. Luciano disengaged and, looking around, motioned to the interior of the old building. He stood, his passion unmistakable through his jeans, and held out his hand. Theresa took it, and he pulled her to her feet before leading her into the dark space.

They kissed again once they'd moved into the entrance a few yards, away from prying eyes, and it was only after a few seconds they registered the flies, which were buzzing in an audible swarm from the depths of the building. Theresa recoiled instinctively from the insects, and Luciano hesitated for a moment before fishing in his pants for his lighter.

Theresa's scream echoed through the quiet area, reverberating off the walls of the nearby residences. A light went on in one of the windows after she screamed again.

Fifteen minutes later, two police cars stood in front of the abandoned machine shop, their lights illuminating the curb as they took statements from the two frightened teens while waiting for the forensics van to arrive. One of the officers logged the time – midnight – while another wrapped the entry with bright yellow tape in a gesture to keep the non-existent crowds from entering the area.

A television van screeched to a stop, the driver having picked up the call from a police scanner he constantly monitored so as to be first at any scene.

Contrary to Amieri's best laid plans, Danny would be front page news the following morning.

❧

The orange rays of dawn were breaking across the Roman skyline when Colonel Gabriel Synthe received a hasty call from his police contact. He listened intently and, after hanging up, mulled over the ramifications of what he'd just been told. He'd need to call Luca and update him on the latest events, much as it irritated him. The only joy was had in knowing he would likely wake the man up. To his dismay, Luca answered within seconds and sounded alert.

"What do you have for me?" he asked perfunctorily, not bothering with any niceties.

"The investigator who arranged for the girl and Cross to get into the basilica was found dead last night. Tortured and strangled," Synthe reported.

"Good heavens. That's two dead in as many days. This can't continue…" Luca exclaimed.

"Nobody's happy about it. The police are increasing the status of the alert for the pair. That's going to make it increasingly hard for us to intervene before they're taken into custody." Synthe reminded Luca of the obvious. "Or until whoever is doing the killing locates them. Either way, this is bad."

Luca took a few moments to digest this latest news.

"Do we have any evidence that the girl or Cross are doing anything but running from a threat?" Luca asked.

"It's safe to assume they're trying to solve the mystery of the Scroll. Why else would they have come to Rome and done a night visit at the basilica?" Synthe reasoned.

"I tend to agree, but the security footage was inconclusive. They're captured by a camera as they enter the basilica, and then as they descend to the middle level, but there are some holes in the camera positions there, and between the gaps we lose them for about fifteen minutes. We don't know what they were up to during that time."

"You've had someone go in and look around?" Synthe asked.

"Of course. I had three men go in the following morning, and they found nothing amiss. But it's a big hall, and without knowing what the girl was looking for, it's impossible to speculate whether she found it or not. By the time my men got over there and looked at the footage, the church was open and crowds were moving through, as were the custodians. We do know that the art was intact – the curators helped to inspect it all, and nothing was touched that they can see. So we're no further along than before, other than knowing that two people in direct contact with the girl were murdered."

"As troubling as that may be, our first priority is still the Scroll," Synthe reminded Luca. The Sentinel had spent half an hour with Synthe for an in-person progress report the prior afternoon, and he'd underscored that he was very disappointed that Synthe hadn't been able to put the matter to rest.

"Yes. But it could be that we're going about this the wrong way. The girl and Cross must know their driver was killed, so they're undoubtedly terrified of everyone and everything. As far as we can tell, the girl doesn't know much about the Scroll, so she may have gone to Cross, not out of a desire to learn its secrets for the sake of the knowledge, but rather as a way to discover what happened to her father, or perhaps to carry out his final work. We just don't have enough information." Luca paused. "I'm thinking about trying a different approach."

What the hell? "That sounds like an extremely bad idea." The last thing Synthe needed was Luca going operational. That could be disastrous.

"Your opinion is noted. But what we're doing right now isn't working, is it? Did I miss something in all of this where we're getting closer to finding the Scroll? Seems to me that it's working exactly the opposite, and we've now lost track of the pair, have no idea what they're doing, and are in danger of losing them, and presumably the Scroll, to a hostile unknown group that kills without hesitation."

Synthe had no facile counter to that. All he could do was restate his position.

"You getting involved is a poor call. You're not experienced with field work, and it will only complicate matters."

"Again. I understand, but with all due respect, matters are already complicated. And not to put too fine a point on it, but it wasn't my job to ensure the Scroll was safe. It was under your 'professional' watch that this disaster happened, and I see no evidence of it improving, having done things your way for the last few days. Whether you like it or not, I am already a part of *this scenario*, as your ilk like to call it, so I don't see what harm I can do that hasn't already been done." Luca's voice had taken on an edge.

Synthe was experienced enough to sense that nothing he said would alter Luca's intent now that he'd dug in. If the idiot wanted to get himself killed, it was better to just step out of the way and let events unfold of their own momentum.

"I will have no alternative but to register my reservations with my superior, then," Synthe fired as a parting shot. Perhaps alluding to the Sentinel would give Luca pause.

"Do what you have to do. I'll advise my superior to expect his call. I will keep you posted of any progress. I expect you to do the same," Luca said and slammed down the phone.

Luca considered his next step. All the subterfuge had gotten them nothing. He didn't see what they had to lose by being more direct. Luca had a feeling that this was the right step, once he put himself into the fugitive pair's shoes. They might be receptive to talking to someone who could make the whole problem just go away.

It was worth a try.

❧

Natalie and Steven took turns driving to Mestre. A little after nine a.m., they pulled into the garage on the lower floor of a small house on the outskirts of the city. A suburb of Venice, Mestre was one of the primary living areas for the workers who kept the tourist machine that was the historical city of Venice running. It was perfect to get lost in – near a massive international destination, and yet completely off the radar. After they had pulled into the single space garage and closed the door with the remote control, they both exhaled a sigh of exhausted relief. Natalie had been quiet for the last few hours, and Steven couldn't get a read on what was going on in her head. He figured she was just beat, as was he.

The house was a two bedroom, two story brick contrivance where the entire living area was on the second story with parking and storage below and was outfitted with modest but comfortable furnishings. Steven carried the bags upstairs to the living room and set them down on the hardwood floor while Natalie explored the kitchen. She exclaimed with delight when she opened the refrigerator, which was stocked with food and beverages, and gratefully opened a container of orange juice and poured them both a glass.

"Home sweet home," Steven said, walking into the kitchen after locking the deadbolts on the door.

"It's not the Ritz, but I don't think I've ever been happier to arrive someplace."

Steven picked up his orange juice and went to the rear of the house to explore the two bedrooms, which were small but adequate. The bathroom was also typical of a home of the size and era; the entire upstairs was around twelve hundred square feet of living space.

When he returned, Natalie was munching on some crackers she'd found in the pantry.

"So what do you think?" she asked.

"It's fine. I vote we get some sleep, and then I'll start on decrypting the Scroll. Shouldn't take all that long, but never say never. I've seen enough to know that it's what you don't see coming that takes your head off," Steven said, finishing his juice and yawning. "I'm going to take a shower and hit the sack. Pick whatever room you want – they're both about the same. I have no preference."

"Then neither do I. Only one bathroom, I guess?"

"You got it. Let's hope the plumbing works reasonably well. My place in Florence was a nightmare," Steven said.

He hefted his bag and threw it on the bed in the first bedroom, quickly hanging his shirts in the wall closet before carrying his shaving kit into the bathroom and closing the door. A pair of thick towels hung from hooks above a small linen cupboard that housed necessities like soap, washcloths and shampoo.

Steven stripped down and turned on the shower, waiting for a few minutes until the hot water made its way up from the downstairs heater and the temperature stabilized. He unwrapped a bar of soap and stepped under the stream, luxuriating in the warmth after spending almost eight hours cramped in car seats. As he washed the shampoo out of his hair, a gust of cool air blew through the small room, stirring the cloud of steam that had formed. He rinsed the suds off his face and out of his eyes and pulled back the shower curtain, to be greeted by the amazing sight of Natalie, naked, standing in her bare feet on the bathmat he'd placed on the floor. For a moment he thought he was hallucinating, and then her lips locked on his, her tongue probing with an urgency that was electrifying in its intensity. After what seemed like an eternity of this essential contact, his arousal was pressing against her belly. She gripped him with a wet hand, stroking him as she stared into his eyes.

"I don't want to sleep in the other bedroom," she said.

Steven turned his head towards Natalie, who was resting easily beside him on the damp bed, partially soaked from their abrupt departure from the shower. Those amazing violet eyes pierced his defenses, and he smiled as he caressed her still-wet hair.

She cleared her throat, and Steven let her speak.

"I've been wanting to do that since the church, but it never seemed like the right time. This probably wasn't either, but you don't always get to pick the perfect moment, right?" she started.

Steven smiled. "That was perfect as far as I'm concerned."

"I thought we should get it out of the way while we have some time alone. I hope you're okay with me taking my lustful urges out on you," Natalie said, returning his smile.

"I'm not easy, under normal circumstances. But these are anything but normal circumstances…"

"I like the way you think. Now do you want to finish the shower, or is there anything else I can interest you in?" she asked innocently.

He gazed at her perfectly-formed breasts, the hint of invitation obvious in her huskily-whispered question, and his body made the decision for them.

Eventually, spent, they returned to the bathroom together and cleaned each other, Steven marveling at how magnificently toned she was as he caressed her with soap suds. Finally, exhausted, they made their way to the unused bedroom, falling asleep in an embrace that suggested they'd been sleeping together like that forever. His last thought as he drifted into the soothing balm of sleep was that Natalie was incredible, and that maybe everything really did happen for a reason.

CHAPTER 28

When they came to, Steven woke first and watched as Natalie's nostrils flared almost imperceptibly each time she inhaled. She smelled like some sort of exotic aphrodisiac, and it was only with considerable restraint that he kept from rousing her in an amorous manner. He studied the contour of her shoulder and considered what had happened. The dam had broken, and almost three years of self-imposed drought had come to an abrupt and memorable end with a woman he knew little about and had known for less than a week. It was amazing, physically, but he didn't know what to make of it on an emotional level. He'd occupied his time with work and trivial pursuits since his wife had died, and he hadn't been much interested in any overtures he'd received, nor had any appetite for the hunt. Then Natalie had blown into his life and upended his comfortable existence on every possible level.

He shifted and reached over to the nightstand for his wristwatch. It was four thirty-five p.m.. He realized he was starving just as Natalie's eyes fluttered and opened, fixing him with her intense gaze.

"Good morning. Or more appropriately, good afternoon," he greeted.

She didn't say anything, preferring to shut her eyes and snuggle against his chest. Her hand drifted down from his pectoral muscle and lazed along his stomach before brushing the sheets. Without opening her eyes, she slid a leg over his waist and straddled him, and all thoughts of anything but Natalie evaporated, along with his doubts.

❧

Forty minutes later, Natalie opened her eyes again, and this time, spoke.

"I'm starving. You?"

"Absolutely. What are you in the mood for?" Steven asked.

"I don't know. I'm thinking…Italian. How about we get cleaned up and head into Venice for dinner? I've never been there, and it might be fun."

"Perfect. When in Venice…I want to program in the cypher before much longer, though, so I'll take a fast shower and do as much as I can before we leave."

"Suit yourself. I'll take twenty minutes. Come on, Doctor. Let's get busy," Natalie said and swung her legs off the bed, standing quickly, with no self-consciousness of her nudity. *I could get used to this*, Steven thought.

They repeated their showering experience, this time focusing on bathing. Steven stepped out after two minutes and quickly dressed, brushing his wet hair back to dry as it liked. He padded to the living room and set up the laptop, then extracted the brass tablet. While peering at the ancient surface, he began creating a table of glyph pairs and letters. It went faster than he'd hoped, and by the time Natalie was ready he was nearly finished.

"I'm almost done," Steven said, admiring Natalie, who seemed to be glowing.

"We can wait if you want to finish it," she said.

"No. It's better if we leave it till later. Once it's all programed, I'll want to do the glyph matching, and then I won't want to stop until I've got it decrypted. It's better if I come back to it. I know myself too well…"

"All right. What's the plan? Drive to Venice, or take a boat?"

"Let's drive over the bridge and park. Way faster. There are a lot of great restaurants, so we shouldn't have too much trouble getting fed," Steven assured her.

"Have you been there before?"

"A few times. But it's been years…" Steven banished the habitual melancholy that loomed on the periphery as he spoke the words. There was no point to wallowing in it under his new circumstances. Antonia would never be replaced in his heart, but the universe was sending him a message that it was time to move on. Much as he still loved her, he felt a pull and realized it was time to let go – to rejoin the living.

"No time like the present, then. Let's hit the bridge. Lead the way," Natalie said brightly.

Steven nodded as he saved the work to his dongle and slipped it into his pocket. He wasn't going to take any chances after everything that had happened. Moody might have been the last honest man on the planet, but that didn't mean that Steven had to leave his hard-fought treasure on the coffee table for anyone else with a key to rummage through. He picked up the brass tablet and stuck it under his arm. Natalie gave him a neutral look.

"Taking it for an outing? Get some air?" she asked.

"I guess it's kind of silly… I mean, if I leave it in the car, the chances of it being stolen are higher than someone breaking in here. And I can't carry it to dinner, like some kind of latter-day Moses…"

"You can do whatever you like, sweetie. I won't laugh, no matter how weird it gets. You can wear my underwear if you want," she assured him with a look of complete insincerity.

He compromised with his doubts by taking it downstairs and hiding it behind the washing machine. Natalie watched him without expression, being true to her word.

They drove across the bridge that led to Venice and she silently took his free hand, holding it loosely to maintain the connection they'd forged so passionately throughout the day. It was comfortable, and he realized with a start that he liked it.

Once parked, they strolled the streets until they came across a bustling restaurant exuding heavenly aromas. They were escorted to a table in a discreet corner by an officious hostess, and before long had chosen a decent bottle of chianti at an exorbitant price, which they savored as they browsed the enormous menu. After some back and forth with the waiter they ordered gnocchi in a truffle reduction to start, and then Natalie chose the baked fish and he got seafood pasta. The pace of service was relaxed, and the meal was the perfect accompaniment to a remarkable day for them both. Yet even as they sipped their wine and ate, Steven was preoccupied by the tablet, as well as the ramifications of his sudden entanglement with Natalie. She sensed his preoccupation, and once their plates were removed, called him on it.

"Where have you been? It's like you're miles away. Hello…"

"I'm sorry. I'm probably still tired, as well as a little surprised by…well…by this."

"Are you complaining?"

"No. Quite the opposite. I mean, it's–"

"If you find my company too distracting, we can always go back to being platonic colleagues," she offered.

"I'm not sure that would work," Steven countered.

"It had better not."

Steven didn't know what else to say. There was a whole world he wanted to talk about, but at the same time, where did one start? He decided to punt it.

"Tell me more about you, Natalie. All the stuff you've been holding back. I'm curious."

"I'd say you know me pretty well, by now," she said, then took a sip of wine.

"Let's see. First off, I don't hop into the sack with every amateur cryptographer who plies me with cyphers. Let's start with that. In fact, I can safely say you're my first amateur cryptographer. In Italy. So far."

Steven took that in, nodding. "I'm not in the habit of showering with every sexy damsel in distress who soaps up next to me," Steven said.

"That's reassuring. I'd hate to think I was just one in an endless line of naked bathing partners you lure to safe houses with lascivious intentions to have your way with."

"Seriously, though. It's been years since I had a…a relationship. Of that kind," Steven admitted.

That put an effective end to the banter, although unintentionally. Steven felt awkward with the situation and was still fumbling his way through. Natalie seemed fine with that.

She took his arm as they meandered down the small winding footpaths that were the only connecting mechanism Venice had, beyond the canals. They made their way to Saint Mark's Square – easily the most famous landmark in Venice. Once there, they watched several wizened old women feeding the pigeons on the massive plaza as dusk cast its final shadows over the long row of gondolas on the waterfront.

Natalie pulled Steven by the hand. "Let's take a gondola ride. I've never done it, and who knows when I'll be back in Venice again?" she pleaded.

Steven couldn't think of a good reason not to, and soon they were meandering up the nearest canal. Natalie seemed delighted with the experience and leaned into Steven and kissed him as they cut through the dark water beneath the Bridge of Sighs. She looked deep into his eyes when they finally disengaged.

"It'll all turn out okay, Steven. You'll see. Everything." Then she returned to kissing him.

They disembarked and made their way back to the car as night fell upon the city. Something important had changed between them, and Steven resolved to just let it unfold, without questioning it or forcing anything. He hadn't signed up to be chased all over Italy, nor had he volunteered for a whirlwind romance, much less to be a hair away from solving one of history's most enduring riddles. Attempting to steer things seemed like a waste of time. He'd simply float along and see where the tide took him. Hopefully, alive.

Once they were back at the house, Natalie had most of her clothes off by the time they made it down the hall, and Steven's focus on completing the remainder of the decryption process was sidelined in favor of more pressing matters. The tablet would still be there in an hour, he figured, so he enthusiastically followed her to the bedroom, kicking the door shut behind him.

❧

Steven sat at the dining room table, having retrieved the tablet from the garage, and was finishing his inputting. In the end, the encryption code was ingenious, and indecipherable absent the key. Some of the letters looked like they were formed by not just two contiguous glyphs, but in a number of cases by a glyph, a meaningless glyph, and then the second relevant glyph in the pairing. And to further complicate matters, if the whole relevant string was preceded with a certain character, it changed it from a letter, to nothing. It would be painstaking to go passage by passage, but there was no other way. Minutes turned into hours as he went character by character, until he finally had the Scroll decrypted – roughly a third of a page of letters which would presumably make sense when broken up appropriately into Latin words. Steven's Latin was passable, but hardly fluent, and he couldn't easily discern any meaning from the letter block.

Which was where his program came in handy. The first stage would be having it create the most likely words from the string, and then break those into likely sentences. He knew from past experience that could result in a host of false starts because the software wasn't intuitive enough to know, if presented with five different possible words from the same six letters, which would have meaning in the context of the document, given the prior and following words. That was where Steven would earn his keep, and he knew that the paragraph could take hours to sort through all of the possible permutations.

The easiest way was to start with just the first letters and filter them into all possible words, assuming that they were in sequence and not randomly arranged. That, he could do with his program, but the likely accuracy decreased the longer the character string became. The earlier messages had been single sentences, making them far simpler and, even so, they'd taken an hour of processing time to group. This could take far longer. He absently wished he was a better coder, but there was no point in recriminations.

Stretching his arms over his head, he resigned himself to practicing patience. He clicked the begin button after configuring for Latin, as well as French, Italian and Spanish – just in case – and watched as the familiar 'in-process' window popped up and the light signaling the hard disk was being hit flickered on and off.

Natalie softly approached from the bedroom wearing one of his T-shirt and shorts ensembles; she stood behind him, her hands on his shoulders.

"What do you think?" she asked softly.

He reached back and put his hand over one of hers.

"It'll take a while. No way of knowing how long. There are a lot of variables to compare, and I'm having it try to create meaningful sentences, not just random words. Words wouldn't take that long. And I'm doing it in several languages. It's probably Latin, but I don't want to assume anything," Steven explained. "What do we do once we know it?"

"I don't really have a plan, Steven. But it seems to me that the only leverage we have is whatever the Scroll is hiding. If we don't have that, we're worm food." She thought about it. "I just can't imagine any medieval secret worth killing over. And knowing whatever it is won't bring my father back, so I'm not sure how it's going to help, beyond that we have it."

"Don't you think there's even more of a chance that the Order and Frank will want to kill us if they think we know it?" Steven asked.

"You mean more than they're already trying to kill us? How can they kill us more than once, even if they want to?"

Score one for Natalie.

"With any luck, soon we're going to know whatever it is, so it'll be time to formulate some kind of strategy. Maybe the best solution will be to disappear and start life over somewhere new," Steven mused.

"I'm not sure they'll ever give up hunting for us. This is priority number one for the Order. I doubt they'll drop it because it's been a few months since we surfaced," she said.

"That's a crummy way to live. Always looking over your shoulder. Trust me, I know," Steven admitted.

"Okay, Mister Mysterious. What's your story? Really? I'd sleep with you to get you to tell me, but it's a little late for that..." Natalie rubbed his shoulder muscles, and he closed his eyes.

"I had the Russian and Italian mobs hunting me for exposing one of their money laundering operations. It started off as something benign, but pretty soon everyone around me was getting killed and I had to run. New identity, new start, and even then, it took years for me to rest easy. I took a bullet at one point, and so did my wife. It was a terrible time, but in the end I was able to create a new existence. Antonia, my spouse, wound up selling her magazine in order to disappear, and I walked away from my entire life with five minutes' notice. It can be done, but it's not easy," Steven explained.

"She gave up everything to be with you? Sounds like true love," Natalie said, no trace of mockery in her voice.

"It was. Then the accident took her from me, and I've spent almost three years sleepwalking." He left out the 'until now' he'd been contemplating. "What about you? What's your story? Besides the FBI?"

"Where do I start? What do you want to know?"

"Just the important stuff. Save the minutiae for later," he said, opening his eyes and leaning his head back to look up at her face.

Her hands lifted from his shoulders and she walked to the kitchen, where she pulled one of the bottles of wine from the rack by the refrigerator and popped the cork, after finding the corkscrew in the drawer below. She rooted through the cabinets and found a couple of wine glasses, then poured them both generous helpings before moving to the couch, beckoning with his glass for him to join her there. Steven complied. The work for the evening was over. He took a sip of the wine and was pleasantly surprised.

"Pretty good," he said.

"It is, isn't it?" Natalie leaned against him. "Hmm...the story of me? Let's see. Only child. My father was the center of my universe, and the smartest, best man ever made. I was a straight A student through high school and college, valedictorian and head of the gymnastics team, and always the good girl trying to please him, impress him. I know he was shocked when I joined the FBI, but he never chastised me or questioned the decision, although I know he was worried about me all the time and didn't understand why I wanted to do it. I think the happiest day in his life was when I quit."

"A couple of years ago."

"Correct. I'd had an ass-full of conformity and being conservative by that point, so the pendulum swung the other direction, and I guess you could say I rebelled in a big way. I wound up working in a no-brainer job near my father, waiting tables in a bar, dating a tattoo artist, just living for the moment with no real direction. Everyone should try it once in their life," she said, sipping some wine. "I dumped the boyfriend after a year and started helping my father with his affairs, which had us in contact almost every day. I eventually made peace with the idea I didn't need to earn his approval and got way happier. Then he got involved with Morbius Frank. You know the rest."

"Not really. Why are you so convinced that Frank did your father in?" Steven asked. That had always been a niggling detail he'd been curious about.

"My father was a stereotype in some ways – the absent-minded professor. But since he hooked up with Frank, he got very withdrawn and sullen and began insisting I make copies of all his work. I'd ask why, and he would say that you never knew when lightning would strike. In the end, he was actively frightened of something, and I intuited it was Frank. I insisted on being part of his scheme, if only as a silent partner, so someone besides my father would know all the details. He never said it, but I know he struggled with his conscience towards the end. As he got closer to attaining his dream, which was to decrypt the Voynich, it's like it ate away at him. In the last week, once he had possession of the Scroll, after the first forty-eight hours, he insisted I take it and put it somewhere nobody could find it. He was worried, and it wasn't about the weather." She took another swallow of wine. "He taped some of his conversations with Frank and let me hear them, and I can tell you the guy is creepy. I had five kills while an agent, which is high, but also a reflection of the work I was doing with the mob, and I can tell you I've seen creepy. Serial killers, psychos, you name it, but just hearing the man's voice sent shivers up my spine."

"Okay, but being creepy is different than being a killer," Steven observed.

"When my father gave me the Scroll, he said that if anything happened to him, to expect the worst and to get out immediately. He wouldn't have said that lightly. He'd gone from sure of himself, to frightened. Over Easter, he'd had too much to drink, and he told me that Frank was evil – that was the word he used. This was not a man accustomed to hyperbole. He thought his partner was evil, but he'd gone too far to back out. In the end, though, I think it's the real reason he decided that Frank should never get his hands on the Scroll."

"At this point, it's moot. We know someone's willing to kill. That's been demonstrated," Steven confirmed, finishing his glass.

Natalie took it from him and went into the kitchen to refill both of their glasses with the remainder of the bottle.

She returned to the couch and handed him his wine. Steven took a big sip, and then asked another question that had been nagging at him. "Maybe I'm missing something, but it seems like you know a lot more about your father's dealings with Frank and their getting their hands on the Scroll than you'd know from your father warning you that Frank was a bad man. What am I not getting?" he asked.

"I was instrumental in planning the liberation of the Scroll from the Abbey. My father didn't have the operational know-how, so he turned to me, hoping that I might have a contact who could carry off the caper without screwing it up. He figured that given my history, I'd know where to look for a specialty contractor to deal with it. He gave me all the details and had me handle the logistics. And he was right. I didn't let him down. I knew probably the only person in the world who could pull this off without opening their big mouth or blowing it." Natalie downed half her wine in a gulp.

"I did it myself."

CHAPTER 29

"You stole the Scroll?"

"Liberated. I *liberated* the Scroll, which no more belonged to the Order than it did to anyone else. But yes, it was me," Natalie replied with a shrug.

Steven studied her with disbelief. *What other surprises was she hiding?*

"That's how you know so much about it…"

"Yes. I helped my father once he'd been given Frank's contact within the Order. I never talked to the man myself, but we got a lot of background information. The Scroll was written in 1450 or so. What nobody knows is that the entire Voynich was created as an elaborate shell around the hidden text in quire 18. But the secret predates the Voynich. After studying everything Frank provided him, my father believed that the Voynich was a copy of an original document, which he thought was written by Roger Bacon in the 1200s. As you know, Bacon is considered to be one of the fathers of the scientific method, but he was also a deeply devout friar who actually spent time at the Abbey. Small world."

Natalie finished her second glass of wine and placed it on the coffee table. "Anyway, during Bacon's reading of the many forbidden and ancient documents that came his way due to his reputation and network of contacts, he discovered a secret that was so sacrilegious that he not only feared for his own life, but also for the continued existence of his order. Back then the Church greeted most new information with death sentences and persecution."

Steven nodded. "Maybe that's why Bacon's name is associated with the Voynich so often. At one point I came to the conclusion that he was the likeliest one who could have written it, in spite of the impossibility, given that he died a century before it was created. It's always been a paradox, and it's that niggling detail that caused me to discard the hypothesis," Steven said. "But why create a copy?"

"The original was in terrible shape after being hidden by those loyal to Bacon for over a hundred years – medieval castles and abbeys weren't the most hospitable places for manuscript storage, long term."

"No, I'd imagine not, given the moisture, and rats, and everything else."

"Exactly. Apparently, one acolyte devoted ten years of his life to creating the current document, from 1440 to 1450, so the secret wouldn't be lost. According to Frank's research, that monk was Christian Rosenkreuz, who later became legendary as the purported founder of the Rosicrucian Order – although in that group's legend he's a doctor rather than a monk and lived a hundred fifty years later," Natalie explained.

"Rosenkreuz was a monk?"

"My father believed that one of the reasons the legend about him started was based in fact, although twisted by history and inventive followers – Rosenkreuz was rumored to know secrets of vast importance, forbidden knowledge, and that got twisted into the Rosicrucian legend after he died. If he was a follower of Bacon and knew the secret, then he would have indeed had forbidden understanding – only not the kind that later got associated with him," Natalie said.

Steven considered this revelation – the saga had just gotten more interesting. He'd decrypted several documents from the seventeenth century that had been coded Rosicrucian communiqués.

Natalie scrunched closer to Steven. "In a way, Bacon did write the Voynich, but not with his own hand – at least, not this iteration, which is all that survives. The original was destroyed by Rosenkreuz once he was done and replaced by what is now the Voynich. Only there was a problem. Two, actually. The first was that he needed to preserve the mechanism for decoding it. In a medium that couldn't be destroyed by time and couldn't be discovered by those who weren't part of the loyal few. That must be where the tablet and the parchment came in. He needed to send instructions to others of his brethren in England and Italy and France, on how to find the decryption tablet, but he couldn't do it in a way that might be discovered," Natalie continued.

The light went on in Steven's head. "He sent encrypted documents to them with coded directions on where to find, not the tablet, but hidden instructions on *how to find the tablet.* Embedded in the middle basilica, which was not publicly known about at the time." Steven finished his wine. "Only a member of the cloth – presumably one of his associates – could have ready access to the upper, new basilica and find the secret way to the middle level. Now that we know the parchment was there, my guess is the existence of the middle and lower levels were passed on as a verbal legacy.

That ensured the secret was safe, with several hurdles in place to keep those not part of the conspiracy from ever discovering the secret. Back then, the Inquisition was in full swing, and even a hint would have gotten someone burned as a heretic," Steven reasoned.

"That's why you've probably seen the crest on other encrypted documents from the same period, which also contained instructions to the Basilica of Saint Clemente, or perhaps to some other site – it could be there's a different location for each encoded parchment sent out. It doesn't really matter and can never be known without decrypting those others. But for our purposes, we have the tablet, which in the end is the key. Without that, there's no way to decrypt the Scroll," Natalie finished.

"I wonder what Bacon could have come across that warranted such secrecy. I mean, it had to be big. During that period, knowledge that had been lost to the West for a thousand years was beginning to make its way into Europe via the writings of the ancient Greeks and Arabs – the study of which ultimately wound up driving the creation of the university system. It was a period of tremendous intellectual upheaval, and at the same time, one of excitement. All the knowledge of the centuries that had been forgotten in the West during the so-called Dark Ages was being rediscovered."

"Our contact didn't know what the Scroll contained," Natalie added. "My father was always curious as to why the Order didn't simply destroy it, versus guarding it all these years, if the secret was that big a deal."

"I think I can answer that. Just a guess, but I suspect they were waiting."

"Waiting? For what?"

"Waiting for someone to decrypt the Voynich, as technology improved. If you want to know a secret that's contained in a document, but you don't know how to decrypt it, you wait until someone comes along who does, or figures out how to. That would account for rumors of scholars deep in the Vatican spending their lives trying to decipher the Voynich. Maybe the rumors about it were true, but like everyone else, they never figured it out?" Steven speculated.

"That makes sense. It also explains why the Church only safeguarded the chapter that held the secret."

"Exactly. Although who actually had possession of the Voynich is unknown for most of its existence, and I don't suppose we'll ever know what happened to quire 16. Could have just fallen out, or been removed at any point in its life." Steven snapped his fingers. "You know, one thing I always found odd was the circumstances by which Wilfrid Voynich came into possession of the manuscript in the first place. It was found among the remaining possessions of a top Jesuit general when he passed away. So there's the Church, again, although not the Order…that we know of. Could be that it was all some convoluted scheme to get the manuscript back out into circulation so modern cryptographers could have a crack at it."

Natalie shrugged. "Whatever. In the end none of this will matter. Soon, you'll have solved the puzzle, and then we'll be in a better position to figure out what to do next." Natalie reached over and toyed with one of the buttons on his shirt. "All this talk is making me sleepy. Are you sleepy yet, or do I need to pour some more booze down your throat first? I'm not above getting you drunk to have my way with you. And it's not just because I'm a crypto-groupie or anything. Although that's probably why you took up the discipline…"

"It was either that or play lead guitar in a rock band," Steven replied.

"I never liked musicians."

"You never heard me play guitar."

"You ready to hit the sack?" she asked, beginning to unbutton his shirt.

"I thought you'd never ask."

The next morning, Steven awoke to the smell of coffee brewing and the chiming of Natalie's cell phone, which she'd left in her purse. He called out for her and then lunged out of the bed to the small dresser where it lay, pushing the gun out of the way in the small clutch to get to the phone. He hit the green call button.

"Hello."

"Steven. I was expecting Natalie. Could you put her on, please?" Moody said without preamble.

"Sure. She's coming."

Natalie appeared at the door and he handed the phone across the bed. She grabbed it and ran back into the kitchen – something smelled like it was burning. Steven pulled on his pants then strode to the living room, where the laptop was waiting for his attention. He moved the mouse, tapped the Enter key, and the screen came to life. A long list of possible sentences stared back at him, and he groaned inwardly as Natalie chatted in the kitchen, rattling pans and doing three things at once.

Steven decided to check his e-mail before he started with the Scroll, which would take an unknown length of time. He got online and opened his web mail, to find over two hundred messages. He looked at the most recent, and sorted by sender. There was a new missive from Gwen that morning.

[Police stopped by again, wanted your cell, gave it to them. Said some sort of problem in Rome? Also, cryptic message from man named Luca. Says urgent you call him about Vornik.]

The mention of the Voynich jarred him. He reread it and then jotted the number down. Steven quickly went through the rest of his mail, forwarding the lion's share to Gwen for attention. It was all business related except for that one.

What the hell was the message all about? A trap? That was the likeliest explanation. But did they really think he was stupid enough to fall for it?

Then again, what was the trap? All he was being asked to do was make a call. Which he could do from anywhere. Even over the internet, if he used one of the myriad online services.

Natalie terminated her call in the kitchen and called out to him.

"Breakfast is ready. Kind of. Hope you like your toast really well done, along with your eggs."

"How did you know? I'm an open book to you, aren't I?"

He approached the round wooden dining room table and sat down, marveling again at how good Natalie looked in her gym shorts and T-shirt as she brought him a plate and coffee. She returned to the kitchen, then came back with her own breakfast and sat across from him.

"What did Moody have to say?"

"The search is heating up in Rome and could go national within twenty-four hours. They have our photos from passport control and immigration. And they found Danny's body – he'd been tortured," Natalie said and took a bite of her toast. "Shit. It's burnt."

"Tortured? What does Moody suggest we do?"

"Stay put until he can get to Venice this afternoon. He's taking a commuter flight within a few hours, and he'll call once he's here. But he says this is getting uglier by the minute. Now it's your turn. What did the computer come up with on the translation?" Natalie asked.

"Well, it's going to take a while to sort out. But I got an interesting e-mail..." Steven described the message to her.

Her eyes widened and she dropped her fork.

"It's probably Frank. Some sort of a trick. I wouldn't call. Certainly not until Moody's in the loop," she said.

"I'm not so sure about that. Where's the trick? If I use a calling card or the web so they can't trace me, what's the trap?" he asked.

Natalie racked her brain, but ultimately had to agree that there was no gotcha immediately evident.

"We should get a calling card and make the call from a pay phone. Maybe something by Saint Mark's Square, in Venice. There are tens of thousands of tourists going through it every day, so best of luck trying to run a trace – if they even could after you put the call through the calling card. And that will give me another opportunity to see Venice...and have a nice lunch there, maybe?" she reasoned. "Now, how long do you think it will take to go through the results on the Scroll?"

"Let me see what we have." He moved to the coffee table with his plate and cup, setting them down next to the laptop before he scrolled through the results. "Give me a couple of hours to translate these and study the possible combinations. Some look like gibberish to me at first glance, but you never know."

"I'll leave you to it and not distract you any further," Natalie said.

"You can distract me any time you want," Steven said, meaning every word.

"Yeah, but we're not getting a lot done, are we?"

"Depends on what you mean by 'getting,' or 'a lot,' or 'done'."

"All right, Doctor. I'll go freshen up while you do your important work," Natalie said, finished with her breakfast. She stood and took her plate into the kitchen, refilling her coffee before moving to the bedroom.

"I can put on a white exam coat and you can call me Doctor later," Steven suggested.

"I'd prefer just the little mirrored head thing and nothing else. Except your boots. Is that a problem?"

"There are no problems. Only solutions."

"That's my boy. Now go solve the most important riddle in the world, would you? By lunchtime, preferably. Stop lagging."

Steven returned to the screen, and cut and pasted the two hundred or so possible sentences into his translation engine, starting with Latin. The computer fan whirred as if it were trying for liftoff, and after a few minutes a new page appeared with all the English variations. He studied row after row of seeming nonsense, pausing occasionally to select the most likely suspect for each section. It was a tedious and painstaking process, but there was no substitute for human selection. One of the ever-present problems was semantics – something that might have been subject to interpretation in Latin could translate as nonsense in English, so once the possible words were segmented in that language, he'd have to go back and do his best to verify he hadn't missed anything.

Time flew by, and before he knew it two hours had passed. Steven rubbed his blurry red eyes and stared at the paragraph he'd assembled. He was used to his thirty-two inch monitor; the laptop screen wasn't nearly as easy to read on. Some of the terms looked like place names, so he began entering them into search engines.

Natalie emerged from the bedroom at noon to see how he was faring. He greeted her with a triumphant grin. She locked eyes with him, and he nodded.

"You didn't," she said.

"Sure did. Although it doesn't look like anything about this damn Scroll is going to be easy. But I think it's safe to say it's given up its secret." He hesitated, then toasted her with his now-cold coffee. "I've decrypted the Voynich."

CHAPTER 30

Gwen was getting ready to go to lunch when her private line rang. There were only a few people in the world with that number, and she didn't think her mother would be calling in the middle of the day. Besides, Mum usually called the cell. She inspected the caller ID, but didn't recognize the number. Roman prefix. She put her purse back down on the desk and, after looking around the room, lifted the handset to her ear.

"Hullo?"

"Gwen. It's me. Don't say my name, okay?" Steven said.

"A…all right. What a lovely surprise to hear your voice. You've been in high demand lately," Gwen responded.

"You don't know the half of it. Listen. You sent me a message. A gentleman caller anxious for me to connect. What can you tell me about him, other than his name? What did he want?" Steven asked.

"All he said was that he needed to speak to you about the Vladnik, and how you'd know what it meant. Said it would be in your best interest to contact him as soon as possible."

Steven let the mispronunciation go. "I don't suppose you ran the number through the reverse directory, did you?"

"Funny you should ask. I know how your mind works by now. Yes, I did, and it came up as one of a group of lines assigned to the Vatican. Are you thinking of converting? Becoming a man of the cloth? Careful with that one, luv, it might be a midlife crisis as opposed to a true calling…"

"You're sure it was the Vatican?" Steven asked.

"Hard to get that wrong, don't you think?"

"Hmm. And what else has been going on during my holiday?"

Gwen cupped her hand over the mouthpiece and turned away from the circle of computers, where Sophie and Ben were busy coding away. "The Roman police sent a couple of coppers round. Seems they want to talk to you big time. I told them truthfully that I had no idea where you were. They wanted to know if I had a contact number, so I gave them your cell. I'm sorry. I hope that wasn't a wrong move."

"That's fine, Gwen. You need to be completely open and honest with the police. As far as my whereabouts go, I'm extending my little holiday for a bit longer. Keeping it open-ended."

"Speaking of which, how's your little friend?" Gwen asked. It was as if she could read his mind. He decided to take the high road and interpret her query in the cleanest possible way.

"She's naturally upset over how things have developed, but holding up," Steven said. "How's everything with the business?"

"Oh, you know, it chugs along, with or without you. Not that you're easily replaceable, but there's nothing we haven't been able to deal with in your absence, so far. Although it does get a bit distracting to have the local five-o stopping in every few days, demanding to know where you are."

"I'm sorry for that. Okay, then. I'm calling with a calling card, so this number isn't a good contact number for me. Sorry. But I'll check back in shortly. In a few days. Hold down the fort, Gwen, and thanks for everything," Steven said.

"Be careful, luv."

Morbius Frank was sitting at a small café in Rome, enjoying the feel of the afternoon sun on his face as he watched the frantic pedestrian traffic. A shadow fell over the table, then Sia Amieri sat down across from him.

"Cross called his office a few hours ago," the big man said.

"And? Do we know anything more than that? Any hint of where he's hiding?" Frank asked.

"No. Nothing in that direction. But there is a troubling new development."

Frank sighed. "Besides having lost him and the girl? In possession of the most valuable treasure in history? Tell me, what could be more troubling?"

"His office got a call from someone at the Vatican. Asking him to get in touch as soon as possible. About the Voynich."

Frank's eyes narrowed to slits. "What? This is bad. First we have the girl turning out to have CIA connections, and now we have the Church in direct contact? We're losing control of this, my son."

Amieri didn't respond. There wasn't anything to say.

"If the Church gets the Scroll back, we can assume that it will disappear forever, and its secret will go with it. I've spent too much money and too many years tracking this down to have that happen," Frank seethed.

"I know. I don't like it either."

Frank took a few deep breaths, composing himself, and Amieri pretended not to notice that his mentor's cup trembled a little as he brought it to his lips.

"Fix this, my son. Whatever it takes. Fix it."

⁂

Natalie and Steven parked at the airport and took a water taxi to Venice, which dropped them in front of Saint Mark's Square. They meandered around and eventually decided to go into a hotel on the waterfront to use the phone. The interior was old Venice, all gold brocade and velvet and polished dark wood. Natalie took a seat at the lobby bar while Steven sought out the bank of pay phones that were situated by the bathrooms.

He dialed the number on the calling card and, when prompted, entered the number. It took a moment to connect, then answered on the third ring.

"Luca."

"This is Steven Cross. You left a message for me at my office?" Steven wanted to keep this as brief as possible.

Luca hesitated for a few seconds. "Ah, yes. Dr. Cross. Thank you for calling."

"How can I help you?"

"I believe we both have an idea. You have come into possession of something that belongs to the Church, and I'd like to discuss a solution before things get any more out of hand," Luca tried.

"Sounds accusatory. Can you prove that the Church is the legal owner of whatever we're hypothetically discussing?" Steven threw out.

This already wasn't going as Luca had envisioned.

"The item in question has been in our possession for centuries. It is clearly our property."

"So possession establishes ownership? I'd say, in that case, whoever possesses it, owns it," Steven observed.

"Ownership of some things entails tremendous responsibility and jeopardy. I was hoping we could discuss how to remove any from your life moving forward," Luca said.

"How do I know you're not a large part of the risk yourself? It seems like it's become a very dangerous world all of a sudden."

"The Church doesn't endorse bloodshed, Dr. Cross."

"Tell that to the folks on the receiving end of the Crusades or the Inquisition," Steven volleyed back.

"I should say that *today's* Church doesn't, and that I personally would never authorize it. Which is why I think we have something worth discussing. Depending upon your objective, I may be able to solve a very real problem for you – namely, how to return the item in question without incurring any retribution or threats. The reality is that whoever possesses the item will forever be a target. In fact, removing it from our custody has already accumulated an enormous toll. I'm clear in my objective here. I want the item returned and am prepared to negotiate to arrange that. Simple," Luca pitched.

"How can I possibly trust you?" Steven asked.

"I'm not sure you're in any position *not* to trust me. I'm trying to put a stop to a very real disaster that has been set in motion, perhaps unwittingly, and in which you are a regrettable collateral player. I think you're a very smart man and can see that being involved with a catastrophe can't end well. For anyone. Besides which, if we can't come to an arrangement, I think you'll find trusting me will be the least of your problems."

Luca had a point. And Natalie didn't have a plan of any kind that she'd shared with him. Perhaps there was a deal that could be brokered with the Church.

Luca continued. "Do you believe in God, Dr. Cross?"

"Not in the sense you do."

"Hmm. Well, I do. Obviously. Very much. What I can tell you is that life on this planet is short and that we all have a destiny, and that yours has nothing to do with the item. It pains me that evil seems to have surfaced and struggled for possession of it. You may not believe in God, but surely you're old enough to believe in evil? You must be worldly enough to have seen it?" Luca asked.

"I'll concede that point, philosophically. I've seen evil. Which is usually nothing more than the actions of greedy, mean-spirited men to satisfy their lusts. I'll agree that evil exists. It's us," Steven said.

"I don't disagree. But just as evil is us, so is good. They are antipodal, and yet co-exist directly because *we* exist. Different ends of our spectrum, if you will. I am not interested in getting into a theological or philosophical debate, or trying to frame a theistic argument. I'm telling you that someone is killing to get their hands on the item – the same someone who likely participated in its theft. That someone will continue until they have it, and you and the girl will share the fate of everyone else who has stood in their way." Luca drove home his point. "In a world of moral ambiguity, perhaps we can keep this simple. Being alive is good. Being killed is bad, or evil, if you like. I'm approaching you to see if we can come to terms that will end this before any more evil occurs."

Steven considered this.

"I have a bargaining chip. Beyond the item, which isn't mine to give or take." Steven had considered the merits of playing his trump card and decided to do so. The only thing the Church would hold more valuable than the Scroll, would be the Scroll's secret.

"There is nothing besides the item. That is all I want. I'm prepared to entertain any terms you might propose," Luca said.

"Is that really all you want? Are you completely sure about that? Think long and hard before you answer."

The line was silent for a few seconds.

"You…you're telling me you've done it?" Luca whispered.

"What do you really know about the item? I mean, really? Do you know what it hides? What it contains?"

Luca composed himself. "I know that what we are discussing is too delicate for the telephone."

"Very well. I'll call you back in a few hours. Take time to speak to whoever you need to, and get clear on what your true, ultimate objective is. Then perhaps we can meet under circumstances that are safe for us both and have a more substantial discussion that will get us both what we really want." Steven let that hang, and then gently replaced the handset in the cradle.

Luca sounded genuine, but Steven was afraid that he might be too low in the hierarchy to seal a deal that would keep both he and Natalie safe in perpetuity. But in the end, Luca was right about one thing. Life was short, and if you didn't have a reasonable assurance that someone wasn't going to kill you at any moment, then you had nothing. He'd been sucked into this, but if he could put an end to it all on terms he, and Natalie, could live with, then he would do so.

Steven returned to Natalie, who was busy enjoying a Kir Royale – the hotel's specialty. He sat down next to her on the elegant booth seat and, after tasting the liquid concoction, he ordered one for himself before relating how the call had gone.

"What? Give it back? That's the best you can do?" Natalie fumed. She was clearly emotional over the idea.

"Natalie. Think this through. As long as we have the Scroll, our lives won't be worth spit. Frank and the Order will pursue us to the end of the earth. So the only option is to give it back to the Order and arrange a transaction where they can protect us. It doesn't play out any other way. We can't give it to Frank, because the Order will still be after us, and if you've described him correctly, he'll just kill us anyway. So we can't keep it, can't give it to Frank…that only leaves one option, as far as I can see."

She thought it over, then stood abruptly and said, "I have to use the bathroom."

She stalked off, still pissed, regardless of the logic.

The bartender brought his drink, and he took an appreciative sip. Natalie returned within a few minutes, seeming more relaxed.

Steven broached the subject again. "The Scroll doesn't have any value to either of us. If it ever did, now that I've decrypted it, the value is gone. It's not the Scroll that had the value, anyway. It's the secret the Scroll contains. My solution to our quagmire is straightforward. You want to finish your father's work and see it through. Fine. I want to help you, and I have the knowledge and capability to do so. But none of this matters if we wind up dead. I'm planning on dying of old age a long time from now, not at the hands of some psychopath's assassins. If you look at this dispassionately, we need to figure out a way to return the Scroll to get everyone off our backs, and we need to finish the job your father started – which we can either try to do on our own, or we can do in some sort of partnership with the Order – a partnership we'll control. Those are the only two options. I don't care which we choose, but I'm not seeing a third."

Natalie regarded him. "Are you always so damned logical?"

"It's what I do, Natalie."

"Not all you do, thank God." She smiled. "Let's say I go along with this. What's the plan?"

Steven told her. Natalie listened without saying a word, and when he was finished, she picked up her drink and swallowed it in one gulp. Smacking her lips, she took his hand and stood.

"Let's grab lunch. Sounds like we've got our work cut out for us."

Just like that, it was decided.

CHAPTER 31

In a dark room in the heart of the Vatican, Luca sat quietly with his superior, His Beatitude Metropolitan Justinian, the leader of the Templars, and the Sentinel, the head of the Order of the Holy Relic. Heavy purple drapes framed the stained-glass windows, adding to the richness of the gold-leaf covered walls. This was an unprecedented meeting, one which Luca had never in his imagination expected to be participating in. Justinian held up a plump hand to underscore his point.

"Diego Luca, no man other than the Sentinel and whoever occupies my office has ever known the full story of the Scroll, or its significance. It is therefore with trepidation that I take you into a confidence that extends to only His Holiness, and the two of us. It goes without saying that you may never share your knowledge with anyone, no matter what the circumstances. You must take it with you into eternity."

Luca nodded, afraid that his voice would betray his emotions.

The Sentinel leaned forward, holding Luca with an iron stare.

"The Scroll contains a secret that the papacy had always believed could bring down or forever change the Church. The author of the document believed it could destroy us if it was known, and that its possessor could literally control the Church with the threat of its exposure," the Sentinel explained.

"What is the secret?" Luca asked, painfully aware of time slipping away.

"That's the problem. Nobody is sure," Justinian admitted.

"What?" Luca didn't understand.

"It is why we have kept the Scroll throughout history and guarded it so jealously. The friar who wrote it originally did so in a cypher of his own devising that was so foolproof nobody has ever been able to unravel it. We know from his statements that he had come into possession of information about something he referred to as the Divine Light, but whatever that was went to the grave with him. Some who have held my office believed that it was the Holy Grail. Others speculated it was something even more precious, beyond imagination, perhaps a gospel written by Jesus himself. All of this was speculation. The friar is dead, and he died without disclosing it to anyone as far as we know."

"Then the secret…is what the Divine Light actually is?" Luca didn't understand.

"Yes. And no. Not *what. Where.*"

Luca looked from one man to the other. "Where?"

The Sentinel nodded. "The secret of the Scroll is where the Divine Light is hidden. The location. And the friar believed that whatever this enigma was would prove so sensitive for the Church that it could never be revealed – but being of a scientific disposition, he also didn't want it to be lost forever, as had been the case with so many other pieces of knowledge through time. He created what is known as the Voynich Manuscript to hide the knowledge. It was only from one of his followers that the Church learned that the secret was written in quire 18 – the Holy Scroll." The Sentinel cleared his throat. "Once that was understood, the Pope, Nicholas V, in 1453 created The Order to safeguard the Scroll until such time as it could be translated and the secret identified. Remember that the history of the Church has been filled with rivalry and power struggles, so Nicholas decided that a separate, secret guardian needed to keep watch, unknown to anyone but a trusted few."

Justinian continued where the Sentinel left off.

"The Scroll is the only record of the location of this Divine Light, which inspired both fear and curiosity at the time – but times have changed since the 1200s, and what might have destroyed a religion then could turn out to be a pillar of faith now. We, as an organization, are chartered with ensuring the Scroll never sees the light of public exposure, but we are fascinated with what the Divine Light might be. If it is the Grail, it could breathe new life into the faithful during a time of waning passion. If it were a new gospel it would revitalize religion, rather than create upheaval as it might have done eight centuries ago. What might have been blasphemous in the friar's age, we now seek to understand through modern eyes."

Luca nodded again, suddenly understanding. "If Cross has decrypted it, discovering what he knows is almost more important than the Scroll itself."

The Sentinel offered a wan smile that chilled Luca's marrow.

"As you say, there is nothing more important than regaining possession of the Scroll – except learning what Cross knows. If he has truly decrypted the document, we must find out what the Divine Light is at all costs and also take it into our possession so His Holiness may decide how best to proceed. But even as the Church has changed, human nature has not, so there will always be factions that would use any knowledge to further their own ends. This cannot be allowed to happen in this case. Hence, the only people who can know of this are myself, His Beatitude Metropolitan Justinian, His Holiness, and now…you," the Sentinel finished.

Justinian cleared his throat. "Diego Luca, it is not common knowledge, but I am ill. My days are numbered and a successor must be appointed. You are to be that successor, so the knowledge being shared with you is merely premature rather than inappropriate. Within a year, you will be the head of the Templars and will be required to work side by side with the Sentinel to protect the secrets of the Church from enemies without and within. That includes the Holy Scroll, and soon, if providence has shined upon us, the Divine Light."

Luca was overcome, momentarily speechless.

The Sentinel sat back and made a series of arcane gestures in Luca's direction with his liver spotted hand, then spoke his final words of the meeting.

"You are hereby granted whatever powers you require, including the full power of my office, and of that of His Beatitude's office, and the Pope's, to make whatever bargain or arrangement you believe is in the best interest of the Church, without exception. Your word or signature shall be the Church's final say on the matter. We impart this to you in extraordinary circumstances because in the coming days you may be called upon to make remarkable decisions that will have permanent effect, and we do not wish you to do so with hesitation or fear of being overridden at a later date. In this matter, yours is the final say, and any amount of money, or property, or sacrifices you deem required, shall be yours to dispense as you see fit. But get the Scroll back, and if you can, get the Divine Light for us, so we can fulfill our destinies and put the era of uncertainty to an end."

The two old men stood and walked around the small table. Luca kneeled before them and kissed the holy rings on their fingers.

"Good luck, my son. You carry on your shoulders the hopes and faith of the Church."

"I won't let you down."

ಘಘ

Steven felt Natalie warming up to the idea of handing off the problem to the Order. If they could negotiate something with the Order, their chances of surviving increased dramatically – mainly because they no longer had what Morbius Frank wanted, but also because the only thing more powerful than an angry homicidal billionaire was the full weight of the Catholic Church. With resources of that magnitude, they could disappear forever without having to worry, or at least they could worry a lot less.

Natalie agreed with his reasoning, although he could tell it went against her grain to capitulate. But the only scenario that made sense was for Steven and the Order to search for the secret together and make finding it a part of the deal. Then, the Church would have possession of everything and the impetus for viewing them as a threat would be nil. But they still needed to get some sort of leverage, just in case, and a plan was rolling around in his head. Perhaps there was a way to leverage Moody's position to act as a prophylactic against future threats or backsliding on their deal.

Natalie's phone rang during lunch; it was Moody, recently arrived in Venice and anxious to meet with them. They agreed to hook up at three o'clock, at one of the numerous small cafés on Saint Mark's Square – the most populated landmark in Venice. After lunch, they ambled over to the rendezvous and watched Moody as he walked into the square. Natalie scanned the crowds to ensure he wasn't being followed; after a few minutes of scrutiny, she went to greet him. Steven and Natalie had agreed to move to a more intimate café down one of the small side streets once they'd verified there was no tail. Steven followed them at some distance when they departed the large plaza bound for the new rendezvous spot.

Within a few minutes, they were all situated at a quiet table in a corner of the garden that served as the outdoor patio for the café. The waitress brought them their order, and once she'd departed, Natalie quickly summarized their situation. After hearing about the latest developments, Moody sat back and whistled.

"Wow. You don't screw around, do you? You believe that Luca can be trusted?"

Natalie shook her head. "No. That's why we need your help. You deal with this sort of thing all the time. What's the best way to buy ourselves insurance so they can't renege on the arrangement?"

Moody toyed with his cup, smiling at the question. "With all due respect, I don't deal with this sort of thing all the time. You're talking about how to get a guarantee with the Church on a bargain to return a stolen artifact. That doesn't fall under my typical job description," he said.

"What are you saying? Can you help us?" Natalie asked.

"You certainly don't do things in half measures, do you? Christ. No offence, but this is as weird as anything I've heard of, and I've seen just about everything. But to answer your question, I can probably help keep you from getting killed in the process."

"How would you lock them in if this was your op?" Steven asked.

"Well, I'd start with a meeting…and a recording," Moody began, and then laid out precisely how to structure the rendezvous as well as the deal.

Steven's respect level for Moody increased as he spoke in a low voice, describing the intricacies and emphasizing why certain things had to be done exactly as he described. Natalie was engrossed, and it was clear he was an expert in his field. She'd certainly gotten the right ally.

Whatever Steven's sentiments about the man, by the end of their encounter it was clear he knew his trade cold.

CHAPTER 32

The following morning at seven, Steven's voice sounded calm to Luca as he relayed his proposal.

"Fly into Florence this morning on the Alitalia flight departing Rome at 9:45. Turn your cell phone on once you're on the ground. I'm assuming this number is your cell. I'll call once you land and give you further instructions. Bring at least two thousand dollars cash to cover logistics," Steven said.

"It will be tight to get to the airport in time to buy a ticket and make the flight. I still need to get dressed, and traffic…"

"You can make it. Get going. I'll see you in Florence." Steven disconnected.

Luca felt a thrill of excitement. Here he was, playing spy, dashing for airplanes while on secret orders from the top. He'd never done anything like it in his life, but there was always a first time. It was more Synthe's area of specialty, but he didn't get the impression that Steven was a threat, so he felt no foreboding – only a tingle of anticipation.

He made it to the airport with just enough time to stand in line, buy the ticket, and jog through security to the gate. Morning rush hour in Rome was notorious, and he wondered if Cross knew what a miracle it was that he'd made the plane.

The flight was smooth, lasting only an hour from gate to gate, and when he landed, Luca thumbed his cell phone on. He disembarked and stood in the arrivals area, waiting for something to happen. After fifteen minutes, his phone rang, and Steven's now-familiar voice gave him his next instructions. He hung up and walked out to the taxi stand and dutifully stood in line, checking his watch. There were six people ahead of him. He tapped his foot nervously as he waited his turn.

The cab took him to the train station, where he booked a first class ticket to Milan. He boarded the train and settled into a comfortable seat for the hour and forty-five minute ride. Once they were underway, a service operative came by and asked him what he'd like to drink. He opted for a soda, as did the man sitting next to him. After half an hour, the man excused himself and went to the bathroom.

Steven took the vacant seat and leaned in to Luca, murmuring a greeting.

"Diego Luca, I presume."

Luca turned to study Steven, who hadn't shaved for three days, as was the fashion for many Italians.

"Correct. I recognize you by your voice, Dr. Cross, although I was expecting someone older," Luca said.

"Sorry to disappoint. Let's get started on this. I've reached an agreement with the girl, and she's willing to give up the item in exchange for a number of things, which I'll tell you about in a few minutes. In the meantime, you should know that I have successfully decrypted the document," Steven said flatly.

Luca's heart rate spiked. "How do I know this is true? After centuries of trying…that you were successful in doing what everyone else couldn't? No offense intended."

"Fair question, and none taken. Let's just say that I know where the Light is located. Is that sufficient?"

Luca played dumb. "The what?"

"The Divine Light. Are you not high enough in the power structure to know about it? Why did they send you?" Steven sounded annoyed.

"I know of it, but always thought it to be a myth. You're saying it's real?" Luca tried.

"According to the Scroll it is. But maybe we should just forget about it and deal with the return of the Scroll…" Steven said.

"I didn't say we weren't interested." Luca's eyes narrowed. "What are your terms? What do you want?"

"In exchange for the Scroll, both the girl and I will require new identities, with passports from a European Union country – within three days of striking any deal. We will also require a guarantee of protection for the rest of our lives. That means you will have to pay for whatever security we deem necessary, anywhere in the world. And I will require a letter, signed by the Pope, thanking me for the valuable service to the Church."

Luca waited for more. Steven stared at him.

"That's it?" Luca asked, incredulous.

"And twenty million dollars."

"Ah… That's more what I was expecting." Luca knew it. Still, the price was laughably low.

"I'm kidding. I don't want your money. I had no part in this, and I'm merely helping the girl return what her father came into possession of. The passports and security are to keep us safe from her father's associates, who won't be delighted over losing the Scroll. But I'm not interested in blackmailing you," Steven explained. "Neither is the girl. All we both want is to be safe and to start someplace new without worrying every day."

Luca couldn't believe his ears. It was completely unexpected.

"I can agree to your terms. Now let's discuss the rest."

"Not so fast. What's your role with the Church? How do I know you have the authority to make important decisions for it and make binding agreements with me?" Steven asked.

"My name is Diego Santiero Luca, and I am a special appointee of the Pope. I answer only to him, and I work under his authority."

"You work directly for the Pope? And your agreement is the same as if he agreed to it? Just to be clear," Steven said.

"That is correct. Now, let's move to the other matter. The location of the Divine Light. What is it, anyway?" Luca asked.

"The Scroll doesn't specify. It merely describes where it is."

"*Merely*. Fine. What do you want in exchange for that?"

"First, I'll need compensation for my decryption work, which I would argue is the best in the world, given that nobody in history has accomplished what I have. For that, and for having to give up my company and uproot my life, I want fair value of the company, which I will sell to the Church. I estimate it would realize one and a half million dollars from a motivated buyer. And the trove of rare parchments I'll have to leave behind is worth half a million. All told, two million dollars. Which, given your reaction to my joke about twenty million, is a steal, I'd say," Steven reasoned.

"I sense there's more."

"There is. I also want to lead the expedition to find the Light. With the Church making all arrangements I require, including travel facilitation under yet another passport, as well as for the girl. So two passports each, for both the girl and myself. First set for the return of the Scroll, second set for travel to find the Light."

"I think I can do that. You don't mind if they're Italian and from Vatican City, do you?" Luca asked.

"Not at all. Oh, and there's one more thing. I want to have unrestricted access to the Vatican archives for the rest of my life."

Luca smiled. "The archives?"

"I'm an amateur cryptologist. Once you pay me, I'll be a professional. As such, I'll want to pore over the most obscure and rare documents in the world – which are in your archives. I won't remove anything, but I will want to satisfy my curiosity for my remaining days. One can have money, and power, but knowledge is priceless. So I want something priceless, in return for giving the Church something priceless – the Light. And I will want that in writing, with the Pope's signature. Irrevocable. You can have him sign it when he's signing the other document." Steven stopped talking.

Luca rubbed his chin and took a swallow of his soda.

"I can speak for the Church. Your conditions are acceptable. How would you suggest we proceed from here?"

"Give me an e-mail address so I can send the passport photos. I can get those to you by tonight – they're already taken. I will also get you the names to use. I know the Church can snap its fingers and make this happen, so I'm not worried about it. On the money, I will give you an account in Lichtenstein for a wire transfer. Once you have the documents from the Pope and the passports in hand, we will do an exchange, and then I will tell you what's required for our expedition. I'm trusting the Church to behave honorably in this, as I am acting, and I hope that faith isn't misplaced," Steven said.

"We're in the faith business. So no, it isn't misplaced. You have my word on that."

"Good. I've taken the liberty of recording this discussion, should anyone on your side ever decide that the world would be a better place without me, or the girl, in it. That tape will go to every media outlet for release along with the entire story if you default or renege. Call it my own way of ensuring the faith isn't misplaced. If you keep your bargain, you have nothing to worry about. Oh, and call off the Order. I don't want to have to worry about them anymore. The girl's father's business partner is enough. Which, by the way, I could also use a hand with as part of our security. But we will touch on that once we have the passports and the money taken care of. Agreed?" Steven said.

Luca realized he had just been set up, but didn't blame Steven. He knew that their transaction might be questioned in hindsight, and an overzealous new Pope might decide to void the deal. The recording would ensure that didn't happen.

"We have a deal, Dr. Cross," Luca said, offering his hand.

Steven shook it. "I never doubted we would. There's always a way when both parties want the same thing. A win-win. Have a good trip. My associate will be returning to take his seat. Don't get up until we arrive in Milan, and when you leave the train, take a taxi directly to the airport or, alternatively, buy a ticket back to Rome on the train. Now, give me your cell phone," Steven instructed.

Luca fished in his jacket for it. Steven removed the battery and passed it back to Luca.

"Pleasure doing business with you. Write the e-mail account on this." Steven handed him a train timetable and a pen. Luca thought for a few moments and then neatly printed an address.

"We'll be seeing more of each other shortly. Safe travels."

Steven moved down the aisle to the connecting door that led to the other cars, and Moody returned from where he'd been lingering by the bathroom. Without looking at Steven as he passed, he ordered a mineral water from the server before returning to his seat next to Luca. He glanced at the cleric and nodded, removed two ear buds from his shirt pocket and put them in place, and then activated his iPod.

Luca picked up the newspaper and returned to reading it, thinking, *what a remarkable encounter.*

In Milan, he opted to take the train back to Rome. It would give him time to think. He had half an hour to kill before it left, so after buying a first class ticket with some of the cash he was carrying, he went to find a cell phone store where he could get another battery.

Natalie threw her arms around Steven's neck when he arrived at the house in the late afternoon.

"How did it go?" she asked between kisses.

"Nothing unexpected. Start picking out names. I promised I'd send them, along with the photos, by tonight."

"That's it?"

"That's it. They agreed to everything, and we'll be game-on within three to four days. We'll return the Scroll, and then we're off to find the Light."

"Where are we going, by the way?"

"Oh, I'd imagine we'll need to start in Israel or Jordan. I'll have to talk with Moody about his contacts there, as well as in Palestine. But that can wait until tomorrow," he said.

Natalie took his hand and led him to the bedroom as he removed his jacket. She turned at the threshold and helped him with his shirt.

It was a long night.

CHAPTER 33

Colonel Gabriel Synthe stood in the parking lot of the Leonardo da Vinci-Fiumicino Airport, watching the planes take off over the Roman hills while waiting for his rendezvous. He hadn't gotten a lot of sleep over the last few days and had a throbbing headache from the tension. The girl and Cross had vaporized without a trace, and the police dragnet had yielded nothing so far. Synthe didn't have a lot of hope on that front – the search was low priority even with the Roman police, and the other cities were probably largely ignoring it.

He idly blew smoke rings to the sky as he stood by his rental car. The lot was deserted at this time of night, so it made for a good clandestine meeting spot. A vehicle approached down his lane and pulled to a stop a few slots from where he was parked. To his considerable surprise, Luca got out of one side, accompanied by the Sentinel on the other. This was unprecedented. His despised counterpart in the Templars was now apparently rubbing shoulders with his superior.

Both men approached Synthe, and neither offered their hand in greeting.

Luca cleared his throat. "We are going to call off the hunt for the professor's daughter and the Cross fellow, effective immediately," Luca said dryly.

"Call it off? Are you delusional?" Synthe spat, dropping his cigarette to the ground and grinding it beneath his foot.

"No. I've solved our problem. We will have the Scroll back within a few days, and this entire episode will be over." Luca held back a victorious smile.

"You mean you *think* you'll have it back. You don't yet, do you?" Synthe sneered.

The Sentinel took a step closer. "Colonel Synthe. While I – we – appreciate your enthusiasm and commitment, the problem has been solved and the Scroll will be in our hands shortly. I'm satisfied that is the case, and I have no reason to doubt that it will happen," he said, ending the matter.

Synthe digested the information and decided to try a different approach.

"That's wonderful news, then. Congratulations. It appears your instinct was the right one, Luca. As the protector of the Scroll for the Order, let me be the first to offer my praise and my support. Anything I can do to help, just say the word. That's the whole point of cooperation between our two groups, right? To get the job done. It's the end result that counts, not our egos," Synthe enthused.

It didn't look as though Luca was buying it, but the Sentinel seemed to be, and that was who he was playing to.

"I share that sentiment, Colonel Synthe," the Sentinel said. "And I want to say that even though the Scroll will be back in our care before long, I want to make some changes to the security precautions – the most important being that I think the tradition of housing it in the Abbey needs to come to an end. It was originally stored there to keep it away from any politically-motivated squabbles within the Holy See, but times have changed and the benefits of keeping it hidden in a remote location are outweighed by the security we can arrange within the Vatican. I am going to ask you to work with me on crafting a foolproof system to house it here in Rome."

"I would be delighted to lend my expertise." Synthe almost bowed.

"There will also be another task for you. Besides security for the Scroll, we will need your assistance with a field operation to recover another enormously important item in the coming days. I will ask you to work with Luca on selecting an appropriate contractor to devise a vault to house the Scroll and this other item, with access limited exclusively to the Pope," the Sentinel continued.

Synthe's respiration increased. "Of course. Whatever is required. But, if you don't mind me asking, what is this other item? It will help to know what I'm to create a plan to protect when designing the system, *no*?" Synthe asked.

Luca and the Sentinel exchanged furtive glances.

"We haven't got a complete description quite yet. But when we do, you'll be told everything you need to do your job," the Sentinel assured him.

"I see. And the field operation? Where will it take place? Here, in Rome?" Synthe inquired.

Luca rubbed his hands together. "Again, when we have more information you will be brought into the loop. For now, all we need you to do is stand down, recall any men you have deployed in the search for the

Scroll, and await further instructions. We should know more in a few days, so you should remain in Rome," Luca said dismissively.

Synthe restrained his natural instinct to punch the pompous ass in the throat.

"Does this few days in any way involve the girl and the cryptologist's return of the Scroll?" he asked.

"Infer whatever you like. You'll be briefed when we have relevant details," Luca said curtly.

The Sentinel eyed Luca, then returned his attention to Synthe. "Colonel, I can appreciate your curiosity, however I am going to ask you to consider Diego Luca your superior in this matter. This is temporary, however, it is necessary for reasons that extend beyond your need to know. Luca will require your cooperation in both the security matter and the recovery matter, and it must be unconditional and unhesitating. Do I make myself crystal clear?" the Sentinel asked him.

Synthe managed a faint smile. "Of course. I shall do as you say and call off the dogs, and await a call when you can tell me more. In the meantime, perhaps you can arrange for me to see the areas you're considering for storage of the Scroll, as well as any blueprints? If I am to create a security scenario that will be more secure than the one at the Abbey, which clearly was not up to modern challenges, I'll need as much time and information as possible."

"That's reasonable. I'll contact you tomorrow with a time for you to be shown the spots." Luca paused. "It goes without saying that everything you've been told is confidential and cannot go beyond our ears."

"Yes. As always." Synthe couldn't think of anything further to add and decided to cut his losses. "I'll await your contact. Let me get going, so I can recall my team."

Synthe saw no reason to drag the meeting out any longer. He needed time to think through a strategy that was tickling the periphery of his awareness.

"Thank you for your efforts, Colonel Synthe. I trust this new arrangement will work well for us all. Remember that it is temporary, and you will report directly to me again once this regrettable affair is concluded," the Sentinel advised.

"I would completely understand if you wished to end our arrangement once this is done, given the loss of the Scroll," Synthe offered. It was virtually mandatory for him to offer his resignation in light of the circumstances.

"We've discussed that, and agreed that, for the time being, we would be better served with you remaining in your position," Luca said. The message was unmistakable. Luca had been discussing Synthe's future with the Sentinel, had participated in deciding his destiny.

"Ah. Just so, then. Whatever best meets your needs, then. I shall await your instructions."

ꕥ

"We're going to Jordan?" Natalie asked.

"Yes. The Scroll doesn't exactly give GPS coordinates, but as near as I can tell, it does the best you could expect for the 1200s. Bacon was a genius, that's for sure. Part of the instructions say to cut several of the drawings here, and here, and here." Steven pointed to the seemingly random blue lines running through four of the illustrations. "Now compare the new composite to this satellite image." Steven had cut and pasted four of the illustrations together to fit, like a puzzle, into one coherent drawing. There was an oblong body of water with several markers surrounding it – a crescent moon, a star, a sideways Y, and finally, the labyrinth crest.

"It's amazing," Natalie observed. "I mean, it would be more helpful if we knew what the symbols meant, but this is a good start…"

"The star fits with the location of Machaerus, which was a fortified complex on the Jordanian side of the Dead Sea. The Scroll specifically calls out the Dead Sea, so that would place the actual location of the fort approximately where it sits in the drawing, give or take…" Steven pointed at the screen, showing Natalie where he meant. "Machaerus is where John the Baptist was beheaded. It would have been a known landmark for centuries."

"Kind of a grisly claim to fame," Natalie said, shuddering involuntarily. Even with her familiarity of death, the vision of a bearded man having his head lopped off had stopping power.

"It is, but that makes it easier to pinpoint. There's not much else I can find in that area that would correlate. The crescent references Lot's wife, which is also consistent with the region."

"Turned into a pillar of salt, if I recall," Natalie said.

"You know your Bible."

"And the Y is?" Natalie asked.

"Looks to me like it sort of matches the Wadi Al Mujib," Steven said.

"The what?"

"It's a river that feeds into the Dead Sea. The Wadi Al Mujib. Which forks off east of the Dead Sea into the Wadi Al Mujib and the Wadi el Hidan. Wadi means river in Arabic. Or more specifically, it refers to a river bed, which may have water in the winter, but which usually dries up in the summer."

"So it's safe to say it gets hotter than hell there?" Natalie asked.

"That would be correct, this time of year. Although the Dead Sea does buffer the heat."

"Okay, we have the fort, Lot's wife, and the Y."

"And the Dead Sea."

"Check. Then it should be a snap to find the Divine Whatever," Natalie said. "So what's for lunch?"

"The Divine *Light* – not to be pedantic. And no, not really a snap. Again, this is rugged terrain in a wasteland, and the map isn't to scale. We have only a rough idea, along with some vague directions. Vague by today's standards, but very precise by standards eight hundred years ago…"

"Not so easy?"

"Is anything in life?"

"You were when I slid up to you in the shower," Natalie observed playfully.

"Your insulting tone with respect to my honor notwithstanding, what we have are some crude directions in Stadia, which are ancient units of measurement – from which the modern term 'stadium' comes. A Stadium is roughly six hundred feet," Steven said.

"That sounds pretty precise."

"Not really. Depending upon the language or the era, a foot varied in length. The two most likely as used in the Scroll are either 294 mm for an Olympic foot, or 308 mm for an Italic."

"That doesn't sound like a lot. Wait. They based a foot on…different sized feet, literally?" Natalie asked.

"Yup. And it isn't much, but when amplified by six hundred, we're talking around thirty feet of difference per Stadium. Put another way, if you calculate using the Olympic measurement, a Stadium is around 577 feet, and if you use the Italic, it's around 607 feet. And the directions, such as they are, tell us that we are to proceed thirty-five Stadia from the point where the Y forks, presumably up the Wadi el Hidan river bed. Once we've done so, we're supposed to go five Stadia north, where supposedly the Divine Light is located. Buried. But when you start looking at the margins of error, just based on the two most common possible variations of what a foot is, you could be off by over a fifth of a mile on the Wadi, and by about a hundred fifty feet once we leave the river bed. It's not impossible, but we're talking a ton of terrain to cover. Add to that we have no idea what we're looking for, and it gets ugly early."

"Then we could be off by huge distances, and won't know until we get there…" Natalie said softly.

"Correct. Trial and error. Which in the sun, in hundred-plus degree heat, is going to suck. We're probably talking about many days of digging around for who knows what in miserable conditions. And that presumes that the Church can get permission. Jordan is predominantly Sunni Muslim, as in ninety percent, so it's questionable how much cooperation they'll get. Oh, and that's a protected nature reserve, or at least parts of it are, from what I can tell online."

"You're making it sound less and less likely to succeed as you go along. Mister Buzz Kill. You're bringing me down," Natalie complained.

"It's like everything. If you don't know much about most things, they look easy. But the more you know about them, the harder they reveal themselves to be. Because most things are hard, or rather, are difficult. This won't be any different, unfortunately. It's just a good idea to have realistic expectations. Mine are optimistic, but pragmatic," Steven said.

"Like I said. Buzz Kill."

❧

Three days later, Luca had the four passports in his hands. The Church had pulled strings with the Italian government and gotten Natalie and Steven one Italian passport each, and the Vatican had issued two Vatican City passports for travel during the search for the Light. Steven was now Arturo Stefano Crossetti, and Natalie was Natalia Pomore Salmagundi.

He also had the agreed-upon signed letters. And two million dollars were ready to be transferred to whatever account Steven chose. He finished typing a message to Steven's e-mail address and pressed send. Now it was just a matter of transferring the cash and doing the handoff.

Luca considered the deal a bargain, but was strangely unenthusiastic about the prospect of getting the Scroll back. Now that Cross had solved the riddle, the relic had little but internal symbolic significance. Still, it was a win for the good guys, and he'd take it.

Cross hadn't told him anything about where they were going. Luca was hoping to discover more at their next meeting. When and where that would be was still unknown, but he figured that he'd soon find out.

A few minutes after sending the message, a chime sounded from his computer, signaling an inbound message. He opened it and read the instructions, nodding as he did so. Tomorrow was going to be another long day.

❧

Steven took the seat next to Luca on the short train ride from Milan to Parma, and wordlessly handed him the box with the Scroll container in it. Luca took it with a sense of disbelief – Cross had used a wine gift box, which was the perfect size, purchased in the morning at a liquor store in Milan, making it untraceable to Venice.

Luca had flown into Milan and they'd repeated the last minute phone call with instructions. Moody had explained to Steven that the method assured them of minimal chance of being tracked, which Steven wasn't hugely worried about, but Moody felt was still a risk. Moody had watched Luca at the airport to ensure there were no phone calls or any suspect contacts attempted, and then monitored him as he took a taxi, watching for a tail. Luca was clean. After ten minutes of waiting at the airport, he'd hopped into a cab and gone to the train station to do the reverse process there, just in case.

Steven was dressed like a businessman this time, wearing a blue dress jacket with a red tie over a blue and white pin-striped Oxford shirt, and gray slacks with a burgundy belt and loafers. There was also something different about his hair – it was slicked back with gel, in the Italian fashion.

Luca took the box from him. "This is what all the fuss was about?"

"Yes. Don't drop it. And keep it somewhere safer this time."

"Noted. We transferred the cash this morning."

"Congratulations on your purchase of the company. It runs itself. You won't have to do much. Although we might have a leak there – I've been mulling over how Frank's people knew we were at the Basilica of Saint Clemente, and the only thing that makes sense is they were given the translation of the first parchment." Steven proceeded to tell him about the two parchments, deliberately omitting the tablet. Why give up the secret sauce that made him look like a once-a-millennium genius?

Luca listened with interest and nodded. "Makes sense. So. Now you have the money and the letters…where do we go from here?" Luca asked.

Steven broke down the various items they would need in order to search for the Light.

"Do you mind if I write this down? It's a lot of detail," Luca said.

"Don't bother. Inside the box, next to the Scroll cylinder, you'll find a piece of paper with the requirements. Basically, permission from the Jordanian government to do some archeological exploration, a list of gear, ten or twelve men to dig, and a way in and out. I was thinking that we should fly into Amman. We'll probably be in Jordan for at least a week or two. The Scroll directions are detailed, but it will still be something of a miracle if we find anything. It's been at least eight hundred years and possibly longer than that, depending upon what we're looking for. I wouldn't expect a lot, but we'll give it our best shot. Oh, and we'll need some weapons. It also might be good if the diggers had military backgrounds," Steven said.

"I'm thinking of some of the Templars who are particularly suited. They receive much unorthodox training, including all types of weapons. They're among the best and very fit," Luca said, unconsciously putting a hand on his stomach.

"I'm also going to bring an observer with us on my team, which will consist of the girl, myself, and my friend. He's in the intelligence field, which could come in handy if we get into a bind in-country. From your side, I want you and the diggers. Nobody else."

"I understand. But I do have a highly-placed colleague who is ex-Mossad, and knows the region intimately…" Luca started.

"Absolutely not. Israeli intelligence would be the last thing we'd want, whether ex or current. The Jordanians are going to be skittish enough without bringing that into the mix. Another thing, I don't want anyone to know where we're going other than essential personnel. Limit it to need to know," Steven warned.

"Fine. What else? Timing?"

"That's up to you, and how fast you can get permission from Jordan. I can be ready to roll in a day. Start pulling strings. Speaking of which, pull some with the Roman police department and get them to back off on hunting for me and the girl. We don't know anything about the driver's murder, except what they do, so it would be helpful if that went to the back burner," Steven said.

"I'll see to it."

"Please do. Now it's phone time again." Steven gestured with his fingers, and Luca obligingly took out the battery and handed it to him.

"Can't you just leave it in the bathroom or something? Finding a battery is a pain," Luca groused.

"That's the whole point. If it's any consolation, I actually trust you. It's my intelligence friend who stipulated this routine, with no variation."

"Very well. I'll look forward to seeing you soon. I gather we communicate as we have, via e-mail?" Luca asked.

"Yes. I'll call your cell if there are any emergencies. Have a safe trip back to Rome and remember not to drop the box," Steven said, as he rose to make his way out of the first-class car.

Luca stared at the non-descript cardboard sheath and opened the top. Inside was the item, so sacred he'd never actually seen it. An ancient cylinder with a host of symbols etched into it. Not much to look at.

Strange that such a seemingly insignificant relic could cause so much commotion. He wondered what the Divine Light would turn out to be. Assuming they found it.

Which, after talking to Steven, wasn't a given by any means.

CHAPTER 34

Heat waves shimmered off the tarmac as the private Hawker executive jet set down on the runway of the Queen Alia airport in Amman, Jordan, its wheels smoking as they struck the scorching surface with a series of screeches. The summer temperatures were just beginning to hit the mid-nineties during the day, and temperatures could easily climb into the triple digits nearer the desert. Fortunately, the dust clouds from the freak winds, the notorious khamsins, had settled over the last few hours, and the flight arrived on time.

Steven and Natalie deplaned along with Luca, trailed by two Templars that Luca had selected for the detail. Both were in their late twenties and had seriously athletic bearings. The most obviously out-of-place member of the group was Luca, who was the oldest and also the least agile.

Natalie powered on her phone and made a quick call as they moved to customs, where the group was passed through as a formality. Luca had worked his magic, and they were welcomed as dignitaries in Jordan – a key archeological team associated with the Church, which had just made several lavish donations to some of the King's favorite charities. Their luggage trundled in a cart towards the charter lounge baggage claim, and within several minutes they were outside in the arid day, watching for their ride to appear.

A passenger van pulled to the curb followed by a Ford Expedition. The driver of the van got out, rounding the hood to greet Natalie with a hug before shaking hands with Steven.

"Robert. Good to see you. Everything going okay?" she asked. Robert was Moody's agreed upon cover name for the trip.

"Been in beautiful Jordan for two days, and so far, no worries. Let's get you loaded up and into the air-conditioning. You want to introduce me now, or later?" he asked, glancing at the rest of the group.

"Robert, this is Luca," Natalie said. "Luca, Robert. He's an old friend and will be facilitating things for us on the trip."

Luca shook hands and eyed Moody warily. "I believe we already met on the train. Always nice to have facilitators helping out," he said noncommittally.

"Nice to meetcha."

"And these two are Arturo and Francois," Natalie continued, gesturing to the young men.

They quickly got the bags into the back of the SUV, and soon they were on the road, departing the city. The two vehicles moved at a moderate pace down the well-maintained highway as Moody briefed them.

"We'll be heading to the Dead Sea, then down the coast until we get to the parking area for the Wadi Al Mujib. There, we have a helicopter that will fly us to the coordinates Steven selected for the base camp. It will bring us in, and then return to Amman for the remainder of the supplies. It would take far too much time to hike to the camp location – days, in fact – and ATVs won't make it due to the water depth in some of the sections. I have a satellite phone for communications; cells won't work where we're going."

"What's the weather been like?" Steven asked.

"Hot during the day and hot at night when the wind's blowing off the desert. Otherwise, you see a thirty-degree drop in a matter of a few hours. Which sounds like a lot, but if it's a hundred during the day that means it gets down to maybe seventy-two at night, if we're lucky. So think of this as a warm-weather holiday, but without the nice hotel rooms, restaurants, or bathrooms and showers. We'll haul our own water in – you don't want to drink the water in the stream. It's probably okay for bathing, assuming there are no parasites in it, but I'd advise using our water supply for that, too. The helicopter will keep it coming, and we'll have a one week emergency supply in case the weather doesn't cooperate." Moody turned to Steven. "Any idea how long we'll be in for?"

"My guess is weeks. But no way of knowing."

"Then we should plan on establishing as comfortable a base camp as we can. It would have been nice to get more guys on the ground, but that was a problem, correct?" Moody asked, leaning his head towards where Luca was sitting.

"Yes. On such short notice we were limited. The agreement was that we wouldn't use any machinery or power tools, that we'd be discreet, and would leave the land largely as we found it. Six was the maximum number of people they would allow on the dig. Believe me, I pushed for another dozen, but it wasn't possible," Luca said.

"Sounds like they were concerned about having a big camp tearing up the hills," Natalie commented.

"That was a part of it. But it also was really more the timing than anything. That, and we had to agree to leave anything we found in place, which we all know isn't going to happen. So the fewer people around, the fewer witnesses, from our perspective," Luca underscored.

"I'd imagine the Jordanians will take the position that whatever we find is their property, being as it's on their soil," Steven pointed out.

"Yes, but we've already taken care of that. We have been assigned an inspector from the state, who you'll soon learn is nowhere to be found. He's probably sitting at home counting his blessings at the newfound wealth he's come into for filing reports saying nothing was located."

The highway came to an abrupt T intersection at the shores of the Dead Sea. They headed south, past numerous large hotels and spas. The area had been developed into a thriving tourist area, where locals and international visitors alike flocked to the complexes in droves.

"Was that a Marriott?" Natalie asked as they sped by yet another massive group of buildings.

"Yup. Unfortunately, we won't be staying there. It's tents and air mattresses for us," Moody said.

The four lane highway narrowed to two and became a steep drop off into the sea. Traffic was light, and once they passed the tourist zone it thinned to nearly nothing. Even with the air-conditioning belting out, they could all feel the heat radiating off the windows, and it ran through everyone's minds that this would probably be the last time they'd be in a cool environment for a long while.

Eventually, the vehicles pulled off at a dirt parking lot along the east side of the road, in front of a group of dilapidated red-painted buildings –

bathrooms for the tourists. A few vehicles were parked abreast of them, but there was nobody to be seen other than a wizened old man who acted as the parking attendant.

"We're here," Moody sang out as he shut the motor off.

When they opened the doors, the withering heat that greeted them was like the blast from an oven, and the group reluctantly crawled out into the harsh glare of the afternoon sun. Moody made a call on his satellite phone, then turned to Steven. "Helicopter will be here in a few minutes."

Steven studied the entrance to the Wadi – a magnificent canyon, carved from the light limestone rock, easily towering hundreds of feet overhead on either side.

"There will be snakes and scorpions and poisonous spiders galore, so try not to get bitten by anything that will kill you. By the time we can get you out of here, you'll be long gone," Steven said.

"He's not kidding," Moody stressed. "There's a first aid kit in one of the bags, but it's not going to do a lot of good if you get the wrong kind of bite, so pay attention to where you're walking. There are enough deadly critters around here to kill us a hundred times over, so remember at all times that this isn't downtown Los Angeles."

"L.A.'s no picnic either," Natalie said. "You obviously haven't been there for a while."

Everyone laughed, relieving the stress that was building from the remorseless ravages of the sun.

A Jordanian military truck pulled off the road and an officer stepped out. He approached the group gingerly, and then deferred to Luca, as the oldest. In broken English, he welcomed them on behalf of the Jordanian government and assured them that their vehicles would be watched over by the attendant, twenty-four hours a day. He seemed uncertain what else to say, so Moody addressed him in Arabic, thanking him for the attention and the courtesy of stopping to see them off.

That seemed to satisfy the officer, who strutted back to the truck and climbed in, patting the roof as a signal to drive on. The message was clear – the military was watching them.

"This is a nature preserve, and you need a permit from the government to hike it. They've stopped handing those out until we've finished with our excavation," Luca said.

Natalie came to stand by Steven's side, gazing up into the canyon. "Steven. It's magnificent. I've never seen anything like it."

She was right. It was incredible, and humbling. The small stream of erosion had taken millions of years to cut through the rock, and the effect was breathtaking. Few people alive would ever get to experience it as they were about to.

The solitude of the moment was shattered by the beating of rotors, and a medium-sized gray military helicopter hovered over the area before slowly descending. Leaning into the swirl of dust, the group toted their bags to it. The flight crew stowed the luggage, everyone boarded, and they lifted off to make the short flight.

Steven watched as they traversed the canyon, veering to the right when they hit the fork in the rivers. After what he knew to be roughly four miles they arrived at the dry, relatively flat area where Steven had calculated they could make camp, at the base of what was going to be their work area. The river bed was gray gravel, with an inclination of twenty feet over its surface of three hundred foot length, but it was large enough to land a helicopter if there was no wind, and he reasoned that they could set up a base camp on the edge and not have the tents blow away by the rotors.

The chopper set down and the small group disembarked, taking their bags from the flight crew. The hold contained several drums of water, as well as various other duffel bags and containers. Ten minutes after arriving, the helicopter was empty, and the crew waved to them as they lifted off. Once the aircraft had departed, the silence was deafening – there was literally no sound but the burbling of the meager river beyond. After only a small amount of exertion everyone was already bathed in sweat – the temperature in the canyon was into the triple digits due to lack of any breeze.

Steven had brought a handheld outdoor thermometer; when he pulled it out of his pack, it read a hundred and seven Fahrenheit. At eleven-thirty a.m.. Anyone with doubts as to whether this was going to be easy duty quickly lost them, and it was with a certain sluggish determination that they unpacked. Several of the unidentified cases contained their camping gear, and they doggedly pitched tents and built a ready-made enclosure for the two latrines. Moody handled the creation of the area for the food and water, and once they were well on their way, he made another call on his satellite phone.

Forty minutes later, the quiet in the canyon was again fractured by the thumping of rotor blades as their chopper approached, loaded with the remainder of their supplies. They were fortunate there was still no wind to speak of, and the landing occurred without drama. The three man flight crew hopped out of the cabin and hurriedly unloaded yet more boxes and crates, which Moody and the two Templars moved to the little camp area.

Ten minutes after it had set down, the helicopter lifted off again, not to return for three days, at the earliest. The muggy air settled on the group like a blanket as they watched it crest the hill towards Amman, their last link to civilization severed. After a few minutes of rest, they returned to setting up the camp for the night before it started to get dark. There were still a few hours of light, and they needed to get the kitchen area up to speed. The helicopter had brought them a small gas-powered generator with several five gallon tanks of fuel, so they could have limited refrigeration in the oversized ice chests using several deep-cycle batteries they could then charge with the generator.

It wasn't Club Med, but it would do.

Steven took bearings with the rangefinder, then retrieved the handheld GPS he'd brought to calculate positions. He powered it on, but nothing happened. Checking the batteries, he tried again, but with no success. After a half hour of fiddling with the device, it was obvious that something had malfunctioned. The adventure wasn't starting off well. Without the GPS, they'd be down to dead reckoning from approximate points on their campsite. That wouldn't work very well, Steven knew, but he would make the best of it for now.

The afternoon wore on as they put the finishing touches on the camp. Just before dark, Luca approached him as he stood near the bottom of the slope, studying the north face of the canyon through his binoculars.

"It's a huge area, isn't it?" he said.

"It is. That's what I was trying to explain on the plane. It's one thing to read the Scroll's directions, but quite another to be on the ground. The place is vast," Steven agreed.

"Do you see anything promising? It all looks the same to me," Luca said, his face red from exertion and sun.

"No. But we have no idea what we're looking for. Whatever it is has been exposed to the elements for many hundreds, or even thousands, of years. So this isn't going to be a matter of seeing two columns from an old temple sticking out of the cliff. If it hasn't been discovered by now, it's because it doesn't look like anything special. Countless generations of nomads have been down this creek, and they'd have noticed." Steven lifted a thermal canteen to his lips and drank some water. "It's not going to be easy. It will be luck, more than skill, that gets us results, I'm afraid. And hard work. A lot of digging. Starting at first light tomorrow."

"That's what I was afraid of. Oh well. Goodnight, Dr. Cross."

"Goodnight. And it's Steven."

"Ah. Right then. Goodnight, Steven. Say goodnight to Natalie for me. And it's Diego," Luca said and moved off in the direction of his tent, walking stiffly, in the wake of the day's demands.

CHAPTER 35

"There."

Steven released the button of the small two-way radio and watched as Arturo, high up on the canyon face, set an orange pole into the steep slope. Steven adjusted the laser rangefinder and shook his head at the futility of it as he waved approval. The absence of a GPS was worse than he'd thought. With the coordinates programmed in, it was far easier to get a bearing on the starting position. This was using a hammer to thread a needle.

He walked over to Moody and took him aside.

"You need to get the chopper back here with another GPS. I have the coordinates in my laptop, but we need the device. Otherwise we're just spinning our wheels for the next three days, exhausting ourselves for no reason," he said.

"Let me see what I can do." Moody moved to his tent to get the Sat-phone.

Their first night had been hot, and the largest, most unexpected problem had been the noise. Or rather, the lack of it. Other than random animals, there was no sound other than their camp, and Steven had realized within a few hours that three of his companions snored. Loudly. Natalie and he had spent the night tossing and turning, listening to the nocturnal symphony of labored breathing, and had gotten too little sleep. Two weeks or more of this would be a kind of hell.

Moody had unpacked the weapons the prior evening and passed them out – several M-4 assault rifles, and six Colt .45 semi-automatic pistols, fully loaded. He'd watched as Natalie had efficiently checked her weapon and then thumbed the safety on and off before putting it by her pillow, doing the same with one of the rifles as she set it next to the bed. It had been a long time since he'd fired one – over twenty years, but the rifle still felt like second nature when he picked it up. Some things were like riding a bicycle, he supposed.

Moody squinted at the sun as he moved to the kitchen area to get a drink, listening intently to a voice on the other end of the phone. He grabbed a water bottle out of the cooler and held it against his forehead.

"All right. See if you can get one here today – we're dead in the water without it. And check to ensure it's operational before you come out. Call me when you know something." Moody approached Steven with the phone in his hand. "They're going to try to find one and fly it out. Hopefully, before dark."

They exchanged glances. It was eight a.m. and already sweltering.

Steven nodded thanks and returned to studying the canyon face for any anomalies.

It wasn't his lucky day.

❧

Arturo and Francois were covered in sweat, taking a break near the section they'd been digging up for hours. The soil was a combination of rock and dirt, sedimentary, with layers of sand, so it wasn't hugely difficult work on the whole – if it hadn't been a hundred and ten degrees. But the heat made it very slow going. They could reasonably keep at it for ten to fifteen minute intervals, and then had to rest for at least that long to rehydrate and replenish the salt they were losing from sweating. They'd created shade with a tarp and several poles, which provided scant relief from the worst of the sun's blaze.

The tarp flapped as a gust blew through the canyon, hot and dry, but still welcome after most of the day had been spent in heavy, motionless air. The two men studied their latest excavation with dismay. It was a meager effort by any measure. They'd managed to get an area twenty feet square dug to a depth of three feet, matching another like it five yards away. Other than the odd scorpion or snake hole, there was nothing to show for their efforts. Whatever it was they were looking for wasn't in that spot.

Cross had joined in digging for an hour, but had been called away by Luca and had never returned. It was just as well, Francois thought. They had a slow but steady rhythm, Arturo with the pick, he with the shovel, and a third or fourth body actually got in the way rather than helping. Francois had mentioned it to the Doctor just before he'd left, respectfully but sincerely. The two were there to provide the muscle. Cross was more valuable studying the terrain for possible signs of whatever they were searching for.

The breeze gusted again, and this time didn't fade, but rather built to a steady twenty knot wind, bringing with it sand from the desert and creating dust in the canyon, partially from their excavation. After trying to continue in futility, the two-way radio crackled to life and Cross called them back to camp. The day was over, at least as far as they were concerned. The two men gathered their water and tools and gratefully headed down the hill to the river bed two-thirds of a mile below, famished and exhausted.

The wind continued to build and by the time they were at the camp, was gusting to thirty knots, threatening to take the tents with it. They secured the kitchen and the latrine and then busied themselves with the others, bolstering the fastenings affixing the tents to the rocky river bed. This was the *Shammal*, a wind that blew from the north, and which Steven had warned could last for a week at a time. Normally not a huge problem, it increased in force due to the funnel effect of the canyon, making the gusting unpredictable.

Moody's satellite phone rang and he barked terse instructions. In a few minutes, the chopper slowly came over the top of the hill, having problems due to the updrafts from the wind. It descended cautiously, the turbulence buffeting it around, and at a hundred feet above the river bed it lurched alarmingly towards the canyon wall, blown by a particularly strong surge. His phone rang again. He plugged his ear with one hand against the noise from the blades and peered through the blowing dust as he held the bulky handset to his other.

"They can't set down. Too dangerous right now. They can try coming back tomorrow, or they can get as low as possible and drop the GPS to us," he shouted to Steven.

"Shit. Okay, let's get that tarp and each take a side. It'll provide a larger surface area for us to catch the unit." Steven called over to Natalie, who was battling with a tent peg ten yards away. "Natalie? Can you come over and help for a second?"

Natalie moved to his side and he quickly explained the plan. They gathered up the tarp from beneath the larger rocks someone had placed on top of it to keep it from blowing away and signaled to Arturo to join them, taking the fourth side of the rectangle. They unfolded it, then positioned themselves below the helicopter, which tried descending one more time.

When it was about sixty feet above the creek bed, the side door slid open, and a head popped out, followed by an arm holding a small cardboard box. The man with the box turned to give the pilot instructions, and the craft shifted a few yards to the left. In position, he released the GPS and they watched as it plummeted towards them.

Another gust hit it and altered the trajectory, and in a split second it became obvious they wouldn't be able to stop its fall with the tarp. Natalie dropped her corner and sprinted towards the stream, eyes never leaving the object, and executed a perfect football catch even as she tripped and fell forward. She absorbed most of the fall with her shoulder, but the round, smooth rocks of the river bed still did damage, and when she stood, triumphantly, box held aloft in her right hand, her left arm was bleeding from multiple lacerations.

Steven ran to her as the chopper lifted back into the sky and, after gingerly hugging her, inspected the damage.

"Good catch."

"Thanks. I was sort of a tomboy in high school, so I got to play a lot of ball." She winced as he touched one of the gashes. "Easy. That hurts."

"I'll bet. Let's get you cleaned up and bandaged. I'll ask for an extra ration of beer for you tonight, in honor of your heroics," Steven said.

"Not to have your way with me…" Natalie murmured.

"You've seen through my evil plan." Steven looked at her arm again. "I'll patch you up and then enter the coordinates into the GPS from my laptop. Tomorrow should be more productive," Steven said. "You need me to carry you?"

Natalie gave him a dirty look. "It's a few scratches, tough guy. But hey, if it works with your barbarian conqueror fantasy, knock yourself out."

Relieved that she was fine, Steven took her good hand and they rejoined the group, which was battening down the camp against the howling wind.

❧

The next morning started better. The *Shammal* was still blowing, as it had all night, but had died down to something tolerable by midnight. Steven stood with Arturo and Francois on the sloping side of the canyon wall near the top, the new GPS in his hand. They were thirty yards from the previous day's digs.

"This is the first section I programmed. From here, to that rock," Steven gestured with the unit, "down to that outcropping. That's our best bet out of the gate. You sure you don't need a hand, Arturo?"

"Thanks, but no. This is what we came to do. Don't worry about it. You'll have your work cut out for you once we find what we're looking for." Arturo smiled. "Which is what, again?"

"I wish I could be more specific. Obviously, we're looking for something buried, something man made. Maybe an old chest, or something crafted out of stone. Anything besides dirt and rocks," Steven said, kicking a stray stone down the hill.

"Buried treasure, *eh*?" Francois commented, shouldering the pick.

"Something like that. I'll stay up here with you, if you don't mind. In case we find anything, it will cut down the time to get all the way up from the camp," Steven offered.

"Make yourself at home. We have a few folding chairs there by the water cooler, and if the wind doesn't get any worse than this, the tarp should stay up for shade."

Arturo wiped the accumulated sweat from his brow with a hand towel he'd brought for that purpose and picked up the shovel. All three looked at where the sun was rising into the hazy sky, promising them another day of its angry, roasting glare. Steven checked his watch. Seven-thirty a.m., and already baking. He headed for the scant shade provided by the tarp, giving the snake holes that riddled the mountainside a wide berth.

Settling in, he pulled his thermometer from his cargo shorts and pressed it on. Ninety-eight degrees, and it had only been light for a little over an hour.

It was going to be another brutal one.

CHAPTER 36

The helicopter lifted off from the river bed and the little group watched as it ascended to the top of the canyon and sailed out of range. After ten days of digging, they'd established a routine. Up at dawn, begin the day's work by seven-thirty, shut down in the heat of the day at two, and prepare for the next-day's excavation while hiding from the devastating effect of the sun until dusk arrived.

The polite courtesy of the first week had gradually been replaced by a kind of curt brevity, as the constant demands of the environment caused tempers to shorten and patience to wane. The unspoken pressure on Steven to perform mounted with each passing day, and the northern horizon was peppered with unproductive excavations, even now fading back into the canyon sides as the relentless winds continued unabated.

They were down to the final few possible sites from the second set of calculations, using Stadium length assumptions of 606.8 feet and 577.28 feet. The longer Stadium had come up dry, and at day six they'd moved down the creek 350 yards and shortened the elevation appropriately, to factor in the shorter unit of measurement. That had yielded another area to be dug up, which, allowing for a margin of error, would take another five or six days. They were nearing the end of that run, and Steven was becoming obsessive about checking and rechecking every aspect of the translation.

That morning, as he sighted with the rangefinder and studied the canyon with his binoculars, watching as Arturo and Francois toiled diligently at their task, he'd had a breakthrough thought – one of the flashes of inspiration that seemed to have deserted him since Antonia's death. What if the calculations, the Stadium length, had been written with a different, more obscure length than what he'd assumed? The logical unit would have been the Italic, given the document, with the more distant possibility the shorter Olympic. *But what if they'd used the Egyptian?* Given the location in Jordan, it wasn't impossible, but it hinted at a far more ancient burial. He did a quick calculation and figured that it would put the starting point for the ascent roughly a thousand yards further east of their original position.

Steven grabbed his binoculars, and Natalie, spying him from where she was working on the computer near the kitchen, wandered over to join him.

"We going sightseeing?" she asked.

"I want to check something out."

He explained his new theory as they trudged up the river bed to the new point, Steven watching the GPS screen as they walked.

"We're here," he announced.

They both looked up the side of the canyon, to see a steep slope interrupted by a ravine leading to the top; evidence of a minor runoff tributary that had etched its way through the rock over the eons. Steven studied the area around the summit with his binoculars, then did a quick mental calculation using the new assumption.

"It's at the top of this ravine?" Natalie asked.

"That would be the instinct, but not what the Scroll said. It said north. That's north-east. The river turned south back there. By my calculations, if we adjust for everything, the new spot would be…there." Steven swung his binoculars back in the direction of the current dig. The new spot was a quarter mile from the original excavation they'd started on the first day. He pointed the rangefinder at it and adjusted a little. Peering back up to the new area, he scrutinized the landscape for any clues. None were forthcoming. Only…

"What?" Natalie asked, hearing his sharp intake of breath.

"There's a rise there that looks promising. I want to take a closer look," Steven said and began striding back along the river bed to the camp. Natalie quickly caught up.

"You seem optimistic. For the first time in days."

"I don't want to get anyone's hopes up, Natalie. This is still needle in haystack territory. I'm just going stir crazy from doing nothing, so maybe I'll go for a little hike and poke around some."

"Cool. I'll go with you."

Steven glanced at her. "Sure. Wear sunscreen," he said.

Back at the camp, Natalie ducked into their tent and emerged a few moments later. They both grabbed shovels and he slung a thermal bag with water in it over his shoulder. Steven entered in the new coordinates he'd calculated and created a waypoint on the GPS. They looked up the canyon face.

Steven shook his head. "That's right along the path up that smaller ravine we've been using to get to the other dig. It's along the natural route we selected to hike up the canyon – the obvious and easiest way to the top."

"What are you waiting for?" Natalie stepped across the shallow river water and was at the base of the canyon within thirty seconds. Steven noted that the outdoors agreed with her – the cargo shorts and army green tank top demanded his attention, even in the heat.

It took twenty-five minutes for them to reach the waypoint, climbing at a moderate pace, by which time they were both soaked in sweat. They stopped, having ascended almost seven hundred feet, and caught their breath. Steven kicked absently at the dirt.

"This seemed a lot easier back at the river. There's a whole lot of nothing here," he commented, studying the ground for a sign of…something.

"Where do we start?" Natalie asked, panting slightly.

"Let's drink some water and take a few minutes. Last thing we need to do is faint. We can begin…here." Steven tossed the shovel a few feet and dropped the thermal bag on the ground, fishing out two water bottles.

Once they were hydrated, they began digging. It was fairly easy for the first foot. By the second foot it became difficult, and by the third they were unable to keep going. They'd hit rock. Steven moved to the side and continued a trench, widening it until it was ten feet long by three feet wide. Natalie worked the other end of it, and when they took another break, they noticed Arturo and Francois waving at them from above. They waved back and then resumed their excavation. Natalie was ready to call it quits after two hours, when her shovel hit something…different. She scraped at it and saw that it was rock, but with primitive mortar bonding it in place. Afraid to be wrong, she continued scraping stone and dirt out of the way, until she was sure.

"Steven."

He turned.

"What is it?"

"Tell me again what we're looking for?"

"I'm not sure. Something man-made," Steven said, wiping trickles of sweat off his face with his arm.

Natalie looked up at him, broiled by the sun, red, in spite of the liberally-applied sunscreen and the baseball hat, giving it a game try on the side of a hill in the middle of nowhere. She felt a sudden and unexpected surge of emotion, a combination of attraction, sympathy, admiration and heartache, and she realized with a twinge that what she was feeling was probably love, for the first time in her life. Different than the love for her father, or the lust she'd felt for sexual partners. This felt altogether…right.

None of which she shared with Steven. Instead, she smiled and said, "I think I found it."

❧

An hour and a half later, Arturo and Francois had joined them in clearing the area of sediment, revealing a crudely-mortared wall, erected from medium sized stones from the river.

"Can you imagine hauling those rocks all the way up here?" Natalie wondered.

"Whoever did this wanted to make sure this stayed in place for a long time. It must have taken a week to build, even though it's not that big," Steven said.

He watched as Luca and Moody arrived from the camp with the sledgehammer and a crowbar, Moody also toting a flashlight.

"What have we got?" Luca asked, puffing from exertions of the climb.

"A wall. Very old, by the looks of it," Steven reported.

"A wall?"

"Yes. Question is what's behind door number one…" Natalie said.

"What's the plan?" Moody asked.

"I'm going to go with: knock down the wall," Steven said.

He took the sledgehammer from Moody and swung it against the upper reach. A rock gave way, falling inward, revealing a dark space behind it.

"Arturo, Francois. Go get more water, and a camera. We're going to be here for a while," Luca instructed the two younger men, who reluctantly gathered their gear and began the hike back to the camp. "I'd prefer to keep this between us for now. I don't know what we're going to find, but I'd rather not have more eyes on it than necessary," Luca said in a low voice.

"It's your ride. You can decide who gets on," Steven said, swinging the hammer again. A rock shifted, but other than that, nothing. He hit it again, and another rock fell in. Moody moved in to help by manning the crowbar in a somewhat practiced fashion.

Twenty minutes went by, and they'd cleared most of the man-made barrier away, revealing a cave behind it – a depression in the limestone that had been there for millennia. Natalie looked back down the canyon at the camp and saw Arturo and Francois loading up a rucksack with supplies. She turned back to the cave and caught Steven's eye.

"Who wants to do the honors?" Steven asked.

Luca gestured with his hand for them to go in.

"Ladies first," Moody said, handing the flashlight to Natalie.

After taking it, Natalie hesitated, then drew a deep breath and stepped into the gloomy cavity. She took a few small steps and waited for her eyes to adjust, enjoying the substantially cooler, if musty, temperature. Steven stepped in after her, carrying the hammer, followed by Moody. Luca brought up the rear. The cave was surprisingly large and deep, stretching for twenty-five feet from the newly-created entry. The walls were the same light limestone as the canyon. Steven realized that his pupils had widened to accommodate the darkness and he could see fairly well.

A crudely fashioned circle of thorned vines sat on top of an ancient stone tablet, atop a primitive pedestal that had been hewn from the soft rock at one side of the chamber, and the group approached it with hopeful trepidation. Natalie shone a beam of light on the coarsely engraved inscription on the rock – they all heard Luca's sharp intake of breath.

"It's...it's beyond belief," he murmured reverently.

"Is that what I think it is?" Steven said.

Luca didn't respond. Steven turned to face him.

"Is it?"

CHAPTER 37

"The inscription. What does it say?" Natalie asked.

"I…it says, 'Heaven sent its son as the Divine Light'," Luca whispered.

"So – this is the crown of thorns from the crucifixion?" Moody asked.

"Perhaps. I mean, in light of the circumstances…" Luca seemed confused.

"I'd say it is, based on the engraving. Which, if I'm not mistaken, is Aramaic," Steven said.

Luca was startled. "You read Aramaic?"

"Just a few words, from some ancient parchment studies I did years ago. But, apparently, you do," Steven said.

"It's not uncommon among those of higher learning in the Church. The Jerusalem Talmud is written in Aramaic, after all," Luca said.

"Keeping up on the competition?" Steven asked.

"I wouldn't put it that way…"

"I'll bet. But even I recognize one of the words. Yêšû." Steven peered at the inscription again. "That would be Jesus, for those who skipped archaic languages in high school," Steven said.

"You're correct, of course," Luca murmured.

"What does the tablet say?" Moody asked.

"It's only a few words. Luca?" Steven prompted.

Luca peered at the primitive lettering and cleared his throat. "I live in each of you. Love one another," he whispered.

"Then…this is the last gospel," Moody said in a hushed voice.

The group regarded the crown and tablet with a sense of awe, in the presence of history. Natalie broke the trance.

"Steven? Come here," she called out, having moved to the deepest part of the cave.

"What is it?" Steven asked softly.

"Another wall."

Steven looked at where she was shining the flashlight. It was another barrier, constructed from the same stones and mortar as the one they'd just broken through. Steven caught Moody's eye and nodded. Steven hefted the sledge hammer and swung it sideways at the edge, where the wall met the cave. It bounced off in a spray of shards, but the sound was of striking something hollow. He swung again, and a stone gave way, just a little.

Moody and he took turns demolishing the obstacle, and after another quarter hour most of it lay in a heap on the cave floor. The noise of the pounding was deafening, but nobody wanted to move out of the cave. It was as though they were rooted to the floor. Even as the dust settled after the final hammer blow, nobody approached the new opening. Finally, Natalie moved to Steven with the flashlight and took his hand. He directed the beam into the depths of the cavity and saw a few items leaning against the limestone wall – a roughly crafted leather satchel, some worn sandals, a battered spear.

Natalie and Steven inched into the crypt, and their light skimmed over the interior, stopping when it came to a form lying on the cave floor. A skeleton lay on its back, staring sightlessly at the ceiling, the fabric of the thin material that had covered it deteriorated to smithereens. The group was frozen.

Moody broke the silence. "Okay, this is too weird. I'm getting out of here. Luca, let me by. I need some air," he said, edging towards the mouth of the cave.

"I'm afraid not," Luca said, as he slammed him in the base of the skull with his heavy steel pistol.

Moody collapsed in an inert heap on the floor, his head making an audible thunk as it hit. A small pool of blood collected beneath his skull as he lay, unmoving.

Steven moved slowly to the side wall as he took in the scene, pulling Natalie with him.

Luca trained the gun on them. "That's far enough," he warned.

Natalie's eyes widened in shocked disbelief. Steven asked the obvious question.

"Why?"

Luca sighed, an exhalation of exhaustion and frustration. "Does it matter?" he asked.

"To me, it does," Steven said.

Luca hesitated, seeming to win an internal struggle, and then started speaking in a quiet monotone.

"The Church is the only family I've ever known. I've given it my life. And yet I've watched as it has lost relevance, even as I've defended its honor and fought the good fight. I knew that whatever we found here would be hidden away while a group of frightened old men debated the possible effects of its meaning on their authority, so in the end, all my work will have been to support a waning institution too timid to do what it should." He gestured with his free hand. "This will be concealed while the powers that be argue whether the world should know the truth. I'm not bitter about it, but as I've grown older, I've also become more pragmatic. I'm a secret warrior for a secret sect of a Church that's afraid to make bold moves to regain its vitality. And I suppose I'm tired of watching it from the sidelines, living a monastic existence devoted to the richest institution on the planet."

"You certainly sound bitter," Natalie said.

"I'm not. It's just that I realized when the Scroll went missing that the Church would do far more and act way more decisively to protect its interests than it ever would to regain the leadership role it used to have in the civilized world. Other religions are boldly evangelizing and spreading their reach. But I'm part of an antiquated system that's afraid of its own shadow, and whatever the Divine Light was, I knew it would ultimately be suppressed. Now that I see the truth, I'm even more convinced I've done the right thing."

Steven shook his head. "*The right thing?* Are you kidding me? Do you have any idea how wrong whatever you're doing is? Whose skeleton do you think this is, anyway, with a crown of thorns the lobby attraction? This is history being made," Steven pointed out, his voice rising in volume as he finished.

"Ah, the passion of the younger man. I almost remember how it was. Yes, this is history – a history that the Church won't be able to make public, no matter what. Do you have any idea what it would do to its legends and reputation if Jesus' body was found? It would turn the Church on its ear. Millions would be devastated. It would mean that the Son of God, proclaimed as such by a hotly-contested vote of Roman cardinals, was a man – a man who clearly didn't rise from the dead after three days and ascend to heaven," Luca said. He cocked his ear, registering a sound in the distance.

Steven gripped Natalie's hand to comfort her. He needed to keep Luca talking and hope for an opening.

"Oh, come on. I think most Christians understand that the Bible is allegorical, and not to be taken literally. Even the Pope has said so. I think you're completely wrong. I think finding the body of Christ along with his last words would rekindle faith and belief and give the Church new legs. It would be proof of a kind. And the last words of Jesus…you have to admit, they're powerful." Steven said.

"I don't disagree. In fact, you're saying exactly what I believe. But the problem is that I know how Rome works, and I can tell you categorically that it would be decades, if not centuries, before any of this was known…if ever. The Church is an enterprise – a business, if you will. It sells faith. But the market isn't as robust as it used to be. Science has encroached on the faith business and taken market share from it. So, like all big businesses with a shrinking market, it either needs to innovate and reinvent itself, or circle the wagons and fight to keep a monopoly going. And I'm telling you, it is more interested in protecting what it has than blazing a new trail. Even the words on that tablet could cause an upheaval – if the Lord is in each of us, do we really require a bunch of robed dignitaries to act as the mouthpiece of heaven? Do you see what I mean?" Luca mopped his brow with the back of his free hand. "While I agree this is a miraculous find and should be trumpeted from the highest buildings, I'm equally sure that the preservation of the Church's position in the faith business will force silence. It's sad, and it's wrong, and I wish I was mistaken, but I'm not."

"Fair enough. Let's say you're right. Why…this?" Natalie asked.

"Because I see the Church for what it is. It's a large, super-wealthy behemoth that's all about money and power, and has little to do any more with faith and spreading the gospel. Truth be told, it hasn't been about that for almost ever. Did you know, that even in the first centuries of its existence, complaints started to surface about priests being the wealthiest men in their towns? These were the representatives of a religion founded on the idea of a savior who sacrificed everything, who lived in poverty and eschewed material possessions. And yet its princes, its bishops, lived in relative luxury while they sat in judgment of lesser mortals. Fast forward to present day and you find an institution founded on those principles of austerity and compassion that has managed to become the richest entity in existence. Doesn't that seem a little odd to you? That the God business should pay so well, when countless generations of humans have lived and died in misery? The hypocrisy is astounding. I should know. I've been a part of it."

Luca motioned with his pistol, and Natalie and Steven flinched as his voice rose. "So, why? *Why*? I'll tell you why. I already know the outcome of this little adventure. The secrets will stay secret, and nothing will change. The rich will get richer. The poor will stay oppressed and poor. I got to thinking that I don't know how much time I have left, so why not do what the Church always has? Why not focus on *my* needs and accumulate something for myself? I've lived in poverty my entire life within rock-throwing distance of palaces, while the religion I pledged my soul to is let down by its servants in the interests of greed. Why not benefit, since the Church always does? I've been an idiot, a naïve and stupid man. But I'm not going to be stupid anymore. Now, no more talking."

Luca glanced at his watch. They stood motionless in the cave for what seemed like forever. Steven tried to edge closer to the wall. Luca shook his head. It was no good; there wasn't enough space to maneuver.

"At least let me check on Robert. He's still out cold," Steven said after a few more minutes had gone by.

"Forget it. Stay where you are and don't move."

"But he needs help," Natalie protested.

"Heaven will help him if he truly requires it."

After another wait, Steven resumed baiting Luca, sure he could suck him in. "Sounds like you've confused stupidity with being honest. Weren't you the one who asked me whether I believed in God? Whether I knew the difference between good and evil? What was that? An act?" Steven asked.

"No. Not an act. I should have framed my question differently. It's not about good or evil. Good men do evil things, and evil men do good things. Hitler loved his dog. It's not that simple. It's not good versus evil. It's rich versus poor, powerful versus powerless. The Church understands that. It knows that with money and power, you can affect outcomes, control things. You can make or break kings, and build or crush empires. The meek don't inherit anything but a cold, shallow grave while their children's lifetimes are spent in indentured servitude. The poor have no power. The rich and powerful allow them the illusion of free will and power so they'll behave and not cause trouble. The privileged allow elections in which all the candidates are owned by them. They allow a choice between their bought-and-paid-for alternatives. No, if you want to do good, or have any power in the real world, you have to have money. That's what I've learned from watching the Church my entire life."

Natalie frowned. "That's a corruption of a concept. By men. How can you stand here, within a few feet from the body of your Savior, and confuse the abomination of power with your belief in Christianity? How can you live with yourself?" Natalie demanded.

"That's *my* point, not yours. That entity with all the power and money will decide whether or not this remains secret, and I'm telling you that it will. There's nothing I'll be able to do to change that. Nor will you. If you accept that I'm right, then the only remaining question is whether you make money from it, or not. I think in that respect, Dr. Frank is absolutely correct. Do you really think that he wants to make the Church dance for him? What do you really believe this is all about? You think he wants these remains for his own? Please. He wants what everyone wants. He's recognized an opportunity in this to make out handsomely, by simply allowing something to happen that the Church also wants to happen. So everybody wins. The Church gets to hide their secrets. Frank makes a fortune. The Church pays him to go away and doesn't even sneeze over the amount. Doesn't matter what the number is. Because there's a bottomless pit of money where that came from. Everyone wins, except me. It just took me a while to realize that I could do what I am being chartered to do by my Church and make my own fortune in the process."

"So this is about money?" Steven spat.

"Isn't everything?" a voice from the cave entrance said, as two shadows momentarily blocked out the shafts of sunlight.

CHAPTER 38

Morbius Frank entered the cave, mopping his cadaverous face with a silk handkerchief. His safari hat was cocked jauntily on his head, lending him the appearance of death on holiday. He was holding a pistol – a Glock 17, its long silencer directed ominously in their direction. Sia Amieri stood to his side, having stopped near the crown of thorns on the podium, his bulk dwarfing his master. Frank took in the situation with a glance and then eyed the crown and the tablet beneath it more closely. He moved towards it but stopped short, as if fearing to touch it. He studied the inscription and nodded.

"Ah… So the legends are true. It does exist. But in the end, like so many things, reality is far different than the stories. It's just a few words," Frank said, as if to himself.

"Who the hell are you?" Natalie asked, almost afraid to hear the answer.

Frank looked her up and down. "Well, what a charming young hothouse flower you are, my dear. Allow me to introduce myself. I am Dr. Morbius Frank. And this is my associate, Mr. Amieri. Pleased to finally make your acquaintance. I've heard so much about you, but I see that it hardly does you justice. You've led us all on a merry chase."

"You're the murdering scumbag who killed my father."

"Tut tut, my dear. Such an attitude and mouth. Your father's death was a regrettable accident. If he had listened to reason, as my friend Diego Luca has, he'd probably still be with us – albeit much richer," Frank said.

"He didn't want to give you the Scroll, so you killed him," she snarled.

"Your father was a fool. An idealistic fool. He felt that the Scroll should remain hidden forever. If he had listened to reason he would have discovered that I, too, feel it should – if the price is right. And for the Church, no price is too high. So we both were after the same end result. He simply didn't pay attention. A shame. An endearing and brilliant man, but with that fatal foolish flaw…and nothing like as nimble as our hero here, Dr. Steven Cross, hmm?" Frank declared, shifting his attention to Steven.

"How much are you getting out of this?" Steven directed the question at Luca, ignoring Frank for the moment.

"More than enough," Luca replied.

"Oh, don't be shy, my friend," Frank said. "It wouldn't do to appear as though you're cheap. You're anything but. The number is one hundred million dollars, young man. As gratitude for a career well served."

Steven whistled. "That's the price of a soul these days? I would have sold mine a long time ago if I'd had any idea you could get that kind of money for one."

Frank laughed – a genuine exclamation of amusement. "Well said. You are a charmer, aren't you? But the number is of no consequence. Money is just a symbol, as are most things. As is this simple crown. Yet many would kill over it, or the few simple words on the tablet. Wars have been fought over the man whose skeleton lies on this cold stone floor – to defend the faith and the honor of his church. In the end, everything is a symbol. A hundred million is fitting tribute for a man with the courage to help bring this plan to fruition." Frank's words dripped with self-importance.

"Why do I think that your number must be far higher?" Steven asked.

"Oh, you've seen through me. Very perceptive. Yes, I am already of secure means, so it takes a larger amount to ensure my cooperation. A much larger amount. But in the end, that too is just a symbol. Although I can't say it is of no consequence because it clearly is. My number is a hundred times greater, and yet the Church can cut a check for it out of their petty cash. I'm not greedy. I could have demanded more." Frank shrugged. "I believe, however, in being reasonable."

"But why? You're already rich. A billionaire, right? Why do all this?" Natalie asked.

"*Because it is there.* Because I can. Because even a man with one billion wants ten. Just as I'm sure that a man with ten will want a hundred. But baby steps. You can't make it all in one day. I'm a patient man." Frank's smile was blood-chilling.

Luca cleared his throat. "Can you keep your eye on these two? I want to take a closer look at…at the remains. This is a once in a lifetime chance."

"Of course, my good man, of course. Take as much time as you like. It's not as though I'm in any rush to get back out into that brutal sun," Frank said, waving nonchalantly with his gun. "You people are really something for enduring that hellish furnace for all these days. I was staying at a top-shelf private resort on the Dead Sea, taking the cure and relaxing this entire time. I couldn't have lived in a tent in this oven, I can assure you. Although my colleague Sia Amieri is more than familiar with this weather." Frank made a head gesture towards the big man.

"He talks a lot, doesn't he?" Steven said.

"Yes, he's quite gregarious, as you've noticed." Frank nodded at Amieri, who moved closer to the skeleton chamber, eyeing Moody's inert body with a casual interest. "Amieri is a man of rare talents and appetites, Dr. Cross. As I'm sure young Natalie will discover before the day is out. But it isn't his fault. He's a victim of society." Frank chuckled to himself. "We all have our crosses to bear."

Luca moved into the crypt and approached the skeleton, pointing his gun at Steven and Natalie as he did so. Steven registered a faint movement at the periphery of his vision in the depths of the darkness. The light was so faint it was hard to tell what was real and what was imaginary in the cave.

Luca reached the skeleton, and Steven could see that he had tears in his eyes. For all his faults and weaknesses, he was a believer, and this was the most important moment of his life. He extended a tentative hand to touch the ribcage, where several of the bones were shattered from the thrust of a Roman spear – possibly the very same one that leaned against the wall.

A hiss emanated from within the bones and a brown blur lashed from the sternum, striking Luca's wrist, causing him to cry out and drop his pistol. Everyone froze for a split second, and then the cave exploded with action. As Natalie lunged for the gun, Amieri raced towards her, his eyes registering surprise and then shock as Steven drove the ancient spear through his chest. He staggered back towards Frank as if in slow motion, the wooden shaft sticking from him, moaning in a low keening voice that sounded nothing so much as a dog's lamentation. Frank dispassionately registered his mortal wound and then fired a single muffled shot to his head, ending his misery as quickly as it began.

Amieri's bulk dropped to the floor, clearing the line of fire between Natalie and Frank. She moved in a crouch and fired, the bullet searing his chest in a spray of blood. Frank simultaneously shot at Natalie, hitting her in the lower abdomen. She went down hard, dropping the weapon, and Steven raised his hands slowly as he backed away from the skeleton. A sinewy brown snake slithered from the ribcage up to the skull, where it wound its way through one of the eye sockets before exiting through the other, and then made its way into the nether recesses of the cave.

Frank clutched his chest with his left hand, the pistol still steady in his right. "You little bitch. You hit me. Fortunately it's a flesh wound, as I surmise from the pain. Grazed my rib. You must be rusty from your Bureau days. I have a feeling I would have been a goner five years ago. Ah, well. Those are the breaks." He squinted at Natalie writhing on the ground, clawing at her abdomen in agony. "I understand stomach wounds are the worst – they can take hours to kill you and are extremely painful. Out here in God's country, there's no way to save you, which I'm sure young Steven has already realized. Judging by the look in his eyes, you've captured his heart in addition to his passions, so it will do me a world of good to know that among his last visions will be you dying a slow death of unspeakable suffering." Frank shifted his view to Steven. "It was nice meeting you, Dr. Cross. A pity we couldn't have crossed swords on a more civilized field. But one plays the cards one's dealt, no?" Frank raised the gun a few inches, drawing a bead on Steven's heart.

Steven's gaze scoured the floor, but he didn't see Luca's gun. Sensing Frank preparing to fire, time compressed as his mind raced for a way out. But there was nowhere to hide, no place to duck behind or dodge to. He inched towards Natalie, who was looking up at him through tears of pain, and when their eyes met he felt something in his chest move. If this was his time, so be it. He reached his hand down to touch her head with a trembling hand. "I'm sorry, my angel."

Snapping back to the immediate, Steven's muscles tensed as he prepared to make a final suicide charge at his would-be executioner, even though he knew it was futile.

He had to, if only for Natalie.

CHAPTER 39

When the shot came, it didn't hurt, which surprised him. Steven heard the distinctive muffled pop of the silenced weapon, even though his ears were still ringing from the concussion of Natalie's gunshot, yet there was no pain. He waited to feel himself drift away or see the light at the end of a long dark tunnel, but nothing happened. After a second he registered movement from in front of him. It was Frank, his chest a mass of spreading blood, sinking as if in slow motion, first to his knees, then to his side, his weapon dangling uselessly from his lifeless hand.

A shadow darkened the cave mouth, and then a figure moved into the cave, gun held at the ready. The newcomer nudged Frank with his toe and then moved to Amieri to do the same. Satisfied that both men were dead, he lowered his weapon and addressed Steven.

"Dr. Cross. I'm not the enemy. You have nothing to fear."

"Who are you?" Steven asked, blinking in disbelief.

"Colonel Gabriel Synthe. Now let's get your friend and the girl out of here before she bleeds out. I have a satellite phone and can have a chopper here in ten minutes or less. I've got one standing by. If we hurry, she can be in Amman within half an hour, which means that, if she's lucky, she'll have a decent chance of making it. Pick her up and bring her to the mouth of the cave, and then drag your friend, Moody, over. I've got to make a call."

As Synthe stepped back into the sunlight, Steven noticed that he was pouring sweat and breathing as though he'd just run a marathon. He fished a satellite phone out of the backpack he'd left outside the cave and spoke softly into it for a few moments. Synthe stabbed the call off and turned to Steven.

"Congratulations are in order. You've made the discovery of the ages."

"Who are you?" Steven repeated.

"I already told you. Gabriel Synthe. I'm with a competitive branch of the Church to Luca over there." He gestured to the back of the cave, where Luca was shuddering in convulsions. "Nothing to be done for him, I'm afraid. I've seen those kinds of bites before. A horrible way to go. There's no anti-venom. We lose more than a few every year that way in Israel. The vipers are notorious."

"The Church? Carrying silenced weapons and killing like a pro?" Steven asked skeptically, cradling Natalie as he carried her to the front of the cave as instructed.

"Call it the operational wing. Dirty tricks and counter-intelligence."

"Ah. The Order?" Steven speculated.

"You're a smart man. How much do you really think it's wise to know? Just call me the guy who's going to rescue your girl after saving your ass, and who will put everything right so you don't wind up in a Jordanian prison for the rest of your lives. You do realize the government would frown if they knew you had automatic weapons and were armed to the teeth, right?"

"Where did you come from?" Steven asked.

"I was tailing them and had to wait until they entered the cave to get up the hill. Quite a run, by the way. Makes me seriously consider quitting smoking," Synthe said, still winded. He reached into the breast pocket of his safari shirt and extracted a pack of cigarettes, fishing one out and sticking it in his mouth.

"That normally would take twenty minutes, at least."

"I made it in under ten. Then again, I was motivated. I didn't know how much time I had before he'd kill you. But I figured that a windbag like him wouldn't be able to resist pontificating, pardon the pun, and whatever was in the cave would probably take a few minutes for him to absorb." He lit the smoke with a gold Cartier lighter. "Today was your lucky day. Hopefully, it will continue when you get to the hospital. Once you're on your way, I'll call ahead to make sure they're ready for her. Here. Let me see what we've got." Synthe said, moving to Natalie. Steven recoiled – he stank of sweat and cigarettes. Synthe lifted Natalie's hand from her stomach and peered at the wound, and then gently laid it back.

"Got her in the lower bowel. Better than the upper, but still not great. If you're a religious man, I'd start praying," Synthe told Steven. He blew a stream of smoke out into the sun.

"But you're not? Working for the Church?"

"The Lord works in mysterious ways, *n'est-ce pas*? Even those who only stand and wait, and so on. Just count yourself fortunate that the Church occasionally dirties its hands with the likes of me. Now, do as I ask and go grab your buddy. Looks like he's got a nasty head wound. Lots of blood."

"Luca hit him with a Colt."

"Did he really? Quite a passive man of the cloth, our Luca. Shame he'll be dead in a few more minutes."

Steven shook his head as though to clear it. "How did they know?"

"Wireless transmitter. I'd imagine Luca pushed the panic button when you found the cave wall. It took them a while to get up the river. The big one you skewered is Frank's enforcer. He was camped out a half a mile downstream from you. Had a permit and everything. Apparently, Frank had some pull with the Jordanians. Amieri took off like a rabbit when he got the signal and killed your two boys in the camp, and then Frank came poncing in on a helicopter. You probably didn't hear it from deep in the cave."

"I think Luca did. You're right, though. The acoustics are deceptive."

"That's the only thing that's saved you from the Jordanian military landing here right now. The shot didn't sound like much, even from just outside. If she'd fired that weapon in the open it would have brought in the cavalry and there would have been a lot of explaining to do – it would have echoed all the way down the canyon and they'd have had to check what had happened. Count your blessings." Synthe walked back into the cave, briefly studying the crown and tablet, and then moved to the skeleton. "Speaking of which, is that who I think it is?"

"Yes."

"Church is going to go ape over this, aren't they?"

"I'd assume so. I have a feeling Luca was right about that. There's no way they'll want this to come out," Steven said.

"Oh well. Do you care?" Synthe asked, studying Steven's face.

Steven thought about it. "Not really."

They returned to the front of the cave and in a few minutes were greeted by the distinctive sound of a big chopper.

"I'm going to have them lift her and your friend out on a stretcher. You'll need to get reeled up on a harness. You okay with that?" Synthe said.

"Fine. Just get her help."

Natalie had passed out from the pain, so at least wasn't suffering for now.

Synthe moved out into the sun again, and Steven waited inside until Synthe called for him. With a final glance at the skeleton, he gathered Natalie in his arms and walked out into the blinding heat.

~

Natalie came out of the operating room after four and a half hours. The surgeon who followed her gurney approached Steven, who was sitting in the hall nervously fidgeting with a can of soda.

Steven jumped to his feet. "How is she?"

The surgeon pulled his mask off and pursed his lips. "The biggest danger now is sepsis. I got the bullet out and sewed up all the damage, but these things can go either way. The prognosis is guarded, but positive. If there are no complications over the next forty-eight hours, I think we're in the clear, although she will need bed rest for a few weeks."

"When will she be conscious?" Steven asked.

"In about an hour. She'll be in a lot of pain, so we're going to be administering morphine for the first seventy-two hours via her IV. She'll be groggy and out of it."

Steven shook the surgeon's hand. "Thank you for saving her life."

"It's all part of the job."

"You speak excellent English, Doctor…"

"Faruk. I went to school at Penn State."

~

The telltale odor of antiseptic hung in the room, an expected companion to the oxygen tubing, the heart rate monitor by Natalie's head and her IV drip pole. The lighting was dim, set that way to promote rest. A nurse entered and checked her vitals. After fiddling with the IV line, she gave Steven a professional smile and exited.

Natalie's eyes flickered open and searched Steven's face, the drugs obvious in her dilated pupils and unfocused gaze. She licked her parched lips and croaked out, "Hello, stranger."

Steven smiled and reached to hold her hand. "You'll do just about anything to get attention, huh?"

"You should know that by now. Did you know getting shot hurts?" Natalie asked.

"I seem to recall it's not a lot of fun. But the doctor says you're going to be fine," Steven said.

"Hopefully, better than fine."

"He actually said you'd be super, but it sounded lame. I figured you'd think I was blowing smoke…"

"Is that an offer?" Natalie asked, her voice dreamy.

"Absolutely."

There was a soft knock at the door, then Moody entered, his head bandaged and his eyes puffy.

"Who let the mummy in?" Natalie rasped.

"You should have seen the other guy."

"You look like a raccoon," she observed, then shut her eyes, drifting back off to sleep.

Steven released her limp hand and moved to the door, motioning to Moody with his head to step out into the hall.

"How are you feeling?" Steven asked.

"Like someone ran over me with a tank. You?"

"Never better. Nothing like a little close-quarters combat to perk up a dull day." Steven eyed Moody's bandage. "What are the odds we can get the helicopter to give us a lift out to the site tonight?"

"Nil. Too much going on. I've been running interference since I got out of the CT room. I have two guys on the ground out there to clean up the bodies and make sure nothing walks off and, apparently, your new friend from the Church has a whole crew sanitizing the area. Between his group and mine, I'd say you're pretty much covered. Why? What do you want?" Moody asked.

"The laptop. A few other things, like clothes, ID…the usual," Steven answered.

"It'll still be there tomorrow morning. You wanna hook up around seven for a chopper ride?"

"I thought you'd never ask. I'm going to crash in Natalie's room – they said they would bring in a cot. Can you meet me back here to pick me up?" Steven asked.

"Sure thing." Moody paused, holding Steven's gaze. "Take care of her. She's one in a million. I probably have some sour grapes that it's you and not me, but if she's happy, that's fine. You're a fortunate man."

"I know I am. And I will take care of her. You can count on that."

CHAPTER 40

The following morning, the river bed was unrecognizable. The tents were stowed back in their containers, the kitchen and latrines broken down and packed, and everything was readied for departure. Steven's and Natalie's bags sat neatly next to Moody's off to one side, with Moody's two men loitering near them, trying to be unobtrusive in the already oppressive heat.

That will be one thing I won't miss, Steven thought as the helicopter set down. Moody slid the door open with a tug, and they both hopped out as the blades slowed to an idle.

"See? Everything's under control. I do have a little experience with these things, you know," Moody said as they walked to their bags. Steven crouched down and did a quick inventory – computer, passports, wallets and money all there. He fished his binoculars out and scanned the canyon side, looking for the cave. All he saw was fresh dirt and sand in a spot three quarters up the north face.

"My guys said that Synthe had a crew out here last night with battery-powered lights setting detonators," Moody said. "They removed the evidence and collapsed the cave, so there's no proof anything was up there. I'll give him credit for being efficient, that's for sure. If you didn't know what had gone down yesterday, you'd never notice anything. And by tomorrow or the day after, the sand and sun will have done their work, and there will be no trace."

"You get the feeling he's done this kind of thing before?" Steven asked, and then turned when he saw Moody glancing over his shoulder. Synthe was approaching from down the river bed. When he arrived on the mound, he shook hands with them both.

Moody spoke first. "I think some thanks are in order for saving everyone's lives, mine included."

"None necessary. Glad I could help out. It's a shame this regrettable incident even took place." He fixed Moody with a neutral look. "Or didn't."

"Exactly. Nothing to see here. Move along," Moody replied.

"May I tear Dr. Cross away from you for a moment?" Synthe asked, taking Steven lightly by the arm, not waiting for a reply. He leaned in to Steven and spoke almost inaudibly.

"My side needs to have a word with you. Some assurances. Luca was working far outside his authority, and I need to know what arrangements he made so I can look at fixing things," he said.

"I was afraid of that." Steven went on to tell him about the tape, and the papal letters.

"When can you be back in Rome? Or put another way: the jet is at your disposal; when will you and the young lady be able to travel?" Synthe asked.

"She'll be here for a week. But I can fly up tomorrow if you want. On the condition that I get a return flight, as well as one more flight for both of us in a week."

"Consider it done."

Steven looked in the direction of the cave again.

"How did you know about Luca, and when?"

"For a while. We were afraid that this had to be an inside job that required more than just a lowly novitiate's level of information, even if he was in the Order and privy to at least some of the secrets. After that, it was just a matter of suspecting everyone until the pieces fell into place. For what it's worth, I don't think he got involved with Frank until the end," Synthe said.

Steven shook his head. "It's a shame. And they almost got away with it." He paused. "I guess you'll have your work cut out for you now, keeping this secret as well. A little harder than keeping a Scroll under wraps."

"Actually, as you may have surmised, that's a big part of why we need to have a meeting tomorrow," Synthe confirmed.

"I got that. Airport at eight?"

"Don't be late."

Steven returned to where Moody was waiting and they gathered their bags and loaded them onto the helicopter. Within a few minutes, they were airborne and heading back to Amman. Steven felt something sharp jab him in the leg, and he fished in his pocket to retrieve the offending object. Then he remembered.

"Moody. I need to ask you to do me a favor, and swear you to absolute secrecy about all of this."

*

Steven sat patiently in the ornately-appointed room at the Vatican. A hushed reverence hung in the air, and even the man who brought him a cup of coffee seemed steeped in formality and dignity. He studied the art on the bejeweled, ornately-engraved walls, and estimated that any three paintings could finance a small nation's army for a year.

A door at the far end of the room opened, and a small, white-haired man entered wearing a simple, anonymous white cassock. He approached Steven, who had stood, and motioned for him to be seated.

"I believe we have some business to discuss?" the man began in heavily accented English.

"It would appear so. I've already met with one gentleman today, who I've described my situation to, and he suggested I speak directly to you, Your Holiness."

"I've been informed of your role in the events of the last week, and I first want to say that you've accomplished an extraordinary feat. Several. You should be extremely proud of yourself. And I don't say that lightly."

"Thank you."

"So play me this tape."

Steven pushed the button on the MP3 player and the room filled with Diego Luca's voice. When the conversation reached an end, he turned it off and took another sip of his coffee.

"It's good coffee, *eh*?"

"Very good."

"Should be. There ought to be some perks to this job."

Steven didn't say anything.

"All right, Dr. Cross, tell me what you want."

"I want what was promised on the tape. I've already gotten the money, so that part is taken care of, as are the passports. But there is still the matter of the letters…and the access to the archives," Steven said.

"I'm told that the perpetrator of this horrible sequence of events was going to hold me up for ten billion dollars."

"Given the circumstances, I think he felt you would have gladly paid that," Steven acknowledged.

"Why do you want to have access to the archives? And why not stick me for ten billion dollars?"

Steven had thought about the answer to that question for a long time. He decided the truth was the best route.

"I have money. I'm not rich, but I'm comfortable. More money won't buy me anything I don't have already. It won't make me younger, it won't find me love, and it won't save me from death. So money won't be of nearly as much value to me as knowledge and the ability to satisfy my passion for discovery. I suppose you could say that I view having unrestricted access as worth ten billion dollars."

He stared at Steven for some time before responding.

"I hear we bought a software company. What do I know about software? I think you should take it back. A man's got to have something to do, and I can't have you in the archives all day, every day."

"You already paid for it."

"Consider it a bonus. You earned it."

"That's very generous. Thank you," Steven said.

The little man sipped his coffee; a look of deep satisfaction spread across his face. "Do you believe in God?"

"Not in the same way you do."

The man nodded. "You can never speak or write of what took place, nor of anything you discover in the archives, unless you have my personal authorization. You understand?"

"I do. I'm not interested in how the Church conducts its affairs, or what it does or doesn't share with the world."

He studied Steven's face. "But what is your opinion? Do you think it is right to keep this a secret? Do you question our wisdom in wishing to deliberate before unleashing this on the world?"

"I personally think it's a mistake. A Church that is more interested in keeping secrets than fostering knowledge is an institution in decline. But then again, who am I to say?" Steven replied truthfully.

"Indeed. I do not make these decisions lightly, nor do I make them alone. But in the end, I must do what I believe is best for the Church, regardless of my personal sentiments."

"I understand. Yet another reason you deserve good coffee."

The man allowed a hint of a smile to play across his face, and then withdrew a single sheet of stationary with an ornate embossing. He picked up a fountain pen and scrawled a missive, then signed it. Finally, he affixed a seal, with his ring.

"Two letters are inefficient. One should do. I just added a sentence at the top about the service to the Church. You now have everything you've asked for, and I trust I can depend upon you to honor your commitment to keep our matter confidential."

"I can speak for myself, and for the girl. I can't commit for the CIA man."

"Don't worry about the Americans. I have pull there." The man finished his coffee with a sigh and shrugged. "Realistically, even if you did talk, at this point, there's no evidence, so it would just be another crazy claim. We hear a lot of those."

Steven nodded. "I understand. It would never make it to theaters."

"Exactly. Too unbelievable."

The two men stared at each other for a few moments, and then both grinned.

CHAPTER 41

Moody sat nursing a mineral water at a table in the back of a restaurant in Florence. The place didn't open for two more hours, but he had an arrangement with the owners, as well as a key. The front door chimed, and Steven entered with Natalie on his arm. They peered through the gloom and saw him wave. Natalie showed no signs of having been shot a few short weeks before, and when she approached his table it was with her usual graceful stride. Moody stood and gave Natalie a kiss on the cheek before shaking Steven's outstretched hand. He sat them down and offered them something to drink.

"I'd like some wine. Red. It's been fifteen days since the surgery, and the doctor said I could have a glass after two weeks, so this is my big chance," Natalie said.

Moody looked at Steven, and he nodded.

"You heard the lady. Make it two," Steven said.

Moody moved across the floor to the wine cabinet near the bar and, after a few moments, returned with a ready-prepared decanter full of deep, dark Barolo. He selected three glasses, removed the cut-glass stopper, and poured them each a generous measure of wine. They toasted, and then Moody got down to business.

"We were reimbursed for all the expenses associated with the expedition, as expected."

"Nice to hear they pay their bills on time," Steven said.

"It looks like the hunt for you two stopped with Synthe's bullet to the good doctor's heart. As expected, Frank's passing didn't raise any stir."

"People die all the time," Natalie said.

"We also did a sweep of your offices and found surveillance equipment. Frank's, no doubt. So your people are clean. It was the phone lines and modem that weren't."

"That's a relief, although I never doubted it. I couldn't see them turning on me."

"Your buddy, Synthe, seems to have fixed things with the Roman police, by the way. My sources say that they dropped you two from their investigation. Something about that part of the file getting lost," Moody said.

"It's a flawed world," Natalie observed.

"We are all cast of imperfect clay," Steven agreed.

"I'll drink to that," Moody added, and they toasted again.

They savored the rich, dark wine, swirling it in the oversized glasses. It was the perfect temperature and opened up nicely, filling the room with its fragrant bouquet.

Natalie stood and excused herself to go to the bathroom. Once she was out of earshot, Moody leaned closer to Steven and spoke softly.

"We did the DNA analysis."

"And?"

"Puts the age at two thousand years, give or take. But there was an anomaly on the rest."

"Anomaly? What do you mean, anomaly?"

"I'm not sure how to say this, so I'll just say it. The bone fragment was human, but it wasn't. The DNA was very close, but it didn't correspond to anything they've seen before. I had to get it classified as top secret to keep anyone from asking uncomfortable questions."

Steven considered the news. Moody nodded.

"Holy shit."

"Yup."

"The world needs to know about this," Steven said, still in shock.

"Not from me, it doesn't. But I agree it deserves to know, for whatever that's worth."

Steven swirled his wine again and took another sip. He studied the light as it refracted through the glass, dancing off the ruby-rippled surface.

Natalie emerged from the back and walked towards them, and Steven rubbed his face before putting his hand down flat on the table.

He fixed Moody with an intense gaze.

"Does it?"

Natalie and Steven ambled slowly down the sidewalk, enjoying the early evening warmth of the new Florentine summer. Hand in hand, they looked happy in the way that only new lovers do.

"The transfer to your account was confirmed today. Two million. I guess you can't say I never did anything for you," Steven said.

"I told you that you didn't have to do that," Natalie countered.

"It was mostly your fault I wound up with the money in the first place, and everything turned out okay, so what the hell…"

"Very gallant. But you're not going to get rid of me that easily."

Steven squeezed her hand. "Ingrate."

"What have you done for me lately?" she asked, and stopped, tiptoeing to kiss him.

He looked deep into her incredible violet eyes and then grinned, thinking he could get lost in them forevermore. She smiled back.

He kissed her again and then whispered in her ear.

"Can you keep a secret?"

<<<< *finis* >>>>

ABOUT THE AUTHOR

Russell Blake lives full time on the Pacific coast of Mexico. He is the acclaimed author of the thrillers: *Fatal Exchange*, *The Geronimo Breach*, *Zero Sum*, *The Delphi Chronicle* trilogy (*The Manuscript, The Tortoise and the Hare, and Phoenix Rising*), *King of Swords*, *Night of the Assassin*, *The Voynich Cypher*, *Revenge of the Assassin*, *Return of the Assassin*, *Silver Justice, JET*, *JET II – Betrayal*, *JET III – Vengeance* and *JET IV – Reckoning.*

Non-fiction novels include the international bestseller *An Angel With Fur* (animal biography) and *How To Sell A Gazillion eBooks (while drunk, high or incarcerated)* – a joyfully vicious parody of all things writing and self-publishing related.

"Capt." Russell enjoys writing, fishing, playing with his dogs, collecting and sampling tequila, and waging an ongoing battle against world domination by clowns.

Sign up for e-mail updates about new Russell Blake releases

http://russellblake.com/contact/mailing-list